Maggie Craig was brought up in Clydebank and Glasgow, the youngest of four children of a railwayman father and a mother who worked in the typing pool of John Brown Land Boilers. Maggie was working as a medical secretary when she met her Welsh husband, Will, when he was doing part of his apprenticeship in a Clydeside shipyard, and she and Will subsequently sailed the world on oil tankers, before settling in Glasgow and starting a family.

Maggie now lives in an old blacksmith's house in rural Aberdeenshire with Will and their two children. THE RIVER FLOWS ON is her first novel, and she is also the author of DAMN' REBEL BITCHES, which tells the story of the women of the Jacobite rebellion.

The River Flows On

Maggie Craig

HEADLINE

First published in 1998
by HEADLINE BOOK PUBLISHING

First published in paperback in 1999
by HEADLINE BOOK PUBLISHING

10 9 8 7 6 5

ISBN 0 7472 5864 3

Typeset by Palimpsest Book Production Limited,
Polmont, Stirlingshire
Printed and bound in Great Britain by
Clays Ltd, St Ives plc

HEADLINE BOOK PUBLISHING
A division of Hodder Headline plc
338 Euston Road
London NW1 3BH

To those who came before me:
particularly all the bright boys and girls
to whom poverty denied an education,
but not a lifelong thirst for learning
and creative expression;

and to the two Sheilas
who helped me find the key to the door.

Acknowledgements

I should like to thank Mrs Margaret Hamilton and Mrs Grace Peace, both of whom started their working lives as apprentice tracers at John Brown's in Clydebank shortly before the outbreak of the Second World War. These two ladies gave very generously of their time to answer my questions, and supplied me with a great deal of useful information.

For help in guiding me through their archives I am indebted to Pat Malcolm of Clydebank Library and Claire McGread of the Glasgow School of Art.

Prologue 1996

'Grandma Kate! Grandma Kate! Look – there it is! Down the river! Hurry up, Grandma!' Michael's young voice was high with excitement, his Canadian accent pronounced.

'*She*, Michael,' Kate corrected gently. 'A ship is always a *she*.'

She smiled at the boy. The sun was warm today and the wind coming off the Clyde a soft one, but her bones were getting old. Michael had scampered down from the car, but she'd followed at a more sedate pace. It wasn't a long journey – down the Boulevard, over the Erskine Bridge and then across to the West Ferry Road at Bishopton – but long enough for her to stiffen up.

She joined the boy at the water's edge. One hand up to shade his eyes, he was peering down the river towards Greenock where the tugs were bringing the liner in to lie at anchor.

'Oh, Grandma Kate, she's lovely, isn't she?'

Her eyes on the ship, Kate smiled to herself. He was a quick learner, this little great-grandson of hers. How strange to think that his grandmother, her own daughter Grace, had once run and played at her side as Michael did now. Funny how the years disappeared while you were busy doing other things.

Kate shaded her own eyes, the better to see. Even at this distance the liner looked big, her smooth and majestic lines not dwarfed by the magnificent backdrop of the hills and the Firth of Clyde, but somehow looking just right against them.

'Aye, Michael, she's a bonnie ship. It's grand to see her back in the river of her birth.' She heard the sudden huskiness in her voice and wondered if the child had caught it. You're an old fool, Kate Cameron, she told herself, greeting over a ship. She blinked her eyes to get rid of the tears.

There was a voice in her head. *It's just a big lump o' iron and metal and wood.* That had been Pearl, scornfully tossing her golden curls. But Pearl had been wrong. A ship was much more than just a big lump of iron and metal and wood – much more.

A ship was the dream in someone's head, painstakingly set down on paper so that she could take shape under hundreds of skilled pairs of hands. A ship was the grimy sheen of sweat on your husband's brow when he trudged wearily into the house at the end of the day; a ship was the calluses on your father's fine-boned hands, the legacy of hammering red-hot rivets into metal for hour after hour; a ship was the pride in men's eyes when they saw her launched. And there had been pride in Kate's eyes also, for she too had played her part.

No, it wasn't so daft to cry over a ship, and there had been tears a-plenty back then. What was it the old folks used to say? It was tears that made the Clyde?

Michael was concentrating on the ship. 'Why do they call her the *Queen Elizabeth II*, Grandma? Was there a *Queen Elizabeth I*?'

'Oh, yes.' She was glad of his eager questions, recalling her to the present. 'Although we just called her the *Queen Elizabeth*. She was a fine ship too, Michael. I was there when she was launched – in 1938, just before the Second World War broke out.'

Michael had turned to look at Kate. Young as he was, he

2

seemed always to be interested in his great-grandmother's stories.

'What was the launch like, Grandma?'

'Oh, it was grand. Real exciting. When she hit the water, she caused this huge wave,' Kate lifted a hand to illustrate the size of it, 'and everyone standing on the other bank of the river to watch the launch got soaked.'

Michael laughed in delight. Kate laughed with him, remembering another occasion. She would tell him that story later.

'And before the first *Queen Elizabeth*, there was the *Queen Mary* – and she was the finest ship of all – the pride of the Clyde.' Her ship, she thought, the *Queen Mary* would always be her ship. Hers and Robbie's. She smiled down into the child's upturned face. His lips pursed in concentration, he was nodding in agreement with her.

'I know,' he said. 'My dad told me all about her. She's in California now, and one day we're going to go and visit her. He says that my great-grandpa helped build her.'

Kate smiled, both at the North American twang in that 'grandpa' and the note of pride she heard in the young voice.

'Your great-grandpa and your two great-great-grandpas *and* your Uncle Davie all helped build ships on the Clyde. Now, isn't that something?'

'Gee.' He exhaled a long breath. It lifted the lock of fair hair which had fallen forward onto his forehead. 'Say, Grandma, maybe *I* could build ships when I grow up.'

Kate smiled sadly. 'No, Michael, I don't think so. There's hardly a shipyard left on the river now. When I was wee—'

'The age I am now?'

'The age you are now,' Kate agreed. 'When I was wee, the river was lined with shipyards.' She turned, lifting her arm to indicate the Erskine Bridge behind them. 'From right up in Glasgow way upriver from the bridge there, down through

3

Govan and Yoker and Clydebank and Dalmuir, along to Dumbarton over there on the other bank—'

He was following her pointing arm. 'Where that big rock is?'

'Yes, where that big rock is,' Kate moved her arm round, pointing downriver in the direction of the *Queen Elizabeth II*, 'and then down to Port Glasgow and Greenock. The whole place was full of men building ships. There must have been over a hundred yards, and now there's only two or three left.' She dropped her arm and looked down at the boy. 'No, young man, whatever you do when you grow up, it won't be building ships. Those days are gone.'

She smiled at him and reached out to stroke his cheek. His young skin was soft and smooth, like the bloom on a peach. And whatever you do become, she said silently to herself, I'll not be here to see it.

'What is that rock over there?' he asked. Kate turned him around to look at it, resting her hands lightly on his shoulders.

'That's Dumbarton Rock. It was a stronghold of the Ancient Britons. That's what Dumbarton means – the fortress of the Britons. Can you see the castle on the top of it?'

Michael nodded.

'When Mary Queen of Scots was a wee girl, she sailed for France from Dumbarton Castle. She was only five years old – two years younger than you – and she had to leave her home and her mother behind.'

'Why?'

'Because her father the King had died, and there was civil war in Scotland. It was too dangerous for her to stay, so she had to go to her relatives in France. That would have been in a sailing ship, of course.'

'Smaller than the *QE2*?'

'Much, much smaller.'

4

Michael swivelled round to face her. 'Did Mary Queen of Scots ever come back to Scotland?'

'Oh yes, but not till she was grown up. And what happened to her after that is a story for another day.'

'I like your stories, Grandma Kate.'

Kate cupped his face lightly in her hands. 'My father told me most of them,' she said.

'And now you tell them to me,' replied the boy.

'That's right,' said Kate, studying his serious little face. It's funny, she thought, how the very young can sometimes see things so clearly.

'What was it like, Grandma?' he went on. 'When all the men were building ships?'

She took her hands from his face. 'Noisy,' she said. 'Very noisy.'

'But the river's quiet now,' said the child, looking out at it, flowing serenely past them.

'Yes,' said Kate, 'the river's quiet now.'

She patted the child's fair curls and turned to look out over the river towards Dumbarton Rock. The breeze lifted her own hair. She had a good head of it but it was white now, not the shining chestnut it had once been. *His nut-brown maiden.* How often had Robbie called her that?

She could hear his voice, low-pitched and mellow, with a rumble of laughter in it. That brought a fresh prickle of tears to her eyes. *You're a daft bisom, Kate Cameron,* he would have said. She squeezed her eyes tight shut and he was there, clear as ever in her mind's eye. He'd had a good head of hair himself, much darker than Kate's – almost black. It had a habit of flopping onto his forehead, the darkness emphasising his pale skin. When she remembered him like this, she could see that characteristic toss of the head to get the hair out of his eyes, and the slow smile lighting up his grey eyes, the slow smile that was reserved just for her . . .

5

'Grandma Kate?' Michael, puzzled, was pulling on her skirt.

Blinking back the tears, she smiled down at the child. She *was* a daft bisom, standing here dreaming of days that were gone. It had all happened such a long time ago. You've been alive a long, long time, Kate Cameron, she thought. And this child, tugging at your skirts and looking up at you out of very blue eyes, was just starting out on that journey.

And while his days and years stretched out before him in a smooth, sunlit path winding up the hill and out of sight, you were coming down that same hill, your own days counted. Would he remember his Grandma Kate in the golden summers to come, the ones she herself would not see? Would he tell his children and grandchildren about her, as she had told him about those who had gone on before? She took a deep breath. She must enjoy him while he was here . . . while *she* was here.

'Come on then,' she said. 'You'll have to give me a hand. I'm getting old and stiff, Michael.'

The child extended his hand to her, his face grave, taking the responsibility of helping her back to the car very seriously. Kate felt her breath catch in her throat. There was an unexpected grace about the gesture. It was those blue eyes – and the way he had held out his hand. It recalled another time and another place . . .

Far too much emotion for one day, thought Kate. First the great ship, then Robbie, then that . . . She smiled down at Michael.

'I think,' she said, 'that after we've had a good look at the *QE2*, we might just ask the driver to take us on round the coast to Largs.'

Michael's gravity vanished. It was like the sun coming out. 'Nardini's?' he asked. The famous ice-cream parlour had become a recognised treat of his yearly visits with his father to the old country.

6

'Nardini's,' confirmed Kate. 'And I'm having a knickerbocker glory!'

Safely ensconced in the car once more, Kate asked the driver to leave the window open a little.

'Are you sure, hen?' he asked. 'It'll get quite blowy once we start moving.'

'I like to feel the wind in my hair,' she said, smiling at him as he bent solicitously over her, laying a rug across her knees as her grandson had asked him to do. *Hen*, indeed! Some things never changed. Thank God.

She recalled the pride in Michael's voice when he had talked about his 'great-grandpa' helping to build the *Queen Mary*. They can't take that away from us, thought Kate – the pride of the Clyde. They can take away the shipyards and fill in the docks, but they can't break our spirit and they can't roll away our river.

And as long as the river flows to the sea, and as long as there are children like Michael to carry the stories on, they can't take away that pride. As long as the river keeps flowing . . .

Beside her, Michael strapped himself carefully in and smiled beatifically at her before lifting his Game Boy. She smiled back, then turned to look out again at the Clyde.

All her life, the river had drawn her gaze. It had always been the magnet, the focus around which her life had revolved. The driver was right. It *was* blowy with the window open, but she was tough – Clyde-built, like those great ships of the past.

Kate closed her eyes and allowed her head to fall back onto the cushioned headrest. The breeze was soft and warm. She could mind the times when the wind off the river hadn't been soft, when it had been hard and biting, cutting right through her and her thin clothes, sharp as a blow . . .

PART I

1924

Chapter 1

Her mother's work-roughened hand stung Kate's cheek.

'Lazy wee bisom! I told you to hang out the washing, not to stand here daydreaming!'

'Aye, Mammy,' said Kate wearily, bending to the big basin still half-full of clothes.

'And shift yourself a wee bit,' was Lily's parting shot. 'Do you know how much we've still to do before the bells?'

Kate sighed as she heard her mother's rapid footsteps tap out an angry tattoo on the path through the back court before the sound disappeared into the close. She knew fine how much work there was still to do before midnight. None better. It was Hogmanay, and everything in the house had to be cleaned – clothes, furniture, people. You couldn't go dirty into the New Year. Everybody knew that.

Old Year's Night – 31 December – was the busiest day of the year – for the women and girls at any rate, Kate thought. The men seemed to get off easy. As long as they submitted to female nagging about having a bath and washing their hair they were considered to have done their bit.

Since early that morning, long before it had got light, the tenement block had been full of activity. Bargains had been struck as to who could have the wash-house when, Mrs MacLean had been tactfully dissuaded from beating the dust out of her rugs too close to Mrs Baxter's washing, and recalcitrant children had been unceremoniously dunked in

11

countless tin baths set before cooking ranges in countless kitchens.

Those same children had been further threatened with a right doing if they got so much as a speck of dirt on themselves or their clean clothes. When Andrew Baxter had fallen in an icy puddle down by the Yoker ferry whilst chasing Towser the dog – who also had to submit to the indignity of a bath before he could be allowed to progress into 1925 – the said doing had been duly administered by Andrew's father. Kate, pegging up her own father's shirt, smiled to herself. The smacks hadn't been very hard. Andrew's father Jim was as soft as butter, though you would never have guessed that from the way his son had screamed and bawled. They'd probably been able to hear him right down the water in Dumbarton – or even Helensburgh.

A hand lifted aside the shirt she'd just pegged out and a tousled dark head ducked under the washing line.

'Ho there, fair maiden. Why do you smile?'

'Fair midden, more like,' said Kate, all at once aware of how hot and sweaty she felt, despite the chill December air. 'I haven't even had time to comb my hair today. Do you think I'll manage it before next year?'

Robbie smiled dutifully. The jokes were another time-honoured New Year custom, although they were more common after the bells than before. Once midnight had passed, it was only a matter of minutes before they started. 'See me? I havenae had a bath since last year.' 'Give me something to eat Ma, I'm starving, I havenae eaten since last year.'

And so on, *ad nauseam*. Or until one of the younger children came out with a: 'See me? I havenae been to the lavvy since last year,' and was swiftly silenced by a clout on the ear from an embarrassed mother or elder sister trying to impress her new young man with how refined her family was.

Robbie's clear grey eyes went to Kate's chestnut curls. 'It

12

looks fine to me, Kate. Anyway, why bother?' He grinned at her. 'I never do.' Taking an apple out of his jacket pocket, he polished it on the lapel of his jacket and offered her first bite.

Kate shook her head. She poked him in the chest. 'You're a toerag, Robert Baxter, always have been.' Robbie grinned again.

'Did they close the whole yard early today?' Kate asked.

'Aye, but Ma asked me to get a few things in Clydebank. That's why I'm later back than my Da.'

In the act of pegging out a threadbare towel, Kate stopped dead, her brow furrowing. 'My father's not back yet,' she said flatly. Robbie correctly read the reason for her anxiety.

'It's all right, Kate. I met my Da on the way in – when I took the messages up to Ma. He's away back along to Connolly's. He'll have one drink with him and then bring him home.' He placed a reassuring hand on her shoulder. 'Come on, it'll be all right. My father'll not let him stay much longer. He'll be home soon. You'll see.'

'Aye,' said Kate, meeting his sympathetic gaze, doubt written all over her face. 'I suppose.'

Robbie gave her shoulder a little shake before releasing it. 'Here,' he said, finishing his apple and lobbing the core with pinpoint accuracy towards one of the bins which stood at the bottom of the back court. 'Shall I give you a hand with the washing?'

His movement had stretched his jacket, showing the outline of a book in his pocket. Kate, pointing to it, asked what it was. He fished it out and showed her the cover – *Kidnapped*, by Robert Louis Stevenson – before putting it back in his pocket and bending to pick up the washing basin.

'One of the managers gave me a loan of it. You'll have heard us talking about Mr Crawford?' Kate nodded and took another of her father's shirts from the basin. It was a relief not

13

to have to keep bending down. 'He says it's a rare story. A real adventure.'

Kate shook out the folds left in the shirt by the mangle. 'Can I read it after you? Do you think Mr Crawford would mind?'

'I'm sure he wouldn't,' said Robbie. 'You can read it before me if you like.'

Kate smiled at him and shook her head. 'Now, knowing you, that really is a generous offer. You'll be itching to read it. What was it Miss Noble used to say? Oh yes, I remember. "Robert Baxter, you just *devour* books, laddie".'

They laughed together, then Kate's smile faded. 'Oh Robbie, I wish you could have stayed on at school, maybe even gone to college.'

Robbie shrugged his thin shoulders. 'Och well, Kate. There's so many of us, you know? We needed another wage coming in – and that's a fact. Maybe one of the lassies or Andrew'll be able to stay on, if things are a wee bit easier by then.'

'I thought maybe you might be able to go to sea once Andrew was out working. You always wanted to do that. One of the companies would easy take you on once you've done your apprenticeship, wouldn't they?'

Robbie shrugged again, but gave her no answer. They worked together in silence for a minute or two, making their way along the washing line.

'What about you, Kate?' he asked tentatively, three nighties, two of Jessie's pinafores and one of Granny's highly embarrassing pairs of pink bloomers later.

'You know what about me,' Kate said, a harsh edge to her voice. 'I'll be leaving school at Easter. Ma thinks I should have left two years ago, when I was fourteen, and I'll be sixteen in April. It's time I was bringing a wage in too. High time. I'll have to start looking for a job as soon as the year's turned. Get

14

something lined up for when I leave. I'll maybe try the Singer's factory. See if I can get a start there. Or Donaldson's.'

It was a bone of contention between Kate's parents. Her father wanted his clever girl to stay on at school. Her mother thought she should have been out working long since. The family couldn't afford to keep Kate on at school for much longer – and they needed the wages she could bring in, meagre though those would be. Kate knew that, but she kept on hoping, crossing her fingers and wishing on bright stars . . . but Lily had finally put her foot down.

Aware of Robbie's silent sympathy, and perversely irritated by it, Kate snatched the next garment out of his hand. He changed the subject.

'So what *were* you smiling at just now?' he asked. Kate told him.

'Poor Andrew. It'll have been the humiliation that bothered him. After all, he's nearly twelve. Thinks he's grown-up. Mind you,' he went on, smiling at Kate, 'no doubt Ma gave him an empire biscuit or some gingerbread to make up for the indignity of the leathering.'

'Aye,' said Kate, trying to smile back. 'She did. She spoils him rotten, you know.'

'I know, I know, but every mother's got her favourite—' He broke off, looking suddenly embarrassed. He let out a long breath, like a puff of steam in the cold air. His eyes were soft as he looked at her. 'Och, Kate, I've gone and opened my mouth and put my big foot in it again, haven't I?'

'I'm the eldest,' said Kate flatly. 'And with four children and Granny to look after, Mammy doesn't have time to spoil any of us.'

'She doesn't appreciate you, Kate, and that's the truth.'

The washing was pegged out at last. Kate pulled the basin out of Robbie's grasp and hoisted it onto her hip. 'Look, Robbie, just leave it, all right?'

15

She looked up at him, thin and narrow-shouldered in his ill-fitting suit. He had a muffler tied round his neck in an attempt to add a bit of warmth to his inadequate clothes. He bit his lip and she was instantly contrite, but before she could attempt to smooth it over, he had taken a step or two back from her.

'I'm sorry,' he said stiffly. 'I'll see you the night. Your Da's asked me to be your first foot.'

Kate looked after his retreating back in dismay. Why had she snapped at Robbie, of all people?

He had always been there, right from the beginning, part of Kate's earliest memory. She must have been three, maybe nearer four, and she was sitting out on the back step, crying, salty tears streaming down her face. Robbie, five years old and a big boy in Kate's eyes, came ambling over, sat down beside Kate and put a clumsy arm around her shoulders.

'Has your Da drunk all his pay again? Come to our house. My Mammy'll give you something to eat. Come on.'

Kate had looked at Robbie, her eyes round and big. 'I've torn my pinafore too,' she wailed, in abject misery, because the pretty flowery thing that Granny had sewn for her had caught on the door handle and ripped when her mother had sent her down to the back court to play.

Robbie, kind, tousled-haired Robbie, who always went about looking like a ragamuffin, despite the best efforts of his mother, had struggled to understand Kate's unhappiness – and failed. Clothes didn't matter, did they? But food did.

'Come on,' he said again, pulling Kate by the hand. 'My Mammy'll give you something to eat. Come on, Kate.'

Mrs Baxter did give her something to eat – a big piece of bread, spread thick with yellow margarine and sprinkled with sugar, straight from Tate & Lyle's refinery down the river at Greenock. Kate had never tasted anything so good. She munched it and smiled, while Robbie's parents exchanged a look she didn't see and Robbie smiled broadly back at her. Kate had stopped crying. That was all that mattered.

It was Robbie who'd come rushing to the rescue when she'd found an old sack at the river's edge with a litter of kittens in it. She'd cried on that occasion too, thinking they were all dead, but then Robbie's voice had gone high and excited.

'Kate! One of them's moving. It's still alive!'

It was Robbie who'd done the unbelievable and persuaded Kate's mother that she could keep the kitten. His own mother would help feed it – find some scraps it could have. There were never any scraps in Kate's house, but Robbie's mother was a good manager. As folk said, nodding sagely, Agnes Baxter was one of those women who could make ten shillings do the work of a pound.

Kate and Robbie named the kitten Mr Asquith and Kate's father laughed and told them they were a couple of daft bairns, but when he was well and not in drink, he would let the little black and white kitten climb up on his lap and stroke it with gentle hands.

Kate walked slowly towards the close mouth, delaying her climb up the stone stairs to their flat on the second floor. Their flight of the stairs would have to be washed, too. No doubt she'd get that to do as well.

'Your Mammy relies on you, Kate lass,' her father always told her, the lilt of his native Highlands still strong in his voice. 'You're her right-hand woman, you might say.'

And Kate would smile reassuringly at her father and say nothing. She'd been nine when he'd come back from the Great War, a sombre sad-eyed stranger, nothing at all like the tall, laughing man she remembered. Mammy had changed too, had looked suddenly older, a permanent little frown of puzzlement settling between her brows as her husband withdrew further and further into himself.

It hadn't always been like that. Oh, there had often been

fights over Neil Cameron drinking too much, but Kate had other memories too. Her mother had beautiful hair, long and golden. Only one of her daughters had inherited the colour, Kate's sister Pearl.

Kate could remember her mother washing her hair and kneeling on the floor in front of the range to dry it, pulling a comb through the long shiny tresses. Kate loved to watch her do it. It was just like the story her teacher had read them at school. *Rapunzel, Rapunzel, let down your hair . . .* Mammy had smiled at her, enjoying the admiration in her daughter's eyes.

Then her father came in, tall and strong and dark. His eyes went immediately to his wife. He crouched down beside her on the floor and slipped his arm around her waist, lifting her to her feet. With a wink to Kate, he turned his head and kissed Lily first on the cheek and then, softly, on her ear. She blushed, swaying in his embrace. Daddy gave Kate a few coins. 'Away and buy some sweeties, lass. Take your sisters with you – and don't hurry back. Go for a wee walk or something . . .' His voice, soft and dreamy, had trailed off.

Kate, standing on the back step, sighed. Five minutes more, she thought, lifting her chin and pulling her cardigan more tightly about her. Five more minutes of peace and quiet and then I'll go in. It was dry but too cold to stay out much longer anyway. She peered anxiously at the sky. All that effort to hang out the washing and it would be wasted if the snow fell. No, it was all right. The sky was grey, but the clouds didn't look heavy.

She lowered her gaze. The river too was grey today. It was always different, sometimes calm and smooth, running down towards the Tail of the Bank, to the islands and the hills, sometimes like it was today, dark and forbidding – and unusually silent.

The yards had closed early today, but normally you could

hear them all from here. To her left, up towards Glasgow, there was Yarrow's. On the other bank of the river there were the yards upriver at Govan – Fairfield's and Stephen's and the rest. To Kate's right, heading downriver, there was Rothesay Dock and then John Brown's at Clydebank. Donaldson's, where her father worked, was halfway between the two. Further down there was Beardmore's at Dalmuir.

Boy, was it noisy sometimes! The sound of hammers hitting iron and the rivets being banged into place echoed all along the river bank. It could be deafening, but it was a good sound. It meant that the men were working – and if the men were working, there was food on the table. Aye, it was a good sound.

And maybe, just maybe, if the orders kept coming and her father kept off the drink . . . maybe Lily would relent about her staying on at school. Maybe.

Kate sighed heavily and went into the close. As the neighbours said, her mother Lily didn't have her troubles to seek. There was the continuous struggle to make ends meet and a husband who too often tried to find solace for painful memories at the bottom of a bottle. And then there had been the twins – Eliza and Ewen – who had died in the 'flu epidemic back in 1919. They had come home from school one Friday and never gone back. Lily kept their schoolbags, in the top drawer of the tallboy in the front room. They were just as the twins had left them, with their spelling cards unlearned, their writing homework half done. Kate had crept in to look at the old jotters once, crying hot and silent tears over the round and smudgy letters of the alphabet.

Robbie's mother was mopping the stairs which led to the Baxter flat on the first floor.

'Well, Kate,' she said, swabbing down one half at a time so that folk could get past. 'It's a struggle, eh?'

19

'It is that.' Kate sighed, thinking about the twins.

Agnes Baxter, dipping the mop in soapy water and then squeezing it out hard in the drainage sieve of the galvanised bucket, smiled at her tone. 'That sounds really heartfelt.' She looked up and the smile was replaced by a swift frown. 'What's the matter, hen? You look gey tired.'

'I'm just fed up, Mrs Baxter. Feeling sorry for myself, I expect.'

Agnes Baxter leaned heavily on her mop. 'You'll have had the lion's share of the chores to do, I'm thinking.'

Kate shrugged. 'Och well, just the stairs to do now.' There was no point in trying to deny it to Robbie's mother. With everyone living on top of each other and the flats being so small, everybody knew everybody else's business.

'And yourself,' said Agnes. 'A bit of titivating for tonight, eh? You know,' she said, putting her head to one side and studying Kate thoughtfully, 'I've got a dress that might do you, if we make a few alterations. Got it from one of my ladies.'

Agnes supplemented the Baxter family income by doing dressmaking for some of the better-off families in Clydebank. She surveyed Kate with a professional eye. 'You're a bonnie girl, Kate Cameron, and no mistake. I wish my lassies had nice natural waves in their hair like you do. It's my Robbie that's got the best of it in that department. Wasted on a laddie, eh?'

Kate hid a smile. Robbie had three wee sisters – Alice, Flora and Barbara. While they had thick and glossy hair like their brother, it was, unlike his, perfectly straight. They were beautiful girls, with big solemn eyes which belied their mischievous natures. Kate thought their hair was real bonnie.

Mrs Baxter, however, unwilling to let nature take its course, subjected her three daughters to what Robbie referred to as 'the instruments of torture' in an attempt to produce waves

20

or curls on the heads of her offspring. Andrew, as a boy, was exempt from this, but the little girls had their hair wrapped up tightly in rags every night to produce smooth fat ringlets which had fallen out by halfway through the next morning.

When they had their hair washed once a week, the wavers were brought out. Like huge steel paper clamps with teeth, three of them were applied to each small head. Terrible threats were issued as to what would happen if they took the wavers out before the next morning. Kate smiled at the thought.

'That's better.' Mrs Baxter nodded approvingly. 'A lassie like you should smile more often.' She nudged the girl with her elbow. 'Laddies like to see a bit of a sparkle, especially a certain laddie we both know.'

'Eh, I'd better get on. I've still got the stairs to do.' Shyly, Kate dipped her head and started past Mrs Baxter. Why did everybody assume . . . ?

Agnes Baxter put a hand on her arm. 'Don't you bother about your stairs. I might as well see to them too, since I've got the mop and bucket out.'

'Och but Mrs Baxter, you'll have your own house to do.'

Agnes winked. 'I've got my lazy good-for-nothing family doing most o' that. I can easily manage another flight of stairs. Now, get on with you. You don't want to go dirty into the New Year, do you now?'

Kate pushed open the heavy door into the flat which she'd left on the latch before she'd gone downstairs to hang out the washing. It gave onto a tiny hall with a door to either side. One led to the room at the front of the house where her parents slept with wee Davie. She could hear her mother in there now, crashing and banging as she got on with some heavy-duty dusting of the furniture. Kate turned. There was suppressed giggling coming from the other room.

This was the living-room, and kitchen, and bedroom for

Kate, her sisters and Granny. The old lady was dottled now, but Kate could mind what she'd been like before. When she'd still been fit she and Kate had gone for walks and Granny had told her what Yoker was like in the old days, before their houses had been built. People had always called it 'the Yoker' then. It had all been fields and there had been an old mill, and where the Yoker burn flowed into the Clyde, men had fished for salmon. Hard to imagine now. The river was always beautiful to Kate, but it *was* dirty. That she had to admit.

Granny didn't always know who Kate – or anybody else – was now, or even what time of day it was. More than once she'd wakened the girls in the middle of the night telling them to come and take their porridge. It was time they were off to the school.

The last time it had happened she'd even started cooking the porridge, left to soak overnight in a big black pan. Nobody knew how she'd found the strength to lift it onto the range which stood on the wall along from the box bed where Kate, Jess and Pearl slept. 'She'll have us burned in our beds!' Pearl had wailed, but Lily had given her a swift clout round the ear and told her not to be so stupid.

The three girls took it in turns to sleep with Granny on the hurly bed which had to be pulled out every night from a cupboard under the box bed. Except that Pearl never wanted to take her turn.

'Oh, hello Jenny. How are you the day?' Jenny had been Granny's sister who'd died of diphtheria when she was fourteen. Kate would normally have gone along with it, answered her grandmother as though she were that Jenny who'd died so long ago. Contradicting the old woman only distressed her and made her more confused.

For now, Kate merely smiled absently at her grandmother where she sat in the corner. Baby Davie was at her feet, snug in his cot made out of one of the drawers of the tallboy in

Mammy and Daddy's room. It was lined with an old sheet, folded several times over to make his wee bed as soft as possible. Judging by the faint smell wafting across to Kate's nostrils, she was going to have to change his nappy soon, but that certainly wasn't the most important thing on her mind at the moment.

Pearl was nowhere to be seen. That was by no means unusual when there was work to be done. As Mrs Baxter was prone to say – 'That lassie could get a job as a magician's apprentice. The disappearing lady.'

It wasn't Pearl who was bothering Kate at the moment. Two heads had snapped up guiltily when she had come into the room – one smooth, one curly. The former belonged to Barbara Baxter. Her mother hadn't yet had time to wield the instruments of torture in preparation for the New Year. The second head belonged to Kate's sister Jessie.

'Would one of you two wee dafties like to tell me what you think you're doing?'

She didn't really need an answer. It was quite clear what they had been doing. They had pulled out a stool to stand in front of the range and put the big enamel basin which doubled as baby bath and additional laundry bucket on top of it. In it, covered in soap suds, one of them perched rakishly over his right eye, sat a very angry Mr Asquith. Only the fact that two very determined little girls were gamely holding onto him was preventing his escape – although that could only be a matter of time. The cat was slippery with soap and rapidly approaching the spitting stage. Kate knew an emergency when she saw one.

'Quick, Jessie. A jug of clean water. Pour it over him to get rid of the soap. Barbara, go and open the front door. Shout down to your mother that he's on his way so she doesn't get a fright.'

Mr Asquith reached the front door in a quivering mass of

outraged wet fur so quickly that Kate, following in his wake, didn't have too many damp patches to mop up. She crooked her finger at Barbara to come in from the landing and ushered her back through to the kitchen.

Kate, hands on hips, had to suppress a smile. The two miscreants were looking at her like prisoners waiting for the judge to put on the black cap. Any minute now they were going to ask for a last cigarette. She saw Jessie extend a comforting hand under the folds of their pinafores to her friend.

'Prisoners at the bar,' intoned Kate. 'What have you to say in your defence?'

The girls exchanged glances. Jessie seemed to have been elected spokeswoman.

'Well, everything else is getting washed for the New Year—'

'You don't wash cats!' said Kate, half laughing, half horrified. 'They do it for themselves. They're very clean animals.'

'Don't tell Mammy, Kate,' pleaded Jessie.

'I'll not tell Mammy,' she promised. She pointed a finger at Barbara. 'But you'd better swear your Mammy to secrecy. And don't let me catch either of you doing such a daft thing again. Promise?'

Chapter 2

'That lassie's nearly asleep. She's needin' her bed.'

'No, I'm not.' Kate started up so abruptly from where she sat in the crook of her father's arm that she nudged his other hand, the one holding his whisky glass. A few drops spilled on his waistcoat. Neil Cameron smiled down at his daughter.

'No harm done, lassie. It hasn't spilled on your drawing, has it?' Kate had been spending some of the long hours waiting for midnight to strike by doing a sketch of the assembled company. The kitchen was full.

Mr and Mrs MacLean from across the landing were in and the Baxters too, except for Robbie. He was staying downstairs till midnight. The bairns of both families were tucked up in bed. Pearl and Jessie had gone only under protest but were now snoring softly behind Kate, the curtains drawn over the bed recess.

She retrieved her sketch pad which had slipped unheeded off her lap some time before and sat bolt upright, trying to look as wide awake as possible. She wasn't going to miss the bells.

Lily jumped up to fetch a cloth from the jaw-box, the sink under the window. Neil accepted her dabbing at his front good-humouredly, lifting his whisky clear of the stain, his long slim fingers curled round the rough tumbler.

Kate had always been fascinated by her father's hands. They were rough and calloused from his work in the shipyard, but

25

there was a fineness about them. Once, he'd told her, he'd wanted to become a painter, an artist. When he'd been a laddie back at school in Lochaber, he'd always been good at sketching.

'And did you ever paint anything, Daddy?' Kate had asked, sitting on his knee and looking up at him with shining eyes, because she was her Daddy's pet, she knew she was.

'Och, no my lassie, I never did, but maybe you will. Maybe you'll become a famous artist one day.' And he had smiled and started singing softly to her. Her favourite song.

'I'll take you home again, Kathleen . . .'

He had sung it tonight, earlier in the evening when everyone had been doing their party piece. The other children had stayed up for that. Jessie had recited 'John Anderson, My Jo', and Kate and Pearl had sung a duet.

'Oh rowan tree, oh rowan tree, thou'll aye be dear to me, Entwined thou art wi' mony ties o' hame and infancy . . .'

Everybody loved 'The Rowan Tree', especially the bit about mother sitting *'wi' little Jeannie on her lap, wi' Jamie at her knee, oh-ho, rowan tree . . .'* Singing of children who had gone on before was particularly poignant in the Cameron household.

When the sweet, sad melody was finished everyone had clapped. Mrs MacLean had cried openly and even Jim Baxter had dabbed his eyes.

'Oh dear,' he said. 'Would that song no' bring a tear to a glass eye?'

Everybody laughed, happy to participate in the peculiarly enjoyable sadness of a Scottish Hogmanay.

There had been funny stories too. Lily repeated the tale of how Kate had got her name. 'Kathleen, he wanted to call her. "It's a bonnie name," he said. "Well," says I to him, "it may be a bonnie name, but everybody will think that we're Irish. Worse, that we're Catholics." And then he says to me – "what would *that* matter?"'

Everyone had laughed at that one. Neil Cameron, when he had first come down to Glasgow from the more tolerant atmosphere of the Highlands, had been unaware of how much it did matter. Lily, in full flood, went on with her story.

'What did it matter? "Well," says I, "there's no Catholic going to get a start at Brown's or Donaldson's, is there? Or a lot o' other places for that matter".'

Mrs MacLean leaned forward in her seat, frowning in perplexity. 'But Mrs Cameron, Kate's a lassie. She wouldnae be looking for the start in the shipyards anyway, would she now?'

'In the name o' God, woman.' That was Mr MacLean. 'Mrs Cameron's talking about the general principle. Is that not right, Mrs C.?'

Kate allowed her concentration to drift. She'd heard the story too many times. She didn't like the way her mother made fun of her father's Highland naiveté, either. Mind you, if she was being fair, she had to admit that her mother had a point. It was hard enough for either sex to get a start anywhere. Being a Catholic made it that much harder. So Kathleen had become Kate. Only her father occasionally used her name in full. And Robbie.

He arrived at midnight, just after the toasts had been drunk. Neil Cameron, as master of the house, got up to let him in. They shook hands formally and wished each other a Happy New Year and many of them. Now that Robbie was away from the school and bringing in a wage, however small, his stock had gone up in the community. Not quite a man yet, but no longer a boy.

He handed over the traditional gifts: a lump of coal for the fire, a bottle of whisky, and some black bun that his mother had made the day before. They were talismans – offerings to the gods. Food and drink should guarantee plenty of the same in the year ahead and coal should ensure that the house would always be warm.

'Thank you, Robbie. Will you have a wee dram yourself, man?' Neil, smiling, threw a quick glance over his shoulder to Robbie's parents. 'Is he old enough? Will you allow him?'

'It's all right, Mr Cameron,' said Robbie. 'I've signed the pledge. I've decided to stay teetotal.'

'Well done!' said Neil, slapping him on the shoulder. 'That's a fine thing for a man to do.' Behind his back, several sets of eyebrows were raised. 'And it makes more for the rest of us. Come away in then, and we'll get you something *teetotal*.' He laughed, emphasising the word.

'Lassie, will you pour Robbie a glass o' yon ginger?' He spun round towards the window. 'Och, would you listen to that? Is that not a rare sound?' Out on the river, the ships were blowing their foghorns, heralding the start of 1925 in their own special and time-honoured fashion.

Kate rose and went over to the draining board of the sink where the lemonade bottle stood. Robbie followed her and spoke in a low voice.

'I've got a wee present for you too, Kate.'

'Oh?' Shyly, remembering how sharply she'd spoken to him that afternoon, she took the proffered bundle, wrapped up in a sheet of newspaper. It was a wooden carving of a robin, perched on a piece of mossy wood. He had painted the bird, its breast a startling splash of scarlet.

'Oh, Robbie, it's real bonnie!' On an impulse she stretched up and gave him a peck on the cheek, then flushed deeply and threw an anxious glance over her shoulder.

'It's all right,' came his soft voice. 'None of them saw.'

Kate's green eyes met Robbie's cool grey gaze with extreme reluctance.

'It's all right, Kate,' he repeated. He seemed on the point of saying something else. Kate wasn't at all sure that she wanted to hear it. He opened his mouth to speak, hesitated, and gestured with a nod of his head to the carving of the robin which she held in her hands.

'I'm not as good a painter as you, but I think I've managed it not bad. There's always these bits of wood left over at work.' Robbie, like his father before him, was serving his time as a cabinet-maker and joiner. 'I found the wee log down by the river. You know yon big trees, past where the rowan trees are? There's a big branch that got snapped off during the gales last month, so I broke this bit off for the robin to stand on.'

Somehow Kate had the feeling that wasn't what he'd started out to say. She also had the distinct feeling that he was prattling on, which wasn't like him at all. Giving her time to recover? Recover from what? Pushing the thought to the back of her mind she smiled at him. 'It's lovely,' she said firmly. 'Did you make a robin because of what Mr Asquith did?'

Robbie nodded his shaggy head. It was less unruly than usual this evening. His mother might not use the instruments of torture on him but she had obviously instructed him to wet his hair to dampen it down before coming upstairs.

'You were that upset when he killed yon wee robin you'd been feeding . . . And I thought, well, he can't get this one, at any rate. Can you, you wee monster?' he went on, stooping to stroke the culprit who was snaking his way around his legs.

'Happy New Year, cat,' he said, scratching the sleek head. 'Gosh, his fur feels real smooth. Has your Ma been polishing him or something?'

When Robbie suggested that Kate come out for a walk with him half an hour later, she opened her mouth to say no, but her mother forestalled her.

'It's too cold out there.'

Neil Cameron and Agnes Baxter exchanged a look.

'Och no, Lily,' said Agnes, 'it's quite mild really. Well, no' exactly mild, but if they go well happed up, they'll be fine.'

'It's too late,' snapped Lily.

'No, it's not. It's Hogmanay. There'll be other people out walking,' said Kate's father, giving Agnes Baxter what looked suspiciously like a wink.

'But—' began Lily.

Neil Cameron's good humour evaporated. 'Enough,' he growled, bringing his fist down hard on the table beside him. 'Am I not allowed to be master in my own house?' The whisky was beginning to do its work.

There was an embarrassed silence. Mr and Mrs MacLean glanced nervously at each other and murmured something about it being time they should be thinking of going home. Lily fixed Kate with a look. 'You heard your father. On you go.' She turned her gaze to Robbie. 'But if the two of you are no' back in half an hour there's gonnae be trouble.'

'Come on, Kate,' said Robbie. 'Where's your coat? And mind and put your muffler on. It'll be real cold by the river.'

It *was* real cold by the river. They had walked the short distance from the house to the ferry in silence, an unaccustomed awkwardness between them. She wouldn't have thought twice about being alone with Robbie before, but something was shifting and changing between them – and Kate didn't like it one little bit.

There was, however, no need to discuss where they were walking. They always headed for the river, first the ferry and then along the path which skirted the grounds of the old distillery.

Kate paused by the railings which guarded the unwary from falling onto the ferry slipway. The river was like black silk, flowing steadily through the night towards the sea, its smooth surface dotted with shimmering reflections of the lights of the houses across the river in Renfrew, everybody up late tonight to see in the New Year. Robbie was silent at her side, waiting for her to speak.

'I'm sorry,' she said at last. 'I bit your head off this afternoon, didn't I?'

'Aye, you did,' he said, his voice slow and considering. Its tone was beginning to deepen as he grew older. 'Och, but Kate, I understand full well why. You've got a lot on your plate. And it's not fair.'

She turned to him. His face looked different in the dim light. And when had he got that much taller than her? He outstripped her now by several inches.

'Oh, Robbie, why do we have to grow up?'

He smiled, his teeth a gleam of white. 'Do you not think that growing up might have some advantages, hen?'

Kate looked at him warily, her eyes growing used to the darkness. There was something mischievous about that smile.

'What are you looking at me like that for?'

His smile grew broader. He took a step towards her. Kate, in response, took a step back, coming up hard against the railings.

'You can't go any further,' pointed out logical Robbie. 'Forbye you want to end up in the river. And,' he went on, raising his eyebrows quizzically, 'as far as I know, Miss Kathleen Cameron, you can't swim. So you might as well let me kiss you.'

The statement took Kate's breath away.

'Kiss me?'

'Aye. Why not? After all, it is New Year.'

She curved her fingers in their woollen gloves around the cold metal of the railings. 'So . . . This is just a friendly New Year kiss, is it?'

'Yes, of course.'

'But,' Kate pointed out, 'you've already had a friendly New Year kiss.'

31

'Well, I want another one. A proper one this time. Without half o' Yoker looking on.' Taking a step forward, Robbie put an end to any further discussion, bobbing his head down and planting a firm kiss on her cold cheek. He lifted his head.

Behind them, the Clyde continued on its silent way. The railings which Kate's fingers gripped were no less cold or hard than they had been before, the ground beneath her feet no less solid. Nothing had changed. Everything had changed.

'Kate . . .' Robbie whispered. They stood so close together that she could feel his breath warm on her face. 'Och, Kate, don't look so worried, hen.' He bent his dark head once more, and this time he kissed her full on the lips. His arms came around her, pulling her against him. Kate's hands released their hold on the railings. She felt . . . she didn't know what she felt. His lips were firm and soft at the same time, warm on her cold mouth.

'No!' she said, struggling in his embrace.

Robbie loosened his hold immediately. 'No?'

'I don't want this, Robbie,' she gasped. 'You're my friend.'

She could hear his breathing, quick and shallow. For a frozen moment they stared at each other. He dropped his arms, allowing her to step out of his embrace. He tossed his head, clearing the lock of hair which had fallen across his forehead.

Kate's own breathing was coming too fast, her breasts rising and falling with the rapidity of it. She put a hand out towards Robbie, but he ignored it.

'Come on then. I'll take you home.' He turned on his heel and headed off without waiting to see if she was following him.

'Robbie?' She struggled to keep up with his longer stride. 'Robbie, I'm sorry. It's just . . . Well, I want us to be friends. I want it to stay that way. The way it's always been . . .'

He didn't answer at once, leading the way back up to the

main road. Then he stopped so abruptly under a streetlight that Kate cannoned into him. His hand shot out to grip her arm in support.

'All right?' he asked.

Kate nodded, impatiently pushing a strand of hair under her knitted hat. She saw Robbie's eyes follow the movement. There was something in that look which made her very uncomfortable.

Just when she was beginning to think that he hadn't taken in what she'd said about being friends, he spoke. His voice was gentle.

'We'll always be friends, Kate. Always.'

Kate looked up at him and wondered why what he had said made her feel so sad.

When she finally got to bed she lay awake, staring into the dark in the silent house. Everyone else was sound asleep. It was a gey lonely feeling. Sometimes, on other nights, she would hear her parents through the wall in the next room, her father's voice a low persuasive murmur, and then she would hear her mother . . . but she didn't want to think about that. She never liked to think about that.

She shifted her shoulders. She wanted to turn over, but the movement would disturb Jessie. The sleeping Pearl had been lifted down onto the hurly bed to lie beside Granny.

Kate blew out a long breath. Why did things have to change? Why couldn't it be like it had always been between her and Robbie? She had placed the carving of the robin on the narrow shelf which ran along the back wall of the bed recess. She couldn't see it, but she knew it was there. He had made it specially for her, spent hours on it probably, getting it just right.

She tried not to think about it. Nor about how his lips

33

had felt on hers, or how strong and warm his arms had been as he had held her against him. And yet, she had started it, with that quick impulsive kiss. She had started it.

Chapter 3

Neil Cameron seemed to have gained another four inches in height.

'He's that puffed up with the excitement of the occasion,' whispered Jessie from behind her hand to Kate. 'I'm scared he's going to burst!'

Mind you, thought Kate, suppressing a laugh and looking around at the other men, you could say the same for all of them. It was launch day at Donaldson's and work had come to a standstill. The men stood eagerly awaiting the arrival of the launch party onto the platform which had been constructed at the bow of the ship.

Kate had to admit that she was feeling pretty pleased herself. It had been decreed that the men could bring their families to the launch. Agnes Baxter had come up with the dress she'd promised Kate back in December. It was a sprigged cotton with a honey-coloured background, decorated with tiny flowers in navy and dusky pink. She'd also found a knitting pattern for a bolero which Kate herself had made. It was navy, picking up the colour of the tiny flowers in the dress.

Jessie had knitted one too. Hers was yellow to go with her best frock – which had been Kate's best frock until she had grown out of it last year. Agnes, looking unusually ferocious with a mouthful of pins, had pronounced the necessity of letting the new dress out at the bust. 'You'll never have a flat chest, Kate Cameron, and that's a fact. Now hop up onto the table so I can check the hem.'

Kate, on display in the kitchen in front of Mammy, her sisters, Granny and what seemed like a sizeable part of the female population of Yoker, had let her hair fall over her face to hide her embarrassment. Fashion might decree a boyish figure and the new bust bodices might be designed to help a girl achieve just that, but Kate knew she was a hopeless case.

Even Mammy had seemed to enjoy all this prettifying. She hadn't even complained when Neil had found the few shillings necessary to buy the wool for the boleros. She had put her foot down about Kate's hair though. She might be nearly sixteen, but she wasn't to be allowed to put it up.

'You're no' going to put your hair up till you're eighteen, my lady, and there's an end to it!'

So Kate brushed her hair till it shone and pinned her old straw hat on top of her head. Agnes had helped out again, finding a new piece of navy ribbon to trim it with.

Kate caught sight of a tousled head about twenty yards away, over to her right. Like her, Robbie was scanning the crowd. When she caught his eye he grinned and waved. With a slight nod of his head he drew Kate's attention to his father standing beside him. Jim Baxter had his face lifted towards the hull of the *Irish Princess*, his mouth curved in a smile of pure pleasure. He had his flat cap, his *bunnet*, clutched to his chest, ready to fling it into the air once she was launched.

'See you later,' mouthed Robbie, and Kate nodded.

'Look,' she whispered to Jessie and Pearl, 'Mr Baxter's going to burst too.' Jessie giggled, but Pearl gave her a very knowing look.

'What?' Kate demanded, resisting the temptation to plant her hands on her hips, fishwife-style.

'Oh, nothing,' said Pearl. 'Happy now that you've seen him though, are you?'

'I can't think what you mean,' said Kate airily. 'Would that wind off the river not cut right through you? You wouldn't think it was April, would you?' Pearl gave her another look, one which a twelve-year-old certainly shouldn't have been capable of.

Robbie was a friend, that was all. There had been no repetition of what had happened at Hogmanay. In her more honest moments, Kate didn't know whether she was happy or sorry about that.

The noise level around them ebbed and flowed. The wind was cold but it was a beautiful spring day, with a blue sky above them – a good omen for the launch of the *Irish Princess*. The men had laid her keel last summer and they were bringing her in well on time, although the launch of a ship was far from the end of the story.

Almost as soon as she hit the river, she would be tugged back into the fitting-out basin for the interior work to be done. There was a lot of carpentry involved in that – internal bulkheads and panels for the cabins, the making of the furniture – beds, tables and chairs.

Destined for the Glasgow–Dublin run, the *Irish Princess* wasn't a big ship, but she was a bonnie one, small and neat with nice lines.

Kate said as much to her father. 'What's that, lass?' He inclined his head to hear her better over the hubbub, rising now in anticipation of the imminent launch.

'Aye, you're right there. Lovely lines.' Neil smiled at his daughter. 'I wish the whole family could have been here.'

Wee Davie was thick with the cold. For one awful, selfish moment, Kate had been scared that Mammy would make her stay home to mind him, but Lily had declared that she herself would do it, Granny being no longer fit to be left in charge of a baby.

'Never mind, Daddy,' said Kate. 'There'll be plenty of other launches they can come to.'

'Aye, lass.' The two words were said without much conviction.

Kate could have kicked herself. It had been the wrong thing to say. There was no guarantee that there would be plenty of other launches. There was another ship on the stocks, a cargo steamer, but once she was complete there was little else on the order books.

Kate's father, like many men, could and did take his skills to other yards along the river, but it was the same story there.

Neil Cameron had no trouble getting work when he came home after the war. He was a riveter, a time-served man, and with half the country's shipping destroyed in the hostilities, there had been plenty of work. Lately, though, things had started to get quiet. Worryingly quiet.

Neil had been laid off twice in the past two years. That had been terrible. She'd nearly had to leave school then. There was dole money, but it didn't go far – and a family didn't get it at all until the Means Test Inspector had been to the house, poking and prying and trying to prove that there was some money coming in to the house from somewhere, that they were lying about what they needed to get by.

Kate's cheeks burned still at the memory of those humiliating visits and the spectacle of her father being forced to put his Highland pride in his pocket in order to beg for the money to keep his family going until he was back in work.

Trying to think of something to say that would lift the frown creasing Neil's forehead, she was interrupted by Mr Crawford, one of the managers, coming round handing out sweets, a launch-day tradition.

'Take a couple, lassies. There's plenty.' Encouraged by his smile, Jessie shyly did as she was bid, dipping her hand into the crumpled paper bag and extracting two sweets, brightly wrapped in coloured paper.

'I'll save one for Davie,' she told Kate.

'So will I,' replied her sister, smiling her thanks to Mr Crawford in his dark suit and bowler hat, the badge of his office.

'Well, I'm going to eat both o' mines myself,' said Pearl, tossing her golden curls.

'You would,' said Kate and Jessie in unison. Arthur Crawford moved on, making his way back through the crowd, seeking out the men who belonged to his own squads.

A murmured comment from a few rows in front of them floated back to the Cameron family. 'Sweeties, is it? And we all know that the bastards in bowlers would pay you off as soon as look at you.'

Neil Cameron's Highland accent was more pronounced than ever.

'Mind your language, man. I've got my family here.'

'Oh, sorry, Neil. I didnae notice. Ladies present too, I see.' The man had turned to look at them. Kate didn't like the way he was looking Pearl up and down. She liked it even less when he did it to her.

There was a bustle behind them.

'Launch party coming through!' bellowed a deep voice.

'Mrs Donaldson,' Neil informed his daughters. 'The owner's wife.'

Mrs Donaldson was a tall woman, rolls of sleek blonde marcelled hair visible under a wide brimmed hat. She wore a light camel-hair costume with a fox fur round her neck. She swept past just yards from the Cameron girls.

'Oh, doesn't she look lovely!' breathed Pearl, staring after her in awe-struck admiration.

'Aye, if you want to festoon yourself wi' dead animals,' said Jessie acerbically.

Kate grinned at her. Mrs MacLean had a fox fur which she brought out, smelling heavily of mothballs, on special occasions. She arranged it like Mrs Donaldson's, with the fox's head hanging down over her bosom. The first time Jessie saw it she had said, 'The poor wee thing!' and burst into inconsolable tears. Kate had to admit it gave her the willies too, glass eyes shining where once the fox's own eyes had been, glittering and alive in the freedom of the night.

Aware of other eyes on her, Kate turned and met the gaze of a girl who might have been her own age or perhaps a few years older. She was walking towards the platform, following the men in bowler hats who, in their turn, were walking behind Mr and Mrs Donaldson.

If Pearl had admired Mrs Donaldson, she was all but speechless now. The girl, tall and willowy – and with practically no bust that Kate could see – was dressed in the latest fashion. Her silk afternoon frock had the new fashionable low waist and the skirt was cut on the bias so that the material hung and clung in the most flattering way. The cloth was almost the same colour as Kate's frock but the pattern on it was abstract, modern and right up-to-date. Kate, so proud a few minutes before of her pretty sprigged cotton, felt dowdy and old-fashioned in comparison. The girl's hair was short and fair, tucked neatly under one of the new little cloche hats. Two long strings of pearls completed the picture. She smiled at Kate and moved on, making her way elegantly up onto the launch platform. Her legs were slim but shapely, encased in shiny silk stockings.

'Well, look who it is. The workers' friend.'

Several heads in the crowd turned and there was a rumble of disapproving murmurs. A couple were hurrying through the crowd – well, they were trying to hurry. The woman looked like a bad imitation of Mrs Donaldson. She had the fox fur all right, but her camel-hair costume wasn't nearly so well cut and it was at least two sizes too small. She was red in the face from what seemed to be unaccustomed exertion.

It was her husband who had caught the interest of the men. After a second or two, Kate recognised him. He was the Means Test Inspector. She glanced anxiously at her father's thunderous face. With a few others he moved to bar the man's progress. The Camerons weren't the only family to have been visited by him in the past couple of years.

'How you've got the brass neck to show your face here—'

'I only do my job, Cameron. Just like you.'

'Aye, but you enjoy it a wee bit too much for our liking,' said another man, his voice a growl of soft menace. The three Cameron sisters exchanged anxious glances. They knew from experience that it often took a lot less than this for a fight to break out.

'My lady wife and I have an invitation,' blustered the man. 'From Mr Donaldson himself.'

'I don't care if you've got an invitation from the Archangel Gabriel.'

'Wullie!' his wife wailed. 'We're not going to to see a *demned* thing.'

Jessie snorted. 'Touch of the pan loaf, wouldn't you say?' she murmured. It was the expression they used for anyone trying to put on airs and graces. Anxiety at the prospect of missing the launch was stripping the mock-gentility from the woman's speech, her working-class origins shining through. Her elocution teacher would have been ashamed of her.

'Gentlemen! Gentlemen!' It was the man who had looked Kate and Pearl up and down. He laid a restraining hand on a couple of shoulders. 'Let's not have any trouble on launch day now. We'll allow the lady and gentleman to pass. In fact, we'll do better than that. We'll find them

41

an excellent vantage point – just to show there's no hard feelings.'

Neil Cameron and the other men fell back without a murmur, bland smiles on their faces. Kate had seen nothing, but somehow a signal had been given. Ushering the inspector and his wife through the crowd, the apparent peacemaker turned and gave her a swift wink. She looked across at her father. There was a definite twinkle in his eye, but he put one long finger up to his mouth in a gesture of silence.

'May God bless her and all who sail in her!' The bottle of champagne broke over the bow. For one awful, heart-stopping moment Kate thought that the ship wasn't going to move at all. The crowd seemed to be holding its collective breath. Jess slipped her hand into Kate's. Even Pearl darted an anxious glance up at their father.

Then, so slowly at first that the movement was barely perceptible, the *Irish Princess* began to slide away from the platform towards the river. All of a sudden she gathered speed and a roar went up from the assembled workforce. She was really moving now, so swiftly that Kate saw why they had to attach chains to arrest her progress towards the Clyde. Huge rusty red clouds of dust rose from them, sparks flew out and there was a noise like the sea washing over shingle – only a hundred times louder. She hit the river.

'Oh, Daddy, she's not gonnae sink, is she?' cried Jessie.

Neil Cameron laughed. 'The Clyde's not deep enough for her to sink, lassie. Just watch what happens now, and keep your eye on those daft laddies right down by the waterfront.' He pointed out a knot of apprentices standing to the right of the slipway and several yards above it. A man and woman stood with them. 'We got the boys to show them a *really* good vantage point.'

Jessie's eyes were dancing. 'Oh, Daddy, you didnae!'

Neil chuckled. 'We did, lassie. We did!'

Just when it looked as though the *Irish Princess* might be going to sink after all, she bobbed and righted herself. The bunnets were flung in the air and a mighty cheer went up. It was followed by a deep rumbling laugh which spread throughout the assembled crowd. When the ship slid into the water, her displacement caused a great wave to come back up the slipway. It was huge and unstoppable, rising several yards to cover anyone foolish enough to be standing near it. The apprentices yelped and ran. The Means Test Inspector and his wife also yelped – and tried to run. It was no use. The end result was the same. They were soaked from head to foot.

The excitement over, people began to mingle. Under cover of the general conversation, Kate asked Robbie about the young woman who'd been part of the launch party.

'Oh, that's Donaldson's daughter, Marjorie. My Ma does some dressmaking for her and her mother.'

'Oh,' said Kate. So that's what the look and the wee smile had been about. Kate was wearing Marjorie Donaldson's cast-offs.

'She's a smasher,' broke in Pearl. 'Don't you think so, Robbie?'

'If you like that skinny, straight up and down look, I suppose,' he said absently, turning to wave to some of the other apprentices.

Kate laughed. Smiling at Robbie, she gestured towards the launch platform.

'A sturdily built structure, eh?'

Robbie grinned back. Pearl looked puzzled.

'I don't think building a platform's very exciting.'

Robbie's dark eyebrows went up. 'Oh, you don't, Miss Pearl Cameron? Let me tell you something. That platform marks a great pinnacle of achievement for me. It's the first thing I've actually been allowed to do any real carpentry on – and it's a good deal better than being sent to fetch some tartan paint.'

Neil Cameron clapped Robbie on the shoulders. 'Och, laddie, you didn't fall for that one, did you?'

Robbie gave him a wry smile. 'That one – and the long stand. Green as cabbage, I was.'

Neil laughed, as did Jim Baxter. Jessie wrinkled her nose. 'What's the long stand?'

Jim Baxter explained. 'When a laddie gets a start, there's a few jokes get played on him at first. One is being sent to fetch the tartan paint and another one is to send him for a long stand. When he gets to the store, the chap there tells him he'll need to wait a while for it.' He turned to Neil for confirmation. 'I've known laddies wait half an hour. Have you not, Neil?'

'Even longer sometimes,' said Neil, nodding his head and smiling at Robbie.

'So eventually the laddie gets fed up and repeats the request – he was sent for a long stand – to which the answer is – you've just had it!'

'Well, girls?' asked Jim when they had all finished laughing. 'What did you think of the launch then?'

'It was great,' said Kate. 'Really exciting. And when she hit the water—'

'Aye,' said Jessie. 'That was rare, especially when all those folk at the front got soaked.' She laughed up at Kate. 'I was scared she wasn't going to move at first, were you not, Kate?'

'It's always like that, lass,' said Neil, putting a large hand out to smooth his youngest daughter's hair. 'Your heart's in your mouth . . . and then she goes down so sweetly, like a seal sliding off a rock into the ocean. It's quite something to watch a ship you've worked on with your own two hands take to the water.' His voice was suddenly husky.

'Aye, Da,' said Kate gently, giving Jessie a quick smile. *'Pride of the Clyde.'*

Neil Cameron, his eyes bright, patted Kate on the shoulder.

'Huh!' said Pearl in disgust. 'Listen to the lot of you. It's just a big lump o' iron and metal and wood. And now she's launched, there'll be no work for the Black Squad.'

Kate could have hit her sister. Her father's face fell and the light which had been in it a few seconds before died away as though it had never been. As a riveter, he belonged to the Black Squad, the team of men who worked on the basic skeleton of a ship. Once the hull was complete, there was no work for them. They either moved on to the next yard on the river which was laying the keel for a ship or they were out of work – for days, weeks or months.

Neil Cameron was still working at Donaldson's because of the small cargo ship still on the stocks, but her hull wasn't going to take long to complete. If another order didn't come in soon, Neil knew as well as anybody what was going to happen. None better.

He was proud of his skills and it pained him to be idle. Kate frowned at her sister behind their father's back. Pearl looked innocently back. She was a minx.

Kate looked up and saw the understanding in Robbie's eyes. At least, she thought, trying to smile at him, there would be plenty of work for him and his father. Carpentry was a good trade. It would take a good few months to complete the internal fitting out of the *Irish Princess*.

Unless one of the yards on the river got another order, however, things were soon going to get hard again in the Cameron household – and Kate's chances of staying on at school were growing smaller by the day.

'Kate! Kate!' Lily's voice was filled with panic. Roused from dreams of ships gliding into the river, Kate sat bolt upright and threw the blankets off. There was a low growl of objection from Mr Asquith, curled up at the foot of the bed. Beside Kate, Jessie gave a small grunt of protest.

'Kate! Your father's having one o' his nightmares!'

Pausing only to hurriedly replace the blankets over her sleeping sister, Kate padded through to the front room, the oil-cloth cold and sticky on her bare feet.

Wee Davie, woken by the noise, was screaming in his drawer-cot, his mother making frantic efforts to calm him down.

Neil was sitting on the edge of the bed, one hand clinging onto the brass bedstead. He was wild-eyed, his hair dishevelled. Lily, lifting Davie to calm him, cast a worried glance over her shoulder.

'It's all right, Mammy,' said Kate, quelling her own rising panic. She crouched in front of Neil. He was muttering to himself, a low-voiced stream of words in the Gaelic none of his family could understand. Kate took a deep breath. She had seen him like this before. Many times. She had calmed him before. She could do it now.

'Daddy,' she said softly. 'Daddy. It's all right.'

He lifted his head at the sound of her voice and focused painfully on her face. His hands shot out and gripped her shoulders. Kate winced. She was going to have bruises there tomorrow.

'He's coming for me! The Devil! He's coming for me!'

'Kate! Tell him not to say these things!' Her mother was sobbing. Wee Davie, held in an iron grip to his mother's breast, was bawling at the top of his lungs. Jess and Pearl would be awake by now, thought Kate grimly. If they've any sense they'll stay where they are.

Kate, her mother screeching in one ear and the whole household roused, spoke quietly but firmly to her father.

'You're fine, Daddy. You're safe. At home with us in the

Yoker.' She had to repeat it over and over again until the glazed eyes focused properly on her and the iron grip on her shoulders relaxed. The tension went out of him and the rigid body slumped. He spoke her name.

'Kate?'

A shaky hand came out to stroke her hair. Kate's deep sigh of relief was cut off by her mother thrusting the baby into her arms. 'Settle Davie down while I attend to your father.'

She bundled Neil back into the bed before fetching a stone piggy to put at his feet, refilled with hot water from the huge black kettle which stood hissing on the range day and night.

Kate's own feet were like lumps of ice by the time she got back into the box bed. Wee Davie had taken a while to settle.

'Is Daddy all right, Kate?' came a small voice from the darkness.

Kate patted Jessie's neat little hand. 'Aye, he's fine now. Away back to sleep, you.'

'Why does he have the bad dreams, Kate?'

'I think,' said Kate, pausing to think how to phrase her answer, 'because of the things he saw in the war. It was terrible for the soldiers in the trenches, you know?'

She wondered if Jessie would ask more questions, but in a few moments she heard her sister's breathing change and knew that she was asleep. Oblivion for Kate took longer to come.

The first glimmers of dawn were creeping through the gap in the curtains before she dozed off. The light allowed her to see the little carved robin, the red splash of paint on its breast growing clearer and clearer in the early morning light.

Red for danger. Red for life. Red for blood. Neil Cameron must have seen terrible things in the war – must have done terrible things too, been forced to do them. How awful that

47

must have been for a man as gentle as her father; how awful
to have memories that tormented you for the rest of your life,
so terrible that you thought the Devil would claim you as one
of his own . . .

Chapter 4

Kate was so happy she thought she might faint with the sheer joy of it. Oh, Mammy, Daddy, wouldn't that be terrible! She straightened herself up in the high-backed chair and concentrated hard on her surroundings. She'd been in tearooms once or twice before but never in one as grand as this.

The Clydebank ones she knew were nice enough, with flowery curtains and comfortable cushions on the chairs, but the design here was entirely different. It was all stained glass and mirrors – simpler somehow, and cleaner. She could see that the stained glass was designed to look like a stylised willow and there was also, she saw, a rose pattern all over the place, but nothing like the roses you saw on flowery chintzes. This rose was purple, or sometimes a dusky pink like the flowers on her dress.

The chair in which she sat was tall and painted silver, with a design of small glass squares set into its high back, three squares across and three squares down forming a larger square. The glass was purple too. It made a beautiful contrast with the silver-painted wood.

'Kathleen?' came Miss Noble's voice. 'More tea, my dear?'

'Th-thank you, Miss Noble.'

Her teacher smiled at her and waited expectantly. 'Put your milk in first, dear. I find it tastes better that way, don't you?'

'Perhaps Kathleen is not a pre-lactarian, Frances.'

Frances Noble smiled at the other woman at the table. 'Miss MacGregor is always ready for a debate, Kathleen. On the most insignificant of subjects.'

Kate smiled uncertainly at the two women. Her teacher, Miss Noble, had arranged a Saturday afternoon visit to the Art School on Garnethill. Not only that, she had then announced that they would go on to afternoon tea at Miss Cranston's, to the Willow Tearooms in Sauchiehall Street. Although, as she'd said with a sigh, Miss Cranston had sold all her tearooms a few years previously, when her husband had died.

Her teacher didn't wait for an answer on the milk question, picking up the jug herself and pouring it into the cup. Kate's father drank his tea out of a saucer. A dish of *tay*, he called it, and there was never any discussion as to whether or not the milk should go in first. They did have china cups and saucers at home. They were kept in her mother's pride and joy, the display cabinet in the front room, but they were hardly ever used; only when the minister came round. The children were never allowed to drink out of them. They had to make do with ugly green Delft cups and saucers.

There was nothing ugly on this table. The china cups had gold edging, there were dainty little plates with even daintier little knives on them. In the middle of the table was a three-tiered silver cake-stand. China plates slotted into it. On the bottom, there were sandwiches, in the middle biscuits and on the top iced cakes. The table itself was covered with a lace tablecloth. Kate thought the whole place was beautiful, and plucked up the courage to say so.

'I'm glad you like it, dear,' said Miss Noble, beaming at her protégée. 'Although I'm not sure that Kate Cranston – or Toshie – would have approved of the lace tablecloths. Plain white damask would have been more in their line, I fear.'

'Toshie?' asked Kate.

'Charles Rennie Mackintosh, my dear,' said Miss MacGregor.

'A man ahead of his time, and unappreciated in Glasgow.' She sighed. 'Ah well, they do say that a prophet is always without honour in his own country, don't they? He and his wife Margaret – a gifted artist in her own right – went off to live in France. What, about five years ago, Frances?'

'About that, I believe,' murmured Miss Noble.

'He's the man who designed the Art School?' asked Kate.

'Yes, it's easy to spot the similarities, isn't it?'

'Oh aye,' said Kate enthusiastically, waving one hand towards the rest of the tearoom in illustration. 'The stained glass, the purples and pinks, the rose design—'

She broke off, suddenly embarrassed. Both women were smiling at her.

'Miss Noble says that you have a good eye,' went on Miss MacGregor.

Kate blushed. 'Well, I do like nice things, I suppose.'

'And you like drawing them too, I hear,' probed Esmé MacGregor gently.

'Aye, I do.'

Frances Noble lifted Kate's plate to the cakestand and deposited two sandwiches on it. 'Not *aye*, dear, say *yes*.'

The light of battle shone in Esmé MacGregor's eyes. 'Now, Frances, I don't know that we should be trying to completely eradicate Scotticisms from the children's speech. Lallans has a robust and honourable history, you know.'

'Not now, Esmé,' said Miss Noble firmly. Her companion gave her a surprisingly engaging grin and turned her attention once more to Kate, who was nibbling on one of her sandwiches and hoping that her table manners were up to scratch.

They thought, they told her, that she should stay on at school, try to get into the Art School next year, when she turned seventeen. If she passed her Higher Leaving Certificate, and Miss Noble was sure that she would, Miss MacGregor could arrange an interview with the Principal for her nearer the time. There were scholarships available for gifted students whose families were in straitened circumstances.

Kate's tea grew cold as they talked.

'See you at school on Monday, my dear!' shouted Miss Noble as they waved her off on the tram. Kate smiled and waved back. Sinking onto the hard wooden seats, she stared out at the street and buildings and people hurrying by. She saw none of it.

Words and images were swirling around her head. They had called her a 'gifted student'. They had shown her the Art School, where she had seen light-filled studios and young men and women working at canvases set on large easels. There had been loads of space for them to work in. Everywhere she'd looked there had been canvases, sketch pads, oil paints and water colours, crayons and charcoal. She had never imagined that such a place existed; a place where she could learn to become an artist.

Scowling at the outside world through the window of the tram, Kate tried to work out how she could be part of it. A scholarship was all very well, even if it did include a small allowance, but it wouldn't be the same as her bringing in a wage. And she had to get through another year at school before she could apply for the scholarship. If only Donaldson's could get another order, or Brown's, or any of the other yards. It didn't matter. The Black Squad would go where the work was.

Only there wasn't any at the moment. Maybe something would come in. She could get a Saturday job – at Woolworth's along in Clydebank maybe. Her frown lifted. Yes, that might do. If she got the scholarship and did a Saturday job – and if Da got work soon. Oh please God, let an order come into the yard!

She closed her eyes tight shut and sent up a heartfelt prayer. She wanted to go to the Art School, to be part of it. Oh, how much she wanted to be part of it! Just one more year at school, that was all she needed. Just one more year!

Robbie was waiting for her when she came off the tram. His face lit up when he saw her and she could tell by the stiff way he pushed himself off the wall he'd been leaning on that he'd been waiting for ages.

'Been waiting long?'

'Och no,' he lied, 'about ten minutes.'

'And the rest,' she said.

He grinned. 'I never could get away with anything with you, Kate Cameron, could I?'

'Nope,' she said cheerfully.

'Well?' he demanded.

It came out in a rush. 'They think I should stay on at school. Then go to the Art School, up in Glasgow. They think I'm good enough. They think I could try for a scholarship. That would pay the fees and give me money for materials, and a small allowance, a living allowance. They really think I'm good enough.' Try as she might, she couldn't keep the bubbling excitement and pride out of her voice. She smiled up at him.

'Of course you're good enough,' said loyal Robbie. 'Have I not always told you that? You're great at drawing and painting and all that sort of stuff.' He smiled back at her, a long slow smile. It brought a deep curve to his mouth and a sparkle to his grey eyes.

'What?' asked Kate.

'Nothing,' he said, still smiling broadly at her. 'Nothing. Come on, let's go and tell everybody.'

Robbie's wee sisters were playing at skipping in the back court. Barbara and Flora were holding a length of rope and

Alice and some other girls were taking their turn at jumping. Barbara and Flora swung the rope gently backwards and forwards and Alice began jumping over it as they all chanted the song.

'*Christopher Columbus was a very brave man, he sailed through the ocean in an old tin can. The waves grew higher and higher and OVER!*'

The last word was the signal for the two rope wielders to change from *rocky* to *coy*, swinging the rope in an arc over the head and under the feet of the skipper. Sometimes a girl was caught out straight away, tangled in the rope, but Alice was good at skipping. All the girls joined in the number count. '*Five-ten-fifteen-twenty* . . .' The winner was the one who reached the highest number without the rope catching her ankles. Towser the dog was watching them with great interest, his eyes and his head following the movement of the rope.

On the way past, Robbie reached out and ruffled Barbara's hair. She scowled at him, but refused to allow the disturbance to break her concentration. Alice was still jumping. '*Eighty-five-ninety. Ninety-five-a hundred* . . .'

The young voices followed them as they plunged out of the sunlight of the April afternoon into the darkness of the close.

'Your mother'll give you a doing, Robert Baxter,' Kate laughed. 'You've just ruined what was left of Barbara's waves.'

Robbie laughed too, his smile a flash of white in the gloom of the close. 'No, she'll not. I'm too big for her now, anyway.' He stopped and laid a tentative hand on Kate's shoulder. 'I'm that pleased for you, Kate—' He broke off. 'What was that?'

It was a voice, echoing down the stairwell – Lily's voice, high-pitched and angry. She was letting rip with a stream of invective. Whoever she was shouting at didn't seem to

54

be answering back. Kate looked anxiously at Robbie. Front doors were opening all around them.

'In the name o' God . . .'

'Neil's for it this time – and that's a fact.'

Agnes Baxter appeared at her door on the first landing. 'Ma!' said Robbie. 'What the hell's going on?'

Agnes's glance slid past her son to Kate. 'Oh, Kate, hen, I'm sorry. Your Da's been paid off. The whole o' the Black Squad. And your Da's not home yet, Robbie . . . Mr MacLean told me that a crowd of them went along to Connolly's and they were there most of the afternoon.'

Robbie took the stairs two at a time, Kate and Agnes following him as fast as they could. Neil Cameron sat slumped in his chair in front of the range. His wife was standing over him, hands on hips. Her golden hair, escaping from its pins, was falling in wisps about her face. She was calling him – or rather miscalling him – for everything under the sun.

Jessie and Pearl, sitting as still as china statues on the edge of the box bed, had eyes as big as saucers. Granny, smiling gently in the corner, was oblivious to the drama being played out in the kitchen. From beneath the curtain which covered the space under the jaw-box sink, Kate saw the tips of two paws and a white nose peeking out. Mr Asquith had obviously decided that discretion was the better part of valour. If the scene hadn't been so tragic, it might have been comic.

Neil Cameron smiled stupidly up at his wife. She lifted an arm, ready to strike him. He made no move to defend himself. He seemed rather to be inviting it, something like a challenge gleaming in his eyes.

'Go on, then,' he said softly to Lily. 'Do it.'

Fleetingly, Kate had another image of them before her eyes; the memory of her mother on her knees in front of the range, combing out her hair, her father stooping to lift her into his embrace . . .

55

The expression on Lily's face was unreadable. She drew her arm further back, ready to deliver the blow. Jessie gasped when she saw her mother's hand go up.

Robbie took two rapid strides across the room. 'Now, now Mrs Cameron. You'll not be doing that. You might regret it later.'

Lily turned on Robbie then, eyes flashing. 'Do you know what he's done? Do you know?'

'I think I can guess,' murmured Robbie, 'but hitting him won't help anybody, now will it?' He put his hand on her elbow. She drew in a breath, staring at him. Then, suddenly, her whole body seemed to relax and she allowed Robbie to lead her to the rocking chair on the other side of the range and push her into it, gesturing to his mother to come and stand by her.

'Has he drunk all his pay, Lily?' asked Agnes, her good-natured face lined with anxious enquiry.

'Aye, he's drunk his pay, the rotten, no-good bloody bugger! There's only half a crown left.' She dug into the pocket of her apron and threw the coin onto the floor. 'And there's no work anywhere along the river. None o' them has got any orders.' She sank her face into her hands. Just as suddenly her head snapped back up and her eyes fixed on Kate.

'There'll be no more school for you,' she said. 'That's you finished wi' that. Come Monday, you're out knocking on doors, looking for work.'

'The lassie's staying on at school!' They had all been focused on Lily and hadn't noticed Neil getting to his feet. He stood there, swaying, dwarfing the kitchen with his height. He repeated it, bellowing the words out. 'The lassie's staying on! To make something of herself!'

Lily, pushing Agnes Baxter's restraining hand aside, rose to her feet and squared up to her husband.

'Like you've made something of yourself, Neil Cameron?'

she demanded. 'You're a waster, that's what you are.' She poked him in the chest with one finger to emphasise her point. 'Och, you were handsome enough. Still are, when you're not guttered, but you'll never amount to anything.'

The kitchen held its collective breath, but the fight seemed to have gone out of Neil Cameron.

'Don't be like that, Lily. It was the war, Lily, that's what did for me . . .'

His voice tailed off in the face of his wife's contempt. 'Other men came back from the war and made a go of it. What happened to you? No backbone, that's your trouble.'

His eyes, terribly, filled with tears. 'Och, Lily . . .'

Kate, stunned with the horror of it all, stood frozen. She should do something, but what? She had no idea. She just knew she wanted it to end.

Agnes Baxter took control. She gestured to Pearl and Jessie to climb down from the bed and ushered them towards the door. 'Girls, away ben to the front room and get your wee brother and go down to our house. Jessie, fetch Barbara from the back court and tell her to give everyone a scone. They're just new baked.'

Jessie and Pearl looked anxiously to Kate for reassurance as they left the room. She couldn't seem to find any words of comfort to offer them. She couldn't even manage a smile.

'Neil, sit down here and I'll make you and Lily a cup of tea.' Agnes pulled Neil back to his chair. Once she had him settled in it to her satisfaction, she stood up straight, turned round and took in Kate's rigid form and white face. She exchanged a glance with her son. 'Robbie, why don't you take Kate out for a wee while?'

Robbie shot Kate a glance, then gestured to Neil. 'Are you sure you can manage him, Ma?' he asked in a low voice.

'Aye, son. The worst's over.' She was right. Both Neil and

Lily were slumped in their respective chairs. Agnes lifted a hand to pat her son on the shoulder.

'There's some money in the silver tea caddy on the sideboard. Why don't you take Kate to the pictures? Take her mind off it, like.'

'Aye, Ma. We'll do that. All right, Kate?'

They took a tram along to Clydebank and saw a cowboy picture. Of that much Kate was aware. She couldn't have told anybody what the story was, or even who the stars were. When they came out of the cinema, Robbie said just one word. 'Home?'

Kate shook the chestnut-brown waves of her hair. 'No. Not yet. Can we – can we walk a bit?'

'Of course we can. There's no rush.'

Kate managed a small smile. 'You're looking after me well. You and your mother both.'

Robbie shrugged.

'You know,' Kate went on. 'Where I was this afternoon – at the Art School and the tearoom I mean—' She paused, lifted her hand to indicate Dumbarton Road. 'Well, it's only up in Glasgow, just a few miles away, but in another way it might as well be on the moon. I'm never going to get there. It's not for the likes of us, that's the trouble, only you keep hoping and hoping that it might be.'

Robbie had fallen silent by her side, his eyes downcast, listening to what she was saying.

'Not for the likes of us,' she repeated softly.

He looked up then, his expression fierce. 'You're not to say that, Kate. I won't have you saying that. There's got to be a way we can get you there, some way you can stay on at school.'

'Oh, Robbie,' said Kate, angry with him, with herself and the whole world. 'You know I can't stay on at school after what happened this afternoon. I've got to get a job. You heard her. She's always on about it. Thinks I've stayed on far too long already. And she's right, I suppose. With my father laid off again, someone'll have to start bringing some money into the house. There's only me as can do it.' To her horror, her eyes filled with tears. She turned her head away quickly, but not quickly enough.

'Oh, Kate,' he said, running an angry hand through his already tousled locks. 'Oh, Kate,' he repeated. He was frowning heavily. 'Come on, let's get the tram along a couple of stops and go for a walk by the river.'

The river. Her refuge. Unchanging and yet always changing. Today it was dark as ink, gliding peacefully in the evening sun to the open sea. The sky was impossibly blue, the clouds white and fluffy.

'You wouldn't think it was near nine o'clock, would you?'

Apart from that one comment, Robbie walked tall and silent beside her. She was grateful for that. He didn't try to offer empty words of comfort. She said as much to him. He stopped dead beside her, twisting his flat cap in his hands and stared at her, his eyes very clear beneath angry black brows. She took an involuntary step backwards.

'Christ!' he said explosively. 'Not offer you comfort! And you're grateful to me for that! Jesus Christ, Kathleen Cameron!'

She stared at him. This was a new Robbie, one whose grey eyes flashed with anger and frustration; one who squared his shoulders and tossed his head back, glaring at her; not a boy any more, but a man. It gave her a funny feeling inside, one she couldn't explain. One she didn't want to explain.

He quietened. 'I'm sorry for taking the Lord's name in vain,' he said stiffly.

'Robbie?' She reached out a hand to him.

'Come on,' he said, moving away from her. 'I think I can

just about afford to buy you an ice cream at Pelosi's. Are you coming?'

'Robbie?' she said again. She caught him up and laid a hand on his arm, her fingers curving round his elbow. He stopped but didn't look at her. The wind off the river lifted his hair.

'Promise me something.'

'What?' His voice was raw-edged.

'That you'll get out of here. That you'll go to sea. Make something of yourself.' She grimaced, remembering when she had last heard that phrase used.

He turned to look at her, his expression softening.

'Och, Kate, maybe it's just a dream. A wee boy's dream. Wanting to have an adventure.' His mouth curved in a self-deprecating smile. 'Wanting to set sail for *Treasure Island* with Jim Hawkins and Long John Silver – you know?'

Her fingers tightened on the rough cloth of his jacket. 'But you can do it. It's within your grasp, once you've served your time. Promise me you'll do it.'

'I don't know, Kate.' His eyes were downcast again, his dark lashes long and feathery against his cheekbones.

'Oh, Robbie, what is there to keep you here? A lifetime of looking for work and then being laid off again. What is there to keep you here?'

He looked her full in the face.

'You, of all people, should know what would keep me here. *Who* would keep me here.'

Kate let her hand drop from his arm. She took a step backwards. He held her gaze, challenging, daring her to drop her eyes.

'Oh, Robbie, don't! You and I . . . No, . . . that's not meant to be. I've told you how I feel. I thought that was all sorted out. I don't want you hanging on waiting for me . . .'

She put out a hand, warding him off, reading quite clearly

his intention of taking her in his arms. 'Robbie, don't! I don't want it!' Her voice was high and breathless.

He hesitated, his face full of warring emotions. Then he smiled, a wry twist of the lips.

'Pick my moments, don't I, Kate? And always the wrong ones. Mr Bad Timing, that's me. Come on, let's go for that ice cream.'

Kate tried one last time. 'Robbie, do you ever listen to me? Did you hear what I just said?'

He took a decisive step towards her, gripped her by the shoulders and planted a swift kiss on her forehead.

'I heard you,' he said.

Chapter 5

'So what exactly does a tracer do?'

'Traces things.'

Arthur Crawford smiled at the bright-eyed girl in front of him. Good. That had raised a wee smile. He sighed inwardly. The lassie didn't have her troubles to seek, he knew that. Her teacher, Frances Noble, was his wife's sister, and he'd heard the story more than once. Clever enough to stay on at school, good enough to go to art college, but no money to allow her to do it. Well, she wasn't the only one, not by a long chalk. He couldn't give them all a start, but Frances had put in a good word for this girl.

He surveyed Kate where she sat on the opposite side of the desk from him. Her clothes were threadbare, but her skirt was pressed and the creamy-coloured blouse with the big collar which she wore had been freshly washed and starched. And the lassie was clever. She'd got top marks in the exam she'd sat, along with fifty other girls, last week. So far, so good. A good tracer didn't necessarily need to be artistic, but she did have to be neat and lively minded.

Like John Brown's, the next yard along the river, Donaldson's set an entrance examination every year for girls hoping to be taken on for a tracing apprenticeship. Only ten new apprentices were taken on each year, so there was a great deal of competition for each position.

Kate's exam paper had been the best of all. Arthur Crawford told her so.

'Oh,' she said, giving him a shy smile and trying not to dip her head in embarrassment at the compliment. 'Well, I enjoyed doing it, really.'

She had been surprised at how wide-ranging the questions had been: English and arithmetic; history; knowledge of the yards and the shipbuilding trade; general knowledge. She'd known that her answers had been good. I'd give me a job, she'd thought to herself, and then wondered if she'd tempted fate by being too cocky during the agonising week's wait for the results.

'It was fine realising that I knew those things – that all that information was in my head.'

Arthur Crawford smiled. 'I believe there would be a position for you here, Miss Cameron – if you're interested in the work, that is.'

Kate crossed her fingers, hidden out of sight at her side by the folds in her dark brown skirt. Interested in the work? No, not really, but what choice did she have?

'I'm very interested,' she said firmly, 'but do Donaldson's need tracers at the moment? I thought there were no orders on the books. I'm not looking for any favours, Mr Crawford.'

As proud as her father, he thought. Until the drink gets to him. There were some who would think him daft to put in a good word for Neil Cameron's daughter, but Neil had been a good man – still was, when he was sober. And, according to his sister-in-law, the lassie's mother was hard on her. She needed a hand up. There was something about this girl – something that needed encouragement, something that made him want to help her for her own sake. Spreading his hands out on either side of the pad of blotting paper in the centre of the desk, he smiled at Kate.

'There's one just come in. The designers are busy on it

right now.' He saw the hope leap into Kate's eyes and knew that it was for her father, not for herself. He put a hand up in admonition. 'There'll be no work for the Black Squad for six months, but the plans need to be drawn up – and then copied.'

He explained further. That when a ship was built there were plans for everything, not just the hull and the superstructure, but for internal decks and bulkheads, cabins, storerooms, pipework, all sorts of internal fittings. There might be as many as fifty drawings for one ship, he told her, for a really big vessel even more.

'So the engineers and everyone else involved need copies of the design drawings. That's where the tracers come in. They get the drawings from the draughtsmen, who do them in pencil. The tracers then trace off a copy in ink, very clearly, very accurately—' He broke off, smiling. 'Some of the lassies would say a lot more neatly than the draughtsmen do them. They're always moaning about having to tidy up messy drawings. After that the drawings go to photography so that everyone who needs a copy can have one. Even the interior designers need plans.'

'The interior designers?'

'Aye, the folk who make the insides beautiful.' Arthur Crawford grinned again. 'Those who decide which colour the internal bulkheads should be and what paintings go up on the walls – even what the cups and saucers in the restaurant should be like. There's a lot of folk work on a ship, you know. It's a joint effort. You could be part of it, lass.'

For the first time, Kate felt the stirrings of real interest. It was the way Mr Crawford had put it – that she, Kathleen Cameron, could be part of building a ship. That *would* be something to be proud of. Struck by the thought, she had a vision of herself at the next launch, watching a beautiful vessel slipping into the Clyde. What had her father said? *Like*

64

a seal sliding off a rock into the ocean. It was a beautiful sight – made you want to laugh and cry at the same time, your heart bursting with pride.

If she got a job here, she wouldn't just be proud for Daddy, or for Robbie, or his father. She would be proud on her own account, because she would have helped the ship on its first journey – that most difficult voyage from an idea in someone's head to blueprints and plans which enabled other skilled heads and hands make that vision real. She could see it now – her family looking at her with admiration. Her mother might even be impressed! She could boast about it to the neighbours:

'My daughter's a tracer, you know.'

Kate jumped when Arthur Crawford stood up, his chair scraping the stone floor. She leaped to her feet, looking at him expectantly. He came round the desk and ushered her towards the door.

'Come on,' he said, 'I'll show you where the tracers work.'

They worked in a building tucked in at one side of the yard, just a hundred yards from the main gate. It had three storeys. On the top floor, Kate learned, the design team were based. Below them were the draughtsmen and below them, the tracers.

The tracers worked in a large airy room, with huge floor-to-ceiling windows along one wall and rows of long tables and stools. Electric lamps were bolted onto the tables at regular intervals.

'For the winter,' said Arthur Crawford, seeing her glance at them. 'Good light's crucial for close work. You'll find that out for yourself.'

Kate had been impressed to learn that the plans were photographed. The knowledge that the tracers had electric light to work by when natural light wasn't good enough impressed her even more. At home they had gas-mantles and still sometimes used the old brass paraffin lamp which had been one of Granny's wedding presents.

'Donaldson's employ a lot of tracers then?' Kate did a quick estimate of the stools. There had to be around sixty. The big room was quiet and echoing today, the tracers too having been paid off when the orders had dried up.

A tall angular woman dressed in a black overall came forward and was introduced as Miss Nugent, the Chief Tracer. She was the only member of the department to have kept her job during the shut-down. She shook hands with Arthur Crawford, listened unsmiling to what he said, peered over pince-nez spectacles at Kate and fired questions at her. Did she have her Third Year Leaving Certificate? Which subjects was she good at? What were her interests and hobbies? What was her father to trade? Where did she live? Was she punctual? Kate saw the infinitesimal lift of the eyebrows when Miss Nugent learned that her father was an unemployed member of the Black Squad, but she seemed at last to be satisfied, and began rattling out information in her turn.

'It's a five-year apprenticeship. We'll pay you five shillings a week to begin with. You'll be taught on the job and you'll be expected to work hard. We also encourage our girls to attend evening classes – in any subject. If you do so, you receive an extra sixpence per week in your pay packet. You look neat,' she went on, scarcely pausing to draw breath, 'and your showing in the examination was excellent. That's what's needed in this job – neatness and intelligence. I understand you have artistic tendencies.' Miss Nugent's tone of voice made it crystal clear that this was not a compliment.

'Y-yes . . .' stammered Kate, taken aback that the woman had finally stopped and seemed to be anticipating some kind of response from her. *Five years!* That was forever. Especially when it wasn't what you wanted to do with your life. The beautiful vision of herself at the launch vanished, burst like one of the soap bubbles wee Davie loved to be allowed to blow on wash day. She wanted to learn how to draw and paint, not be under this dragon's thumb for the next five years.

The dragon was looking at her over the little gold specs perched on the end of her bony nose. Kate wondered if she really needed them or if they were a prop to help her look at you as though you'd just crawled out from under some stone. A father in the Black Squad *and* artistic tendencies? Dear me. Miss Nugent made them both sound like hanging offences.

Her next words confirmed Kate's worst fears.

'Your artistic talent is not necessarily an advantage,' Miss Nugent was saying sternly. 'The artistic *temperament* is certainly not required here.' She allowed herself a little smile, directing it at Arthur Crawford. Her eyes came back to Kate and the smile faded.

Any minute now, thought Kate, she's going to wag her finger at me. This is like being back at school. Worse – Miss Noble would never speak to me like this. Artistic temperament, indeed! What does she think I'm going to do? Dance naked around the room with a rose between my teeth? Her rebellious mouth curved at the thought. Miss Nugent's eyes narrowed and her mouth pursed.

'All my girls must pull together and it's hard work, mind! There's no place here for slackers. Bearing that in mind, are you still interested in being considered for a position at Donaldson's, Miss Cameron?'

Stung, Kate drew herself up to her full height. At five feet four, this wasn't particularly impressive, but bullies like this one needed standing up to.

'I'm used to hard work, Miss Nugent.' Oh, Mammy, Daddy, what was she saying? Did she really want to spend five years with this tyrant? Did she have a choice? No – she didn't. There was, however, one last question to be answered before she committed herself.

'What about the girls who were laid off? Won't they all expect their jobs back?'

Miss Nugent looked shocked. 'The decision on who gets a position here is taken by Mr Donaldson, his management – and trusted members of staff.' A conspiratorial smile to Arthur Crawford left no doubt that Miss Nugent considered herself – and him – to belong to the latter group.

'Half of them'll have gone to Singer's anyway,' he put in.

Kate knew that to be true. The Singer sewing-machine factory up on Kilbowie Hill was doing well – had even increased its workforce. Miss Nugent was speaking again.

'With a new order on the books we at Donaldson's have vacancies, especially for beginners like yourself whom we can train up.'

Kate knew what that meant. It was an old shipyard trick. Once the apprentices completed their time, they were paid off and new apprentices taken on in their place. It saved the bosses from having to pay a time-served man the pay he was due.

That five shillings wasn't going to go very far. Lily would expect her to hand over almost all of it. And a five-year apprenticeship! Her dreams of the Art School were receding by the minute.

Kate gave herself a mental shake. Both Arthur Crawford and Miss Nugent were looking at her, waiting for her answer. Who did she think she was, keeping these trusted members of Mr Donaldson's staff waiting? A tiny and inappropriate bubble of humour surfaced. And her only the daughter of a riveter, too. The lowest of the low.

One day she would show them. She would become the best tracer Donaldson's had ever had. She would rise through the ranks. Maybe she would even become a – what had Mr Crawford called them, '*the folk who make the insides beautiful*' – interior designers, wasn't it? Yes, that's what she would do. One day people would ask each other if

68

they'd seen the beautiful designs Kathleen Cameron had done for the new ship – a transatlantic liner, of course, like the *Lusitania* and her sister ships, all built next door at John Brown's. None of your rubbish. That would show Miss Nugent.

Amused by her thoughts, she gave the woman a lovely smile. I'll be gracious, thought Kate – like the young Duchess of York whom she'd seen on a newsreel last week. What was her name again? Princess Elizabeth.

'Yes,' she said, extending her hand the way she'd seen the Duchess do in the film, so dainty and lady-like. Maybe Miss Nugent'll kiss it instead of shaking it, she thought. *Aye, and then I can look out of those big windows and see the pigs flying past.* Kate smiled again. 'Yes, I should like to be considered for a position here.'

Arthur Crawford saw her out, escorting her to the main gate. The shipyard was unusually silent, only a few men having been kept on to keep things ticking over. Even Robbie and his father had been laid off. Kate, remembering the boisterous and light-hearted crowd on the day of the launch of the *Irish Princess*, shivered.

'Watch your feet.'

Glancing down, she saw a patch of oily water, and stepped around it. They were at the gate. Arthur Crawford nodded to the gatekeeper who sat in a small office to one side of the huge double wooden gates, and opened a smaller door built into one side of them. Signalling to her to go through in front of him, he came out behind her into the sunshine of Dumbarton Road. He held out his hand.

'Well, goodbye then, Miss Cameron,' he said, 'and well done. You can give yourself a wee pat on the back.'

Kate, tucking a strand of hair behind her ear, smiled at him and took the plunge. A tram car, bound for the terminus at

Dalmuir, clanked and rattled past them. She waited until the noise died away before she spoke.

'Mr Crawford . . .'

'Yes, lass?'

'When you need the Black Squad again . . .'

Arthur Crawford coughed. He knew full well what Kate was asking. He patted her on the shoulder.

'Your dad's a good man, pet, and we'll be needing the Black Squad back in soon, but he has to cut back on the drink. We can't have that. We really can't. It's dangerous, for one thing. Can you and your Ma try and keep him off the bevvy?'

Kate sighed. 'I'll try, Mr Crawford, I'll try.'

'Good girl.' He took his hand off her shoulder, lifted his head and looked across the main road. 'There's Robbie come to meet you – to see how you've got on, no doubt. You've got a good lad there, hen.'

'He's not—' began Kate but Arthur Crawford had already disappeared back into the yard, the small door within the gates swinging shut behind him.

Robbie, smiling, darted between two trams to cross the road to her. 'How did you get on?' he asked eagerly.

'I start in August.' And then, forgetting modesty, and because she knew how pleased he would be for her, 'I got top marks in the exam.'

His face broke into a delighted smile.

'Oh, Kate, that's magic!' Seizing her by the waist, he swung her around.

'Robbie, put me down!' She was laughing, one hand resting lightly on his shoulder to help keep her balance. An old couple walking past on the pavement smiled at them.

'She's just got a start,' Robbie told them, 'as a tracer.'

The old man gave Kate a toothless grin. 'Well, hen, that certainly is something to celebrate.' He touched his bunnet to her and walked on. Robbie laughed down into Kate's face.

70

'You're a right clever wee thing, Kathleen Cameron—' He broke off suddenly, setting her down on the pavement and whirling around, his head turned to listen. From the other side of the main road came the sound of a handbell being rung – fast, loud and insistent.

The laughter died out of Robbie's face. It was replaced by a determined look and his grey eyes grew steely.

'It's an eviction. Come on, Kate!'

Grabbing her hand, dodging between a tram and a horse-drawn coal lorry, he pulled her across the road in the direction of the frantic ringing.

Chapter 6

The woman looked terrified. She also looked very young. Despite the baby she held in her skinny arms, clutched tightly to her breast, and despite the two children clinging onto her shapeless skirt, Kate realised with a jolt that she was only a few years older than herself. She and her children stood in front of a pathetic pile of furniture which was growing larger as a group of men carried the family's possessions out of the tenement block from which they were being evicted.

'It's a damned disgrace,' a woman shouted, 'putting the lassie out while her man's not in the house.' The voice was familiar. Standing on tiptoe to peer over Robbie's shoulder, Kate saw that it was Agnes Baxter. With three or four other women she was squaring up to the removal men and a man holding a sheaf of papers who seemed to be in charge of the proceedings.

There were shouts of, 'Shame!' from the people gathering in front of the tenement, spilling off the broad pavement into the street.

One by one, half a dozen men detached themselves from the crowd and moved through it to surround the girl. One of her older children whimpered at their approach, re-doubling his grip on his mother's skirt so fiercely that she nearly lost her balance. One of the men, tall and straight, gave a deep, reassuring laugh, bent down and lifted the boy onto his shoulders, turning tears to delighted laughter within seconds. Kate gasped. It was her father Neil.

'My Da and your Ma,' she whispered before she realised that Robbie was no longer in front of her. He too was one of the men now standing around the little family like a guard of honour, shielding their trembling bodies from the man Kate had now worked out was the sheriff's officer, and the men he had employed to carry out the eviction. It was a scene which had become all too familiar in Clydebank in recent months.

A mere fifty years before, within living memory, the town hadn't existed at all. When J. & G. Thomson decided to build a shipyard downriver from overcrowded Glasgow in 1871 – the yard which was later to become the world-famous John Brown's – they had chosen an area of green fields known as the Barns o' Clyde. There had been nothing there but a few cottages.

By the time the American Singer company started building Europe's biggest sewing-machine factory eleven years later, other companies had moved in and Clydebank – named after Thomson's yard – was set to boom. Houses for the new and rapidly-expanding workforce, some of them built by the companies themselves, were hastily thrown up.

Too hastily, in many cases. By the 1920s, when landlords tried to introduce rent rises for tenement flats which were often damp, poky and badly constructed, tenants had decided that enough was enough. They banded together and called a rent strike, refusing to pay the increased rents unless and until improvements were made.

The landlords fought back. Some tenants found that their arrears of rent were being stopped from their wages – an indication that many employers were in cahoots with the land-lords' factors. As the dispute escalated, the landlords became heavy-handed, taking tenants to court for non-payment. The law too seemed to be on their side, and eviction orders were not hard to get.

Political leaders – men like the local Labour MP Davie Kirkwood – had advised people to put the rent money to one side, so that when it came to the crunch, families would be able to pay the arrears and not have to face being thrown out onto the street. With so many men out of work, however, the idea of being able to keep any money by was a bad joke.

The outside world called the rent strike militancy and gave the town, along with its bigger neighbour Glasgow, a nickname which was to endure for decades: Red Clydeside. There were many who took pride in that name. Others felt it did more harm than good, putting new companies off from setting up in the town. Most Bankies, pushed beyond endurance by the struggle to feed and clothe large families in small, damp and overcrowded houses, living constantly with the threat and the reality of unemployment, thought their rent strike was a simple matter of survival. Kate knew that her father was one of them – and Agnes Baxter.

It was she who'd rung a handbell to summon assistance, a strategy which had rapidly been adopted as the evictions had increased. It was a signal which brought everyone within earshot running – particularly the women. More likely to be at home during the day, they had come to play a leading role in what had rapidly developed into a war between the people and the factors. The latter had tried carrying out evictions at dinner-time, just as wives were cooking and dishing out meals for hungry husbands, assuming that women wouldn't break off from their household duties. They had been wrong.

The strategy changed again. The factors began to carry out the evictions at night. An appropriate response was mounted. Kate's father had joined the Vigilantes, a group which patrolled the town during the hours of darkness. If they couldn't prevent an eviction they at least found someone to take the affected family in and give them a roof over their heads.

Agnes Baxter had stopped ringing the bell and was haranguing the men removing the furniture from the flat. They were looking nervously to the sheriff's officer for guidance. The crowd was big enough to be intimidating, and the phalanx of men standing around the evicted family all looked as though they meant business.

'Youse ought to be ashamed o' yourselves!' Agnes waved an angry hand at the young mother. 'Where d'you think this lassie and her bairns are going to spend the night, eh? Answer me that!'

'That's no' our concern, missus. We've got a job to do. Now, if you'd just let the men get on wi' it . . .'

Agnes put her hands on her hips. She wasn't a big woman, but she had personality enough – and anger enough – to present a formidable obstacle. Kate saw Robbie glance sideways at his mother, his mouth quirking. She caught his eye and he gave her a wink and the ghost of a smile. Neil Cameron, the young boy still riding high on his broad shoulders, moved forward to stand beside Agnes, laying a reassuring hand on her shoulder. She glanced behind her to see who it was, and gave him a quick nod of recognition. Then she turned her attention once more to the sheriff's officer, standing uneasily in front of her.

'Putting women and children out o' their houses, is it? Think that's *man's* work then, do you?'

The look she gave him, from his head to his toes and then back again, was one of unmistakeable sexual appraisal. A slow blush spread over the man's face, creeping up from his stiff white collar. There were some sniggers, but the crowd remained curiously quiet, awaiting the outcome of this encounter with edgy anticipation. Kate knew that it could go either way. An eruption into violence might be only seconds away. She sent up a swift prayer. *Please God, don't let anybody get hurt.*

Robbie's mother, however, knew what she was about. She gave her victim a cool smile, then a look of withering contempt, and she took a step towards him. The officer made the mistake of taking a step backwards. The crowd hooted its derision and erupted, but into laughs, catcalls and whistles.

Kate laughed too. The man was at least a foot taller than Agnes. It was a ridiculous sight – the majesty of the law humbled by a wee woman from Yoker with her hands on her hips and a gleam in her eye.

Another voice, deep and authoritative, sounded out over the hubbub.

'Be off with you, man – and your carrion crows. There's not a man jack of us in this crowd that doesn't need a job – but there's some work no decent man would undertake.'

Neil Cameron shot the waiting helpers a look of haughty disdain, his soft Highland accent underscoring the contempt in his voice.

'Be off with you,' he said again. 'There'll be no eviction here today.'

To huge applause, the removal men left, the sheriff's officer making a series of blustering threats as he departed which convinced no one. Strange, thought Kate, nothing other than peaceful resistance had been offered. Yet a distinct threat had hung in the air – along with something much more wholesome. The little family had been given the protection of the community. Neil, Robbie, Agnes, the other men who had surrounded the mother and her children – they had all quite literally been prepared to stand up and be counted.

'Lizzie! Lizzie!' There was a frantic voice from behind them and the crowd parted to let a young man through. Neil Cameron set the boy down off his shoulders so that he could run to his father. The young man, who also looked little more than twenty, scooped up his son with one arm and stretched the other around his trembling wife, baby and other child. The girl breathed his name, looked up into his face and sagged against him. Her relief at his presence was palpable. His arm tightened about her thin shoulders.

'Lizzie,' he said. 'Och, Lizzie.'

'Well,' said Agnes Baxter, her voice ringing out, 'are any o' you lazy lot gonnae help us put the furniture back in the house?'

Her question signalled a change in atmosphere. Men were shaking hands and clapping each other on the back. Women began laughing and chatting, going over what had just happened. Agnes reached up and kissed Neil Cameron on the cheek – at which point he blushed furiously and told her not to be so daft. He turned, his face bright with laughter, and spotted Kate in the crowd. She pushed her way through to him.

'Och, Daddy, you were,' she paused, searching for the right word, 'magnificent!' she burst out.

'You think so, lassie?' He was grinning broadly. 'Magnificent? Well, it's a fine word.' He spied Robbie and gestured to him to join them. Then he struck his forehead.

'Och, Kate, I nearly forgot. How did you get on?'

'She's got the job, Mr Cameron,' said a proud Robbie. 'She starts in August. *And* she got top marks in the exam,' he added for good measure, beaming at Kate as he said it.

Neil's face, happy already, broke into a beatific smile.

'Och, Kate, my darling lassie. Och, Kate,' he said again, squeezing her shoulders. 'My girl going to be a tracer.' His eyes were wet. 'It's only the really clever lassies that get taken on for that.'

His pride in her achievement made Kate ashamed of herself. It *was* a good job and she *was* lucky to have been taken on. She ought to be counting her blessings instead of feeling resentful that she couldn't go to the Art School. Her father turned to Robbie.

'We'll have to do something to celebrate. Shall the three of us—'

'Neil, man,' came a shout. 'We're off to Connolly's for a dram. A wee celebration, like. Are you coming wi' us?'

Kate held her breath. He'd been making heroic efforts to stay off the drink. Being one of the Vigilantes had helped. It had given him a purpose, despite Lily's constant nagging that he was going to get himself in trouble with the law, and then where would they all be?

Behind her back, Kate carefully crossed her fingers – only those on the right hand, of course. Everyone knew it didn't work if you crossed both. If you were telling a wee fib you could cross both, but not if you were wishing for something. And she was wishing for something. She was wishing so hard . . .

Neil, his attention caught briefly by the man who had shouted the invitation to him, bent his gaze again to Kate. He flung the next words over his shoulder, never taking his eyes off his daughter's face.

'Another time, Bill. I'm away to take my daughter for an ice cream and a glass of ginger. For our own wee celebration, like. She's just got a start at Donaldson's. As a tracer,' he added, unable to keep the pride out of his voice.

There were shouts of congratulation and Kate's hand was seized and shaken several times.

'That means there's going to be a new ship then?' asked the man called Bill.

'Aye, Mr Thompson,' said Kate. 'Good news, eh?'

She smiled furiously at him, screwing up her eyes to hold back the tears. Her father had been offered whisky – and he had chosen to go and drink lemonade with his daughter.

★   ★   ★

When they got home an hour later, the girls were out in the back court, playing at beddies. They had marked out the hopscotch court on the paving slabs with chalk. Robbie joined in with the game – to hoots of laughter from his sisters and Jessie Cameron. Deftly nudging the peever – an old shoe-polish tin – with one foot, he hopped up the beddies court to where it had landed.

'Help! I'm gonnae fall over!' he yelled, pretending to lose his balance, waving his arms wildly in the air.

'Och, Robbie,' giggled Barbara Baxter, 'you're daft. You're on four and five. You're allowed to put both feet down there.'

Neil Cameron, leaning on his elbows against the wall which divided their back court from the next, smiled and turned to Kate, who'd hoisted herself up to sit on the wall beside him. She'd been on the point of going in when her father had suggested staying out for a wee while to enjoy the sunshine.

'Well, lass, and how do you think you'll get on at Donaldson's?'

'Fine. I think I might quite enjoy it. The pay's not that great,' she told him how much, 'but I think I'll earn more in a year or so. It's not exactly what I wanted to do—'

She broke off. Neil Cameron was nothing if not quick on the uptake. He was also stone cold sober, with nothing more than ice cream and lemonade inside him, and deeply ashamed.

'Kathleen . . . I'm sorry, lass. About the Art School.' Leaning against the wall beside her, he seemed to slump, become once again the defeated man of that dreadful scene in the kitchen, not at all the magnificent warrior of an hour ago. She wanted that man back. The tall, brave, laughing man she remembered from before the war. Oh, how she wanted that man back!

'It's all right, Daddy,' she said. 'I don't mind. Not really.'

She should be crossing all her fingers and toes for that one. She should be crossing every part of her anatomy.

Silence fell between father and daughter. It was punctuated by the yells and shrieks coming from the girls and Robbie, still busily – and tactfully – playing the fool. Somewhere, not very far away, a blackbird was chirping. It sounded like a warning. Mr Asquith must be out on the prowl.

Neil Cameron spoke, his voice low and hesitant. 'Could you not maybe go to evening classes, once you're working? I'll make sure your Ma doesn't take all your pay off you,' he added grimly.

Kate, her head bowed, shrugged. Miss Noble had given her the Art School prospectus to look at on her last day at school. Her heart had leapt. There were so many different subjects you could study: sketching, water-colour painting, oil painting, life drawing, still life, ceramics – she'd had to read the class description to find out what that was – pottery, which was making things out of clay and decorating them with your own designs. She'd love to have a go at that, but it was all out of the question. Staring at the ground, she bit her lip, and was unaware how Neil Cameron's face softened when he saw the gesture. His voice grew gentler still.

'How much does it cost, lass?'

'Two guineas,' she said flatly. 'Two guineas for the year's session, and then there's all the materials.' She lifted her face to the sun and gave Robbie, who was glancing across at father and daughter, a tight little smile.

'Oh,' said Neil.

She turned to him. 'It's all right, Daddy, honestly. It's all right.'

'It is not all right,' he said fiercely, 'Kathleen, it is not all right. Let's see now, if the Black Squad get taken on again for this new ship, and with you working yourself . . .'

'Oh, Daddy,' burst out Kate, 'I've done all the calculations.

80

It still wouldn't work. If I save really hard, I might just have enough money for my tram fare up to Glasgow every week!' She bit her lip once more, fighting back the tears of disappointment.

Miss Noble had made a tentative offer of a loan. Kate, of course, had stiffly thanked her, but refused. The Cameron family had had enough of charity. If she couldn't pay her own way, she just couldn't do it at all. It was hard, but there you were. Life was hard.

She thought of the young woman who'd almost been put out of her house. Life was harder for her. Three children to look after, a husband out of work and an eviction order hanging over her head. Kate straightened her shoulders. She was an ungrateful bisom. She was young and healthy and she had a job. A good job. She ought to be counting her blessings. She turned to her father.

'See me?' she told him. 'I'm going to be the best tracer Donaldson's have ever had. And,' she added, 'I thought you were a hero today, Daddy. I really did.'

'A hero?' His voice was very dry. 'I don't think so. But you're a good lass.' She turned towards him. The smile didn't quite reach his tired eyes, but he leaned forward and kissed her gently on the forehead.

'I don't know what I did to deserve—'

'Barbara? *Barbara!*'

Robbie's voice was shrill. Turning round in alarm, Kate saw Barbara in mid-hop on the beddies court. The girl was swaying, her eyes closed and one hand up to her forehead. On the seven, thought Kate stupidly. She can't put both feet down there. The swaying grew more violent. Her brother caught her just in time, sliding his arm around her shoulders seconds before the back of her head would have made contact with the paving slabs.

Robbie cradled the girl in his arms while Kate, Neil and

the other children gathered anxiously around the two of them. Jessie Cameron's eyes were as big as saucers as she looked down at her friend. Barbara's eyes were closed and her face was as white as paper.

'Barbara?' asked Robbie again. Kate could hear his conscious effort to calm himself down. 'Are you all right, hen?'

His anxious words were falling on deaf ears.

Barbara Baxter regained consciousness ten minutes after Robbie carried her upstairs and laid her carefully on their parents' bed in the front room. Twenty minutes after that, Dr MacMillan arrived, fetched by Neil Cameron from his home in Yoker Mill Road. Kate and Agnes Baxter had already shooed everyone away from the bedside, and Lily had taken the three youngest Baxter children to the Camerons' flat.

Leaving Agnes and Jim in the front room with the doctor, Kate closed the door quietly behind her and went through to the kitchen. Robbie was sitting in the rocking chair by the range, staring into space. Jessie was by herself at the kitchen table, hands clasped neatly in front of her. Kate didn't like the way she looked. If they weren't careful the doctor would have two invalids on his hands. She crossed the room and knelt down beside Robbie.

'I'm going to get Jessie to help me make some tea,' she said. 'Unless you'd like us to just go.' He hadn't changed position, but he covered the hand which she'd laid on his knee with one of his own.

'I don't want you to go.' His voice sounded odd, not like himself at all. 'This has happened before, you know. About three months ago. She just *went* – fainted, like she did just now. *Why*, Kate? I don't understand it.'

Kate moved her hand, lacing her fingers through his. He loved all his family, but there was something special between him and Barbara. Sometimes the little girl drove

82

him demented. Sometimes he teased her, but despite the difference in their ages, there was a close bond between them. They sparked off each other, made each other laugh.

His hand felt cold and clammy. He was scared. Kate squeezed the fingers she held. He looked up at that, doing his best to snap out of it.

'Tea would be fine. I daresay the doctor will be wanting a cup when he's finished.'

'I daresay,' she said. 'And Jessie needs something to do,' she added quietly.

That roused him, as she had hoped it would. He turned to look at the girl sitting so still at the kitchen table. 'Aye. On you go, Kate. Thanks.' He cast his eyes down to their linked hands, his dark lashes thick and feathery against the paleness of his skin.

'No bother,' she said, her voice very soft. Sliding her hand out of his, she rose to her feet, moved across to the kitchen table and put an arm around her sister's narrow shoulders.

'Come on then, Jess. Everyone'll be wanting tea soon. Let's get organised.'

Jessie raised huge eyes to her. 'What's wrong with Barbara, Kate? One minute she was fine and the next she wasn't. What's the matter with her?'

'I don't know, Jessie,' said Kate, and then with a cheerfulness which she was far from feeling, 'but I'm sure Dr MacMillan does. Now, up you get and see if there's enough water in the kettle.'

Over Jessie's head, her eyes met Robbie's. They did their best to smile at each other.

In the event, Dr MacMillan didn't know what was wrong with Barbara. Nothing to worry about at the moment, though, he told the Baxters confidently, the lassie was fine now. Lots of rest over the next few days and keep an eye on her. It might just be an isolated incident, but since it had happened before, they should bring her in to see him if it occurred again.

Then Barbara herself came skipping through, apparently as right as rain and none the worse for her experience. Robbie rose to his feet, glowered at her and told her in no uncertain terms to sit down and stop dancing about like a wee daftie. Barbara ran up to him, cocked her head to one side, and said, 'Och, Robbie.' He sank to his knees and wrapped his arms around her.

Kate, seeing that the grey eyes visible over Barbara's shoulder were too bright, immediately caused a diversion, insisting that everyone sat down at the kitchen table for their tea, and sending Jessie to fetch the rest of the family. The Cameron family came with them and the evening became one of high spirits and gaiety. They talked about the eviction and Neil and Agnes's part in preventing it. They discussed Kate's new job. Jim Baxter joked that his wife had pressed Dr MacMillan to stay for two cups of tea and a large buttered slice of her home-baked fruit loaf because he was a handsome young man, not long qualified.

'But a fine physician,' said Neil Cameron in his deep, soft voice, holding out his own teacup to Agnes for a refill.

'He is that,' agreed Jim Baxter, 'and a fine man, too. "I'll get my fee the next time," he says to me when I saw him out. "I know everyone's a bit short at the moment." That's what he said. A fine man.' Jim looked round the table for confirmation.

Kate caught Robbie's eye and knew exactly what he was thinking. Please God, don't let there be a next time.

Lying in the box bed that night, Kate found sleep elusive. It had been an eventful day. Faces swam in front of her mind's eye: Miss Nugent, stern and disapproving, peering at her over those ridiculous glasses; Robbie and her father, so delighted that she'd got a start; Agnes Baxter saving the day at the eviction.

How had she done that? By making fun of the man – turning aggression into ridicule. The way she had looked him up and down . . . Kate turned onto her back, eliciting a sleepy protest from Pearl.

Then there was Barbara, lying so still and silent in her brother's arms; Jessie, desperately worried about her best friend, not understanding what was wrong; Robbie, staring into space . . .

She had felt so tender towards him tonight. Had wanted to put her arms around him and comfort him, draw his head down onto her breast and let him bury his face there and cry like a child if he wanted to.

Yet earlier, when he had stood shoulder to shoulder with her father and the other men, she had seen quite clearly that Robert Baxter was no longer a boy, but a man. And that was a most uncomfortable thought, especially when taken in conjunction with her desire to hold him to her breast. She turned once more onto her side.

'Kate, in the name of the wee man, go to sleep.'

She stared into the darkness, towards the shelf at the foot of the bed. The thought of holding Robbie like that . . . it made her blush. Thank goodness it was so dark in here. She would never hear the end of it if Pearl or Jessie caught her blushing over Robbie Baxter. Ridiculous!

Pearl was snoring again. Kate wished she could fall asleep, too. Two other faces replaced Robbie's in the blackness – the young couple who'd been saved from eviction. This time. The factors and the sheriff's officer would be back, as sure as fate – and perhaps at a time when no one was around to stop them.

It was a terrible way to live. No money, no prospects, no hope – maybe not even a roof over their heads. Oh God, wouldn't it be awful to have no home? What did that pair today have? Their children? Love?

In her mind's eye Kate had a picture of the woman's face when she had seen her husband elbowing his way through the crowd to get to her. There had been love there, all right, as they had clung onto each other. They had both been so thin, their clothes so shabby . . . Probably, like so many people in Clydebank, they starved themselves so that their children could have enough to eat.

People with no money shouldn't really have children, should they? But children went along with love. The thought of the mechanics of how that happened made her blush again. She was a bit hazy about the details, but she knew enough to find it a bit frightening. It must hurt . . .

Her own father and mother had once been in love. Look what had happened to them. Lily seemed to have nothing but contempt for Neil, and he drank too much – because of the war and because life had defeated him. Both her parents were disappointed people. Is that how love always ends up, she wondered. At least for people like us?

The blankets were moving at her feet. Mr Asquith was making his way up the bed.

'Come here, baudrons,' she whispered. 'Come and give us a cuddle.' She adjusted her position as far as she could so that the cat could settle into the curve of her body at her waist. Oh, he was nice and warm. 'You're the only man for me, Mr A.,' she told him. The cat began to purr, a soft and comforting sound in the darkness.

Sleep was still a long way off. Try as she might, she couldn't stop thinking about the Art School and she couldn't stop doing calculations in her head. The trouble was, no matter how hard you added money up, it didn't make it grow any more.

Something came back to her, pushed out until now by the

events of the day. Hadn't Miss Nugent – the old battleaxe – said something about an extra sixpence if you went to night school? Cat and sister murmured their protests as a restless Kate moved yet again.

'Sorry,' she muttered, more to the cat than to Pearl. She stroked the former, a little absent-mindedly, but it was enough for him to deign to remain in position and resume his purring.

Kate barely noticed. She was on to something here. There were lots of evening classes held in Clydebank – there might even be a painting one. It wouldn't be like the Art School, of course, but it would keep her going. The local ones weren't nearly as expensive – between about a shilling and half a crown a session. If she could scrape that out of however much of her five shillings pay her mother let her keep, she could earn more money which she could save towards the Art School. It wouldn't leave much over for anything else, and she was going to need some new clothes – and an overall – for work.

Her brain was busy calculating. Sixpence extra a week over fifty-two weeks made one pound six shillings. It would take her almost two years to save the two guineas – and then there was the cost of materials – so it might take three years. If she did two evening classes – maybe a dressmaking one so that she could make her own clothes? She'd have to pay for the cloth, of course, that would cut into the money a wee bit . . . This needed careful working out, but it was a real possibility.

She laid a light hand on Mr Asquith's smooth fur. She could do it. It might take her two or three years, but she could do it. She'd have to think of a safe place for the money she was going to save. Lily would have it off her like a shot, and if her father found it in a weak moment it would end up in Connolly's Bar. Maybe she would ask Agnes Baxter to keep it for her – or Miss Noble.

She hugged the thought to her. It made her feel as warm

as the cat under her hand. It's going to be different for me, she thought. I don't want the life my mother has or that girl Lizzie endures. I don't want to have a baby every year or be thrown out of my house because I haven't got the money to pay the rent.

I *am* going to make something of myself. For a start, I'm going to the Art School. Come hell or high water. *However long it takes*.

PART II

1926

Chapter 7

In the two years Kate had been working at Donaldson's she had never known Miss Nugent raise her voice. She didn't have to. By sheer force of personality, and by the position she held over them, she ruled the tracers with a rod of iron. The Chief Tracer had strict rules of conduct for her girls, and she made sure that they were obeyed.

One of the strictest was that contact with the men working in the yard was to be avoided at all costs. This was not too difficult, given that the girls worked office hours. By the time they arrived at work at ten to nine, the men had been in for over an hour, and went home correspondingly early. That arrangement, Kate had to admit, had a lot to recommend it. The girls arrived and left by the small door within the main gates which Kate had used on her first visit to Donaldson's. For the 3000 men who worked at the yard, the gates had to be thrown open wide. When the hooter sounded at the end of the working day, no one wasted any time in leaving the workplace. Finding yourself in that stream of humanity flowing joyfully out into the street on its boisterous way home might well be an overwhelming experience for any girl.

The measures taken to prevent Miss Nugent's young ladies from coming into contact with the trainee draughtsmen working on the floor above them, seemed, however, to have less to do with safety. They too worked office hours, but were required to be at their drawing boards five minutes before the girls started and left five minutes later than they did at night. That didn't stop them leaning out of the windows and wolf-whistling while the girls were crossing the yard on their way home, much to Miss Nugent's tut-tutting disapproval.

It had embarrassed Kate at first, but she had learned to take it in her stride. Like the other girls, she soon became adept at throwing the occasional bit of banter back up at the smiling faces. Despite retaining a good measure of her own natural reserve, she was quite capable of giving as good as she got. After all, she was over eighteen now, no longer a schoolgirl.

If she did, very occasionally, meet any of the draughtsmen on the stairs, they were unfailingly polite and courteous to her, especially, it had to be admitted, a young man called Peter Watt. The other girls teased her about him – until they found out about Robbie.

He had waited behind one wild winter's afternoon to see her safely home – a fatal mistake. Kate had told him off for it, but by then the damage had been done. All the girls had seen him, standing by the main gate and turning with a smile as Kate approached. When Bella Buchanan, one of the girls who'd started with Kate two years before, had spotted her and Robbie at the cinema two weeks in a row, the bush telegraph had swung into action. Within twenty-four hours every tracer in Donaldson's knew Robbie's name, what age he was, where he worked in the yard and that he and Kate lived up the same close in Yoker.

'Childhood sweethearts!' Bella declaimed. 'That's *dead* romantic!'

Aware of the tendency among some of her charges to hang back for that five minutes which separated their departure time from that of the draughtsmen, Miss Nugent wasn't above coming into the large washroom where they all went to comb their hair and put on their hats before leaving, in order to shoo them home.

Nor was there much chance of meeting and chatting to the draughtsmen during the day. The drawings emanating from that office, which provided the girls with their tracing work, were either delivered to their own room, or fetched by Miss Nugent herself.

Kate always smiled when she remembered how Bella had tried to circumvent that rule.

'Shall I go up and get the next batch of drawings, Miss N.?' she had asked innocently, turning her sweet, blue-eyed gaze upon her supervisor. 'To save you the climb up the stairs?'

'Thank you, Miss Buchanan, but no. I think I can cope with the stairs. I'm not quite in my dotage yet.' Miss Nugent had smiled frostily at Bella over the pince-nez specs.

'In the name of the wee man!' Bella declared that lunchtime as the girls congregated in the washroom to comb their hair and titivate in front of the mirrors. 'How does that old witch ever expect me to find myself a man?'

Kate smiled at Bella, who stood with her hands on her hips, her full bosom straining against the buttons of her overall. She could be coarse sometimes, but she was good-hearted.

'There's plenty out there, Bella.' Drawing a comb through her own shiny chestnut locks, she nodded with her head towards the shipyard.

'Huh! I don't want one of them. I want a man who does a clean job.' She smiled suddenly, a knowing curve of the lips. 'Don't you, Kate? I mean, maybe not a draughtsman – like Peter Watt, for example.' She paused, shooting a sly smile at Kate, who merely smiled back at her. 'Someone like a cabinet-maker, then?' Bella continued. 'Tall, dark and handsome, and just coming to the end of his apprenticeship – a time-served man?'

'If you think I'm going to rise to that one, Isabella Buchanan, you must be dafter than you look.'

*   *   *

One day in the August of 1927, Kate found one of the new intake of apprentices sitting on the floor of the washroom crying her eyes out because Miss Nugent was insisting she used her right hand instead of her left.

'I would do it if I could, Kate,' sobbed the girl, Mary Deans, 'but I cannae. I've always been left-handed. Got the strap for it at school until the teachers gave up on me.' She gulped, and wiped a grubby hand across her eyes. She looked up at Kate, bending solicitously over her. 'It comes out all messy if I use my right hand. You've got to be neat at this job. I'll never make a tracer if she doesn't let me use my left hand. I've tried, I really have. I just cannae do it!' she wailed, bursting into a renewed bout of weeping.

'Wheesht,' said Kate gently, patting the girl on the shoulder. 'I'll sort it out for you, Mary. Don't you worry. Wash your face and comb your hair and go home for your dinner and I'll speak to Miss Nugent about it.'

Mary's soft brown eyes were huge. 'She's that fierce though, Kate, d'you no' think so?'

'I'm feeling a bit fierce myself this morning,' said Kate. 'Go home for your dinner, Mary. I'll sort this out.'

Peter Watt was clattering down the stairs as she saw Mary out into the corridor. He gave a low whistle of concern when he saw the girl's face and registered that she'd been crying.

'What's up?'

Kate explained the situation to him and, on a sudden brainwave, asked him to see Mary home. That, she thought, watching them both go, Peter's arm solicitously under Mary's elbow, might just kill two birds with one stone. Mary was a bonnie girl.

Peter's parting shot echoed Mary's words.

'Are you sure you're fit for the old battle-axe, Miss Cameron?'

Kate marched back into the tracers' office, her head held at a determined angle. Yes, she was fit for Miss Nugent. As she'd told Mary, she was feeling fierce – and tired too. They'd had a difficult night with Granny, who'd had them all up three times, havering about having to put a washing on and get the dinner cooked for the men. It had been a hard job to convince her that she didn't need to do either of these things. Years and years of worry had left their mark. Granny's whole life had been spent in washing clothes, cooking meals and cleaning houses. Running after other people, never having time to think about herself.

After they'd got her back to bed for the third time, Granny had one of her 'wee accidents' which Kate had cleaned up. Jessie would have helped, but Kate had seen the distaste on her sister's face and taken pity on her. Pearl, as usual, had managed to make herself scarce – some doing, at five o'clock in the morning.

Kate was worried about Barbara Baxter too. After that incident just before she herself had started at Donaldson's, the girl had been fine for well over a year, but then the dizzy spells had started again. She'd had three in the past six months. Dr MacMillan had sent her up to the hospital, but the doctors there couldn't seem to find anything wrong with her either. The Baxters were worried sick, and Robbie was developing a permanent little frown of anxiety between his dark eyebrows.

It all made Kate uncharacteristically blunt. She marched up to Miss Nugent's table, set on a platform from which she commanded a good view of the entire room. Dimly aware that another woman was standing beside the supervisor, Kate made a request to have a few words with the latter which came out more like a demand. The Chief Tracer heard her out in silence, peered at her over the little gold-rimmed spectacles and spoke, finally, once Kate had drawn breath.

'Are you *quite* finished, Miss Cameron?'

The icy tones brought a flush to Kate's cheek.

'Y-yes . . . I'm finished. Thank you,' she added, thinking it was an absurd thing to say. 'So you'll stop making Mary use her right hand?'

'I shall give it my consideration, Miss Cameron.'

'But . . .' began Kate.

Miss Nugent's voice, frosty already, sank to Arctic levels.

'I believe, *young lady*, that I have previously had occasion to remind you that decisions here are taken by senior members of staff in consultation with Mr Donaldson himself.' Her nostrils flared as she drew in a long breath. It made the pince-nez glasses rise. 'Decisions are most definitely not made by apprentices who seem to have acquired ideas above their station.' She inclined her head – a fraction of an inch. 'That will be all, Miss Cameron.'

If Kate hadn't been so tired and fed-up, she might have had the sense to stop there. She didn't. Exasperated with Miss Nugent's attitude, and incensed by the way she was being dismissed, she put her hands on her hips. Shades of Bella Buchanan and Agnes Baxter, she thought briefly. She had an inspired thought.

'What advantage is it to Donaldson's to have an apprentice they aren't making the best use of?'

There was a throaty chuckle, not from the Chief Tracer, visibly bristling at the criticism all too obvious in Kate's voice, but from the girl who stood by her desk.

'She's got you there, Miss N., don't you think?'

Startled, Kate turned her head and found herself looking into the face of Marjorie Donaldson. The girl smiled and stuck out her hand.

'How do you do – Miss Cameron, is it?' There were freckles across the bridge of her nose. 'Your father works here too, I think. Didn't I see you with him and your sisters a couple of years ago? At the launch of the *Irish Princess*?'

Yes, thought Kate, you would remember that. I was wearing your cast-offs. Marjorie had red-gold hair and the creamy complexion, translucent like fine porcelain, which so often goes with it. She looked like a pale angel Kate decided, except that the grin which now broke over her features was more devilish than angelic.

'That was the day that stupid man and his wife got soaked by the launch wave. I never saw anything so funny in my life!' She was still holding out her hand. 'I'm Marjorie Donaldson,' she added politely – and unnecessarily.

'I know who you are, Miss Donaldson,' said Kate, taking the proffered hand with some reluctance, and ignoring the implicit invitation to share in the memories of the *Irish Princess* launch. She'd seen her a few times since then, but only from a distance – once during the dreadful few days of the General Strike last year. Marjorie had been one of the Bright Young Things who'd volunteered to keep things going when the workers of Glasgow and Clydebank had joined their fellows all over Britain by downing tools in support of the miners.

They'd all seen her, going through Yoker on a tram. Kate could remember it vividly. Marjorie had been acting as the clippie. She'd even managed to get a conductress's uniform from somewhere. She'd been standing next to the driver, a handsome fair-haired young man, throwing her head back and laughing at something he was saying. The pair of them had obviously seen it as a good laugh, a bit of a lark.

Andrew Baxter, coming up to fourteen and passionately interested in politics, had shouted after them. They were strikebreakers and blacklegs, dirty capitalists, exploiting the workers and grinding the faces of the poor.

'Hark at Comrade Lenin,' Pearl had said flippantly. Jessie Cameron, of course, had leaped to Andrew's defence. She always did.

Kate brought her thoughts back to the present. The boss's

daughter was as elegant as she'd been on the day of the launch of the *Irish Princess*, her clothes in the latest style, of the best material and beautifully cut. I'll bet she's never had to clear up after her grandmother, thought Kate.

Marjorie Donaldson, however, wasn't pretty. She was slim, with a fashionably boyish figure, and she had that beautiful pale red hair and creamy skin, but her face was long and plain, her nose too big. Some might have described her as horsey. Kate, staring unsmiling at her as she dropped her hand, saw all this, and chided herself for the uncharitable thoughts. You couldn't choose how you looked.

Marjorie Donaldson did have a lovely mouth and a wide and generous smile. She seemed totally unabashed by Kate's lack of response to it. And she had introduced herself, hadn't she? Beautiful manners then, thought Kate. Unlike my own, marching in here and doing an Agnes Baxter, without so much as a by-your-leave. The girl was saying something, asking her a question.

'Yes.' Miss Nugent answered for her. 'Miss Cameron did design the menus for the last launch.'

During a slack morning Kate had occupied herself doing a drawing of an old sailing ship, basing it on a painting which hung behind Miss Nugent's desk. She had added a border, in swirling scrolls of burgundy, gold and green, and then printed the name of the new ship in beautiful black Gothic lettering.

Without Kate's knowledge, Bella and some of the other girls had shown the drawing to Miss Nugent, who in turn had shown it to the chief draughtsman on the floor above. It had gone all the way up to the design team, who had decided to use the drawing as the theme for the menus and programmes for the launch. The extra work had earned Kate a bonus of ten shillings which had gone straight into her Art School fund.

'I thought your designs were lovely,' Marjorie Donaldson

was enthusing. 'So – kind of . . . *medieval*, I suppose. Have you studied art, Miss Cameron?'

'A little,' replied Kate. Marjorie Donaldson wasn't to know that she'd studied art at Yoker school, and for the last two years at night classes in Clydebank, fees and materials carefully eked out of her wages – or what Lily let her keep of them.

'You should think about going to classes in Glasgow,' said Marjorie. 'The Art School holds them most evenings and Saturdays too, mornings and afternoons. Do promise me you'll think of it.'

'It's kind of you to take an interest, Miss Donaldson.' Kate's tone was very dry. Miss Nugent shot her a warning glance. It sent a clear message. *This is the boss's daughter, you know, and you, Miss Cameron, are in enough trouble as it is.*

'You should think about going to classes in Glasgow.' That was priceless. Kate thought of little else! She had hoped to make it for the start of the autumn term this year, but she was still too short of funds. Every month she visited her old teacher, Miss Noble, taking whatever she could spare out of her meagre wages. Miss Noble, who had learned painfully not to mention the possibility of a loan to her former pupil a second time, had gone with her to show her how to open a savings accounts at the Post Office. Kate had asked her to keep the passbook for her. If her mother found it, she would have it cleared in five minutes flat. She felt a wee bit guilty about that – but only slightly. As it was, she thought she might be going to have to break into it. It was coming to decision-time about Jessie.

Kate gritted her teeth. She was determined that her clever wee sister was going to stay on at school to train as a teacher. That meant she couldn't risk the Art School this September. Her own fund might have to be plundered to compensate for the delay in Jessie going out to earn a living. A teacher in the family! That would be worth a few sacrifices.

Kate scowled at herself in the mirror of the washroom. Another year, then – at least. Oh, but it was hard to be patient!

'Hurry up, Kate!' shouted someone. 'The dragon'll be in here breathing fire any moment now.'

'Leave her alone!' shouted one of the other girls. 'She'll be getting ready for Robert Baxter. Boy, has he got it bad for our Kate!'

For Robbie, despite Kate's telling-offs, still occasionally waited behind to see her home from work.

There was laughter and a few teasing comments.

'He's that good-looking, too.'

'With a *lovely* smile.'

'And Kate just keeps him dangling. How do you do it, Kate?'

'I'll bet she's never even let him put his hand on her knee!' yelled Bella Buchanan. 'If it was me, he wouldnae have to ask twice, but our Kate's that lady-like, is she no'?'

Kate smiled sweetly. She had learned that it was the only possible response. They soon got tired if you didn't rise to the bait. She drew a comb through her short hair.

She and Pearl, greatly daring, had gone up to Glasgow a few weeks ago and come back with their hair shingled. Pearl had even bought lipstick and powder in Woolworth's, and they'd applied them in the Ladies' at Central Station, giggling all the while. Jessie, although she'd accompanied her sisters on the expedition, had declined to participate in either activity, sniffily disdainful of such vanity.

'You see, Pearl,' Kate had said, smiling at her youngest sister to take the sting out of her words, 'Jessie's the intellectual of the family. She's above this kind of thing.'

'The intae-what?' Pearl had asked, her pretty face such

100

a study in puzzlement that it had been Jessie and Kate's turn to burst out laughing. When they had recovered, Kate explained.

'Jessie likes books and studying and discussing ideas, Pearl. She's not interested in make-up and frivolities like that. Boys, for instance,' teased Kate.

Pearl tossed her newly cropped head. 'Oh, really? Well, she may be an intae-whatever it is, but she isn't above fancying boys. Have you seen the way she looks at Andrew Baxter?'

Jessie had gone an immediate deep shade of red and Kate had had to step in to separate her two sisters.

Smiling at the memory, she plonked her cloche hat onto her smooth head, and following the other girls out, running across the yard to the gate. She smiled again, remembering how her father's mouth had dropped open when he'd seen two of his daughters shorn of their crowning glories.

'What have you daft lassies done to your bonnie hair?' he'd asked, his voice so mournful that she and Pearl had taken a fit of the giggles, until he'd asserted his authority and thundered at them to 'get that muck off your faces!' Robbie hadn't liked her with short hair, either.

Well, she liked it. It made her feel grown-up, and modern. And Robbie Baxter didn't own her, not by a long chalk. She supposed people did think that they were walking out, but going to the pictures together once a week didn't make them boyfriend and girlfriend, not in Kate's book. She waited for a Dalmuir-bound tram to clank its way past before crossing the road to her own stop.

She and Robbie went to the pictures together every Monday night – a carefully neutral evening. They went Dutch on the tickets, at her insistence, and although they sometimes walked home together afterwards, enjoying each other's company, that was all there was to it.

Well . . . if she was being honest, she had to admit that

on one occasion there had been a bit more to it than that. It had been late summer last year and they had strolled along the river in the twilight, chatting quietly, but had both fallen silent, stuck for something to say, by the time they reached the Renfrew ferry. As they walked into the darkness of the close mouth, Robbie had suddenly pulled her to him, his voice rough-edged and his breath warm on her face.

'Let me kiss you, Kate. Please?'

So she had let him. Just to see what it felt like. To see if it felt any different from that Hogmanay when he had kissed her. She couldn't say it had been unpleasant, but when his hands had begun, very tentatively, to explore her body, she had pulled back, breathing heavily, panic rising in her throat. Then the leerie had come in on his nightly rounds to light the gas mantles in the close and made a coarse comment, and it had all descended into farce, with Kate running up the stairs and Robbie calling after her in a frantic whisper, so that neither of their families would hear. She had avoided him for a week after that and had agreed to resume their weekly trips to the pictures only on the strict understanding that their friendship was to be just that – nothing more.

Kate sighed. She knew Robbie wasn't happy with the situation, but it was all she could manage. She tried to encourage him to go to the dancing on Friday and Saturday nights – there were plenty of halls – in the hopes that he might meet someone nice.

'I've already met someone nice,' he always said, his mouth set in a mutinous line. Kate sighed again.

As her tram pulled up to the stop she caught a glimpse of herself in her new cloche hat, reflected in the gleaming windows. Not bad, she thought. Not bad. She had succumbed to it last Saturday afternoon in the millinery department of the Co-op. She made most of her own clothes, so the hat had been a big treat.

Granny had taught her to knit when she was a wee girl and she went to night school for dressmaking with some of the girls at work, with Agnes Baxter always on hand if she had a problem with anything. She hoped she was getting a bit better at it and that her skirts and blouses didn't look too home-made.

Anyway, she thought, jumping off the tram at Kelso Street, her clothes might have cost a fraction of those Marjorie Donaldson was wearing, but they were as fashionable as Kate could make them. And she'd made and paid for them with her own money and her own efforts. Could Marjorie Donaldson beat that? Kate doubted it.

The first thing she heard when she got in was Pearl's voice, going on at Jessie. That was nothing new.

'What do you know about life, you wee nyaff?'

'That's enough,' said Kate, coming into the kitchen and taking off her hat. 'Is there any tea on the go?'

Jessie leaped up from the schoolbooks open in front of her.

'I'll get you a cup, Kate.'

'Where's Ma and Davie?' She didn't ask where her father was. The rent strike had all but collapsed, suffering a terrible blow when Andrew Leiper, one of the leaders of the protest, had died in August after being knocked down by a car. Now that the Vigilantes had been disbanded her father had lost a role – and he'd consoled himself in the only way he seemed to know how.

'Up at the Baxters',' said Pearl.

Kate sat down at the table and looked with interest at the book Jessie had been studying. Botany. She turned over the pages. There were some beautiful illustrations of plants and flowers, and she said as much to Jessie. The girl turned eagerly towards her, her face lighting up as it always did when someone took an interest in her studies.

103

'Aye, they're dead artistic, aren't they?' She set a cup of tea down in front of Kate, well away from the book. 'D'you want a wee biscuit, Kate?'

Kate shook her head. 'You know, when I finally get to the Art School I think I'd like to do something like china painting – maybe try painting flowers and trees and that sort of thing, but onto crockery.'

Jessie smiled. 'You'd be real good at that, Kate, I bet.'

Pearl, sprawled in their father's chair at one side of the range, yawned ostentatiously.

'Listen to the pair o' you. One wants to bury herself in books, and the other wants to paint cups and saucers. Me, I think life's about having fun.'

Kate shot her an old-fashioned look. Pearl was an attractive girl, clad now in the smart black dress with white collar and cuffs which she wore for her work serving behind the counter at a confectioners in the West End of Glasgow. Her smart blonde bob and the make-up Kate knew she applied once she'd left the house and their father's disapproving gaze, made her look much older than fifteen. Kate had a shrewd idea that her sister equated what she called *fun* with young men – or maybe not even young ones. Her conversation was peppered with tales of well-spoken gentlemen who came into the shop and were so light-hearted with her as she sold them elegant boxes of chocolates for their wives.

'What's that look for?' demanded Pearl, sitting up in the chair and squaring her shoulders. She made a move towards her handbag, lying on the floor beside her, and then checked it.

'Just be careful, that's all,' said Kate. Her eyes flickered from the bag up to her sister's face, suffused now with a pale rosy glow. 'Fun's fine, but watch that it doesn't get you into trouble.'

They all knew what she meant by 'getting into trouble'.

'And if you're going to smoke,' Kate went on, 'at least get rid of the smell out of your hair before you come home.' Pearl, about to take offence at her sister's previous comment, allowed her hand to fall protectively towards her handbag. I am right then, thought Kate. She's got a packet in there. Just lately, in bed at night, lying next to Pearl, she'd caught the faint whiff of something.

'Daddy'll hit the roof if he finds out you've started smoking.'

Pearl shrugged. 'He can't talk. With his drinking, I mean.'

'Don't speak about him like that!'

Pearl shrugged again. 'Why not? It's the truth. Where d'you think he is now?'

Kate was saved from saying something she might regret by the sound of her mother's key in the lock. Also, perhaps, by her own honesty.

Frances Noble smiled at the pretty girl standing on the door-step of the neat little house she shared with Esmé MacGregor in Scotstoun.

'Come in, my dear, come in!'

She ushered Kate into the parlour, talking all the while. Esmé was out, but she'd be back very soon. She particularly wanted to see Kate, so would Kate wait for her, take some tea perhaps?

'I don't think I will, Miss Noble. Perhaps I could just leave the money for my savings account with you.'

Frances Noble looked at Kate more closely. The girl was bunching up the cloth of her skirt with her hand. It was an unusual gesture for a young woman who, although shy, was extraordinarily self-possessed for her age. And she had expressed no desire to know why Esmé MacGregor wanted to see her. That, too, was unlike her. She was staring fixedly at the silver framed photo on the mantelpiece, the one of

Miss Noble's brother Alan, who had died on the Somme back in 1916.

'Is something the matter, my dear?' Frances indicated the two armchairs at either side of the fire. 'Won't you sit down and I'll make us some Russian tea?'

Kate turned sombre green eyes on her.

'Miss Noble . . .' Then, as though making up her mind, 'Miss Noble, do you know anything about brain tumours?'

Frances Noble came forward and took Kate's hand between two of her own.

'Who is ill, Kate? You?'

Kate shook her head vehemently. 'Oh, no. It's Barbara – Robbie's wee sister – the daughter of our neighbours,' she added, but her initial method of describing Barbara Baxter told Frances Noble more than Kate knew.

'Sit,' she commanded, 'and to hell with tea. I'll fetch the sherry.'

Esmé MacGregor came home during Kate's retelling of the story, letting herself into the house and bouncing into the room. She was halted immediately by her friend putting a finger up to her lips with a brief, 'Go on, Kate.'

It was a relief to pour it all out: the Baxters' anxiety over the past two years; Barbara's dizzy spells; the additional symptoms which had appeared recently – double vision, bumping into things – until, finally, the hospital doctors to whom Dr MacMillan had referred the girl had said the dreadful words. Barbara had a growth on her brain – a tumour. It was the first time Kate had heard the word. She was to come to know what it meant only too well.

'They say they may have to operate, but not yet. They're going to wait and see if it grows any more. Sometimes they shrink, apparently. Disappear completely.' She looked at her listeners. 'Have you ever heard of that happening?' She asked the question with a pathetic eagerness which caused Esmé MacGregor and Frances Noble to exchange swift glances of sympathy.

'Of course we have,' said Esmé MacGregor stoutly. 'I'm sure it happens all the time.'

Kate looked doubtful. Frances Noble added the weight of her opinion.

'What you have to do, Kate, is to remain positive – for the sake of Barbara and her family. I know that's hard to do, but you've got to be strong for their sake. So any time you need to talk about it, don't forget that Miss MacGregor and I are here. And we're always pleased to see you. Aren't we, Esmé?'

Kate's bottom lip was trembling. Esmé MacGregor poured her a second glass of sherry and patted her on the shoulder.

'There, there, my dear. There's no need to say anything. We understand.'

Kate tried to smile. They were both so kind.

'Was there something you wanted to see me about, Miss MacGregor?'

'And who,' asked Esmé MacGregor, watching her friend closing the door behind an astonished Kate half an hour later, 'might this Robbie be?' His name had come up several times in the conversation. Frances Noble pulled back the lace curtain which covered the small window to the side of the door and waved to Kate before turning to answer. Her voice was thoughtful.

'That girl's soulmate, I think.'

The eyes of the two women met.

'You're a good person, Frances Noble,' Esmé murmured.

Frances smiled and, coming forward, slipped her arm through Esmé's.

'Another wee sherry before dinner?'

* * *

A grant! Kate had never imagined that such a thing existed. She'd even suspected Miss Noble of trying to fool her into letting her pay for classes at the Art School by pretending that Miss MacGregor had discovered the existence of a bursary for part-time students. But no, it was all there in black and white. Miss MacGregor had shown her the paperwork. Incredibly, she had applied for the bursary on behalf of Kate and it had been decided to award the sum to her – a whole ten pounds!

Kate, walking slowly back home from Miss Noble's house, couldn't believe her luck. Ten pounds was a fortune. Miss MacGregor had explained how it worked. Any class Kate took would be paid for and a certain sum would be set aside in her name at the supplies shop, so that she could go in and choose what she needed, when she needed it. Each month she would be able to go to the bursar's office and collect a small sum of money for fares.

The two women, as excited as Kate, had fetched their copy of the Art School's prospectus. Between them, they decided that she would start with a still-life class held on Saturday afternoons. As if that wasn't enough, a shining-eyed Kate had then realised that with a grant of ten pounds and her own carefully saved money, she could afford to pay for two years at the Saturday classes, and maybe even take another class on a weekday evening. She knew exactly what she wanted to do – ceramics.

Oh, it was that exciting! To have waited so long and then to have suddenly got what she wanted! Then, crossing Dumbarton Road and nearly home, she remembered about Barbara Baxter. Was it wrong to be this happy for herself when Barbara was ill and everyone was so worried about her? The thought troubled her so much that she stopped dead when she reached the pavement, wrinkling her brow in perplexity.

No, she decided at last, it couldn't be wrong. Maybe she

wouldn't do the ceramics class, though. Perhaps it wasn't fair to be out too much. Jessie might need her around – or Robbie. She could always do it next year.

Turning out of the evening sunshine into the darkness of the close Kate made her way up the stairs. Her news might even cheer Jessie up a wee bit – might help Robbie too. Cast down as he was by Barbara's illness, she knew that he would find it in himself to be pleased for her. He always did.

Chapter 8

Kate wished that a great big hole would open in the floor and swallow her up. She had wanted this for so long. Now she was here, she was conscious only of how nervous she was. There were butterflies in her stomach and her skin felt clammy. This was a new world she was about to enter, one in which she didn't know the rules. At work she was Miss Cameron, almost halfway through her apprenticeship and good at her job. Here she was just a wee girl from Yoker, with ideas above her station.

It had taken all the nerve she possessed to steel herself for the walk up the hill from Sauchiehall Street to the Art School. Looking up at the building as she toiled up the steep brae of Scott Street on the first Saturday afternoon of term, it seemed monstrous, looming over her like some great fortress.

Built in solid blocks of red sandstone to Charles Rennie Mackintosh's design, it had been completed in the year Kate was born, just eighteen years before. Although red sandstone resisted dirt more than lighter-coloured stone did, the walls were already grubby, bearing the grime all Glasgow's buildings acquired from being in a big industrial city, with shipyards, locomotive works and forges belching their pollution into the air, day in, day out.

The college was no less imposing for that, thought Kate, looking up at its enormously long windows. Divided into small panes of glass by black horizontals and verticals, the effect was a bit like the bars of a prison. Prisons kept people out as well as in, didn't they? Who did she think she was, that the doors were going to open for her?

Turning the corner onto Renfrew Street, she felt her heart pounding and knew that it had nothing to do with the exertion of the climb. She paused for a moment, pretending to admire the front of the building.

Pretending was the wrong word. She *did* admire it, loved the wrought-ironwork with which Toshie – wasn't that what Miss Noble had called him? – had decorated the frontage. Looking up, she spotted 'the Glasgow rose' – a stylised version of the flower to which he had returned again and again in all his designs, exterior and interior. She lowered her gaze. The lettering above the door was also in Mackintosh's distinctive style. *The Glasgow School of Art.* She really liked his style of printing. She wondered what Miss Nugent would say if she used it on the blueprints at work. *None of your artistic tendencies here, my girl.*

Kate Cameron, she told herself sternly, stop dithering and get into that building! Taking a deep breath, she climbed the flight of stone steps leading up from the pavement and pushed open the door.

Once inside, she found a blackboard in the hall directing her to the appropriate room for the still-life class. She asked a girl who was passing where it was and was directed up a light, airy staircase and along a corridor. Taking another deep breath she walked into the room. It was large and bright with huge windows, probably those she'd seen from outside. Easels and sloping desks were arranged in a circle around a plinth which was draped with a piece of cloth on which stood various objects. The room was also full of her fellow students. She must be one of the last to arrive. Maybe she should come straight from work next week, instead of going home for her dinner first as she'd done today. She glanced nervously about her, and for the second time in ten minutes wished that a great big hole would open at her feet.

She was far too smartly dressed. She'd gone to some effort to be just that, but she saw at once that she'd made a mistake. Everyone else was wearing loose, paint-spattered clothes. Old shirts and casual flannels seemed to be the order of the day for the men. Even some of the girls were wearing trousers, with men's shirts acting as their painting overalls. Why hadn't she thought to bring one of her father's old ones? She clutched her bag tightly to her, blushing as she thought of the neat flowery pinny inside it. Mrs Baxter had made it specially for her, they both having decided that her grey work overalls were too shabby, covered as they were with the black ink she used for tracing. That flowery pinny was going to give this lot a real laugh.

She heard a suppressed giggle. In one corner of the room, a girl with very short black hair and bright red lips was saying something to the man beside her. He seemed vaguely familiar and he glanced across at her, the way you do when someone says, 'Don't look now, but . . .'

He was tall and fair and as impossibly sophisticated as his companion, who was one of the girls wearing trousers and an old shirt. Even from across the room she could see that his eyes were a piercing blue. With miserable certainty, Kate knew that they were commenting on her appearance.

She had thought she looked quite nice in the cream-coloured jumper in artificial silk yarn which she'd knitted herself. It was tunic-length, with a deep lacy border at the hem and a collar and tie at the neckline. Combined with her neat brown wool skirt and topped with her new beige cloche hat she had thought she looked just the ticket when she'd got on the tram. Smart, but not *too* dressy. Now she realised that her outfit was completely inappropriate. Totally out of place. Other heads swivelled to look at the newcomer.

Sharp tears pricked her eyes. Furious with herself, she ducked her head, turned on her heel and headed for the open doorway, colliding with someone coming in.

'Sorry,' she mumbled. The girl she'd bumped into grabbed her by the arm.

'Don't I know you from somewhere?'

Kate lifted her head. She recognised the voice, and the face, immediately.

'I doubt it, Miss Donaldson, but I know you.' It was the boss's daughter. 'Would you excuse me, please?'

Marjorie Donaldson still had her by the arm. 'Why, it's Miss Cameron! What are you doing here?'

Having ideas above my station, thought Kate briefly, but Marjorie Donaldson, beaming at her, her pale face animated with what looked like real pleasure, had now let go of her arm and was shaking her enthusiastically by the hand. 'Hello, how are you? It's so nice to see you here. I'm glad you decided to take *this* class.'

Kate, stopped in her headlong flight, hesitated. Marjorie Donaldson did sound genuinely pleased to see her.

'Weren't you coming to this class?' Marjorie gestured back towards the room, and its chattering young men and women, their momentary interest in the newcomer forgotten. She looked into Kate's face. 'Are you upset about something? Did one of this lot say something they shouldn't have? Most of us know each other from last year, you know. I'll soon sort them out.'

She's got even more freckles than the last time I saw her, thought Kate, studying them where they overlaid the creamy complexion on the bridge of her nose and high up on her cheeks. Yes, they would all know each other, wouldn't they? That just made it worse. The tears threatened again, but she wasn't going to cry in front of Marjorie Donaldson, of all people.

'I've just changed my mind, that's all. Now, if you'll excuse me,' she said politely.

'But you can't leave. Come and sit by me at the back. There's a spare easel there. Are you using oils?'

Kate opened her mouth to protest. Nothing came out. Marjorie, one hand on Kate's elbow, propelled her towards the spare easel. To her horror she found that it was positioned between Marjorie and the couple whom she'd been sure had been laughing at her. The black-haired girl looked her over with a glance which took in everything – the cheap shoes and skirt, the home-made jumper, Kate's obvious discomfort. She turned and murmured something to the fair young man at her side. He shot another glance at Kate and chuckled.

Marjorie, sorting herself out ready to begin, picked up a paint-stained rag from the ledge which ran along the bottom of her easel and flung it at him. He laughed, caught it easily and flung it back. Kate suddenly remembered where she had seen him before. It had been that time during the General Strike when she had spotted Marjorie working on the tram. This ill-mannered young man with the remarkable blue eyes had been the driver.

'Behave yourselves, you two. This is Kate Cameron. She's a friend of mine from Clydebank – works for my father. *And* she's a very gifted artist.'

Startled, Kate looked at Marjorie. Acquaintance, maybe, a very distant one, but *friend* was surely stretching the point a bit. And how did she know whether Kate could paint or not? Then she remembered the designs she'd done for the menus and programmes for the last launch, the designs Marjorie had admired so much. The girl was talking, introducing her friends to Kate.

'These extremely rude people to our left are Suzanne Douglas and Jack Drummond. Say hello to Kate, children.'

'Hello to Kate, children,' chorused Suzanne and Jack.

114

Then they looked at each other and dissolved into laughter.

'Ignore them,' advised Marjorie. 'Have you got a smock or something, Kate? You don't mind if I call you Kate, do you? We're very informal here. And do call me Marjorie.'

Oh aye, thought Kate, that'll be right. You're only my boss's daughter and my father's boss's daughter, but of course I'll call you Marjorie.

I'm not staying, she thought. I'm not staying here with these horrible people. I'm going to walk back over to the door and down the stairs and out of the front door and down Scott Street to Sauchiehall Street and get on a tram and never come back here again. Never ever. Just then the tutor walked in and closed the door behind him.

'Good afternoon, ladies and gentlemen,' he said. 'Shall we get on?'

Kate turned huge green eyes to Marjorie. 'I can't do this. I can't stay here.' Her voice came out as a whisper. Behind Marjorie, she saw Jack Drummond's face. He was looking directly at her.

'Stuff and nonsense,' said Marjorie. 'Of course you can. Don't you think you owe it to yourself?'

For one frozen moment, Kate swithered, fighting the overwhelming urge to bolt from the room like a frightened rabbit. Then she realised that Marjorie Donaldson was absolutely right. She owed this to herself – and to Miss Noble and Miss MacGregor too – and to Daddy and Robbie. It had taken her a long time to get this far. Was she going to let these two rude people put her off? No, she was not. She lifted her chin.

'Of course I can.' She gave Marjorie's words back to her and was rewarded by a beaming smile.

'Now, where's your smock?' Taking Kate's bag from her unresisting hands she pulled out the flowery pinny.

'Oh!' said Marjorie, holding it up. There were further

giggles from the corner. 'I don't think this is really very suitable. Why don't I lend you a spare shirt?' She laid the pinny to one side and delved into a large leather bag sitting on the floor beside her. She brought out a blue and white striped shirt, collarless and unstarched.

'One of my father's cast-offs,' Marjorie went on cheerfully. 'It's really much more practical and it'll cover the sleeves of your jumper better. It's so pretty, it would be a pity to get paint on it. Did you knit it yourself? I do so admire people who can make their own clothes.'

There was still suppressed giggling coming from the corner. The tutor, a short round man with a neat beard and a mane of white hair combed back from his forehead, lifted his eyebrows and his voice.

'Miss Douglas? Mr Drummond? Is there some problem there at the back?'

The room settled down to work. Kate squared her shoulders and did so too, dwelling only briefly on the extraordinary fact that here she was in the Glasgow School of Art wearing a shirt which had once belonged to one of the biggest shipyard owners in the west of Scotland, a man who had something akin to the power of life and death over the Cameron family. Not only that, she and that man's daughter were now on first-name terms. Supposedly.

When she turned her attention to the task before her, she forgot everything else. The still life arranged in the middle of the forest of easels consisted of a wooden bowl filled with several red and green apples and one orange, set on top of a dark green satin cloth whose folds, draped over the tall plinth, fell gracefully to the floor.

Sketching the shapes in with charcoal wasn't a problem. She did a lot of sketching at home. It was the easiest thing to do sat at the kitchen table. Her night classes in Clydebank over the past two years had taught her a lot about shape and

116

form and perspective. She'd also learned how to use water colours. She'd liked that, but was determined to master oil paints too.

The apples weren't going to be too difficult, she thought, frowning in concentration, but it was going to be hard to get the texture of the orange right. Clutching one brush in her mouth, she absent-mindedly scratched her nose with the hand in which she held the other. Sparing a thought for how she was going to tackle the folds of the green satin cloth and the shadows they cast, she re-applied herself to the orange.

'Miss Cameron, isn't it?' She jumped, let go of the paint-brush clamped between her teeth, scrabbling furiously as it slid down Mr Donaldson's old shirt, smearing green paint all over the blue and white stripes.

'Miss Cameron?' asked the voice again. The tutor was standing beside her, looking at her work. *Her work!*

'Y-yes,' Kate stammered. 'Yes, s-sir. I'm Kathleen Cameron.' She managed to get it out and then stood in an agony of anticipation as he stood, head cocked, studying her infant picture. Narrowing his eyes in concentration, he bent forward and peered at it.

'Your technique needs a great deal of work,' he pronounced at last. Kate's heart sank. Was he going to tell her she was no good? That she wasn't up to the standard of the class? Maybe she should just take the shirt off and pack up now.

The tutor stroked his beard and took a step or two back from the painting. 'Mmm,' he said. He turned and smiled at Kate.

'Technique we can teach you. Talent is God-given. The Good Lord has been generous to you, Miss Cameron. Very promising,' he murmured. 'Very promising. We'll start on your technical education next week. Continue.' He flicked his fingers in a gesture of dismissal and left an open-mouthed Kate staring after him as he progressed to the next student.

Aware of eyes on her, she turned her head. Jack Drummond was looking at her. He inclined his head to her in a gesture which indicated that he was impressed.

'Glad you stayed?' asked a quiet voice.

Kate turned her head and gave Marjorie a lovely smile. 'Yes, I'm glad I stayed.'

With a shy goodbye to Marjorie, Kate left quickly at the end of the lesson, hurriedly packing up her things and slipping out into the corridor. She could have got to the ground floor without using the stairs. She was walking on air. No, she was floating on a cloud, not a pink one, but a red and green and orange one. She grinned at the extravagant thought. *Very promising, with a God-given talent.* The words swam deliciously around inside her head. She would probably get on to the green cloth next week. She'd give it some thought beforehand, work out how to approach the folds and the shadows—

'Miss Cameron! Miss Cameron!'

Startled, she turned. It was Suzanne Douglas, the flowery cotton pinny in her hand. She was standing on the landing in the turn of the stairs.

'You don't want to forget it,' said Suzanne coyly, letting it fall from her outstretched hand, so it could clearly be seen for what it was. Behind her, Jack Drummond was grinning. Another two or three students, clattering past them, looked amused. Kate felt the smile slide from her face. Running swiftly up the flight of stairs, she snatched the bright fabric out of the girl's hand. Then, turning without a word, she went back down the stairs so quickly that she slipped just before she reached the bottom, recovering herself only by gripping the banister so tightly that she heard her knuckles crack.

'Hey,' called Suzanne Douglas after her as she crossed the entrance hall, 'Miss Cameron! Can't you take a joke?'

Kate, her breath coming faster because she'd almost fallen

inside the building, went down the stone front steps onto Renfrew Street at a slower pace.

'Miss Cameron!' This time it was a man's voice. 'Miss Cameron! Stop! Please!'

Her foot poised to go from the last step onto the pavement, Kate had just made it when Jack Drummond caught her by the arm. She wobbled. Strong fingers tightened their grip on her arm.

'Careful,' he murmured, his mouth very close to her ear. 'We don't want you to fall now, do we?'

'I'm fine,' said Kate, but her breath was still coming too quickly. He released her but came immediately to stand in front of her, barring her way, laughing into her face.

'You've got a smudge of paint on your cheek.' He smiled. 'Green, to match your eyes.'

Knowing that she was blushing – she could feel the heat spreading over her face – Kate lifted a hand to rub at the offending mark. The street was quiet. Where on earth was everyone else? Surely Marjorie Donaldson and that Suzanne girl were still in the building? She hadn't noticed them come out. At this precise moment, she'd have welcomed the presence even of the latter, with her smartly bobbed hair, her bright red lips and the malicious gleam in her dark eyes.

Kate wet her fingers – now her tongue would be as green as her cheek – and applied herself with renewed vigour to cleaning her face.

'You're making it worse, you silly girl.' He's got a lovely voice, she thought. Well-spoken, of course, round and mellow and deep. Pity about the rest of him.

'Come here,' he said.

He fished a handkerchief out of the pocket of his flannels, wet it with his tongue, and started to rub at the mark on her cheek. Kate jumped as though she'd been stung by a wasp. 'Stay still,' he commanded. 'We could do with some turps,

119

really . . . no, that's it. There! That's you done. Pretty as a picture once more.' He thrust his handkerchief back into his trouser pocket.

'Thank you for cleaning my face. Goodbye.' She made as though to go round him, but he put a hand out to stop her.

'Look,' he said, 'I'm sorry. Suzanne and I behaved very badly in there.' He gave a nod of his head to indicate the college behind him. 'I'd like to apologise for both of us.'

Kate tossed her head. 'Did Marjorie Donaldson make you come after me?' She glanced up the steps to the double doors of the Art School. The two other girls still hadn't come out. Was Marjorie hanging back to allow this apology to take place?

'Maybe. Or maybe I retain just enough good breeding to know that I was damn' rude to you in there. Unforgivable. Only I hope that you will – forgive me, I mean.'

He was very good-looking, his handsome face wreathed in a broad smile. A confident smile, which showed that he expected her to forgive him. Kate doubted if he'd ever been refused anything in his whole spoiled life. Well, there was a first time for everything.

'Excuse me, Mr Drummond.'

'Hey, come on. I'd like to know that I'm really forgiven. And the name's Jack.'

'Excuse me, Mr Drummond,' Kate said again.

'My, but you're fierce,' he said admiringly.

Kate did what her mother would have referred to as 'giving him a look'. She knew from experience that it was enough to wither any of the young draughtsmen who might try it on during a works outing, but it just seemed to make Jack Drummond laugh. No doubt he expected her to come back at him with some witty rejoinder. Didn't they call it *repartee*? Only right now she couldn't think of one single smart remark.

'I have to get home. Would you let me past, please?' There was a tremble in her voice. If she'd heard it, she supposed he had too. She dropped her lashes and put one hand out to rest on the curved wall which bounded the stairs. The stone felt cool and solid beneath her fingers. There was a silence, during which Kate was aware of those blue eyes resting on her.

'We did upset you, didn't we?' came a quiet voice. 'I'm sorry, Miss Cameron, I really am.'

Startled, Kate looked up. He did sound sorry. Had she misjudged him? He smiled at her and ran an impatient hand through his fair hair.

'Look,' he said, 'some of us are going on for afternoon tea. A pleasant custom which developed last year. You'd be very welcome to join us.'

'No, thank you.'

'We have some great discussions – about art and architecture and all that sort of stuff.'

Kate would have loved to discuss *all that sort of stuff*. She did a quick mental review of the contents of her purse. Knocked off balance by a yearning to do just what he'd suggested, by this whole conversation and, most of all, by Jack Drummond himself, she told him the truth. 'I have precisely two and threepence in my possession, Mr Drummond, and it has to last me till next Friday.'

He raised elegant eyebrows.

'I thought you had a job at Marjorie's father's place. Don't tell me the old skinflint doesn't pay you enough?'

'Mr Donaldson pays me an adequate wage, thank you, but I give most of it to my mother. My father's a riveter, one of the Black Squad.' There was no apology in Kate's tone – rather the reverse – and she said it with an unconscious lift of her chin. 'He gets laid off regularly and my family needs my pay.'

'I'll treat you, then.' He grinned. 'Or Marjorie will. She's got enough dough to treat us all.'

121

Kate's eyes grew cold. 'I don't think so.' Taking him by surprise, she turned and walked off in the opposite direction.

He followed her, falling into step beside her, adjusting his long stride to hers as they turned the corner and went down Dalhousie Street.

Kate stopped dead. 'What do you think you're doing?'

'Seeing you to your tram. Are you walking out with someone, Miss Cameron?'

'No.' Should she cross her fingers for that one?

'Strange,' mused Jack Drummond. 'All the fellows in Clydebank must be blind, then.'

Suzanne Douglas was waiting for him as he ran back across Sauchiehall Street.

'Tea? On to cocktails, later?' he asked. 'Thanks for keeping Marjorie busy, by the way.'

Ignoring both the comment and the question which had preceded it, she inclined her head towards the retreating tram.

'Rejected your advances, then? The little mouse?'

'For the moment,' agreed Jack equably, extracting a gold cigarette case from his inside pocket, opening it and extending it to her.

'Thanks.'

He brought out his lighter and lit both their cigarettes. Suzanne put hers to her bright red lips and took a draw. Then she fixed Jack with a hard stare, which, she would have been horrified to learn, corresponded exactly to Lily Cameron's definition of 'giving someone a look'.

'You won't get anywhere with her, you know. Working-class girls are incredibly strait-laced.'

He paused, his cigarette halfway to his lips, a faint look of surprise on his face. 'Give that girl a bit of attention and she'll open up like a rose.'

Suzanne, her own cigarette held in one elegantly upraised hand, narrowed her eyes at him.

'Jack . . . You're not really smitten, are you? With a wee girl from Clydebank?'

'Don't be ridiculous, darling. I just think it might be fun to introduce her to . . . things. Expand her horizons a bit.' He drew deeply on the cigarette and blew the smoke out in rings.

A small child, passing by on the pavement in front of them, turned and stared up at him, fascinated. Her mother pulled her round, but not before her own face had registered her disapproval of Jack and Suzanne. Only fast people smoked in the street.

Jack went on in a dreamy tone of voice, 'She's got an absolutely luscious figure, as far as one can tell under the shapeless garments you girls wear nowadays. Do you think she'd let me buy her an evening dress?'

'No, and I don't think she'd be prepared to pay for it either. Not in the way you have in mind.'

The blue eyes crinkled at the corners. 'Now, there's a challenge.'

'Do you have *any* scruples, Jack?'

He tapped some ash onto the pavement. 'Not many.'

'It'll get you into trouble with Marjorie. She seems to have taken a liking to little Miss Cameron for some reason. Wants to take her under her wing.'

'Marjorie doesn't have to know, does she?' Jack Drummond's voice was very soft. The blue eyes which held Suzanne's gaze were not. He took another draw on his cigarette, looked up at the buildings across the street and then back at Suzanne, the blue eyes once more clear and innocent.

'You're a swine, Jack Drummond.'

'But you love me all the same?'

'You'll never know how much.' Just for a second there

was naked longing in Suzanne Douglas's eyes. An expression which held genuine sympathy passed across Jack's face.

'I have to marry money, sweetie. You know that.'

The smart, brittle mask was once more in place. 'So you come over all sympathetic to the little mouse while I continue to play the wicked witch?'

'You do it so well, darling,' he murmured.

'And you don't want Marjorie to know.'

'Correct. I've no desire to queer my pitch there. Sooner or later I'll have to bite the bullet and *press my suit* –' he said the last three words in a tone full of irony and with one fair eyebrow raised '– but there's no reason not to have a bit of fun first, is there?'

'And that's all it is – a bit of fun?'

'Of course, my darling. What else?'

They stood for a moment or two in silence. Jack turned to look along Sauchiehall Street in the direction of Charing Cross. After a while he spoke again. 'She's rather good-looking, don't you think – for a wee girl from Clydebank? Not beautiful, exactly, but very attractive. Lovely smile.'

Suzanne frowned. Then she dropped her cigarette and ground it out on the pavement with a twist of her crocodile-skin shod foot. 'Are you coming?' she asked abruptly.

'You run along. I'm going to have another cigarette.'

Suzanne turned, once, on her way to the tearoom. Jack Drummond was standing where she had left him, nonchalantly smoking a cigarette and staring along a Sauchiehall Street from which Kate Cameron's tram had long since disappeared.

Kate, by this time clanking past the Art Galleries and swinging into Dumbarton Road on the tram, had dismissed Jack Drummond from her mind. The trouble was, he kept sneaking back in. Just when she was hugging to herself the praise from the tutor and thinking how pleased her father and Robbie and Jessie would be for her, she would see those mocking blue eyes again, laughing with Suzanne Douglas at her home-made clothes. Or she would hear his voice. *My, but you're fierce. The name's Jack.*

Fancy suggesting that Marjorie would pay for Kate's afternoon tea – and his, for that matter! The men she knew would be horrified at letting a woman pay for them – or even for herself. What a fight she'd had with Robbie when she'd insisted on paying for her own ticket to the pictures! Posh folk were different, she supposed.

She could still feel Jack Drummond's fingers, wiping the smudge of paint from her cheek . . .

'Kate, hen!'

Kate looked up. The tram had stopped at Partick Cross and Mrs MacLean, one of their neighbours from Yoker, was making her way up the gangway – with some difficulty, as she was carrying a huge basket of shopping. She settled her comfortable bulk beside Kate.

'This is me since Tuesday,' she announced, not just to Kate but to everyone sitting within earshot. Kate hid a smile. It was a common opening gambit, and was usually the preamble to a long description of what a hectic week the speaker had just had.

'Have you been getting the messages, Mrs MacLean?'

It was all that was needed. Her neighbour launched into a discourse on the merits of the shops in Partick versus those in Yoker and Clydebank. As this included all the people sitting around them, Kate, so long as she contributed the occasional 'Oh, aye?' or 'Do you tell me that?' was free to let her thoughts wander. The fact that they so frequently took a route back to green paint and blue eyes was entirely her own problem.

Chapter 9

Marjorie Donaldson was holding forth about a pottery demonstration she'd seen on a recent visit to London.

'It was marvellous – held at Waring and Gillow – that's one of the big department stores, you know.' She divided a smile between the group sitting around the table. 'Fantastic colours and patterns, all designed by this potter called Clarice Cliff. She's got these girls working for her and they were painting the things there and then. That was really interesting – to see the work actually being done. And Miss Cliff is beginning to experiment with different shapes.'

'How can you make a cup or a teapot a different shape?' asked Suzanne Douglas, slanting a smile across the table at Jack Drummond.

Marjorie turned eagerly towards her. 'Well, that's just it – you can. There are restrictions because of the function of the thing, of course, but there are innovations to be made. It's just a matter of looking at things from a different angle, with fresh eyes.' She stretched out an impulsive hand and touched the arm of the girl sitting silently but attentively next to her in the tearoom. 'You'd have loved it, Kate, you really would.'

Kate smiled. To her own amazement she had warmed to Marjorie Donaldson. When she was interested in something – as she was now – her enthusiasm for it bubbled over and infected everyone around her. She could make even the sophisticated Suzanne drop the pose of languid disinterest in everything and everybody.

Kate had discovered that it was only because of Marjorie that Suzanne and Jack were regular attenders at the Saturday-afternoon class. 'Because you insist we have to do *something* useful with our lives, Marjorie darling,' Jack Drummond had drawled in explanation.

From what she'd been able to gather, Jack Drummond's life seemed to be an endless round of amusement. He didn't work and still lived with his mother in Bearsden. That seemed odd to Kate. He was twenty-six years old. She knew that for a fact, because it had come out in conversation. Surely he would prefer to be working and in a place of his own?

He and Suzanne Douglas talked merrily of cocktail parties, golf parties and weekends staying with friends in the country.

'Only,' Suzanne Douglas had said a couple of weeks ago, a gleam in her dark eyes, 'Jack keeps turning down weekend invitations these days. I wonder why that is, darling?' His only answer had been to lean forward and light her cigarette.

Marjorie was part of the circle too, but she was more serious-minded than the other two. Kate wouldn't have gone so far as to claim her as a friend, but she was beginning to like her – very much. A few weeks after the start of the term, Marjorie had persuaded her to join the midweek ceramics class which Marjorie herself had been attending for the past couple of years. Since Barbara Baxter's condition seemed, at least for the moment, to have levelled out, and since the grant made it possible, Kate yielded to temptation.

As soon as she felt her hands on wet clay and began learning how to form it into shapes, she knew she'd found something special, something she really wanted to do. Getting her first pieces out of the kiln, fired and ready for decorating, had been a huge thrill. Next week she was going to be allowed on the potter's wheel for the first time.

It was a passion which united the two young women, Kate forgetting her shyness and her consciousness of the differences between them in their shared enthusiasm. Marjorie, who'd been attending classes for the past three years, was talking about opening her own studio next year, and Kate got caught up in the excitement of it, flattered when Marjorie consulted her about different aspects of the project.

The other girl had even managed to persuade Kate to join the rest of the group for tea after class, which was why Kate, on a Saturday afternoon in December, was sitting in a tearoom in West Regent Street.

Outside the mullioned windows the city was locked fast in a typical Glasgow fog – thick, yellow and smothering. They had found their way down from the Art School with great hilarity, scarves around their mouths and noses to keep it out, linking arms and holding on to each other's belts as though they were climbers caught out on a mountainside in the dark. Kate had managed to avoid being next to Jack Drummond at any point, which hadn't been easy, as the giggling group – five girls and three boys – had been constantly shifting position, deriving as much amusement as possible from the journey. This was their last meeting before Christmas, and they were as light-hearted as schoolchildren about the holidays ahead.

Since that first day, she hadn't exchanged a word with him alone. She was, nevertheless, all too aware of him – in class, at the occasional evening lectures she had been to with Marjorie, in company afterwards. She got the distinct impression that he was full of contrition for his rudeness to her, and then, being Kate, wondered if she was flattering herself. Probably he hardly knew that she existed. Yet once or twice she had looked up from her easel and found him studying her with a little self-deprecating smile, as if to say, 'Am I forgiven yet?'

His behaviour towards her now was impeccable – almost too good. In a group which prided itself on its informality, and where first names were the order of the day, Jack Drummond insisted on addressing and referring to Kate as 'Miss Cameron'. Once or twice she had intercepted a look between him and Suzanne Douglas and had wondered if the two of them were laughing at her, but she didn't think so. Jack did seem genuinely contrite. Had she been too hard on him? Maybe it was Suzanne Douglas who had led him on to behave badly and he, being chivalrous, had gone along with her.

Inside the restaurant, in contrast to the pea-souper which was blanketing the outside world, all was bright and cosy. The tablecloths gleamed white and waitresses in black dresses and equally spotless white lace-trimmed aprons and caps moved smoothly about the room serving tea, coffee and orangeade for the children, enjoying afternoon tea with their parents as a Saturday treat.

There was a standard charge, which suited Kate perfectly. The first time she had gone with them, Marjorie had tried to pay for her too. She hadn't tried again. Kate had bristled the way Mr Asquith did when another cat had the temerity to walk into his back court. She couldn't help noticing, however, that Jack Drummond and Suzanne Douglas were quite happy to let Marjorie pick up their bills as well as her own.

Kate loved the conversations the group had. They held passionate discussions on the meaning of art and how important it was for the artist to be honest. They talked about politics and their trips to Europe, and whether there would ever be another war. They talked about love and marriage and women's rights and of how different they were from their parents' generation. They talked about everything, and they exchanged books and magazines and newspaper articles on all possible topics of interest.

Kate had learned a lot – about the new style called Art Deco, named for the exhibition of *Arts Décoratifs et Industriels* held in Paris a couple of years before. According to Jack Drummond, this style was poised to take over from Art Nouveau, which had dominated design since before the turn of the century. Kate was surprised how knowledgeable he was about it. He evidently didn't spend all his time drinking cocktails and playing golf.

Kate loved what she had seen of Art Deco style. It was clean and pure and modern. The new generation of artists and craftworkers used bold primary colours, contrasting them with sharp black, white and silver. They represented nature in a totally new way, and delighted in using such diverse images as geometric shapes and the fluid lines of the female form. She had seen photographs of beautiful little statuettes of women – usually dancing – their bodies caught in movement and their clothes flowing. It was all so different and fresh – a dramatic contrast to the fussy styles which had preceded it.

Marjorie was still enthusing about Clarice Cliff, while Suzanne was still arguing with her about the impossibility of a teapot's being able to be any other shape than the conventionally accepted one.

'Of course it can,' said Marjorie robustly. 'Don't you think so, Kate?'

'Oh yes,' began Kate, leaning forward over the table and forgetting her shyness in her interest in the subject.

'The little mouse speaks,' Suzanne Douglas murmured through her scarlet lips.

'Shut up, Suzanne,' Jack Drummond growled. 'I want to hear what Miss Cameron has to say, even if you don't.'

Kate blushed and stuttered and somehow managed to finish her sentence.

Later, at the coat-stand behind a screen in a corner of

the room, getting ready to venture out into the fog, Kate glanced up at Marjorie's new coat. It was beautiful, in a mixture of red and dark green velvet, the swirls of the pattern resembling the Glasgow rose. The coat had square shoulders, tapering to a narrow hem, and a deep shawl collar in plain green velvet. She couldn't resist stroking the luxurious pile of the material, soft and deep under her hand. With a sigh, she swung her own herringbone tweed coat – one of Agnes Baxter's acquisitions – around her head, ready to put it on. Other hands took it from her and helped her into it.

'Oh! Thank you,' she said, turning around when the operation was complete. Had he seen her touching the collar of Marjorie's coat? She hoped not, uncomfortably aware that the gesture had been all too revealing. She longed to be able to afford beautiful clothes like Marjorie's.

Jack Drummond, however, said nothing. Smiling politely at her, he turned to take down her muffler which had been hanging underneath her coat.

'Wrap up warm now – and make sure you have this round your mouth. It's pretty bad out there. Where did you put your bag?'

Bemused by his attention to her welfare, Kate covered her confusion by turning away to the big mirror, heavily framed in oak, which was on the opposite wall of the lobby created by the screen. The muffler pulled up over her mouth, she turned again to take her leave of Jack Drummond. He was holding the big bag in which she kept her painting gear and he was smiling. He put a hand out and tugged gently on the diminutive brim of her cloche hat.

'Between this and the muffler, all I can see of you are your eyes.'

There was a brief pause. She should say something. Something sharp and funny. She managed it easily enough with the lads at the yard, but Jack Drummond was a different kettle of fish entirely. He held out the bag to her.

'See you after the holidays. Mind how you go, now!'

Emptying her bag at home that evening, she pulled out Mr Donaldson's old shirt. Marjorie had insisted she kept it. Her father had laughed for days at the thought that his daughter was wearing one of the boss's cast-offs.

'Oh!'

The exclamation was surprised from Kate by what she had found underneath the striped shirt. It was a package, beautifully wrapped in paper printed with Regency stripes of silver, green and red. Her bag *had* felt heavier than usual. Curiously, she lifted it out. It was fastened with red ribbon, finished off with a beautifully tied bow. A small green envelope, tucked in behind the bow, was addressed to *Miss Kate Cameron*.

Looking guiltily around from the box bed on which she had rested her bag, prior to stowing the contents away in the drawers underneath, she saw only Granny snoring in her chair and Mr Asquith fixing her with his yellow eyes from one of his favourite spots, on top of the small hearth rug which covered the oil-cloth flooring in front of the range. From the other side of the wall behind the bed came the murmur of voices – her mother and Davie. She didn't know where everybody else had disappeared to. Right at this moment she was just grateful that it was only the cat who was looking at her.

'You'll not clipe on me, son, will you?' whispered Kate. Mr Asquith continued to give her an unblinking stare which seemed to tell her not necessarily to count on his discretion.

Why, in any case, should she be feeling guilty because someone had given her a present? Stupid question. She knew exactly why. She also knew that she wasn't going to have to call in Sherlock Holmes to help her work out who had slipped the gift into her bag. Turning her back on the cat and the room, she untied the ribbon and removed the paper.

'Oh!' she breathed again. She was holding a beautiful box of chocolates in her hand, the lid decorated with a picture of a huge vase of flowers. She laid it carefully on the bed and, fumbling, opened the little green envelope and found a white card inside. The handwriting sloped elegantly.

I behaved very badly at our first meeting, and I'm sorry for it. Please tell me that I'm forgiven. Merry Christmas. It was signed simply with his initials. *J.D.*

'What have we here then?'

Kate let out a yelp. Pearl was right behind her, peering over her shoulder. She thrust the box of chocolates under her sketch book and turned hurriedly. Mr Asquith, she saw, had dived for cover under the sink curtain. Had she screamed that loudly?

'Pearl! What a fright you gave me. You shouldn't creep up on people like that. I was just putting my painting things away,' said Kate.

'Oh, aye? Is that what you were doing?' Leaning forward, Pearl scooped up the box of chocolates from under the sketch book where Kate had tried to hide them – unsuccessfully, it appeared now.

'Gosh,' said Pearl, her eyes growing wide in her pretty face. 'None o' your rubbish. This is our most luxurious line. Whoever he is, these must have cost him a packet.' She looked Kate straight in the eye.

'He's just a friend,' said Kate quickly. Too quickly. And he wasn't a friend, anyway. Was he?

'That's what you say about Robbie,' observed Pearl shrewdly, giving her older sister a very worldly-wise look. 'Only it wasn't Robbie that gave you these. What's his name?'

'Mr Nobody,' said Kate smartly, snatching the box of chocolates out of Pearl's grasp. With her free hand, she cleared a space on the bed and sat down on the edge of it. She looked up at Pearl, trying the worldly-wise look herself.

'Would you like a chocolate, sister dear?'

Pearl gave her a smile which told Kate quite clearly that she wasn't fooled one little bit by this apparent lack of concern.

'Of course I'd like a chocolate. Three or four if you want me not to tell Mammy about them,' she added complacently. 'Or about Mr Nobody. Are you sure he's not Mr Right?'

'Don't be daft, Pearl,' said Kate, her tone sharp. 'Of course he's not.' She dropped her eyes, concentrating on removing the outer wrapper and opening the box of chocolates. Lifting the lid, she offered her sister first choice. Jessie would have to get some too, of course, and wee Davie. She'd need to swear them both to secrecy. Pearl popped a chocolate into her mouth and began chewing it with relish.

'We're not allowed to eat these ones at work. Too posh for the likes of us.' The knowing look stayed on her face. She arched her eyebrows. She had plucked them to a thin, perfectly-shaped line, which she had then filled out and defined with a black make-up pencil.

She finished the chocolate and picked out another.

'Mr Nobody?'

'Mr Nobody,' said Kate firmly. With sudden decision, she leaped to her feet. 'Here, take your other two. I'm putting this away now.'

Jack Drummond most definitely was not Mr Right. That much she *was* sure of. Men like him weren't interested in girls like her. Well, only for one thing, and if he thought she was that kind of a girl, he had another think coming.

However, it wasn't that robust thought which lingered in her head over Christmas and New Year, but Pearl's question to her that kept popping up at the most inconvenient moments. *Are you sure he's not Mr Right?* Ridiculous though that was.

134

Chapter 10

She had to thank him for the chocolates. She might be poor, but she'd been brought up to have good manners. She thought about writing him a letter, then realised that she didn't know his address. That meant she would have to wait till the class resumed in January. That raised a big problem. If she thanked him in front of everyone else, they would know that he had given her a present, and they would ask why, and then people would start teasing and it would all get too complicated for words.

She could just imagine the interested gleam in Suzanne Douglas's eye. That made her think of Pearl, whose sharp eyes never missed a trick – or a handsome man. Kate allowed herself a moment's amusement at how horrified Suzanne would be by the comparison to someone she would no doubt consider, if she thought of such people at all, as a little shopgirl.

The alternative solution to Kate's problem was to try to get a few minutes alone with Jack Drummond. Oh Mammy, Daddy, that was just as bad an idea!

When the class started up again in January, Kate had the distinct feeling that Jack was well aware of her predicament – was even gently amused by it. He kept glancing across at her, giving her little smiles when no one else was looking. She delayed packing up her things at the end of the lesson, hoping he would get the message and wait behind too. Then she could quickly say thanks for the chocolates and leave. He would go down Dalhousie Street to join the others somewhere in Sauchiehall Street and she would go down Scott Street to get her tram. She had already told Marjorie she wasn't going to make it for tea today.

He got the message. Only too well.

'They've all gone.'

Kate looked up from the third and totally unnecessary rearrangement of the contents of her bag. He was right. The two of them were alone in the big bright room. The sun, gathering its strength before sliding into the early winter twilight, slanted through the long windows and transformed his fair hair into a gleaming helmet. Like an angel, thought Kate, or a knight in shining armour. He's real handsome, standing there so relaxed in his casual clothes, smiling at me . . .

'A penny for your thoughts,' came the soft and well-spoken voice. He sounded amused.

'Oh, nothing. Th-thank you for the chocolates,' she stammered. She seized her bag and clutched it under her arm, poised for flight. 'They were lovely,' she said shyly. 'My sisters and I enjoyed them very much.'

'You mean there are more at home like you?'

But Kate, her little speech out, had dipped her head and made for the door. Jack got there before her, however, neatly overtaking her, closing the door and standing in front of it with his arms folded across his chest, barring her escape route.

'Hey! There's no need to rush away.' The handsome face was open and friendly. 'Stay and talk for a while, now that I've finally got you to myself.'

She glanced up at him, completely tongue-tied. He laughed softly.

'You look terrified. I don't bite, you know. That's better,' he said, nodding his head in approval of her reluctant smile. 'You're a very pretty girl, you know.'

'Why, thank you, kind sir,' murmured Kate, sparing one hand to tuck the strand of hair she could feel on her cheek behind her ear. 'You'll be turning my head.'

She had surprised him. She could see that by the subtle change in his expression. There was a re-evaluation of her going on behind that handsome mask. His smile, which had faded, began to creep back, curling the corners of his mouth.

'Not the little mouse you pretend to be, then?'

'You'll never find out.'

Now, where had that answer come from? It sounded like a challenge. Kate lifted her chin with a smile and realised that she was enjoying herself. This man liked her, wanted to get to know her better. It was out of the question of course, but she was woman enough to enjoy the knowledge of her power. Her smile grew broader. Jack Drummond was still smiling in return, but there was a hint of puzzlement in those very blue eyes. Standing up straight, he unfolded his arms.

'I like you,' he announced. 'I think you're sweet.'

'In a little mouse-type way?'

'In a female-type way.'

Now he had knocked her off balance again. He saw it immediately.

'Sorry,' he said, 'I shouldn't have said that.' He sounded completely sincere. More than ever Kate was convinced that it was Suzanne who'd been the guilty party on that first day.

'Would you consider coming out to lunch with me?' he asked suddenly. 'Before the class next week? I'll pick you up from your work in my car. What time do you finish?'

'No,' she said firmly, the colour rising in her cheeks. 'Thank you, but no.' But, heavens, it was a lovely thought! She'd seen his car, a sporty little Morris Cowley. It might be worth it, just to see Miss Nugent's face – and Bella Buchanan's.

Jack Drummond put on a hangdog look, turning his head to one side.

'Don't you like me at all, Miss Cameron? Not even a little bit?'

She bit back a smile. 'We're not discussing whether or not I like you. We're discussing the fact that I'm not going to go out with you.'

'Why not?' he demanded.

'Use your loaf,' said Kate acerbically.

'Do you really think that sort of thing matters in this day and age? It is the twentieth century, after all.' He hadn't insulted her by pretending not to understand what she meant. She liked him for that, but she still wasn't going to go out with him and she told him so.

He sighed theatrically, turning to one side and raising the back of his hand to his forehead. 'Oh, you're so cruel. Cruel, cruel, cruel Miss Cameron!'

'You ought to be on stage at the Glasgow Empire. And for heaven's sake stop calling me *Miss Cameron*. My name's Kate!'

He dropped the dramatically upraised hand and beamed at her.

'Well, Kate, if you won't come out to dinner or lunch with me, will you come to Kelvingrove tomorrow to look at the paintings?'

Kate narrowed her eyes at him. 'Who else will be there?'

His blue eyes crinkled at the corners when he smiled. 'Och, you're so suspicious, Miss Cameron! The rest of the group, of course – part of our artistic education. What's the matter? Don't you trust me?'

'Not as far as I could throw you.'

Jack Drummond threw back his head and laughed. I'm

getting better at this, she thought. Maybe there wasn't much difference in dealing with fresh apprentice draughtsmen and well-off young men like Jack Drummond after all. He laid a hand, lightly and briefly, on her shoulder.

'But you'll come, won't you, Kate – to look at the paintings? Twelve o'clock at the main door of the Art Galleries?'

She was almost a quarter of an hour early, but he was already there, standing at the top of the steps under the portico. The building, solid and stately, stood with its back to the River Kelvin as though it had been there for centuries, an impression confirmed by its ornate towers, which gave it the look of a palace.

It had been completed, in fact, less than thirty years before, the centrepiece of the great exhibition held in Kelvingrove Park in 1901. Glaswegians loved to tell each other that the Art Galleries had been built the wrong way round, as a result of which the architect, unable to cope with such a catastrophe, had committed suicide.

The truth was a bit different. The building had been constructed to face the river and Glasgow University's magnificent new neo-Gothic home high up on Gilmorehill, on the other side of the Kelvin. It was the right way round, the architect hadn't killed himself and, in any case, Kate always thought that the mellow red sandstone building looked just as nice whichever angle you looked at it from.

Crossing the driveway which led from the main road to the entrance, Kate raised her hand to return Jack's wave. She was picking her way carefully. There were some nasty little icy patches underfoot. Glancing up with relief as she reached the salted steps, she saw him running nimbly down the broad flight to greet her.

'Are the others already inside?' she asked, looking up and trying to see through the big revolving door. Something about the quality of Jack Drummond's silence caught her attention. She turned to look at him. He was wearing a long dark overcoat, a white silk scarf just showing under its lapels.

'The others aren't coming, are they?'

She could see his breath when he spoke, a white cloud in the crisp January air.

'Don't be angry with me. It was the only way I could think of to get you to have lunch with me. We can still go and look at the paintings. Please?'

'All right,' she said reluctantly. 'Let's look at the paintings. I'm not so sure about lunch, though.'

'You've got to eat. I've brought a picnic and it'll go to waste if you don't share it with me.'

'A picnic?' She looked pointedly behind her, at the icy patches through which she'd walked. 'Are you aff yer heid? We'll catch oor deaths o' cold.'

Kate's accent had adapted to the people with whom she was now mixing, but sometimes there was no substitute for the vernacular.

'Aff my heid?' It sounded funny in his well-bred voice. 'Yes, I think I am "aff my heid". That's the effect you have on me.' Their eyes locked. She thought he was going to touch her and she took a half-step backwards. He bit his lip. It was the smallest of acknowledgements of her withdrawal from him. When he spoke again, he sounded hearty. It didn't fool her for one moment. That tiny movement of hers had upset him. Mr Sophisticated had feelings – deep ones at that.

'We won't be cold if we sit in my car. I'll put a rug over your knees and we'll be nice and cosy. What d'you say?'

'In your car?'

'Yes, it's parked round the back.' He grinned. 'Or the front, if you prefer the old story. Come on, Kate, it'll be fun.'

'Uh-huh.' She raised her eyebrows. Now they were back

140

on safer ground. 'In your car. You must think I came up the Clyde on a water biscuit, Mr Drummond.'

His smile was like the sun coming out. 'Do you always say exactly what you think?'

She thought about it, head turned to one side. 'Not with everybody.' She thought about it a bit more. 'Not with most people.'

His teeth flashed white. 'Then I'm honoured.'

'Uh-huh,' said Kate again, giving him a look. 'You are.'

He was a knowledgeable guide, with lots to say about the different paintings in the gallery. He smiled ruefully when she complimented him on it.

'Well, I don't work, Kate, so I fill my head with lots of useless information. I'm what you Red Clydesiders would call a capitalist parasite, living off money earned by my father and grandfather.'

'I wouldn't say it was useless,' she replied, giving him a sideways smile as they stood in front of Rembrandt's *Man in Armour*. 'What have you got to say about this one, then?'

He folded his arms and rocked back on his heels. 'No – I've been doing all the talking. What do *you* think of it?'

'Me?'

'Go on,' he encouraged. 'You probably know more than you think.'

She wanted to tell him that she thought the man in the painting was like him – a man in armour, hiding his true feelings. She wanted to tell him how she had seen the sun striking his golden hair yesterday, making a helmet of it, but she was too shy, so instead she studied the painting carefully, self-consciously using the vocabulary she'd heard used at the art appreciation lectures she'd attended with Marjorie.

'Well, the painting depicts a soldier, in profile and at rest. His eyes are closed, I think . . .' she paused, and looked more closely at the canvas '. . . or he's looking at something on the ground. If he is, I think he's using it as a thinking post – not really seeing it. I get the impression that his his thoughts are far away.'

She glanced at Jack, who nodded his fair head in encouragement.

'Maybe he's thinking about some battle he's been in, but I'm not sure about that. He looks very calm, doesn't he? Like a man at peace with himself, yet you would think soldiers always had unhappy memories—' She stopped short.

'Is anything the matter?'

She found herself telling him about her father and his nightmares. Jack listened carefully, his blue eyes fixed on her face.

'I suppose I should be grateful that he came back,' said Kate, her voice sombre. 'Lots of people lost their fathers in the war, didn't they?'

'I was one of them,' said Jack, his voice low and suddenly rough.

'Oh Jack, I'm so sorry!' Kate laid a swift, impulsive hand on his sleeve. 'What age were you?'

Smiling wryly at the depth of her sympathy, he covered her hand with his own. Kate couldn't quite hide a little jump at the touch of his warm fingers, but she left her hand where it was. This was definitely a different Jack Drummond she was seeing today.

'Thirteen. It was harder for my mother. She's never really got over it.'

'But she's got you to keep her company, at least.' So that was why he still lived with his mother. That put a different complexion on things.

'I can't bring myself to leave, Kate – and that's the truth. Can you understand that?'

'Oh yes, I can, I can!'

'I knew you would be able to.' He made a funny little sound, halfway between a sob and a laugh. 'You won't tell anybody else what I've just told you, will you, Kate? I don't think I could cope with people thinking I was noble. I have my devil-may-care reputation to protect, you know.'

'Well, I think it is noble,' she said, squeezing his arm. 'And very kind, too.'

'How earnest you sound, little Clydebank girl.' He was smiling, but there was a frown between his brows as he studied Kate's upturned face. 'I'm not kind at all. In fact, if I were you, I'd have nothing to do with me, I really wouldn't.'

'Why? Are you mad, bad and dangerous to know?' Kate asked, one of Miss Noble's lessons on the life of Lord Byron coming back to her. She laughed into his face, wanting to tease him, to help him forget the sad things they'd been talking about, to forget her own worries, to have some fun. There was, however, no corresponding teasing glint in Jack Drummond's cool blue eyes. He looked very serious and it was a minute or two before he spoke.

'Answer me a question. Are you happy? Right now, at this moment? Being here with me?'

'Yes,' she said. 'I am.'

He smiled. 'Then let's go and have that picnic.'

So she went and sat in his car with him and he behaved like a perfect gentleman. Apart from tucking a tartan travelling rug around her knees, as promised, he didn't touch her. He had brought sandwiches, and soup kept hot in a silver flask – and champagne.

'On a day like this there was no trouble keeping the champagne cold. I do think it makes a picnic, don't you? Can you hold the glasses, Kate?'

Kate took them from him and stared at him – and the bottle he was opening – in utter amazement. Champagne? He had

143

removed the wrapping round the cork and was untwisting the wires which held it in place.

'I never thought people actually drank champagne. I thought it was just something you saw at the pictures – and at launches, of course.'

He raised his eyebrows. 'You've never drunk it?' Carefully easing off the cork, which gave a satisfying *pop*, he poured the foaming liquid into the two glasses. Then he bent forward, slid the bottle to lie on the floor between his feet, straightened up and took a glass from her.

'To us,' he said softly, 'and your beautiful green eyes.'

And your beautiful blue ones, thought Kate. She took a cautious sip.

'Oh! The bubbles are going up my nose!'

Jack Drummond threw his head back and laughed. 'Drink some more then. It's the only cure.'

'Oh dear,' she said, laughing with him after she had taken another sip. 'Robbie would really disapprove if he could see me now. He's signed the pledge.'

Jack's beautiful blue eyes narrowed. 'Robbie?'

Was it just a wee bit tactless to mention one man when you were drinking another's champagne? 'Robert Baxter,' she explained briefly. 'A friend.' Better change the subject quickly.

'You remind me of the *Man in Armour*.' She told him why. Well, she told him half of it – how she had watched the sun strike his hair and make it look like a gleaming helmet.

'I'm flattered,' he murmured. 'And here was I thinking that you had hardly noticed me.' He chuckled at the look of disbelief she directed at him.

'You laugh a lot, don't you?'

'Isn't that what life's about?'

Kate lowered the champagne glass into her lap. Barbara

144

Baxter's face had suddenly appeared in her mind's eye. 'Not always,' she said.

'Now you're sad,' observed Jack. 'Want to tell me why? Is it to do with this Robbie you mentioned?'

'Not exactly.' She looked away from him and out of the window at the park. The sun was stronger now. It had melted all the icy puddles. No, she thought, she didn't want to tell him why she was sad. She turned away from the view and looked at Jack Drummond. He was sitting back on the bench seat. He appeared very relaxed, but his eyes were watchful.

'I don't want to talk about sad things,' she said.

He gave her a searching look and then a long slow smile. 'Then, my dear *Miss Cameron*, you're come to the right man.' He bent to retrieve the champagne bottle. 'Have some more.'

Afterwards, when Kate had admitted that she'd never been in a car before either, he insisted on driving her home, although she made him let her out two tram stops before Yoker Ferry Road. He raised his eyebrows at that.

'Ashamed of me, Kate? Or don't you want to make your friend Robbie jealous?'

Kate blushed and denied both vehemently. She struggled to put it into words as Jack pulled into the kerb and stopped the car.

'Today's been really special for me. I just don't want to have to – to *explain* anything to anybody!'

She was turned towards him, an appeal in her green eyes. Jack Drummond took her hand.

'It's been really special for me, too. How about doing it again soon? We could go for a spin – out to Loch Lomond, perhaps?' He raised his fair eyebrows in interrogation.

She wanted to say yes, to speed through the countryside in his car, laughing and chatting as they had today, but if she did, was she agreeing to something more? He saw the conflict raging in her face.

'Go on, Kate, say yes. We could have some fun together, you and I.'

'Just fun? You wouldn't want anything else?'

'Just fun. I promise.'

She should say no, she really should, stop this right now before it went too far. But oh, how she longed to have some fun!

'Yes,' she whispered. 'Yes, please.'

Chapter 11

Mr Asquith, lying in front of the range, stretched luxuriously.

'Makes you feel warm just to look at him,' said Neil, smiling at Jessie, who was sitting on the rug beside the cat.

'Mmm,' she agreed, sending Mr Asquith into paroxysms of pleasure and demented purring by stroking him from the tips of his ears to the tip of his tail. 'Look how long he is when he does this.' She beamed up at her father. He had wee Davie on his knee and he was singing to him.

'This is your big sister's song,' he told his son, before launching into *I'll take you home again, Kathleen . . .*

Kate, sitting at the table reading, exchanged a glance with her sister. Neil was making another heroic effort to stay off the drink. It had been nearly a month now since he'd been to the pub and there was no alcohol in the house. So far, so good.

She bent her head to the magazine which Marjorie had lent her. It had an article devoted to new developments in ceramics, complete with photographs. There were so many interesting things going on. Down in England a potter called Susie Cooper had joined Clarice Cliff as one of the names to watch.

In Glasgow too, small studios were springing up to produce pottery with a difference – miles away from the mass-produced ware most people, rich and poor, had in their houses.

Finishing the text of the article, Kate studied the pictures in detail. Ideas were forming in her head. She reached for her sketch pad and pencils, lying at the ready on the table in front of her.

Granny was in her usual corner, diagonally behind Kate where she sat facing the range.

'Jenny!' she hissed.

Kate threw her the swiftest of smiles over her shoulder. 'Sorry, Granny,' she muttered, more to herself than to the old lady, 'but I've got to get this down on paper.' Ideas were like that, she'd found. They seemed so clear in your head, but they disappeared like snow off a wall if you didn't capture them right away.

There was a knock at the front door. Kate hardly heard it, absorbed in the sketch growing under her pencil.

'I'll get it,' sang out Pearl, always eager for distraction.

A rowan tree, thought Kate – that would make a good *motif*. If she drew it naturally first, and then worked out how to stylise it . . . Engrossed in the work, the familiarity of the voices at the door didn't penetrate her consciousness until the visitors were actually in the room.

'Kate's communing with her muse,' drawled a light, amused voice.

'Yes, her tongue's sticking out in concentration.'

Kate's head snapped up. Suzanne Douglas and Jack Drummond were standing on the other side of the table smiling down at her. Behind them she saw Marjorie's face, peering over their shoulders.

'You don't mind, Kate, do you?' she asked. There was a tinge of anxiety in her voice. 'We thought we'd just drop in.'

'As we were in the neighbourhood,' murmured Suzanne, turning her head and laughing up into Jack Drummond's face. He gave her a lop-sided smile and turned to look at Kate, his fair eyebrows slightly raised, as though in enquiry. *Is this all right?*

148

Kate caught a glimpse of her mother's face as she hovered behind the unexpected visitors. Lily looked completely panic-stricken. No, it damn' well isn't all right, thought Kate, a pang of sympathy for her mother, as intense as it was unexpected, shooting through her. People like these, in their expensive and beautiful clothes, with their cultured accents and exquisite manners, were like some alien species to her. Lily could have dealt with the King and Queen coming to the door more easily than she was going to be able to cope with Marjorie Donaldson and her friends.

Lifting Davie gently off his lap, Neil Cameron spoke.

'You'll be Kathleen's friends from the Art School?' he asked in his soft accent. 'Let's see if we can find you all a seat. Lily?'

As he rose to his feet, drawing himself up to his full height, Kate saw Suzanne Douglas give him an appraising look.

Lily recovered herself. 'Perhaps youse would all care to step through to the parlour?'

Jessie cringed. Their mother was unsuccessfully putting on the pan loaf. Kate saw Suzanne Douglas smother a snigger. She also saw Marjorie elbow her discreetly in the ribs.

'Oh no, Mrs Cameron, it's fine and cosy in your kitchen. It is Mrs Cameron, isn't it? I'm Marjorie Donaldson.' She held out her hand. Lily took it – and bobbed a curtsey.

Jessie, Kate knew, was about to die of embarrassment, any second now. Her own sympathy for her mother had been swallowed up by irritation. Why didn't she know how to behave?

Kate was suffering from a considerable amount of embarrassment on her own account too. It was one thing to sit in a tearoom with her fellow students, as equals, setting the world to rights. It was another to look at paintings and then sip champagne with Jack Drummond, or drive out to the country with him, chatting merrily all the way. They'd had

149

several Sunday afternoon dates although, at Kate's insistence, without the champagne. Usually they went into some little place for lunch or afternoon tea.

It was, however, quite another thing for her Art School friends to visit her here, in the poky and cramped two rooms which housed the Cameron family. How must it look through these sophisticated eyes? Poverty-stricken? Squalid?

Maybe she would just join Jessie, thought Kate wryly. They could both slide gently to the floor and regain consciousness once the visitors had left. Pity there wasn't really enough space to do it.

Marjorie, a friendly smile on her face, ignored Lily's disastrous gesture and turned to Neil, obviously determined to manage the introductions single-handedly if she had to.

'Mr Cameron? I hope you don't mind us dropping in like this. I believe you work with my father, don't you?'

Neil Cameron smiled down at her from his great height, his handsome mouth quirking.

'I'm not just sure that *with* is the right word, lass, but it's nice of you to say so. May I introduce the rest of my family?'

Kate was proud of him. Their house might be too small and more than a little shabby. There might be laundry hanging down from the pulley above the range, but the Cameron family was going to rise to the occasion.

This, Kate felt sure, had been Suzanne Douglas's idea – a bit of a wheeze, a good laugh. 'Let's go slumming, see where the little mouse lives.' Jack, in his usual relaxed fashion, had gone along with it. If he'd thought about it for two minutes, he must have realised how embarrassing it would be for Kate. Honestly, he was hopeless!

Behind the backs of the visitors, Lily was making frantic signals to her and Pearl. Pearl shook her head. Kate fixed her with a look, and with a murmured excuse, grabbed her sister's wrist as unobtrusively as she could, and led the way out into the lobby.

'We havenae got enough good cups and saucers, Kate,' said Lily in a furious stage whisper, 'and no' even a biscuit to give them a cup o' tea anyway. What'll we do?' she wailed.

'It's all right, Mammy, I'll go down and borrow some cups and saucers from Mrs Baxter and ask her if she's got anything in her tins.' She could be confident enough about that. Agnes Baxter devoted one day per week to baking for her family – enough to last the week, kept fresh in airtight biscuit tins. 'She'll maybe have some empire biscuits or shortbread left.'

She patted her mother awkwardly on the arm. It was a strange feeling this, a mixture of irritation and sympathy. How could she expect a woman like her mother to cope with the likes of Suzanne Douglas? 'We can do a baking the morn and give it back to her then.'

'Aye,' said Lily, nodding her head vigorously, 'that's what to do – but Pearl and me'll go.'

'Oh, Mammy,' wailed Pearl in her turn, 'I want to stay and talk to the visitors.'

Lily gave her a swift clout on the ear. 'Kate'll talk to them – and Jessie. They've both got the gift of the gab wi' folk like yon.' She gave Kate a look which made it clear that this was not a compliment.

Jack Drummond stood up as Kate walked back into the kitchen, then sank once again into her father's chair. Marjorie sat opposite him, chatting animatedly with Neil, who'd perched himself on the old stool beside her. Suzanne Douglas sat on an upright chair between them, looking round the shabby room with a little smile playing on her lipsticked mouth. She looked like an exotic bird of paradise in a farmyard full of old brown hens.

Mr Asquith, rudely evicted from his place in front of

the range by the arrival of the visitors, jumped onto Jack Drummond's lap.

'Hallo, cat,' he said, glancing down and stroking the beast with his beautiful hands. He looked up suddenly, catching Kate unawares. Blushing, she turned away. Seeing Jack sitting in her mother's kitchen was strangely unsettling. When it came to watching him smooth the cat's fur with those long elegant fingers, unsettling didn't begin to cover how it made her feel. Suzanne caught her eye. Kate didn't care at all for the look the girl gave her.

She couldn't know – could she? By tacit agreement, she and Jack had kept their developing relationship to themselves. Kate wasn't quite sure why. Except that she was more comfortable having him drop her a few streets away when he brought her home from their Sunday-afternoon outings. Except that she was happier allowing people to think that those afternoons were spent with a group of friends, and not one particular one. Kate had a shrewd idea that Pearl had her suspicions – maybe Robbie, too. She wasn't sure. It had been ages since she'd had a decent conversation with him. They no longer went to the pictures together and they had lost the old camaraderie. Since she had met Jack Drummond.

Lily and Pearl returned, bringing Robbie with them. He walked stiffly into the room and Kate guessed that Lily had asked him to come and help out in the conversational line. More introductions were made. Marjorie looked up at Robbie with a genuine smile, Suzanne tried a vampish look from under her blackened eyelashes and Jack extended a languid hand to him.

'So you're the famous Robbie!'

If looks could kill, thought Kate, I *would* be lying dead on the floor, whether there's enough space or not. Robbie's dark brows, meeting in a reproachful line, spelled the message out quite clearly. Kate Cameron had discussed him with another man, and he didn't like that one little bit.

Not that he had anything to worry about. Not really. Jack Drummond didn't go in for deep conversations. Their afternoons together were about having fun, he declared. They laughed and joked and enjoyed the countryside. Kate had started letting him kiss her – but nothing more than that. 'Fun,' she would remind him, pushing him away. 'Remember?'

'Are you artistic like Kate, Mr Baxter?' Suzanne was asking, laying a hand on Robbie's jacket sleeve as he settled into a seat beside her, hurriedly placed there by Jessie. He flashed her a quick smile of thanks over his shoulder as he sat down.

'I'm a cabinet-maker, Miss Douglas,' answered Robbie. 'I don't know whether you consider that artistic.' The smile he'd thrown to Jessie faded as he looked at Suzanne. One lock of dark hair, as usual, flopped onto his forehead. A kitchen full of handsome men, thought Kate, even if one of them is only just managing not to glower like a thundercloud. Pearl'll be in seventh heaven.

'A cabinet-maker, how fascinating!' exclaimed Suzanne Douglas, her arm resting lightly on Robbie's. 'Do tell me more.' She'll be purring soon, thought Kate sourly. She could give Mr Asquith a run for his money. Lost in the thought, she looked up and found Jack Drummond's eyes on her. He raised one of Mrs Baxter's best china cups to her in salute. Kate had the feeling that he knew exactly what she'd been thinking.

Pearl *was* in seventh heaven, her eyes nearly popping out of her head. Suzanne was dividing her attention between Robbie and her, basking in the younger girl's unabashed admiration of her clothes and make-up. She glanced away occasionally, smiling at the other men in the room. Anything in trousers, thought Kate, and was absurdly cheered up when she saw the expression on Robbie's face grow more and more disapproving as he watched Suzanne Douglas.

Marjorie, she had to admit, seemed to be taking a genuine interest in her father. She'd even managed to draw a terrified Lily into the conversation, asking her the occasional gentle question so she wouldn't feel left out. Marjorie was talking to her father now about his childhood in the Highlands.

Jack, on the other hand, had hardly participated in the conversation, just sat there looking around him, taking in the shabby, cramped room, the drying clothes, Granny snoring gently in the corner. Maybe this hadn't just been Suzanne's idea. Had they both thought it would be fun to come and gawp, as they might have gone to Wilson's zoo in Sauchiehall Street to look at the animals?

Robbie, who had also dropped out of the conversation, saw it too. Kate could tell that by the look on his face. Like her, he was getting angry. As soon as was reasonably polite, he rose and excused himself.

Kate followed him, murmuring something about seeing him out. Opening the big front door, she followed him out onto the landing, pulling the door closed behind her.

'Don't go yet.'

Ready to head off down the stairs, he looked at her quizzically.

'Why not? You've got your smart friends in there, haven't you? What do you need me for?' But he stayed, all the same, leaning on the cool painted wall of the landing, tilting his unruly head back against it and letting out a long breath before he spoke.

'I'm surprised they didn't bring us bags of monkey nuts. See if we would do some tricks for them.'

'Robbie . . .'

'What?' His eyes were fixed on the long window on the opposite wall. During the day it flooded the stairs with light.

There was nothing to be seen out of it now but the moonless night sky.

'What?' he asked again. He was very pale in the dim light of the gas-mantle above his head, his eyes and hair dark against his white skin.

Kate shook her head. The two of them had always had the uncanny tendency to share the same thoughts. She couldn't disagree with what he'd just said.

Robbie looked at her for a moment. Then he let out another long breath.

'I'll be off, then.'

Kate took them both by surprise when she suddenly leaned forward and kissed him on the cheek. His skin was cool under her lips.

He went completely still. 'What was that for?'

'It wasn't for anything. It was just for you.'

'A farewell kiss?' he suggested, his voice raw-edged. 'Good-bye Robbie, and thanks? It's been swell?'

'Robbie . . .'

'Don't bother, Kate. Go back to your friends. They'll be wondering where you are.'

Dismayed, she stood and watched him go down the stairs. He didn't look back up at her.

Chapter 12

'So the gallant Robbie is my rival for your affections? Is it his witty conversation or his dashing character which appeals to you most?'

'Don't make fun of him.'

Jack, sitting beside her in the confined space of the Morris Cowley, turned those very blue eyes on her.

'Oh, so that's how the wind blows, is it?'

'No, it is not. I just don't like you talking about my friends like that.'

Before he could stop her, she had the door open, and was crunching noisily over the shingle on her way to the edge of Loch Lomond. When she got there she stopped and looked across to the mountains on the other side. It was the middle of March, a bright and sunny day, but cold. She wrapped her arms around herself.

She heard footsteps on the stones behind her and then two strong arms slid round her waist, under her own. His voice was a warm murmur against the chilly flesh of her ear.

'Cold, Kate? Why don't you come back to the car and let me do something about that?'

Angrily, she broke away from him and started walking along the shore. They were at Millarochy Bay, north of Balmaha on the eastern, and quieter, side of the loch. Once the weather got better it would be busy on a Sunday afternoon, full of campers and cyclists and hikers, but today it was deserted.

Since the very beginning, Jack had shown a preference for quiet and lonely places. Even when they went in somewhere for lunch or afternoon tea, as they had today at Drymen, he chose the quietest hotel or inn he could find.

'Kate.' He had caught up with her, lain a restraining hand on her arm. She whirled round, her voice quivering with rage.

'Are you ashamed of me? Because I come from a poor family?'

He took out his gold cigarette case, extracted a cigarette and lit up. Kate watched him hungrily. Every gesture had an easy grace which spoke volumes about his background and the easy wealth with which he'd been brought up.

'Your background doesn't matter to me one little bit. Quite the reverse, in fact. I think you've done marvellously to get on as much as you have. You'll probably never have any idea how much I admire you. For sticking to your principles, among other things.'

She met his blue eyes. Sometimes he said things she didn't understand. Oh, she knew what the words meant, but she couldn't figure out whether he was being his usual determinedly light-hearted self, or if something deeper was being said. He dropped his cigarette onto the beach, his eyes following it, so that she couldn't see the expression in them.

'Maybe I'm ashamed of myself sometimes.' His fair head snapped up. 'After all, my little Red Clydesider thinks I'm a wastrel, doesn't she? A capitalist and a parasite?'

'I think,' Kate said severely, hugging herself and trying to suppress a shiver, because it really was cold, 'that you should get yourself a job. You're an educated and intelligent man, after all.'

'And if I – distasteful as the prospect is – got myself a job, would you look on me differently?'

157

Kate's stomach lurched. What was he asking? There was such a huge gulf between them . . .

'Do you know why I really want to keep our outings to ourselves?' he asked her then.

Still hugging herself, Kate shook her head.

'Because when we're together like this, and there's no one else around, we can be ourselves – Kate and Jack – with nothing to separate us. With you, I can just be truly myself – and I'd like to thank you for that.' His voice was husky.

Kate's anger evaporated in an instant. Closing the distance between them, she lifted her hands to rest on his upper arms, her gloved fingers sinking into the warm wool of his overcoat.

'I want you to be yourself. And you can tell me anything you like – really you can. You don't have to bottle things up.' If only she could make him see that, encourage him to show her the man she'd only caught glimpses of up till now, the vulnerable boy behind the confident exterior.

A wistful smile flitted across his mouth as he looked down at her. 'So earnest, my little Clydebank girl. So sweet. But I won't tell you sad things. You have enough of those at home. And you forgive me, don't you? For wanting to keep you to myself, for landing on your family, for being a swine sometimes?'

'The appalling thing is,' said Kate, 'that I find that I do.' Good heavens, she was even beginning to sound like them now. With that thought came another. Maybe that gulf wasn't so huge after all. Maybe she could learn how to cross it.

He put his arms around her waist. 'Give us a kiss, Miss Cameron, and then come back to the car with me.'

'Are we leaving?'

'Not yet, no.' He was happy again, and she was glad. He bent forward to kiss her. One hand slid onto her breast. Kate

158

lifted it and repositioned it on her shoulder. Jack sighed, his breath warm on her face.

'You did say that you admire me for sticking to my principles,' she murmured.

'I say a lot of very foolish things. I thought you knew that.'

She threaded a hand through the thick soft straw of his hair, pulling his head down towards her. She was glad he couldn't see her face. That way he wouldn't see the hope in her eyes, nor the urge to give in to him, to let him have what he wanted, to offer him the comfort of her body – as well as the love in her heart.

At home that night she was thoughtful and distracted. Had he hinted at a proposal today? Or was that wishful thinking on her part? He did seem prepared to wait, allowing her to push him away with a fairly good grace, as he had done today. He got irritated sometimes, but that was natural. Men liked that sort of thing, and women had to resist it. Although she was a bit shakier on that than she used to be.

When she found her thoughts drifting to what it might be like to let Jack do what he wanted, she resolutely pushed them down and went off to take over from Jessie, who was listening to wee Davie's reading. Five years old, and just started at school, he was the family pet. They all doted on him, and he in turn idolised his sisters, especially Kate, who always had a threepenny bit for him when she got her pay. He was allowed to go down to Pelosi's on his own now, and he usually handed the coin over in exchange for three penny caramels. The thick chewy sweets kept him going for most of the weekend.

Sitting side by side so that she could help with the difficult words, Davie snuggled into her. Kate put her arm around the small shoulders, smiling at his concentration as he read to her, his downcast eyelashes resting like dark feathers on his downy cheeks. That reminded her of Robbie.

Sometimes she thought men were like wee boys. They pretended to be big and brave and bold, but inside they were sweet and trusting like wee Davie, hungry for love and reassurance and comfort.

The stream of words stopped abruptly. One had stumped him. He looked up at his big sister, confident that she would be able to help him.

'Apple,' said Kate, pointing to the picture of the fruit which went with the story. 'Now you say it.'

Davie repeated it obediently.

'Clever boy,' said Kate, giving his shoulders an encouraging squeeze. 'Now, can you read what it says on the next page?'

She was sure there was a wee boy inside Jack Drummond. She had caught glimpses of him now and again – on that first day they had spent together at the Art Galleries, and on a few occasions since, like today. He always covered it up quickly, as though he were scared she would think him weak if he showed her how he really felt. How silly men were! Knowing that life sometimes made him feel sad or scared or small just made her love him all the more.

There was so much she could do for him – let him be himself, encourage him to see that there was more to life than having fun, that hard work could be rewarding. Why, she could be the making of Jack Drummond! She caught herself on, laughing inwardly. What a big-head!

Davie's small body was warm and heavy against her own. It was a nice feeling. She'd like children of her own one day. Lots of them. And if she was beginning to visualise them all as fair-haired with beautiful blue eyes . . . well, who could blame her?

There were always exhibitions being held at the Art School

– official ones, ones organised by the different clubs and societies, ones held by individual classes. Not to be outdone, Marjorie declared that the Saturday-afternoon class would mount its own show of work just before the School broke up for the summer holidays. They would send out personal invitations to everyone they could think of in the art world – and friends and family. That way, they would be sure of getting a good attendance. Kate, she decreed, would show her very first painting, the still-life she had done last September, a subsequent water colour of a rowan tree, plus the cup and saucer which she'd decorated with the same *motif* at the ceramics class.

'When you're famous, people will boast of having seen you during your Rowan Tree period!' she said, beaming at Kate.

Jack Drummond, who had nothing to show because he never finished anything, was deputed to compose the invitations and write descriptions for cards which would accompany each exhibit. Marjorie herself would show some of her own pottery, and the rest of the class would show a variety of paintings and sketches.

Caught up in her friend's enthusiasm, Kate threw herself with gusto into the preparations for the show. She'd had no idea how much organising such events took. Once Marjorie had discovered how good Kate was at lettering, she had been dragooned into doing the invitations and the descriptive cards, thus giving her and Jack Drummond a legitimate excuse for spending time together. It was a relief to be able to talk about him openly, and at home too, his name began to pepper her conversation.

Marjorie made up a list of people who should be invited to the show. Kate was surprised by the response, until Suzanne Douglas made a rather snide remark querying whether the interest was purely artistic, or whether the fact that Marjorie was the daughter of one of the biggest shipbuilders in the west of Scotland might just have something to do with it.

Unwilling to agree with Suzanne, honesty nevertheless compelled Kate to admit that she had a point. All the same, she couldn't help being thrilled that her own work was going to be seen by some very influential people. She proudly sent out an invitation to Miss Noble and Miss MacGregor. They would be pleased, she hoped, with what she had achieved and it would be a small thank you for the help they had given her in securing the grant. After a moment's hesitation, she took out a second invitation card and carefully filled in another name – *Mr Robert Baxter*. She delivered that one by hand and Robbie thanked her gravely and said he would be delighted to come.

A week before the show, scheduled to be held on the last weekend of term, Kate arrived early at the Art School so that she could have a look at the room where they were holding it. A few of her fellow students were coming in on the Thursday beforehand to set everything up. She herself had been able only to get Friday afternoon and Saturday morning off – without pay, of course. Miss Nugent obviously thought the time off was a huge concession in itself. Kate, unwilling as always to be given any special treatment, suspected that Marjorie had secured it for her, but when she challenged her friend, Marjorie simply held up her hands, smiled and said, 'Ask me no questions and I'll tell you no lies.'

They were having a discussion in class today on how the room should be set up. Kate, having a good look round so that she could make her contribution to this, turned as she heard the door of the room open. It was Jack. Glancing round to make sure they were alone, he planted a swift kiss on her mouth and, with a flourish, presented her with a white envelope.

'What's this?' she asked, smiling up at him.

'Open it, my dear Miss Cameron, and all will be revealed.'

It was an invitation, but not one of those the two of them had designed for the class show. Printed in gold lettering on thick white card, it had gaps which were filled in with green ink. It invited Miss Kate Cameron to join Mrs John Drummond for lunch at her home in Bearsden the following Sunday.

Jack was beaming when Kate lifted her head.

'It's to celebrate the exhibition. I'll drive you out there as soon as the show closes. That's one o'clock on the Sunday, isn't it? Maybe we could even go half an hour earlier?'

'But what about the clearing up? We'll have to help, won't we?'

'Leave that to other people,' he suggested with a lazy smile.

Kate narrowed her eyes at him, and he laughed, laying a hand lightly on her shoulder. 'Oh dear, you always think I'm so workshy. How can I prove myself to you, I wonder?' He bent forward to kiss her but she stopped him, putting a hand flat on his chest.

'Get yourself a job, you capitalist parasite. Go and work for your living for a change.'

He struck a dramatic pose, seized her hand and clasped it between his own. 'Darling! Then would you look on me more kindly?'

Was he serious? She could never tell. She changed the subject.

'Who's coming to this lunch party, then?'

'There'll be eight of us. Suzanne, of course.'

'How nice,' muttered Kate. Jack grinned and chucked her under the chin.

'My Mama, Marjorie, a couple of art critics who, of course, will think that your Rowan Tree crockery is just the very thing.'

He held a hand up as if to forestall a protest. 'I know exactly what you're going to say. You haven't got anything suitable to wear. So how about I take you along to Tréron's this afternoon after class and buy you something? Nothing too fancy that you won't be able to explain away to your parents. Just a little afternoon frock, Kate? I'd love to see you in something really nice. Please let me do it.'

'Do I get a word in edgeways?' asked a bemused Kate. It was all a bit much to take in. Mrs Drummond inviting her to lunch, people who might like her work going to be there, Jack offering to buy her a frock – from Tréron's too. None of your rubbish.

'Only if you say yes. Oh, go on, Kate – because we've got something else to celebrate.' He was beaming at her.

'What?' she asked, intrigued.

It came tumbling out of him. Marjorie's father had offered him a job – at Donaldson's plush city offices in Bath Street in Glasgow.

'Oh, Jack, that's wonderful!' Kate clasped her hands in delight. 'That's just great!'

Smiling at her reaction, he put his arms to her waist and swung her around. 'Does it earn me a kiss, then?'

It did. When they separated, she looked up at him, her green eyes shining. 'So what exactly will you be doing? What sort of a job is it?'

'Oh, I'm not quite sure,' he said airily. 'Anyway, I don't start for ages – not till after the summer, but isn't it marvellous? I'm going to be a wage slave, Kate, a sober citizen, a useful member of society and approved of by Miss Kate Cameron, spinster of this parish.'

There was a sudden silence. Then Jack reached for her hand, raised it to his lips and kissed it.

'Though perhaps not for very much longer,' he said.

*   *   *

She let him buy her the dress. He seemed to take such pleasure in it, making her try on half a dozen different ones before she chose a simple little sleeveless frock in crêpe-de-chine with a dropped waist and a scooped neckline. The minute she tried it on, she knew it was right for her. The skirt hung so beautifully and the colour – eau-de-nil – made a lovely contrast with her smooth chestnut-brown bob. Even the formidable saleslady, whose polite manner didn't quite conceal a certain disapproval, agreed with her.

As soon as she emerged from the changing room Jack said, 'Oh, yes.' He was sitting on a plush sofa, eyes narrowed as he surveyed her. He gestured with his hand for her to do a twirl, and she did, dipping her head shyly.

'We'll take it,' he said, 'but she'll need a wrap. Something pretty and light.'

The saleslady went off to fetch a selection. Kate, entranced by the dress, was checking her back view. The material felt lovely, light and cool against her skin.

'Like yourself, do you?'

Blushing, she looked down at him. He was smiling in tolerant amusement.

'Oh, Jack, it's lovely! I've never had anything so nice!' She frowned suddenly. 'But I don't know if I should be letting you do this – and a wrap, too.'

He rose smoothly to his feet and walked over to her. 'Of course you should. You want to make me happy, don't you?'

He put a finger under her chin and lifted her face. The green eyes were troubled.

'Silly little goose,' he said. 'So proud.' His eyes fell briefly to her mouth. 'So lovely too, especially in this dress. Please let me buy it for you, Kate. It would mean so much to me.'

Where had the saleslady got to? It seemed suddenly very quiet. Even the noise of the Saturday-afternoon traffic on

Sauchiehall Street, audible through the closed windows, had diminished. Jack was very serious, his eyes searching her face. She did want to make him happy . . .

'All right,' she whispered. Smiling, he bent and kissed her. There was a discreet cough from behind them.

'Would Madam perhaps care to look at these wraps now?'

They settled on a lacy white stole, decorated with beads in the same colour. She told her mother they had both been sale items. She thought she'd got away with that. With Pearl she wasn't quite so sure. Her sister gave her one of those sly looks which never failed to make Kate uncomfortable. The invitation from Jack's mother caused enormous excitement. Lily showed it to everyone in the close, including Agnes Baxter. She, in turn, standing at her own front door, showed it to her son as he trudged up the stairs on Monday night coming home from his work.

'Look at the circles our Kate's mixing in, Robbie. Bearsden for her dinner! Up among the posh folks. Just fancy!'

Pearl Cameron, who had come in close on Robbie's heels, rolled her eyes. '*Lunch*, Mrs B. Posh folk have their dinner at night.'

Robbie took the card thrust into his hand – he could hardly do otherwise – read it and handed it back to his mother without comment. Joining them, Kate felt a flash of irritation. Couldn't he at least try to be pleased for her?

Chapter 13

Kate was experiencing a strange mixture of emotions: elation, irritation and embarrassment. Elation because of how well the show had gone. Her work had been admired by many people, including the influential art critic of a respected Glasgow newspaper, who was to be one of the guests at the lunch in Bearsden the next day. He and others like him had said lots of nice things. They had called her talented and advised other people that here was a name to watch. It might have turned her head if it hadn't gone hand in hand with barely concealed surprise that a working-class girl should turn out such fine work. That was where the irritation came in.

Kate thought of all the folk she knew who were, in one way or another, talented: men who, in their spare time, took and developed photographs, or mended intricate clocks, or spent hours painstakingly building model ships, which they then displayed in a bottle; women who made clothes or turned out beautiful knitting and embroidery; men and women who wrote poetry and songs; the pianists and the accordion players and the singers who were so much in demand at local weddings. They worked on their hobbies in their few spare hours, going to evening classes or joining clubs with other like-minded people.

Clydebank was overflowing with people like that. There were horticultural and operatic societies, drama groups, evening classes in a wide variety of subjects. With very little spare cash, and not much free time, people went to enormous efforts to express their creativity. It was a safety valve, a way of saying, *This is what I am capable of, this is the real me,* and a very necessary antidote to the hard physical labour of their daily grind. Some of the people Kate had met this weekend had seemed surprised that she could walk and talk at the same time, let alone turn out pottery to her own design. She said as much to Marjorie.

'Whereas my problem is that I don't know whether the praise is really genuine, or because I'm my father's daughter!'

'Your stuff's excellent, Marjorie,' said Kate stoutly. 'We all know that.'

Marjorie patted her on the shoulder. 'You're a good friend, Kate.'

'And you're a good potter.'

Marjorie grinned, the freckles dancing on the bridge of her nose. She glanced over Kate's shoulder.

'Oh look, Kate, it's your family!' She moved forward, hand outstretched, her plain face wreathed in smiles. 'Mr Cameron, how delightful to see you again.'

That was where the embarrassment came in – oh, not because of her father or Jessie. Despite their shabby clothes, she could never be ashamed of either of them. They both looked attentively at all the exhibits. Her fellow students were quite taken with her father and sister, she could see that, even if there was a hint of condescension in their reactions. Imagine a working man asking such intelligent questions about art!

Seeing her father standing with his arms folded in front of a painting, head cocked as he listened to the artist – a rather shy young man – explaining his picture, Kate felt a real pang. If only her father could have expressed himself this way, she thought sadly, instead of trying to find the answer to life's problems at the bottom of a bottle. Why did life defeat some people, and not others?

Her mother hadn't come, of course. She tried not to feel too disappointed. Lily would probably only have been an embarrassment – like Pearl, who was completely ignoring the paintings and pottery and happily flirting with every man in sight, including Jack Drummond. She darted sly little glances at Kate every so often to see whether or not she had noticed. Suzanne Douglas did, smiling her cool and sophisticated smile. It was a relief when Pearl finally left, trailing reluctantly after her father and youngest sister.

Half an hour later Kate was standing in a small group, discussing how they were all going to manage to get out for a bite to eat.

'We'll operate a shift system. Six of us can go out at a time. What d'you say, Kate?' asked the shy young man who'd been talking to her father. He'd come out of his shell quite a bit this morning. He'd never called her by her first name before. Then she heard her name again.

'Kathleen,' came a quiet voice from behind her. Laughing, she turned around, and experienced embarrassment of a different sort. Robert Baxter, flat cap held between his hands, stood there.

'Robbie,' she said in surprise. Then, recovering herself, 'I'm so glad you could come.' She gestured round the room. 'Have you had a look at all the exhibits?'

'I'm only interested in yours.'

The comment fell into a silence which seemed all at once to descend on the whole room. Kate saw eyebrows being raised. Robbie pulled himself up to his full height.

'I've come to invite you to dinner. L-lunch, I mean,' he said, clearly all too aware of the number of ears which had pricked up. 'If you're free,' he added. His voice was clipped, his face unsmiling.

'Sounds more like an order than an invitation,' murmured Jack, who had strolled over to join the group. There were a few stifled giggles. Robbie glanced without interest at him and bent his grey gaze again to Kate.

'Will you come?'

Jack took out his gold cigarette case and extended it to Robbie. His eyes flickered. 'I don't smoke, thanks.'

'Nor drink, either, I hear,' drawled Jack. 'How terribly good of you.' Suzanne Douglas came up behind him and put a hand on his shoulder, then draped herself over him – as fluid as a piece of silk, thought Kate. The two of them looked Robbie up and down, taking in his smartly pressed but old suit, his stiff collar and neat tie and his obvious discomfort. Compared to them, he was over-dressed. Like her on that first day, she thought, when she hadn't known any better.

'Don't you have *any* vices, Mr Baxter?' purred Suzanne. 'A good-looking chap like you?'

Robbie's grey eyes flickered again. He spared the two of them the briefest of glances and turned once more to Kate.

'Will you come?' he asked again. 'I thought we could go to Sloan's in the Argyle Arcade. I – I've booked a table,' he added self-consciously. Out of the corner of her eye, Kate saw Suzanne's mocking reaction. That, if nothing else, made her mind up.

'Of course I'll come,' she said, impulsively reaching out to touch his arm. 'Just let me get my coat.'

Robert Baxter was ill at ease, and it had nothing to do with his surroundings. In fact, thought Kate, glancing surreptitiously at him from behind her menu, he fitted in quite well. Put him in better clothes and he would be more than a match for any of the men enjoying lunch at the tables round about them.

Her childhood friend had matured into a broad-shouldered and quietly handsome young man, who normally had an air of quiet calm about him. Not today, though. He was jumpy about something.

Could he be worried about Barbara? No, she dismissed that straight away. If Barbara's illness had got worse, her mother would have heard about it from Agnes. And if anything had happened, Barbara's brother certainly wouldn't be sitting across a restaurant table from her today.

She had hoped he might relax once they got away from the Art School, but he had stayed tense on the short subway ride down to St Enoch's. Sitting silently beside each other, experiencing the traditional 'shoogly' motion of the train, she had considered the fact that the world in which she had come to feel so much at home was unfamiliar territory to him. She had changed and he hadn't. She was leaving him behind and she was sorry about it. Perhaps, she thought, with a sudden burst of affection for him, there was some way for them to stay friends, even if she and Jack did . . . but that was counting her chickens before they were hatched. His mother might have invited her to lunch, but Jack hadn't yet asked the crucial question – not in so many words anyway.

Robbie relaxed slightly during the meal but passed only the briefest of comments on her exhibits at the show, and then only when pressed – and that wasn't like him at all.

'Ice cream?' he asked at the end of the meal, returning the menu to the waitress who stood hovering, waiting to take their dessert order.

'Cheese and biscuits,' said Kate, smiling up at the woman.

'Then I'll have cheese and biscuits too. Coffee or tea, Kate?'

When the waitress had gone, Kate looked at him. 'You called me Kathleen earlier on. It's only you and my father who do that. It sounds so formal.' She laid one hand flat on the white damask tablecloth.

Robbie extended his own hand and put it over hers. There was an abruptness about the movement.

'Maybe I called you Kathleen because I wanted to be formal today.'

Kate's heart started to thump, so loud in her ears that she was sure the other people in the restaurant must be able to hear it. She glanced around, but no, they all seemed to be involved in their own conversations. She was not at all reassured when Robbie took a visible deep breath and squeezed her hand.

'Kate . . . Kathleen . . . you know that I'm time-served now. I've got a good trade. Things might not look too rosy at the moment, but there's always work for a good cabinet-maker. If the orders dried up, I could go to sea, although I'd hate to do that and leave you all alone.'

'Leave me all alone?' Kate's voice sounded as though it belonged to someone else.

Robbie nodded his head. The unruly lock of hair escaped as usual, falling over his pale brow. He had been staring fixedly at the table. Now he looked up, tossed his head, took another deep breath and plunged in.

'Och, Kate, I'm making a bit of a hash of this. What I mean is, well, Kate . . . Kathleen, I mean . . . I suppose what I'm asking is – will you marry me?'

The waitress brought their biscuits and cheese.

Robbie jumped back, lifting his hand off Kate's so quickly that it caught one of the plates the waitress was setting down on the table.

'Tut-tut. Now, never you mind, sir, we'll clear this up in a jiffy.'

Kate looked away, but not before she had seen that Robbie's colour was up. She knew he was in an agony of impatience for the woman to leave them alone. She also knew that when the waitress did go, she herself was going to have to utter words she'd rather have left unsaid. Something gentle and kind, but a refusal, all the same. When the woman finally left, she steeled herself to meet Robbie's grey eyes, but he had one hand up in a gesture of rebuttal.

'Before you give me an answer, let me just say this.' He stretched his free hand across the table. His voice was very soft. 'Give me your hand again?' Reluctantly, she did as he asked.

'You know I'd never stand in the way of your art and your pottery. I'm a modern man. I would hope we'd have children, of course, but apart from that, I'd want you to keep doing all that.' He nodded, a gesture which took in the Art School and the exhibition and her friends there and everything which was, she knew, so alien to Robert Baxter. He was rubbing her hand now, gently drawing his thumb backwards and forwards over her knuckles. 'We could go out, to places like this – or to tearooms . . . Well, we couldn't afford it every week, but maybe once a month, or something.'

'Oh, Robbie!' He was offering her all that he had, putting in everything he could think of to tip the balance of the scales in his favour – and it wasn't enough. He knew that as well as she did, which was why he wasn't looking at her now, scared to read the answer in her face.

She knew him so well. He'd been her best friend for as long as she could remember – always there, ready to comfort, ready to talk, ready to help her forget the raised voices and angry silences between her parents. She couldn't imagine life without Robbie in the background somewhere. She had a shrewd suspicion that when she gave him her answer she was going to have to.

He looked up. 'Kate, for God's sake. Do you want me to go down on one knee, hen? Because I will. Here and now.' He was trying so hard to look relaxed and amused, but the hand which wasn't on top of hers was gripping his linen napkin so tightly that his knuckles had gone white.

She moved her hand, threading her fingers through his.

'Robbie,' she said, and then stopped. How could she put this in a way that wouldn't hurt him? In the end, he saved her even from that, reading the answer in her green eyes, soft with pity for him.

'The answer's no, then?'

Kate tried to think of something to say, some way to soften it. She should have expected this. It had been brewing for a long time. She had been so taken up with the Art School and her new friends that she had thought Robbie had given up on her. He knew as well as she did that she was about to leave him behind, so he had spoken now, trying to catch her before she soared off into the new life which seemed to be beckoning her ever closer.

'The answer's no. I'm sorry.'

'Not as sorry as I am.' He pulled his hand out of her grasp and turned his head away, his lips set in a rigid line.

They both made a half-hearted attempt at finishing the meal and Robbie asked for the bill.

'Should I leave a tip?' he asked quietly.

'It's customary,' said Kate. Jack always left a tip, usually a generous one.

Once they were back out on Argyle Street, Kate stole a glance at him. He looked completely dejected. Suddenly she couldn't bear being in his company for a moment longer. She stopped dead in the middle of the pavement. That made him stop too.

'Well,' she said brightly, 'thank you very much for lunch. I'll just get the underground back up to Cowcaddens.' Absurdly, she held out her hand. Robbie ignored it.

'Come down to the river with me.' His voice was raw, the words rattled out, as though he'd had to summon up all his courage to put the request.

'Robbie . . .'

'Please. Just for a wee minute.'

So she went. They walked through St Enoch Square, past the imposing railway station, down onto the river bank and then a few steps out onto the suspension bridge which linked the city centre with the Gorbals. Not until they got there did Robbie speak again, fixing her with one of those looks which meant that he was determined on getting an answer to his question.

'Is it because of him – Jack Drummond? Are you in love with him?'

She was beginning to get angry. She had said no, and she was sorry, but what was the point of prolonging the agony? She drew in her breath. 'I'm not sure that's any of your business, Robbie.'

He flinched, but went doggedly on. 'Has he asked you to marry him?'

'Maybe.'

'Maybe?' His voice rose in disbelief. 'How can someone *maybe* ask you to marry him?'

'Things are . . . understood.' Were they? She swallowed and turned away to look at the spires and steeples of the city, reaching their smoke-blackened fingers up towards the sky.

'But he hasn't actually asked you?' The voice was quiet, the questioning relentless. Robert Baxter would have his answer, whether she wanted to give it to him or not.

She tossed her head, smooth and neat in the little cloche hat. 'No,' she admitted, 'but we have an understanding.'

'An understanding? Och, Kate!'

She turned to look at him then and saw that now it was his turn to gaze at her with sympathy. That was too much to bear. Kate's green eyes glittered.

'Just what gives you the right to ask me these questions, Robbie? Is it anybody's business but my own? And Jack's?'

Something flashed in those grey pools when he heard her

say that name. All sympathy gone from his face, he said sharply, 'Don't be so stupid, Kate. People like them don't marry people like us.'

A dart of pure anger shot through Kate's chest. How dare Robbie Baxter stand here and say that to her? She drew herself up to her full height. It didn't come close to matching his, so she took a couple of steps back so that he wouldn't have such an advantage.

'Perhaps, Robert . . .' Her tone was icy. She never used his full name – except when she was joking – which she most certainly wasn't now. 'Perhaps you might like to consider that *you're* the stupid one. Maybe I've moved on. My friends and I at the Art School don't pay any attention to all those outdated ideas about class!'

'That's a brave wee speech, Kate,' he said dismissively. He closed the distance between them. Now she had lost the advantage. She had to tilt her head back to look at him. He had folded his arms across his chest and was looking down his nose at her. It was a stance designed to infuriate her – and it did. She glared up at him. Where were the clever words when you needed them – the ones that would wound and hurt and show Robert Baxter what was what?

'Cheer up, hen, it might never happen!' The man who had spoken, crossing the bridge from the Gorbals into town, clutched his mate in mock alarm when Kate turned and gave him a look. He sketched Robbie a mocking salute. 'I'd give her the elbow, pal – that look could turn you into stone!' The two men passed, their raucous laughter floating back to the couple who stood so still on the bridge.

Did his lips twitch? Did he stretch a conciliatory hand towards her? Kate was too angry to notice – too angry to find those clever words. She resorted to those of the playground.

'Mind your own business, Robbie, and I'll mind mine. Thank you for lunch.'

Turning on her heel, she stomped off. She didn't look back.

People like them don't marry people like us. How dare he? HOW DARE HE? Shoogling her way back up to Cowcaddens on the subway, she kept hearing those words, matching themselves to the noise of the train-wheels like the chorus of a song. *People like them. People like us.*

Kate stared out of the train window, scowling into the blackness of the tunnel. She wasn't *people like us* any more. She was an artist and she wasn't going to live like her mother did – or that girl Lizzie. She and her family had been evicted in the end – her children split between relatives and her husband off on the tramp somewhere, looking for work.

Kate's life was going to be different: different from the only one Robert Baxter was able to offer her!

So why did she keep seeing his face, the hurt in his grey eyes unsuccessfully hidden behind the sharp words he had flung at her. She squeezed her eyes tight shut. That was a mistake – it just brought him into sharper focus. The train hurtled to a stop at Cowcaddens. She got off and ran up the stairs to ground level. The underground had its own peculiar smell – stale, like cabbage which had been boiled too long – but oddly refreshing, because there was always a breeze running through the tunnels, along the platforms and up the stairs.

She had to slow down climbing the hill to the Art School, a stitch in her side. Can't wait to get back there, she thought ruefully. That's where I belong now. The picture of those hurt grey eyes was proving difficult to shake off. Damn you, Robert Baxter, leave me alone.

It stayed with her all afternoon: even as she laughed and joked with her fellow students; even as she politely conducted visitors around the exhibits; even when Jack, finding her alone in the corridor after she had shown an important visitor out, grabbed her hand, pulled her round a corner and into his arms.

'We'll get caught!' she squeaked. Laughing, he overrode her protests, but even as he kissed her, Robbie's face was still swimming before her eyes.

It all made for a very uncomfortable afternoon. Kate felt like a wrung-out washing clout by the end of it, her emotions swinging wildly from elation about the reception her work had received to a miserable realisation of how unhappy Robbie must be by now. But he shouldn't have said those things to her, should he? Thinking of that made her angry again. More than that: it made her defiant. She was aware too of an emotion normally foreign to her – recklessness.

Chapter 14

At the show the following morning Jack was subdued, but it wasn't until he was driving them out to Bearsden that he told her why. His mother had remembered a prior engagement and wasn't going to be able to host the lunch-party after all.

'Oh!' Kate had been enjoying the view of Cairnhill Woods through the window as they bowled along the Switchback. She hadn't slept well and the fresh air was clearing her head. She turned anxious eyes on Jack.

'Is it still all right then? Maybe we should have made other arrangements.' She wasn't quite sure what those would have been. Her own mother would definitely die of shock if they all turned up at Yoker. *Mother dear, could you fix us a spot of lunch?* That'd be right.

'Don't frown,' said Jack, taking one hand off the steering-wheel and patting her knee reassuringly. 'It's all right. Cook will have everything ready. I'm just a bit disappointed that my Mama's not going to get to meet you.'

Touched at the way he had put it, and seeing that there were lines on his own brow, she returned the gesture, patting his hand as it curved round the steering-wheel. 'That's all right. I'm sure it was something really important that she had to miss the party for.'

'Are you?'

How odd he sounded. Had he had an argument with his mother? She hoped it hadn't been about her.

They drove through Canniesburn Toll and up Drymen Road which was lined with large houses set in well-cared for gardens. Grounds would be a better word for some of them, thought Kate, looking curiously around her. She was only a few miles from her home in Yoker, but it was a different world up here There were trees everywhere, cool, green and leafy.

Jack drove through Bearsden Cross and then turned left, shortly afterwards pulling into the driveway of a beautiful honey-coloured sandstone villa. He helped Kate out of the car with due ceremony, extending his hand to her with a flourish.

'Welcome to my humble abode.' She looked around. The driveway was made of small red granite chips. Not a weed marred its perfect surface. Between the house and the road was a lawn which wasn't so much cut as manicured. There were four rose beds on it, with a small fountain at their centre. A jet of crystal-clear water, shooting a yard up, sparkled in the sun as it fell down again into a stone basin in the shape of a large shell.

'You like?' he asked. He was smiling, watching her reaction.

'I like,' she said.

He reached for her hand. 'Think you could get used to it?'

All at once, the tiredness and unhappiness of the day before left her. They *did* have an understanding. Didn't the question Jack had just asked prove that?

'I think I could get used to it,' she said, smiling and waiting for him to kiss her, but he was looking over her head. Kate heard the sound of tyres on the stones and turned her head.

'Ah,' he said smoothly, 'the others have arrived.' Dropping her hand, he walked forward to greet his guests.

Kate liked all of it, delighting in the beautifully cooked

meal, the elegant lace tablecloth, the sparkling wine glasses, the unobtrusive service provided by two parlourmaids, neat and demure in black dresses, white aprons and caps. Even Suzanne Douglas was on her best behaviour. Her eyes sweeping over the eau-de-nil dress into which Kate had changed in the ladies' cloakroom at the Art School, she told her that she looked very nice.

Marjorie, characteristically, told her that she looked perfectly lovely, and kissed her on the cheek. She linked her arm through Kate's and went with her into the dining room, but not before Kate had caught a glimpse of herself in the full-length mirror in Mrs Drummond's lobby. She didn't look half-bad, at that. She had put vinegar in the rinsing water when she had washed her hair last night to make it shiny. She'd had it trimmed the week before so that it hung in a short, neat bob, emphasising the curve of her neck and the shape of her shoulders, and the dress was a dream, definitely her colour, and skimming to just on her knees, making her legs look long and shapely – well, shapely, anyway. She could never aspire to Marjorie's willowy height. One of the maids had relieved her of the feather-light stole when she came into the house, had even called her madam as she did so. Fancy! And her just a wee girl from Clydebank.

She had too strong a sense of humour to allow it to go to her head, but yes – she could get used to this. Encouraged by the admiration in the eyes of the men at the table, she began to emerge from her shell, laughing and talking and paying scant attention to how often her glass was being re-filled. She drank the champagne and the white wine which followed it with appreciation. It was refreshing – like liquid sunshine, or the sparkling water which played on the fountain in Jack's garden. When the parlourmaid went to fill her glass for the fourth time, however, Kate put a hasty hand over it to prevent her.

Marjorie looked across the table in mock-alarm. 'Don't let

Kate have any more to drink, Jack – she'll get tight.' She grinned at Kate to show her that the comment was meant only in fun. Kate watched as Jack lifted Marjorie's hand to his lips and kissed it.

'Don't worry, darling, I'm driving her home in my little bus. She'll be quite safe.'

'That's all right, then,' said Marjorie. She turned to talk to her partner on her other side. She was blushing, and Kate saw something she should have realised months ago. Marjorie was in love with Jack. A pang of sympathy pierced her. It was true what they said, then – money couldn't buy you happiness. Jack wanted to marry her, not Marjorie. Was that why he had wished to keep it quiet – so as not to hurt their friend's feelings? Oh dear. Marjorie would have to know soon, and that could make life *very* complicated.

Suppressing a sigh, Kate lifted her almost empty wine glass to her lips. Greatly daring, she had put on the thinnest smear of lipstick when she had changed into the new dress. The three glasses of wine she had drunk had probably rubbed it all off by now. She set the crystal glass down on the lace tablecloth. The dark wood of the table was showing through, its glossy dark patina making an attractive pattern when seen through the white lace. She was staring fixedly at it when she felt her eyelids droop. With a start, she caught herself on. She had woken several times during the night from troubled dreams which had evaporated as soon as she had tried to remember them.

Suzanne Douglas was smiling at her. She must be dreaming then – or having a nightmare, but she would be gracious, as befitted a woman who might soon be mistress of a beautiful house like this. Then Kate reprimanded herself. She must be getting tiddly, letting her thoughts run away with her like that. Jack hadn't even asked her. Not yet.

*   *   *

The lunch-party broke up at half-past three. Suzanne Douglas was the last to leave. She hovered on the doorstep as one of the boys, who was giving her a lift, impatiently sounded his horn.

'Bye, darling,' she said, kissing Jack full on the lips. 'Sure you don't want me to stay and act as chaperone?' She gave Kate an arch look.

'The cook and the parlourmaids can do that,' said Kate sweetly, coming forward to put her arm through his. Jack had told her to be ready to leave in ten minutes, but there was no reason for Suzanne to know that. 'We wouldn't want to put you to any trouble, would we, Jack?'

'The cook and the parlourmaids?' Suzanne was staring at her. Then she turned to Jack. 'Jack, haven't you—'

He cut her off, giving her a gentle shove out of the door.

'Shut up, Suzanne. Now say cheerio like a good little girl.'

Kate drew her breath in sharply. She had never heard him be quite that rude to anybody. Suzanne glared at him, her eyes glittering, but she went. He closed the glass-panelled inner front door behind her and leaned against it. Now that the guests had left he looked, all at once, as tired as she felt.

'Jack . . . is anything the matter?'

'Not a thing.' He smiled. 'Let's open another bottle of champagne. Just for the two of us.'

Kate lifted her hands in a gesture of exasperation. 'Let's not. I've had more than enough to drink and I think we should talk.'

'Talk?' His face wore a pained expression, as though she had made the strangest request imaginable. 'What would you like to talk about?' The mask was back in place, an expression only of polite interest on his face. He pulled out his cigarette case. 'You don't mind, sweetie, do you?'

183

Striding forward, Kate snatched the case out of his hand and laid it down on the hall table which stood by the door.

'Yes, I do mind. I want some answers. I want to know what Suzanne was talking about there. I want to know why so many things are left unsaid between us. I want to do more than just have *fun*!'

He took a deep breath. 'Would you like to see round the house?'

'Jack, please . . .'

'It's a serious question,' he said, looking at her gravely from out of his blue eyes, 'and it might give you some of those answers you're looking for.'

He showed her the downstairs rooms and then he took her upstairs to look at his mother's bedroom. It was exquisitely decorated and furnished and completely dominated by a huge painting which hung on the wall opposite the luxurious bed.

'Your mother?'

He nodded and Kate went to stand in front of the painting. It was a conventional society portrait, the sort she secretly despised, where it was the painter's job to do as flattering a job as possible on the subject, posed in her best gown and showing off the family's wealth by the jewels decorating ears and wrists and ample white bosom.

She'd never met Mrs Drummond, but in this case she had the feeling that flattery hadn't been necessary. She was a lovely woman – too much a female version of her son for there to be much doubt about that.

'She's beautiful,' said Kate.

'Oh, yes, she's beautiful.'

She turned, intrigued by something she heard in his voice. He was standing leaning in the open doorway, his arms folded.

'Do you know why she's really not here?'

184

Kate shook her head.

'Because she's off visiting some titled friend in the Highlands. Only asked her last week. She knew fine well that I wanted her at the party today, but she just doesn't care. She's not interested in anything I do. I can never match up to my father, you see. He had the good luck to die a hero's death – at an early age – so all his faults are forgotten and all his virtues are magnified. Whereas, because I'm here all the time, it's the other way round for me.' He ran a hand through his hair, and gave her a lopsided smile. 'Sad, ain't it?'

'Oh, Jack!' Kate's eyes were full of compassion. She knew only too well what it was like to have a mother whom you could never please. She crossed the room towards him and laid a comforting hand on his arm.

'I thought maybe she disapproved of you seeing me.'

'She doesn't know about you.' Seeing Kate's eyes widen, he hastily amended this to: 'She doesn't know that you're special.'

'Am I special?'

'You know you are.' He bent forward and kissed her, a gentle nuzzling of the lips. Then he leaned his forehead against hers and laid his arms on her shoulders – heavy, warm and possessive.

'My bedroom's along the corridor,' he whispered.

Kate pulled her head back and smiled sweetly at him. She too, spoke in a whisper.

'Forget it, Mr Drummond.'

Jack Drummond threw his head back and laughed. 'Oh, Kate! What would I do without you?'

She let him open another bottle of champagne.

She had definitely had too much to drink. Oh, she wasn't tight, not by a long chalk, but she felt warm and mellow and she was doing things she normally wouldn't. Like lying on a sofa in his mother's drawing room, with her shoes kicked off and her head in his lap – telling him about Robbie. She hadn't wanted to, but he had badgered and cajoled and made her drink two glasses of champagne.

'If you must know,' she said, too tired to resist any longer – maybe she could have a wee nap before he drove her home – 'he asked me to marry him and I said no.'

Jack's fair eyebrows shot up. 'Why would that be?'

'Can't you guess, you idiot?' She stretched her neck and squinted up at him.

Jack dropped his eyebrows and and smiled broadly. 'Darling! I do so love it when you give me a good ticking off.'

Kate's heart turned over at that *darling*, even though she knew that he and Suzanne and Marjorie tossed the word around between themselves so much that it meant very little.

He leaned forward and kissed her lightly on the lips. Fine. There was nothing wrong with kissing him, was there? They'd done that lots of times. He kissed her again. This time it was harder and his hand slid round to rest on her left breast. She tilted her head and gazed pointedly down at it.

'Going to come over all respectable, are you?'

'Is there anything wrong with that?'

He gave an ostentatious shudder. 'Everything. And you an artist too. As all these people here this afternoon told you.'

'What's that got to do with it?'

'Respectability's so *boring*, Kate,' he drawled. 'Don't you think so?' The hand resting on her breast began to move, stroking her through the thin fabric of her dress. Deep within her, something leapt into life.

'Stop that,' she said.

'Not a chance,' he replied smoothly. 'You don't really want me to.' He slid his hand down to her knee and smoothed her dress up, exposing her stocking tops and suspenders.

'Ooh, nice.' He bent forward, adjusting their positions so that he could delicately kiss the exposed flesh.

'Stop that,' she murmured once more.

'No.'

'I'll scream,' she said, but her hand was stroking his hair.

'Scream all you like. There's no one else in the house.' He turned his attention once more to her mouth, his hands roaming over her body, alternately sliding over cool crêpe-de-chine and warm skin.

'What about the cook and the parlourmaids?'

'They've gone off for the afternoon,' he mumbled. 'They don't live in.'

That seemed odd, but she let it go for the moment. There was silence, broken only by the sound of heavy breathing. Was that her – or him?

'Jack, we shouldn't be doing this . . .'

'Hush, now. Of course we should. Stand up.' He moved, pulling them both to their feet and stopping any further protests with a succession of passionate kisses. She tried one last time, laying her fingers on his lips to prevent him kissing her again. She couldn't think straight while he was kissing her.

'This is wrong.'

He smiled, his eyes tender. 'Have you any idea how lovely you look?'

'Jack, please . . .'

'How can this be wrong? We love each other, don't we?'

'Jack,' Kate said again, but she said it on a little moan of desire. It was all he needed. He loosened his hold and held out his hand to her. It was such an elegant gesture.

'Come on, Kate,' he said softly. 'Come upstairs with me.'

Kate Cameron looked at that outstretched hand and at the handsome face behind it. And because he had said '*We love each other, don't we?*' and because she was entranced by the

187

house and the party and the champagne and the flattery, and – above all – because she thought she could see past that handsome mask to the vulnerable little boy within, she put her hand in his and let him lead her upstairs to his bedroom. And once they got there she let him do what he wanted to.

She was crying. Quietly, so as not to waken him up. It had all been so beautiful, with Jack laughing and kissing her and telling her how lovely she was . . . Then he had changed – become urgent and demanding . . . overpowering . . . and he'd been so strange afterwards – distant and cool. She had expected him to take her in his arms, to kiss her and hold her, but he had simply patted her arm and turned away.

'Have a little snooze,' he'd said. Just like that, as though what they'd just done had meant nothing.

She stifled a sob. The body lying beside her stirred.

'Why are you crying?'

'I'm not.' She sniffed and turned quickly away from him, rubbing her eyes with her hand, pulling the sheet up to cover herself.

'That's all right, then.' She felt the bed dip. He was getting up.

'Sorry if it hurt. It'll be better next time.' She heard the rasping sound of a match being struck. A second or two later the smell of tobacco reached her nostrils. 'You'd better clean yourself up. I need to do something about the sheet.'

Kate turned just in time to catch the look of distaste on his face. He raised the cigarette to his lips. *Sorry if it hurt?* As though he'd stepped on her foot?

He was looking at her in exasperation.

'Get a move on, Kate! It's nearly seven o'clock. What time did you tell your parents you'd be home?'

'About eight,' she said, her voice dull. They'd planned to go back into the city early, just the two of them, collect her things from the Art School, and have a bite to eat somewhere. She'd thought he might be going to use the opportunity to ask her a question – the same one Robbie had posed yesterday. She didn't think so now.

He pulled up, as usual, two tram stops before Yoker Ferry Road. Tonight of all nights Kate wouldn't have minded being taken all the way home, but he hadn't given her the option. They'd barely exchanged a word during the drive from his home to hers. People said that men lost respect for girls who let them do what she and Jack had done this afternoon. Was that why he had gone so quiet and cold?

Yet when he leaned across to open the door for her, he smiled and kissed her cheek. She made no move to get out of the car, looking at him with a mute appeal in her green eyes.

'Shall we see each other again next Sunday? As usual?'

She was hoping he wanted to see her earlier than that. He smiled and lifted a finger to stroke her cheek.

'Sorry, sweetie. I'm going to a house party near Dumfries next weekend.' She waited for him to say more, to suggest another date. He didn't. It was left to Kate to stutter something about having to collect her things from the Art School, not just her clothes but her two paintings and her pottery – an awkward load for her to bring home on the tram by herself.

'I'd forgotten about that,' he murmured. 'Why don't you meet me there on Wednesday night – about six o'clock?' He glanced at his watch. 'Look, Kate, I've really got to be going.' He dropped another light kiss on her mouth and then somehow she was out of the car, standing on the pavement. Usually she waved to him, but tonight she didn't, turning her face for home, listening to the sound of his car disappearing in the other direction.

The tears weren't far away. She could feel them rising in

189

her throat. She had to get home before she disgraced herself by crying in the street. She quickened her pace and stopped suddenly, wincing. It *had* hurt – more than she'd expected – and what hurt even more was the way Jack had been afterwards, as though he didn't want to know her after he had got what he wanted.

'Hello there, Kate. Been out on the town?'

It was Mr MacLean, touching his bunnet to her as he passed. She gave him the briefest of smiles and turned her burning face away, sure that the man must be able to see her for what she was.

You were supposed to save yourself for your husband. She knew that. It was the way she'd been brought up. Girls who didn't were fallen women, laughed at and gossiped about, unworthy of any decent man or woman's respect. She, Kate Cameron, had broken the rules, crossed a line which could never be re-crossed, because she had thought . . . But there had been nothing in return – no words of love, no promises, not even a comforting hug when she had been crying.

Maybe all men were like that afterwards. Perhaps it was just the way things were. Kate shook her head angrily. She didn't want to believe that. She tried to think of another explanation for Jack's coolness. Could he be feeling guilty? Embarrassed that he had succeeded in persuading her to forget her principles? Perhaps he needed a few days to come round, was feeling just as confused as she was. And he had spoken of the next time. Surely that meant he loved her really?

By the following evening Kate had made some decisions and come to some conclusions. There wasn't going to be a next time – at least not until after they were married. She loved him and she thought he loved her. Didn't the fact that their feelings had carried them away show that? Caught up in those powerful feelings, he had panicked about marrying her, worried about the social difference, worried about how his mother and his friends – including Marjorie – were going to react. Being Jack, he had covered up by being flippant and trying to pretend that nothing had happened. She, Kate Cameron, was just going to have to sort all those confused feelings out. No bother. She could do that. As long as they loved each other, that was all that mattered.

She was at work on Tuesday when all the doubts came sweeping back in. Was she fooling herself? Had she been just another conquest? Jack was a sophisticated man in his late twenties. Did she really imagine that she was the first girl he'd ever made love to? With miserable honesty she admitted to herself the answer to that question. He was experienced. Any fool could see that, so where did that leave her theory about him being worried and confused?

It left Kate worn out and exhausted, tossing and turning that night, going over it all again in her head at work on Wednesday. By the time she got the tram into Glasgow that evening and walked up the hill to the Art School, she knew only one thing. She had some straight questions for Jack Drummond and she wanted some straight answers.

Brave words. She felt anything but brave as she headed for the stairs, nodding at the porter on duty. There was no sign of Jack.

'The building's closing at seven, miss,' the man said. Kate smiled an acknowledgement. Most students, she assumed, had collected their bits and pieces by now, halfway through the first week of the summer holidays. She found her own exhibits quite easily. She tied her two paintings together, face to face, with some string, fashioning a handle out of it to make them easier to carry.

Somebody, Marjorie probably, had already wrapped her Rowan Tree cup and saucer in tissue paper. Kate found a small box to put them in. Then, glancing up at the clock on the wall and seeing that it was already quarter past six, she went out into the deserted corridor to look for Jack. Still no sign of him. Pushing down the thought that he might have stood her up, she walked along to the cloakroom. She would splash some cold water on her face and comb her hair. That would make her feel better.

She pushed open the door of the cloakroom. The girl who stood there, smoking and leaning against the wall, looked as though she'd been waiting for some time. She straightened up, stretching stiff shoulders, and smiled at Kate, her mouth, as ever, painted a perfect scarlet. The glittering eyes looked her over from head to foot.

'Well, well, well . . . If it isn't the little mouse,' she drawled.

Chapter 15

Suzanne Douglas sauntered across the room.

'I have to hand it to you. You kept him dangling longer than most. Can't figure out the attraction myself. The Little Miss Innocent act, I suppose.' She leaned forward and hissed the words into Kate's face. 'Not so innocent now, are you? A sinner like the rest of us.'

Kate felt her face drain of colour. 'He told you about us?'

Suzanne smiled her hateful smile. 'You have no idea, do you? Not a clue about how the world works.'

Then she told Kate how the world works. Told her about herself and Jack Drummond, told her that he had planned Kate's seduction, told her how the price for the job at Donaldson's was marrying the boss's daughter.

'After all,' said Suzanne callously, fitting another cigarette into her holder, 'she's no oil painting, is she? And Old Man Donaldson would do anything to keep his little girl happy – even take on a penniless charmer like Jack.'

Kate's mind was frantically trying to throw up barriers to the poison dripping from Suzanne's mouth. She fixed on one word.

'Penniless?'

Suzanne took a puff. 'Fooled you, did he? He advised his mother badly – they've lost a lot of money on the stock market over the last couple of years. I can't imagine why she thought Jack was worth listening to, except that she's devoted

193

to him. Thinks he can do no wrong.' She caught sight of the expression on Kate's face. 'Don't tell me you swallowed the neglected little boy story? I thought he'd given that one up.' Her speech had grown calmer. She was beginning to enjoy herself, drawing the veils from Kate's eyes.

'The cook and the parlourmaids at the party? Hired in for the day. They had to let all the servants go in March. No, if dear Mrs Drummond and her little boy are going to continue to live in the style to which they're accustomed, Jack has to marry money – or Marjorie, which amounts to the same thing.' She gave Kate a bitter little smile.

'But he doesn't love Marjorie! He loves me!'

'You? Don't make me laugh! You were just an amusement to him – a game he was playing.' Suzanne put the cigarette-holder once more to her lips, drew on it and blew the smoke out in rings, taking her time over it. 'He told me all about it; he always does. That's the game he and I play, you see.' Just for a second, the poise faltered. There was an edge to the mocking voice. 'Jack Drummond can be very cruel.'

She must be lying. Wasn't she?

'Kate! Are you in there?' It was Jack, banging at the cloakroom door.

'Why don't you come in, darling?' Suzanne called out. 'We're having such an interesting conversation in here – your little girlfriend and I.'

He was through the door in a second.

'Tell me she's lying,' whispered Kate, turning stricken eyes on him.

He let the door close behind him and advanced further into the room. His eyes were narrowed. 'What has she told you?' he asked cautiously.

Suzanne gave a short bark of laughter, and stubbed her cigarette out in a wash basin. 'The game's up, Jack. I've told her everything.'

'Tell me she's lying,' said Kate again. She was beginning to tremble.

'Oh, Kate!' There was a peculiar expression on his face – a mixture of affection and exasperation, and something else she couldn't decipher. 'Oh, Kate!' he said again, moving closer to her. The trembling became a violent shaking. She was getting hot and it felt as though someone had tied a bandage around her forehead and was pulling it tighter and tighter. Making it into one of the toilet cubicles just in time, Kate was violently and comprehensively sick.

Slumped in an upright chair which stood against one wall of the cloakroom, Kate lifted her head and looked around. 'Where is she?'

Suzanne, her mischief-making done, was nowhere to be seen.

'I got rid of her,' he said grimly.

Kate stared at him, green eyes glittering in a face as white as paper. 'Why did you tell her about us?'

'I didn't,' he said tersely. 'She guessed. She's got sharp eyes. You know that, Kate.' He put a hand under her elbow to lift her to her feet. 'And I didn't know she was going to be here either – don't go thinking that! We were at a party together on Monday night and I must have mentioned that I was meeting you. I'd no idea she was going to lie in wait for you! Come on, now. Let's get you out of here. You and I have to talk.'

He drove to the Art Galleries. It seemed the appropriate place. They sat in the Morris Cowley in the cool evening air and looked up at the University, high on Gilmorehill, and they talked. Well, Jack talked – and smoked – and Kate listened as he demolished, brick by brick, those defensive walls she'd tried to throw up against Suzanne's words.

Suzanne had broken it a bit brutally, but it was true. He

195

had to marry Marjorie Donaldson, had no choice really. Of course Kate hadn't just been an amusement! She knew what a bitch Suzanne was. How could Kate think he thought of her like that? She was special – his little Clydebank girl – and he loved her. Hadn't Sunday afternoon proved that?

'People who love each other get married,' sobbed Kate, laying her head on his shoulder. 'People who *make* love to each other get married.'

'Oh, Kate,' said Jack Drummond, his arm around her. 'What would we live on?'

'You could get a job, a different job. You're clever – there's lots of things you could do. You could train to be an art teacher – you know a lot about that.' She lifted her head and clutched at the lapel of his jacket. 'I can wait to get married, I wouldn't mind.'

He reached out and smoothed her hair. 'You're a sweet kid.' He gave an odd little laugh. 'It's a lovely dream, but it just wouldn't work, my pet. It really wouldn't.' His blue eyes were very soft.

'But you don't love Marjorie. That's not fair to her either!'

The eyes lost their softness. He lifted her fingers off his jacket and sat up straight.

'Don't be silly, Kate. Love doesn't have anything to do with marriage. Not for people like Marjorie and I, anyway.'

Dumbstruck, she stared at him. It was an echo of what Robbie had said to her last Saturday. She too straightened up, shrugging off the arm which lay loosely about her shoulders. They sat in silence for a few minutes. She found one last weapon. Surely, if he truly loved her, he wouldn't be able to withstand it. Flushing a deep scarlet, she got it out.

'What if I'm . . . after Sunday. What if I get . . . well, you know what I mean.'

He shifted in his seat and coughed before he spoke. 'There are people who get rid of mistakes, Kate.' He turned to her and said quietly, 'If you need the money for that, just let me know. I may be broke, but not that broke. Now I really think I should get you home.' He started up the car.

When he pulled up at the kerb to let her out, two tram stops from home as usual, he reached over to kiss her, looking at her in surprise when she pulled back.

'Goodbye, Jack. I'll get the dress and the wrap cleaned and send them back to you.' Her hand was on the door handle when his came over it, pulling her around, forcing her to look at him.

'What are you talking about, Kate? What would I do with a frock? It's yours.'

'You think I earned it, do you? Last Sunday afternoon?'

'Kate – don't talk like that.' His eyes were searching her face. 'Is this goodbye, then?'

She couldn't speak, but she nodded. Despite her best efforts, two fat tears rolled slowly down her cheeks.

'Won't we see each other again?'

'No.' She managed the word and then had to clamp her mouth shut. Let me go, let me go, she was praying silently. Before I give in and agree to see you again – a man who's going to marry my best friend.

This was the last time she would ever be close to him. He was so handsome, especially at this moment, looking at her with that peculiar expression on his face – a mixture of regret and affection and enquiry. She knew very well what the question was. She had grown up a lot since Sunday.

'No,' she said again.

'It's your choice then, Kate,' he said softly. 'Not mine. Remember that.'

She got out of the car and turned, taking one last look at him.

'None of this was my choice, Jack. None of it.'

She walked away, determined not to look back. That was hard, especially when she heard no sound behind her of the car engine starting up. Was he waiting for her to change her mind? To run back to him? But the only thing he could offer was a clandestine affair which would betray Marjorie. She couldn't do it. She just wasn't made that way.

Lifting her chin, she quickened her pace. Behind her, she heard his car start up, turn and move away, back towards Glasgow. The sound grew fainter and fainter until she couldn't hear it any more.

It must be nearly nine o'clock. How on earth was she going to explain away how late she was? As it turned out, she didn't have to. As she came up to her own close, she saw Jessie. She smiled automatically as the girl ran up to her. Then she saw the expression on her sister's face. She had been crying and her voice was high and frightened.

'Kate, Kate, Barbara's in the hospital! I think she's real bad this time! Oh, Kate, I don't know what's happening to her!'

All thought of her own predicament flew out of Kate's head. She lifted her hands to grip her younger sister's thin shoulders.

'Jessie, it's all right. Calm down, now. When did they take Barbara in?'

The answer didn't matter at all, but it might just give Jessie's mind something to fix on. Before the distressed girl had time to answer, however, Kate heard footsteps beating a rapid tattoo on the floor of the close. Agnes Baxter was the first to appear. Lily Cameron was beside her, her arm about her shoulders. As they emerged into the evening sunlight, followed by Jim Baxter, Lily saw Kate standing there. Her face cleared.

'Agnes and Jim are going back up to the hospital,' she burst out. 'Robbie's still there – he went in the ambulance with

Barbara this morning. Agnes is worried about Flora and Alice, but I've told her we'll look after them, won't we, Kate?'

Kate wondered if anyone else could hear the note of entreaty in Lily's voice, and it came to her that while her mother was doing her best to comfort Agnes Baxter, she herself was looking to Kate for support. It gave her a funny feeling in her chest, as though she wanted to burst into tears and smile at the same time.

'Aye,' said Kate, 'of course we will. Don't you worry about the girls, Mrs Baxter – or Andrew. We'll look after them. Ma and me – and Jessie too.' She patted her sister's arm.

'You're a good lassie, Kate,' said Agnes, and then could say no more. Biting her lip, her tired eyes shiny with unshed tears, she gripped the girl wordlessly by the hand. Jim Baxter shook his head at Kate.

'Robbie'll not leave her. He's been there all day. I couldn't get him to come home for a rest.'

'You know Robbie, Mr Baxter,' Kate tried to joke. 'Stubborn as a mule.'

Jim's smile flashed briefly. 'Aye, hen, you're right there.'

They waited with the Baxters until the tram came, standing for a moment to watch it swaying along the road. There would be time enough for Robbie to rest, thought Kate as they made their way back to the house to offer what comfort they could to the Baxter children. Soon there would be more than enough time.

Barbara died just after midnight. Kate, head slumped on her arms at the kitchen table in the Baxters' flat, was wakened by a light touch on her shoulder about an hour and a half later. It was her father. His face told her the news. Standing up, she stumbled into his arms, stupefied by tiredness and shock. Not grief. That would come later. And then not so much for herself as for the Baxters, and Jessie – and Robbie.

'All right, lass?' he whispered in her ear. 'Bear up now, for their sakes. Will you make some tea?'

She nodded and moved out of his strong arms to head for the range. Behind him, just letting themselves into the flat, were Jim and Agnes, a white-faced Robbie following them. He looks so tall, thought Kate, still half-asleep, or is it that Jim and Agnes have shrunk?

Neil Cameron ushered all three Baxters to sit down at the table. Lily, who'd gone upstairs about eleven o'clock with a pale and tearful Jessie, had also slipped into the room. Her husband stood behind her chair, his tall figure oozing sympathy for the people who sat so quietly round the table. Kate, who'd had a kettle simmering since she'd helped put the Baxter children to bed, made the tea, moving about the kitchen to fetch cups and saucers, biscuits from Agnes's tins, a plate to put them on, the stand for the teapot.

'Thanks, Kate, hen,' said Jim Baxter, as she set the table. Agnes stared fixedly at some point in the middle of the cloth, with eyes which saw nothing. When Kate brought over the teapot, Jim rose from his chair.

'Here, lass, you'll be needing a seat yourself.'

There was a squeaking noise as the chair opposite him was abruptly pushed back.

'Kate can sit here. I'm going out.' White-faced, swaying with tiredness, Robbie was on his feet.

'Will you not have a cup of tea first, lad?' asked Neil Cameron gently.

Robbie took a deep breath and said, 'No,' his voice rough and raw-edged. Kate, watching the two men, saw a look pass between them.

'Aye,' said Neil Cameron, laying a hand on Robbie's shoulder. 'If that's what you need to do, laddie.'

When he came back after closing the door behind Robbie,

Kate, having poured out the tea and slid the tea cosy over the pot, came round the table.

'Should we have let him go, Daddy?' Her gaze slid past her father's head towards the door. 'Maybe I should go after him.'

She bit her lip, undecided. He'd still be going down the stairs. She could catch up with him if she went now. If they hadn't had that stupid quarrel last Saturday she wouldn't have thought twice about it.

'Leave him be, lass.' Kate pulled her gaze away from the door. 'Sometimes a man needs to think things out on his own. He'll be needing you later, I'm thinking.'

Kate looked up into her father's face. His tired eyes were full of understanding.

'Aye, Daddy,' she agreed, her speech slurred with fatigue. She wasn't at all convinced that he was right.

When Robert Baxter didn't come home for breakfast, his mother began to get worried. When he didn't come home for his dinner at midday, that worry began to cross the line into panic.

'He was that fond of her,' Agnes kept repeating. 'I'm scared he'll do something daft, I really am. He was in a real funny mood before all this happened anyway. He shouted at me on Saturday night, and he's never done that before. Och, Lily, what if he does something stupid?'

Kate, woken from restless sleep at half-past eight as Lily tried in vain to comfort Agnes, who sat weeping noisily in the Camerons' kitchen, felt torn in two that morning. She wished Jessie would cry too, but the girl sat still and pale, like a wee white ghost, obediently drinking a cup of tea and nibbling a piece of bread when Kate made her, but keeping her grief for the loss of her best friend locked up inside her. Only when Kate tried to leave her side did she make a little inarticulate

201

sound and reach for her big sister's hand, clutching it so tightly that both their palms became hot and slick with sweat.

How could she leave her? How could she not go and look for Robbie? Aside from relieving his mother's distress, it was Kate's fault that he'd been in a 'real funny mood' on Saturday. He had enormous stores of love and respect for his mother. If he'd been driven to shouting at her, that could only have been because of the quarrel he'd had with Kate – and her rejection of his proposal. What if he *did* do something stupid? A hundred times that morning, swimming in a river of tea as neighbours called past to offer sympathy, Kate ached to get up and go to him. Then she would look at Jessie's face again, and stay where she was.

When young Dr MacMillan, calling by in the early afternoon to express his condolences, supplied the information that Robbie had apparently gone back to the hospital in the early hours, but had left the building about seven o'clock in the morning, Kate could stand the look on Agnes Baxter's face no longer. Firmly pulling her hand out of Jessie's grasp, she stood up and spoke quietly but decisively.

'I'll go and look for him, Mrs B.,' she said. 'I think I might know where to find him.'

Jessie was looking up at her, a mute appeal in her eyes. *Don't leave me, Kate.* Kate caught her father's eye. He gave her a nod. Crossing the kitchen, he scooped Jessie up in his arms and sat down with her in the big armchair, cradling her with his work-roughened hands as he had done all of his children when they had been babies and toddlers.

'Coorie doon, lass, coorie doon,' he whispered. One large hand rested lightly on Jessie's hair, drawing her head down onto his shoulder. 'I'll look after you. There's someone else needing our Kate the now.'

She found him, as she'd expected, down by the river. He

was standing just beyond the rowan tree, leaning on the rail, staring down into the murky waters of the Clyde. The afternoon sunshine struck a gleam of brown from his bowed head. Funny, she always thought of his hair as being black.

His shoulders were hunched, his head bent, his back curved and vulnerable. For the first time in her life, Kate understood exactly what people meant when they said 'my heart went out to him'. Hers did then, reaching him several minutes before her feet did.

A couple, chatting away to each other and walking a few yards in front of Kate passed behind Robbie. He took no notice. Kate, her heart overflowing with sympathy, paused. Was she intruding on his own private grief for Barbara? Had she any right to be here? Would he want any comfort she could offer him – especially after the bitter words they had flung at each other a few days ago?

He evidently recognised her light step, or perhaps it was her quietness and stillness as she stood, hesitating and uncertain, a few feet behind him. Looking over his shoulder, he saw her and turned, giving her a smile so brave and sad that it made Kate's heart turn over in her breast.

'I thought I'd find you here,' she said softly. 'Your Ma was worried about you being away so long. I'll go and tell her that you're fine, shall I?'

'Don't run away. Stay for a wee while.' He extended a hand towards her. Kate managed to avoid taking it, but she came forward and stood beside him, glancing up at him.

'You're sure you wouldn't rather be on your own?'

Robbie shook his unruly head. 'No. I'm glad you came looking for me.'

His chin was dark with stubble, his eyes bloodshot. He must be exhausted, she thought. He had probably walked all night and then ended up here, as she had known he would.

'How's Jessie taking it?'

Kate shrugged. 'Well, she's terribly upset. You know . . .' How like him to think of Jessie in the midst of his own grief. She felt a lump grow in her throat. It wasn't fair. Robbie, of all people, didn't deserve this. She looked at his hand lying on the rail which separated them from the river. Impulsively, she covered it with her own.

'I'm sorry, Robbie. I'm really so sorry.'

'Aye,' he said, exhaling his breath on a long sigh. His hand moved under hers. He turned it palm upwards and interlaced his fingers through Kate's. She wondered if he was remembering when they had last held hands. Could it just be a few days ago? Since then, the world had turned topsy-turvy. Barbara Baxter was dead and Kate Cameron was a fallen woman. That didn't seem to matter very much now.

Robbie's eyes were downcast, his eyelashes resting on his cheekbones as he studied their entwined hands.

'I keep seeing her, Kate. Wherever I look. I look at the river and I look up at the sky and all I can see is her. It's as if I'm at the pictures – only the film's stuck and all I can see is her, lying there in that hospital bed – but it's not her. It's only a doll that looks like her. And I think – how can that be? She was so lively and full of fun.' He lifted his gaze. 'She was, Kate, wasn't she?'

Kate choked back the tears and forced a smile.

'Aye, Robbie, she was that. Full of mischief, too. Mind yon time she and our Jessie gave Mr Asquith a bath?' She squeezed his hand, trying to get him to give her a smile in response. He did his best, but it was a dismal effort, fading from his tired features as quickly as he tried manfully to put it there.

'I went back to the hospital last night – this morning, I mean. It just didn't seem right to leave her there, all alone.' His grip tightened painfully on Kate's fingers. If he exerted any more pressure her knuckles were going to crack. Not for all the tea in China would she have uttered a protest.

'The nurses had clasped her hands on her chest and put some white lilies under them, as though she was holding them . . . but she was dead, Kate, she wasn't able to hold anything.' He sighed and lifted his shoulders and the pressure on Kate's fingers eased – not a moment too soon.

'So I left the hospital and I've been walking all night.' He looked at her. 'To tell you the truth I've no idea where I've been, but somehow I ended up back here. By the river.'

'Where the two of us always end up.'

'Aye. Where the two of us always end up.' A smile was there, faint, but genuine. She lifted her free hand to his face, feeling the smoothness of his cheek and the roughness of his chin under her fingertips.

'You're cold, Robbie,' she said gently. 'Come on home with me and get some tea, and something to eat. You must be tired, too.'

He shook his head. 'I don't feel tired, Kate, nor hungry either. I've been standing here for ages, trying to think of her alive, trying to see different pictures of her – skipping, or playing at beddies, or washing Mr Asquith – or driving me nuts when I was trying to concentrate on something, cheeky wee bisom that she was . . .' His voice trailed off to a raw whisper.

'Oh, Robbie,' breathed Kate. Wincing, she extracted her fingers from his grasp and slid her arms around his waist, and as her father had done with Jessie, she lifted a hand to the back of his head and pulled it down onto her shoulder.

'I wouldn't mind if you wanted to have a good greet,' she whispered into his ear. 'There's nobody about.' She glanced around to check what she had just said. It was true enough. The path was deserted and there were no boats within sight. 'Maybe it would help you a wee bit.'

Loosely held in her embrace, his shaggy head jerked up. 'Don't be daft, Kate. Men don't cry.'

'Don't they?'

The grey eyes and the green eyes met. He looked down at her for a long moment. When, at last, she saw the tears well up and slide down his face, she sent up a silent prayer of thanks. Lifting a hand to the back of his head, she laced her fingers through his hair and gently drew his head once more down onto her shoulder. Her arms tightened about his waist. His came about her.

'Cry for her,' Kate commanded softly. 'She was worth it, wasn't she?'

The heavy head on her shoulder nodded. Then she felt her neck grow wet with his tears.

She could not take his pain away. She wasn't able to draw a curtain over the pictures in his mind's eye. He had to bear it all himself, but she could try to share it with him, give him comfort, offer him what strength she had.

'I'm glad we're friends again, Robbie,' she whispered soundlessly into his hair.

Chapter 16

'You're two weeks late.'

'Nearly three, actually,' said Kate calmly. She was aware of mild surprise that her mother should have noticed. Then again, living in such close quarters as they did, it perhaps wasn't surprising, even with three daughters to keep an eye on.

Lily wasn't in the mood to beat about any bushes.

'Whose is it? Robbie Baxter's?'

Kate didn't answer. Was she relieved that her mother knew? She wasn't sure. She wasn't sure about anything at the moment. Normally as regular as clockwork, she had nevertheless tried hard to convince herself that there was some other reason for her period being late. Unhappiness at breaking up with Jack, perhaps; worry itself. She'd stopped believing that a week ago.

Seated with her elbows on the kitchen table, Kate let her head fall forward, threading her fingers through her hair. She'd washed it the day before. It felt smooth and shiny and cool, just like the crêpe-de-chine frock . . . There were fingers on her chin, jerking her head upright.

'I asked you a question, young lady.'

Kate had to moisten her lips before she could speak. 'Not Robbie,' she managed. 'Just . . . just someone I know . . .' Her voice tailed off at the look on her mother's face. Lily, her colour up, put both hands on her hips.

'One o' your fancy Art School friends then, is it?' She spat the words out.

Kate nodded.

'Does he know? About the bairn, I mean.' Lily gestured towards Kate's stomach. Kate felt panic flutter up from her abdomen to her throat. What was she going to do when she began to show? When the tongues started wagging? Oh God, what would her father say? He'd be so disappointed in her. She'd have to give up her apprenticeship, too – with less than two years of it to go.

'Yes.' Behind her back, she crossed her fingers so that the lie wouldn't count.

'Will he do the decent thing – marry you?'

Kate laughed, but the sound had no mirth in it. 'People like him don't marry people like us.' That made her think about Robbie. She wondered what he was going to think of her.

'But he'll support you? Give you some money? He's had his pleasure with you. He'll have to pay for that.'

Kate winced and the thought came, unbidden, that there had been very little pleasure in it, at least for her. Her voice, when she spoke, was dull and flat.

'He offered to pay for . . . for . . .' She couldn't say the words. *People who get rid of mistakes.* A dreadful numbness was creeping over her, sliding up from her toes. It crawled past her knees, then it was at her waist. She couldn't have moved from the chair if the King and Queen themselves had walked into the room.

'For you to get rid o' it? Well, maybe that would be the best thing.' Lily nodded sagely.

Kate lifted stricken green eyes to her mother's face.

'Mammy, I couldn't do that, I just couldn't!' Unconsciously, her hand went to her stomach.

'That's all very well, my girl,' said Lily, folding her arms over her chest, 'but you've only got two choices. Either you get rid of it or you find someone else to marry you.'

'Someone else? Who else would . . . ?' Frowning in puzzlement, Kate stared up at her mother. Then the penny dropped. She felt the blood drain from her face. 'You don't mean . . .'

'He asked you, didn't he – before Barbara died? Agnes doesnae know for sure, but she thinks he did.'

The numbness had worn off. Kate leaped out of the chair and went to stand by the range, looking back across the kitchen at her mother with horrified eyes.

'Ma, I couldn't do that to Robbie, it wouldn't be fair! It's not his child!'

Lily snorted. 'He wouldn't be the first man that's been fooled.' She too moved, crossing the room to lift the kettle off the range before taking it to the sink to be filled. The cold water gushed noisily out of the tap.

'I can't do it, Ma,' said Kate firmly. 'It wouldn't be fair.'

Lily turned the tap off, lifted the kettle over to the range and reached to one side for the teapot.

'You'll have to get rid of it then,' she said implacably. 'You can't keep it and no' be married.'

Kate opened her mouth to protest and closed it again. Lily, having made all the preparations possible before the kettle boiled, which was a long way off, turned and looked at her daughter. Miserably, Kate looked back at her. They were standing only a foot apart. She could see no sympathy for her in her mother's blue eyes – blue like *his*, she thought.

'You were supposed to be the brainy one,' Lily reproached her daughter. A drop of water, falling from the spout of the kettle, hissed as it hit the hot surface of the range. 'Not daft enough to let a man have his way wi' you without a ring on your finger.'

Funny, thought Kate, with that part of her brain which was watching all this go on as though it were happening to someone else, she's not worried about my morals. She's just got contempt for my stupidity.

'It'll kill your father, you know,' Lily said quietly. 'You've always been his favourite. Out of all of us.' Her eyelids flickered. 'Two choices, my girl. And make them quick. Men might be stupid, but they can usually count. You haven't got much time to make up your mind.'

The woman who got rid of mistakes lived in Dalmuir. There was a wee park opposite her house. After a moment's hesitation Kate crossed the road to it and went in, carefully closing the heavy gate set into the railings behind her. Sliding onto a green-painted bench she studied the roses in the flower bed in front of her. They were beautiful, a mixture of white and yellow, just beginning to bud.

There was a light breeze in the air. It made the rosebuds sway on their stems like impossibly graceful dancers.

The words were ringing round her head. *It'll kill your father. You were supposed to be the brainy one. Let a man have his way with you.* Was that all it had meant to Jack Drummond? That he'd had his way with her? Wasn't love supposed to come into it somewhere?

If she kept the baby . . . But how could she? Jack didn't want to know. Could she go away, start a new life somewhere else? Buy a cheap wedding ring in Woolies and pretend she was a widow? Use your loaf, Cameron, she upbraided herself. Where would you get the money to live on? She couldn't go out to work, not with a wee baby in tow.

The door of the house opposite opened. A neat maid, in black dress, white cap and apron, waved a tablecloth free of crumbs. What time was it anyway? Kate had eaten nothing since breakfast that morning. There was a crisp banknote in her purse, enough to pay to get rid of her mistake.

'You'll get it back from him, mind!' That had been Lily's

parting shot, her lips set in a firm line. Kate had miserably agreed, knowing that she would rather be torn apart by wild horses than ask Jack Drummond for the money.

The maid had gone back in, the door was once more closed. It was painted a shiny black, like the railings around the little park. The door had a well-polished brass letter box and a knocker in the shape of a lion's head. All she had to do was get up, walk across the road and lift the lion's head. That was all. She would hand over the money and the rest would be taken care of. Her mistake got rid of, she could get on with the rest of her life: finish her apprenticeship and continue with her art studies. She sighed and tilted her head back to look up at the sky. It was blue, filled with fluffy white clouds.

Kate's eyes fell again on the roses. They were so beautiful. Yet they were so fragile. Someone could come along here and lop their heads off and they would never get the chance to burst forth into their full beauty and grace.

Slowly, as though she were walking in her sleep, Kate stood up and made her way to the park gate. She turned once, to look at the roses.

'I thought I'd find you here,' came a quiet voice from behind her. Kate turned from her scrutiny of the oily surface of the river.

'We must stop meeting like this.'

Robbie gave her the briefest of grins and ran his hand through his hair. 'Aye.'

'How are you?' she asked.

He shrugged and walked forward to join her at the handrail. 'Och, you know.'

'Aye, I know,' said Kate softly, thinking how tired and pale he looked.

He grasped her hand and slid it through the crook of his arm. She took a deep breath and straightened her shoulders.

211

She felt rather than saw Robbie's sidelong glance at her and he took a step away, allowing her to pull her arm out of his. The air between them crackled with tension. With his usual perception, he had guessed that something was coming.

She had spent the previous night tossing and turning, eliciting numerous moans from Pearl. Her sister's irritation was nothing compared to the torment going on inside her own head. She wasn't at all sure that she could go through with this.

Yet she had made her decision yesterday, in the little park looking at the roses. Her life had taken a turn she hadn't expected, but it had to be faced up to – and dealt with. There was a price to be paid, of course.

The fact that it was Robbie who, all unwitting, was going to have to pay most of that price was what made her hesitate. But he loved her; she knew that. He wanted to marry her . . . but it was deceiving him – in the worst way possible.

He was silent, waiting for her to speak. He loved her. She kept coming back to that. And she would try her best to be a good wife to him, to make him happy. She had two lives to think of now – her own, and her baby's. And because of that other small life, so utterly dependent upon her, she turned at last to Robert Baxter and spoke.

'Robbie,' she said. 'Mind you asked me a question, that day you took me out to lunch, three weeks ago?' *Three weeks!* Was it so recent? So much had happened since then: Barbara's death; her own small tragedy.

'I remember,' he said gravely. 'What about it?'

The blood was pounding in Kate's ears. She turned and looked at him as though she were seeing him for the very first time. He was pale, and very serious. It was a warm evening and he was in waistcoat and shirt-sleeves. He had taken his tie and collar off, and undone a couple of shirt buttons. she looked at the skin of his throat, exposed to the fresh air. It made him look curiously vulnerable and boyish. His thick hair was, as usual, tousled. Could she really do this to him? Did she have a choice?

'Would you ask me again?'

He went very still, and it was some time before he spoke. 'I thought you had an understanding with someone else.'

She dropped her head, shame flooding through her. Maybe she was going to have to tell him the truth after all, see his grey eyes fill with condemnation and hurt.

'Has something happened to change that?' he asked.

'Yes,' she mumbled, 'something's changed.'

'Look at me, Kate.' His voice was quiet, but implacable. With a toss of her chestnut-brown waves, Kate forced herself to meet his eyes.

'Are you sure you're doing this for the right reasons?'

Her stomach lurched. Did he have a crystal ball?

'I don't want you to say yes because things haven't worked out for you, or because you're feeling sorry for me about . . . about Barbara.' He managed to get his sister's name out and then clamped his mouth tightly shut. There were to be no tears today. 'I don't want you marrying me out of pity, or on the rebound from . . . someone else.' He was finding that name difficult to say, too. 'You gave me a pretty definite no three weeks ago.'

Kate tucked a strand of hair behind one ear. She hadn't expected this interrogation – although she should have. It was how he was: honest and straight and always needing to get at the truth. How was she to convince him? Nervously, she got something out about feelings having changed.

'Is it your feelings that have changed? Or his?'

He had hit the nail on the head as usual, asking the only question which really mattered. She had to steel herself not to drop her eyes again before his level gaze.

'Mine,' she whispered. It was the only possible answer, but

she crossed her fingers as she said it. Hope leaped into his eyes. She saw it – a tiny flame; saw also how he made a move towards her, then checked himself, hands held stiffly at his sides.

'If I ask you again, I have to ask you two questions. The second one depends on the answer to the first.'

Squaring his shoulders, he looked her full in the face, preparing himself for the blow she might be about to inflict on him. 'Do you love me, Kathleen Cameron?'

She had to lick her lips before she could speak and, once again, she gave him the only possible answer.

'Yes,' she whispered.

Robert Baxter wasn't giving an inch.

'Say it,' he insisted. 'Say the words.'

'I love you, Robert Baxter.' She smiled up at him. It was hard to smile when you had tears in your eyes.

'Say it again.'

'I love you, Robert Baxter.' Her voice was stronger this time.

'Then prove it,' he said, reaching for her. She could feel the warmth and strength of his arms through the thin cotton of his shirt-sleeves. His lips were cool and firm on her mouth. Swept away on a tide of emotion, Kate found herself kissing him back. He gave a small grunt, tightened his hold on her and redoubled his efforts. Fighting the urge to struggle, Kate forced herself instead to relax against him – and felt the unmistakeable response in the body pressed so closely against her own. He let go of her just in time.

So swiftly that she didn't realise what was happening until he'd got there, Robbie slid to one knee in front of her. He was smiling at last, his face bright as he looked up at her.

'I think this is what I did wrong, the last time. Not going down on bended knee.' Laughing down at him on a surge of relief, she hardly heard the words. 'Will you marry me, Kate?'

'Yes,' she whispered, 'yes.'

His arms came round her waist, pulling her to him, his head warm on her stomach. 'You're a daft bisom, Kathleen Cameron.' His voice was muffled by her body but she could hear the joy in it. Waves of gratitude and relief swept through her. It was going to be all right. Everything was going to be all right. Kate sent up a prayer of mingled thankfulness and apology. If You forgive me, God, I swear I'll make it up to him. I swear I'll make him happy.

Just let me marry Robbie and keep my baby. I won't mind about giving up the Art School, or my apprenticeship – or Jack Drummond. I'll shut all those memories away in a box in my head, and never look at them again. Just let me keep my baby and I'll make Robbie happy. I'll be a good wife to him, I swear I will. The words swirled round her head, like a litany, a plea both for forgiveness and a promise to their future together.

That night, for the first time in two weeks, she slept through without waking. That was good. She had to think about her health now – for the baby's sake.

It was only when she opened her eyes the next morning, clutching at a few more moments in a warm bed before she got up to go to work, that she remembered that she hadn't crossed her fingers when she had told Robbie she loved him.

She thought about it. She had told him too many lies yesterday. She had no desire to tell him any more. They had always been honest with each other, right from when they were children. She frowned, trying to puzzle it out. Then her face cleared. Of course she loved him. Like a brother, of course, but it was still love. She just hoped it would be enough.

215

Chapter 17

They married two weeks later – quietly, in the vestry of the church, with only the two families present, as was fitting when the groom was in mourning for his sister. Robbie had made a token protest about the loss of Kate's apprenticeship, but it hadn't taken much to persuade him that their wedding should take place soon. Fearful perhaps that she might change her mind if they delayed at all, he didn't even suggest waiting a decent interval. His family, relieved to see him so happy, put no obstacles in the way of a quick, if quiet wedding, much to the relief of Lily Cameron.

'We'll just have to hope that this bairn's a wee one,' she told Kate. 'Then we can say that it's arrived early.' Kate winced, and hated the deception afresh, but then determinedly put the thought into that mental box. Robbie was happy. Any fool could see that.

Andrew Baxter complained that his elder brother was going around 'grinning like an eejit' at everyone.

'Then he remembers about Barbara,' Andrew went on, 'and he's away down in the dumps again.'

'Well, I think it's dead romantic,' sighed Pearl Cameron. 'I wish I was getting married. *And* they're going to have a place o' their own. A right wee love nest – eh, Kate?'

'A love nest!' snorted Andrew Baxter. 'Likely it'll be damp.'

'Och, you, you've got no romance in your soul. Has he,

Jessie?' asked Pearl, batting her eyelashes at Andrew and winking at Kate as she put the question to their sister.

Jessie nodded listlessly. Kate was growing increasingly worried about her. She'd been tired and droopy since Barbara's death, even seemed to have lost interest in her studies. Maybe, once she and Robbie were married, Kate could think of ways of cheering her younger sister up, perhaps have her to stay sometimes at their own wee place – their love nest, as Pearl called it.

Robbie, puffed up with pride, had come home three days before the wedding and announced that he'd got them a flat in Clydebank – very central, at the foot of Kilbowie Road. It wasn't much, he told Kate apologetically, just a 'single end', – a room where they would sleep and eat and live, but it was a start. Astonishingly, he had then further announced that they were going to have a honeymoon – four days at Millport on the Isle of Cumbrae in the Firth of Clyde.

When Kate asked him how they could afford either of these, he went rather red and mumbled something about having been saving up for a while. When she pressed the point, he admitted that he'd had a savings account at the Post Office for the past three years.

Darting a quick glance up at her from where he sat in the armchair by the range – her father being at the pub and Lily and the rest of the children downstairs at the Baxters' discussing the food for the wedding celebration – he had gone on to tell her that he'd called this nest egg his 'marrying Kate' account.

Kate, in the process of putting the kettle onto the range, raised her eyebrows at that one and gave him a look her mother would have been proud of. The heavy kettle safely set to boil, she folded her arms over her chest and said, 'And what if I'd said no the second time? Would this have been your "marrying some other lassie" account?'

Half-amused, half-angry, she stood there tapping her foot, waiting for his answer. When it came, it took her breath away.

'There's only ever been you for me, Kate. If you'd kept on saying no, the money would have been my "taking my broken heart off to sea" account.'

He reached out for her, pulling her down to sit on his knee.

'Give us a kiss,' he said, 'before the hordes come back and we start another of those conversations about how much shortbread your Ma's making and how many empire biscuits mine is.'

He was trying to lighten the conversation, but Kate knew full well that he was deadly serious. When Robbie Baxter made up his mind to do something, there was no shifting him. He *would* have gone to sea – especially after Barbara's death. She'd only just caught him. The thought gave her the queerest little flutter of panic, not all related to her predicament.

He bent forward to kiss her, but she laid a hand flat against his chest to stop him.

'I know it's just a single end we've got, but d'you think maybe Jessie could stay with us now and again? Would you mind?'

He put his hand round the back of her neck, lifting the ends of her bobbed hair. 'I wouldn't mind,' he said. 'Just not all the time, eh? I'm looking forward to getting you to myself. Being able to kiss you as much as I like, whenever I like. Among other things,' he murmured, giving Kate a long slow smile.

That smile – and the twinkle in the grey eyes which went with it – gave Kate goosebumps. How odd it seemed to be contemplating doing *that* with Robbie. Embarrassing, even. She thought of him as a brother. He would expect it, though, of course he would. And she had to let him

218

do it. Otherwise there would be no point at all to this deception.

Robbie wore his Sunday suit for the occasion and Kate a new print dress. It was a simple little yellow cotton frock, nothing at all like the dress *he* had bought for her. She'd given that to a delighted Pearl, on condition that she didn't wear it at the wedding. Robbie bought Kate a string of glass beads as a wedding gift.

'One day I'll buy you pearls,' he told her, lifting the long strand over her head, smooth in her little cloche hat. 'I know how you like bonnie things.'

'These are bonnie things,' she assured him, touching the smooth, cold globes. They were dark green, almost exactly the same colour as the beautiful vase Esmé MacGregor and Frances Noble had given her when they called the night before the wedding to offer their best wishes.

Kate's heart had sunk when she had opened the door to them. She had taken the coward's way out by sending them a letter informing them of her forthcoming wedding. She had told them of another letter too, one she had tried, and failed, not to cry over. It had been to the Art School, formally giving up any claim to the second half of the grant and stating that she would not be returning to the part-time classes when they resumed in the autumn. Maybe someone else could get some use out of the bursary . . .

Expecting reproaches, feeling that the two women who'd done so much to encourage her were perfectly entitled to make them, Kate had been enormously relieved when Miss Noble had simply handed over the gift and wished her all the best for the future.

She'd even managed to derive some secret amusement from the way Robert Baxter, a grown man, had leaped to his feet at the sight of his old teacher, standing to attention and only just managing not to salute her, the traditional way generations of boys had greeted their schoolmistresses each morning.

'I trust, Robert,' said Miss Noble, 'that you are still reading as much as you used to.'

'Oh yes, Miss Noble, I'm the library's best customer. I'm reading a lot of poetry at the moment.'

They had gone off into a discussion on the relative merits of Keats, Shelley, Byron and Burns, interrupted only when Esmé MacGregor caught her friend's eye.

'Ah yes,' said Frances Noble, stopping in mid-flow. 'Miss MacGregor and I have something we wish to say to you, Robert – apart, of course, from congratulating you on your forthcoming nuptials.'

Impatient with this shilly-shallying, Esmé broke in. She drew herself up to her full height – which was a good foot less than Robbie's. The contrast between the tall young man and the short middle-aged woman should have looked absurd. It didn't. Fixing Robbie with a piercing stare, Esmé prepared to do battle.

'Young man, are you aware that your wife-to-be is a very gifted artist?'

Kate shifted uncomfortably and Robbie cleared his throat.

'I am indeed, Miss MacGregor.' His voice was grave. 'I'm very proud of Kate's talent and I see absolutely no reason why she shouldn't continue to develop as an artist – through classes, or through practice. I shall certainly put no obstacles in her way. Quite the reverse. I intend to encourage her as much as possible.'

Kate looked at him in surprise. That little speech hadn't sounded at all like the Robbie Baxter she knew. Could it be that there was a man she didn't know hidden behind the years of childhood friendship? One who had grown up in this last year while the two of them had been slowly drifting apart? It was an intriguing thought.

Esmé MacGregor was looking intently up at Robbie, study-ing his face. Whatever she saw there seemed to satisfy her. She gave a funny little nod, then stuck out her hand.

'In that case, young man, I congratulate you most hearti-ly.'

They shook hands solemnly. Miss Noble came forward, smiling, and kissed first Kate and then Robbie, who went bright pink. Then Agnes Baxter opened one of the two bottles of sherry she'd bought for the wedding and they all drank to the future.

Theirs was not the only awkward visit Kate had endured. Marjorie had also called, bearing Kate's pottery and paintings from the Art School, condolences from her mother and herself to Agnes Baxter on Barbara's death, and congratulations – and a set of fluffy white towels – to Kate and Robbie. She also had some news of her own in that department, she told Kate with a smile. Her left hand was adorned with a beautiful diamond ring.

That was the day Kate discovered a hitherto unsuspected talent for acting – born out of sheer desperation, she sup-posed. She did, it was true, have a few moments to collect herself while the assembled womenfolk oohed and aahed over Marjorie's ring, although that brief respite turned out to have a sting in the tail. Pearl, eager for details, elicited the infor-mation that Marjorie's fiancé had popped the question when they had both been guests at a house party near Dumfries.

'The weekend after we broke up from Art School,' she told the girl, laughing at Pearl's enthusiasm.

The weekend after he had made love to her. *I may be broke, but not that broke.* Obviously not too broke to find the money for a ring for Marjorie either – an investment in his future, no doubt. Just in time, Kate stopped herself from allowing her reactions to show on her face. Robbie was watching her, his dark brows drawn together in the way he had when he was trying to puzzle something out. She remembered the question he had put to her. *Is it your feelings that have changed? Or his?* Kate leaped to her feet and shook Marjorie by the hand.

'Congratulations,' she said brightly, 'and please give Jack my best wishes too.' There. Her voice hadn't even wavered when she had said his name. Marjorie stood up and threw her arms around Kate's neck.

'Oh, Kate! We're both going to be married ladies. Just imagine! Only I've got to wait until next February – a winter wedding.' She beamed at Kate. 'I'll tell you all about the arrangements when we start back at the Art School in September. You are coming back to the class, Kate, aren't you?' She shot an anxious glance at Robbie. 'There's no reason why a married woman shouldn't take a class, don't you think so, Mr Baxter?'

It's not him who's going to stop me, Marjorie, thought Kate, he's not that kind of a man. I won't be coming back to college because I'll be having a baby – just about the time you and Jack Drummond are getting married.

She saw Marjorie downstairs. Should she say something? Tell her to be careful, that she might be making a terrible mistake? As they walked out of the close onto the pavement, Kate saw that a group of excited children were gathered around Marjorie's car. Her friend turned and smiled. Happiness had transformed her plain features. She looked almost beautiful.

'Do you want to have children, Kate? I know I do.' She turned and hugged her friend once more. 'I'm so happy,' she whispered. 'I can't begin to tell you how happy I am to be marrying Jack. I hope you're just the same with your Robert.'

Neil Cameron cried as he gave his daughter away.

'Chicken-hearted!' scoffed Lily afterwards, repeating the words to anyone who cared to listen. Kate didn't think he was

222

chicken-hearted. She found a moment during the wedding breakfast to have a quiet word with him. He was in the front room, sitting by himself at the window.

'Are you all right, Daddy?' she asked, looking at the glass of whisky in his hand, and wondering how many he'd had.

He looked up at his daughter, and lifted his free hand to her. She took it between her own. Such a large hand, but still fine-boned and delicate, despite the calluses and hard skin which his work had put there.

'Aye, my lassie, I'm fine.' His eyes creased at the corners. 'Well, I suppose you're not my lassie any more, you're Robbie's lassie.' There was a catch in his voice.

'I'll always be your lassie,' she said, looking intently into his soft green eyes, so like her own, and willing him to know how much she loved him. She wished she could just have told him, simply have leaned forward and kissed his forehead, but things weren't done that way in the Cameron household. Lily had the Scottish dislike of public displays of affection in full measure, and she'd inculcated it into her family.

'Ready, Mrs Baxter?' came a voice in her ear. Robbie, smiling broadly, put his hand on her back. She could feel the warmth of his fingers through the thin dress, splayed out over her back. He's taking possession of me, she thought, staking his claim. She turned to him, uncomfortably aware of his closeness.

'It's not time to go yet, is it?' She hoped she didn't sound as panicky as she felt. In a few hours' time, they were going to have to get closer still. She might still be her father's daughter, but she was about to become her husband's wife.

Neil Cameron rose slowly to his feet and extended his hand to Robbie.

'You take care of my girl now, Robert.'

Robbie shook his new father-in-law firmly by the hand. 'You can depend upon it, Mr Cameron.'

Chapter 18

Kate was coming slowly out of sleep, the events and images of the day before replaying themselves in her head: Robbie, so proud and happy, slipping the simple gold band onto her finger; her father – proud too, but sad to lose his wee girl; her mother, relieved that they'd pulled it off; her own sick realisation during the wedding ceremony of what she was doing; her unhappiness at how she was fooling Robbie – a man she cared for deeply – a man she did not love as one should love a husband.

Then there had been the sail 'doon the watter' from Craigendoran: the little steamer chugging her way through the waves, the magnificent scenery of the Firth of Clyde, its hills and sea lochs and islands, the gulls following the boat. There had been a wee laddie with his grandparents who'd fed his piece to the gulls, shrieking with delight as the birds had swooped low to snatch the pieces of bread from his outstretched fingers. At any other time Kate would have relished it all – the sights, the sounds, the fresh air on her face, the sea breeze lifting her hair.

'Oh good, you're awake.'

Struggling up onto two plump pillows – what luxury! – Kate saw Robbie struggling into the room with a huge tray.

'No, don't get up,' he said, seeing her pushing back the blankets. 'This contraption's got legs.' Kicking the bedroom door shut behind him, he crossed the room towards her.

'Sit up,' he said cheerfully, 'and pull the covers up. There.' Deftly moving his hands so that foldaway legs fell down at both ends of the tray, he set it on the shiny dark blue counterpane.

'Scrambled eggs and sausage, tea, toast, butter and marmalade. Breakfast is served, madam.' Dressed for the day in new flannels and an open-necked shirt, he sat on the bed facing Kate, one leg bent, the other dangling over the side.

'How did you persuade the landlady to do this?' asked Kate, finding her voice at last. If they kept to neutral subjects, maybe they could manage to get through today. Maybe.

Robbie, concentrating on his scrambled eggs, didn't look up.

'Och, she says that a lot of new brides feel shy the first morning. After the wedding night.' He was eating calmly, but Kate hadn't missed the tiny hesitation between the two sentences. Their wedding night had been a disaster.

By the time they had landed at Millport and got the bus the short distance along to Kames Bay, Kate had been wound as tightly as a watch spring, her emotions swaying wildly between guilt and apprehension. She shouldn't have done this to him, but now that she had, was he going to be able to tell? One problem was solved when the landlady took her quietly to one side and pointed out a bucket of cold water sitting discreetly under the curtains below the sink in their bedroom.

Kate, hideously embarrassed, had made out only a few words about taking off the small draw sheet which, the landlady explained, was on top of the main sheet, and steeping it overnight.

'That'll take the bloodstains out fine. If you just do it straightaway, pet – as soon as young Mr Baxter's finished with you.'

Under different circumstances Kate might have allowed herself a smile at that last statement. As it was, she felt only huge relief. When the time came to go to bed, she insisted on the lamp being put out, despite Robbie's gentle pleading to be allowed to light it again.

'I want to see you, Kate,' he whispered in the darkness. 'Please?'

'I can't,' she mumbled. 'I can't . . . I'm sorry.'

'You're shy,' he said, matter-of-factly. 'Come here then, my bonnie lass, we'll just have to find each other by touch.' He was smiling. She could hear it in his voice.

She tensed when he reached for her, remembering another voice saying sweet and soft things in her ear, other fingers caressing her skin. Robbie was very gentle, yet she had to steel herself not to shrink from the touch of his hand on her body.

'Kate?' Now he sounded puzzled. He doesn't deserve this, thought Kate, angry with herself. Pull yourself together, Cameron. Make an effort. She lifted a hand and laid it on his shoulder, above her in the dark. His skin was smooth and warm.

'It's all right. I'm just nervous. Go on.'

'Is that what you want? For me to go on?'

The question hung in the air for a few seconds. She moved her hand on his shoulder, stroking it.

'Yes.'

She hadn't convinced him.

'I think I could stop now. I might not be able to, later on.'

Oh God, she couldn't do this! Not with Robbie. But she had to.

'That's all right.' She could hear for herself how wooden she sounded.

'Are you sure—' he began again, but Kate, her nerves at breaking point, snapped at him.

'Oh, for heaven's sake, Robbie. Just get it over with!'

She could feel his hurt, sense his emotional withdrawal from her, but confused as he was, he did as she asked. It wasn't long before she realised that he had reached the point where he wasn't going to be able to stop. Slowly and gently, he entered her – and she froze, every part of her recoiling from this intimacy with him. He took her reaction for pain and would have pulled out, only by then it was too late.

Afterwards, once she had whipped off the draw sheet with its non-existent bloodstains and dunked it in the pail under the sink, Robbie took her stiff body in his arms and drew her, all unwilling, into his warm embrace. He kept apologising for having hurt her, until she wanted to scream at him to shut up. He hadn't hurt her at all, that was the whole problem. At last, unable to bear the contact any longer, she pulled herself out of his arms and turned onto her side, facing away from her new husband.

'Kate?' He was leaning over her, trying to work out what was wrong.

'What's the matter, Kate? Can't you tell me?'

No, she couldn't. Tell him that she was a fraud, that she had fooled him?

'Go to sleep, Robbie,' she had said dully. 'Just go to sleep.'

When they had finished breakfast, Robbie suggested a walk along the prom to Millport. It was a beautiful day, the sky blue and the clouds white and fluffy as cotton wool. She walked by his side in silence, responding when he asked her a question or pointed out something in the bay, but her replies were monosyllabic. He tried to take her hand as they walked, but she pulled it out of his grasp.

Kate gave her head an angry little toss. She had to snap out of this, for his sake. This whole mess was her fault, not his. She had used him, taken advantage of the feelings he had for

227

her. Should she tell him the truth? See his face cloud over, see the bitter disappointment in his grey eyes? Shatter all his illusions?

It would give him the chance to walk away from her. But what then? They were married, fair and square. American film stars might get divorces – you read about it sometimes in the newspapers and magazines – but not people like them. People like them just put up with it. You made your bed and then you lay on it. She felt as though her head was going to burst. She stopped suddenly – because he had. She was a pace or two ahead of him. She had to turn round to look at him.

'What?' She hadn't heard him speak. Kate forced herself to concentrate on what he was saying.

'I said – d'you fancy hiring a couple of bikes and going round the island? It's only eleven miles. We could take a picnic – stop round on the west coast somewhere. Maybe we could even get a tandem. What do you think, Kate?'

How many times in the last twenty-four hours had she heard him say her name with that anxious question in his voice?

'Oh, Robbie!'

Kate turned to look out at the bay. There wasn't a breath of wind this morning; the sea was glassy and flat, the water sparkling in the morning sun. It was going to be a hot day. A seagull flew past their heads, his squawk loud and discordant. She closed her eyes and saw the little boy on the boat yesterday, face wreathed in smiles as the birds took the bread he held out to them.

Robbie's voice floated to her from where he stood, a few paces behind her, on the esplanade.

'I'm sorry, hen. Maybe bikes aren't such a good idea today. I should have realised.' He hesitated and then asked, his voice low and concerned, 'Are you very sore?'

'Robbie . . .' she murmured. Embarrassed and ashamed, she took a few more steps away from him. An elderly man, out for his morning constitutional, touched his hat in polite greeting. Kate barely acknowledged him. Robbie had followed her to the ornate handrail separating the promenade from the rocks and sand below. He was right behind her – so close that she could feel his breath warm on the back of her neck.

'Kate?'

She put her hand out to the wrought-iron rail and curled her fingers tightly around it. Sore? She should have been, shouldn't she?

'Talk to me, Kate.' There was something in his voice that might have been amusement – and might not. 'At least tell me what I've done wrong. Then I might be able to work out how to put it right. At the moment, I'm kind of struggling in the dark. Like last night, in fact,' he joked clumsily.

She wheeled round at that, looking up into his face. He was trying to keep things light, but his forehead was creased in a frown and his grey eyes were wary.

'You've done nothing wrong,' she said at last. Her voice sounded odd. She coughed to clear her throat. 'You've done nothing wrong,' she repeated in a stronger voice. 'It's me.'

'Do you mean that you're having second thoughts?' he asked in a low voice. 'That you wish you hadn't said yes to me?' As though afraid of the answer he might read in her face, he turned away from her and looked out over the water.

Oh, Robbie, thought Kate, that's exactly what I wish, but it's not your fault, it's not. He leaned forward, resting his elbows on the rail and staring fixedly in front of him.

'I suppose,' he said, 'if you really don't like it . . . I know a lot of women are supposed not to . . . I suppose I could try not to want . . . I could try not to bother you too much . . . in that way.'

They were both scarlet by the time he had finished speaking, stumbling his way along, leaving most of the words unsaid. He tossed his head, flipping back the rogue lock of hair from his forehead.

'Let's walk,' he said abruptly, the colour fading slowly from his face. They fell into step together, automatically heading in the direction of Millport. Robbie made no move to take her arm, or hold her hand.

God forgive me, thought Kate drearily, for what I've done – and to Robbie of all people. She looked at the houses they were passing – big, solid sandstone mansions, like *his* house. She turned away, back to the view out over the Firth of Clyde. She would not think of him. That was over. Kate lifted her face to the breeze. And made a decision.

She stopped and pulled on Robbie's sleeve.

'Not that way,' she said, 'this way. Where it's quiet.' He slanted an odd look down at her, but allowed her to turn them around.

'Can I take your arm, Mr Baxter?' she asked, consciously lightening her voice. He would never know the effort it cost her. He must never know, if her plan were to work. He studied her face. Whatever he saw there smoothed out the frown on his brow and lifted the corners of his mouth, but he was cautious, unwilling to let the smile go any further. They walked in silence for ten minutes, until they had left the fine houses of Kames Bay behind.

When Robbie spotted a bench looking over the narrow channel which separated the island from the mainland he steered them both to it and sat down, pulling Kate with him.

'Talk to me,' he demanded, 'or I'll go off my rocker.'

Kate took a deep breath. She had made her bed and she had to lie on it – with Robbie. There was no reason why it had to be uncomfortable for him too. She put a hand out and touched his leg. His eyes fluttered closed for a second and he gave a funny little moan.

'Oh, Kate.' His voice was very soft. 'I said I would try not to bother you, but if you only knew the thoughts I have about you. They would make you blush, lassie.'

His grey eyes were as soft as his voice. When he covered her hand with his own, Kate felt oddly breathless. It was like her father's, she thought, rough and work-calloused, nothing like . . .

But she would not think of *him*. Robbie was what mattered now. Robbie who loved her. Robbie whom she had cheated. Robbie who was now looking at her with a rueful smile.

'They make *me* blush sometimes,' he confided. Embarrassed, she dropped her eyes, studying the hand which held hers captive.

'I'm hungry for you, Kate.' She looked up, startled by the edge to his voice. His eyes were narrowed in concentration, searching for the right words. 'No, it's more like thirst. I'm in the desert, crawling across the sand . . . and then I see an oasis – like in that picture we saw, remember? A beautiful oasis of cool, clear water and shady green trees. You're my oasis, Kathleen Cameron. Cool, clear and shady. Somewhere I can rest and be myself. Find myself, somehow, in a way I can't explain yet. Maybe I'll never be able to explain. I just know that when I'm with you, I feel as if I've come home.'

'Robbie,' she began, her voice cracking. 'I don't want you to think that I don't love you . . .'

He was looking rueful again. 'You love me like your brother. I know that now. I also know that you married me for your own reasons. Maybe because of Barbara . . .' His voice tailed off. 'I just hope that, given time, you'll be able to love me like your husband. Which I am, Mrs Baxter.' Leaning forward, he kissed her gently on her slightly parted lips.

'Robbie, I . . .'

He tapped her mouth with his forefinger. 'You don't have

to say anything. I don't want you to say anything. Let's just give it time, eh?'

'But I do love you,' said Kate urgently. 'I *do*. And I'll try to be a good wife to you, and try to like . . . that. You can *bother* me whenever you like. Oh, Robbie, you know what I mean – and stop laughing at me!'

'I'm not,' he protested. 'Honest.' But he was grinning widely. He stood up and extended a hand to pull her to her feet, too. 'Give us a kiss, Mrs Baxter.'

Kate did her best. She knew it wasn't quite good enough. She knew he knew it too, but he was still smiling when he released her, his eyes full of hope. She couldn't extinguish that. Maybe, if she tried really hard, she could make him happy, never let him know that he'd been second best.

'Right, madam, what do you want to do today?'

'Whatever *you* want,' she said earnestly.

Robbie's dark eyebrows shot up. 'I know you promised to obey me, but I didn't think either of us had taken that seriously!'

'I took my wedding vows very seriously.'

There was a pause which went on for just too long.

'Did you?' His tone was neutral. She forced herself to look at him. He couldn't know. Could he?

His apparent composure cracked. He took her by the shoulders and gave her a shake. 'I don't want a wee doormat, Kate. I want you. Full of life and full of ambitions. The Kate I know and love. *My* Kate.'

He finished on a quick, rapid breath, looking intently down at her.

My Kate. He must never know that she'd been someone else's Kate. Never. She lifted her face.

'Give us a kiss, Mr Baxter.'

Robbie took her in his arms enthusiastically and did as she asked, then held her in a loose embrace.

'Will you do something for me?'

'Anything,' she promised recklessly.

He lifted his hand to her head, touching the short chestnut-brown strands.

'Grow your hair for me? It's so bonnie, and I'd like to see it dancing on your shoulders again.'

'Dancing on my shoulders? You've definitely got a way with words, Robert Baxter,' she teased. 'Yes, I'll grow my hair for you.' It was a small enough thing for him to ask.

'Good.' He took her hand. 'Why don't you do some painting while we're here? You can look at the sea and the rocks and I can look at you.'

'I didn't bring my water colours. Not even my sketch book.'

'No, but I did. I got Jessie to smuggle them out for me.'

She turned to him, genuinely touched. 'Och, Robbie, that was kind of you! Whatever made you think to do that?'

'I reckoned,' he said, trying to look severe, and failing miserably, 'that if I didn't keep my promise to encourage you, yon wee Miss MacGregor of yours would have me hung, drawn – and quartered.' He dropped a kiss on her nose. 'Come on, bonnie lass, let's go and fetch your stuff now.'

PART III

1931

PART III

1921

Chapter 19

'Daddy! Up!'

The childish voice was imperious. Robbie, arms folded over his chest, looked down his long length at the child. Arms outstretched, she was reaching up to him.

'Bit of a dictator, aren't you? Like that chap in Italy, what do they call him again? Mussolini. Come on then, you wee horror.'

Reaching down for her, he hoisted her up onto his shoulders. One chubby leg down each side of his neck, Grace Baxter chuckled with delight, and sank her fingers into the dark waves of her father's hair.

'Ow, you wee bisom! Don't pull my hair! Shall we run?'

Grace relaxed her iron grip on his head and clapped her hands.

'Aye, Daddy, aye!'

Robbie immediately broke into a slow, but deliberately jerky run, designed to shake his passenger up like a sack of potatoes. It provoked delighted chortles of glee from Grace. Kate, following at a more sedate pace along the riverside path, smiled after them. They got on well together, that pair.

Now and again her conscience still pricked her – when she was having difficulty in getting to sleep at night, or if she woke early on a spring morning. However, as time had moved on it had become easier to consign those kind of thoughts to that box of hers and slam the lid on them.

Occasionally, they got out again. Like when, worried by her seeming inability to conceive again, she had consulted young Dr MacMillan about the problem.

'What's your hurry, Kate?' he had asked. 'Why not just relax and enjoy Grace? You and Robbie had no problem having her, after all. Quite the reverse, as I recall,' he added, a distinct twinkle in his eye.

Kate, embarrassed beyond words, had dropped her eyes under that amused gaze. The doctor could obviously count quite well. Baby Grace had obliged her grandmother Lily by being just five and a half pounds at birth, light enough for it to be casually mentioned that her birth was a few weeks premature. If there were some raised eyebrows at that, Kate knew that most people assumed, as Dr MacMillan did, that she and Robbie had simply jumped the gun a wee bit. Robbie himself, stunned by the strength of his own reaction to the birth of his daughter, had paid such details scant attention.

He adored the little girl and spent a lot of time with her. It was two and a half years now since she'd come into the world and Robbie had been there right from the beginning, scandalising the midwife by wanting to be present at the actual birth.

'You cannae do that, Mr Baxter,' the woman had said. 'It wouldn't be decent.'

Surrounded by the disapproval of the womenfolk from both families, Robbie had been forced to bow to the inevitable. He laid a cool hand on Kate's sweaty forehead just before he was hustled out of her mother's front room.

'I'll be back just as soon as this gaggle of harridans will let me through the door,' he said softly, in a voice intended only for Kate's ears. 'Don't go away.' Bending, he had dropped a kiss on her cheek. As he straightened up, reluctant to take his leave of her, their eyes locked. Kate had never forgotten the look on his face that day. It spoke volumes, had said all the things she knew he longed to say to her, about how much he loved her, about the way he loved her.

She couldn't return that love in full measure, knew bitterly that she wasn't worthy of it, but she cared for him very deeply. He was her husband, her companion and her best friend, and she would have trusted him with her life – and that was love, too. Of a sort.

She'd seen too that he was scared, terrified of relinquishing her to the risky process of giving birth. She was frightened too, but for his sake she screwed up her courage, smiled at him and managed a few words.

'I'll be here.'

Grace, set down by her father, was running back to Kate, ready for another game of which she never tired. Spreading out both arms at her sides, Kate dodged from side to side across the path. Grace pretended to try to escape. She never did. That was part of the game.

'Caught you!' Crouching down, Kate wrapped her arms around the stocky little figure of her daughter, nuzzling her face into her neck. She couldn't get over the beautiful smoothness of Grace's skin, or how wonderful it smelled, soapy and fresh and new.

'I think I'll just eat you for my tea,' she told her daughter, 'you taste so good.' Planting a kiss on the young cheek, smooth as the bloom on a peach, Kate felt a shadow fall across her, and raised her head. Robbie was smiling down at both of them.

'Well, Grace Barbara,' he asked, 'shall we go home and see if your mother can find something else to feed us on?'

He bent down and planted a kiss on the line of Kate's jaw, just under her ear.

'You taste good too,' he whispered passionately. 'It must run in the family.'

Discomfited, she took Grace's hand, so that the child

walked between them, prattling away as they strolled back to Clydebank after a Sunday afternoon visiting both sets of grandparents in Yoker.

She wished Robbie wouldn't say things like that. As husband and wife they had evolved an easy companionship, their family life revolving around Grace, who had arrived so early in the course of their marriage.

Their partnership was a democratic one. Robbie had astonished Kate, at the end of their first week of living together, by presenting her with his unopened pay packet from the yard. She had taken it from him and looked, uncomprehendingly, first at it and then at him.

'What do I do with this?'

'Keep the house, of course,' he said easily. 'Give me back a wee bit for pocket money, and divide the rest between rent and food and anything else we need.'

'Oh,' she said, 'is that how it's supposed to work?' An unexpected shaft of sympathy for her mother pierced her. How often had her father drunk the lion's share of his pay before he'd even got home? Lily hadn't had it easy. Robbie, watching the emotions chase themselves across Kate's face, put a hand over hers, sealing the pay packet between them.

'I earn the money and I trust you to work out how to spend it. My pay belongs to both of us. I go out to work, you stay at home and run the house. We've both got our jobs to do – and I want you to take some pocket money for yourself.'

She seldom did. Emulating Agnes Baxter, she established an emergency fund instead. Kate's was in a box in the middle drawer of a sideboard she'd bought cheap at a saleroom. Increasingly restless as her pregnancy progressed, she had stripped the piece of furniture back to its original wood and set about repainting it in an Art Deco style, covering it first of all in white paint and then applying the decoration

– the Glasgow rose alternating with her own *motif* of a rowan tree.

The project gave her a lot of satisfaction. She missed the Art School a great deal, and wondered sometimes if she'd been too hasty in relinquishing the grant. She could hardly have gone back straightaway – not when she was growing larger every month with Jack Drummond's baby – but perhaps it could have been put in abeyance for a year or two. Robbie, she knew, would willingly have minded the baby on Saturday afternoons or one evening a week, but she *had* given it up and she knew very well that she had no chance of getting another one, not once she had become a wife and mother. When she was feeling sorry for herself, she told herself firmly that once she'd had the baby and it was old enough she would go back to the local art classes. She wasn't sure how she would afford supplies, but she would cross that bridge when she came to it.

She missed the daily companionship of her workmates, although some of them came to visit during the evening or at weekends. Mary Deans, now happily allowed to use her left hand, was one of them. She was walking out with Peter Watt from the Drawing Office. He and Robbie had become firm friends. Mary and Peter were going to wait to marry until Mary had completed her apprenticeship.

Kate privately wished she could have done the same. In low moments she was bitterly disappointed at the waste of her training. She'd been good at her job and she'd enjoyed it. All *his* fault, she caught herself thinking one day, and then immediately berated herself. Jack hadn't forced her, she had been an all-too willing partner. And despite it all, she knew that she still loved him.

With too much time on her hands as she grew larger and Robbie nagged her to rest more, she found herself spinning fantasies about Jack Drummond. In her mind she went back in time, imagined him chasing after her that night she'd walked

241

away from his car, begging her to marry him after all . . . Then don't be so daft, Cameron! she told herself. Or so ungrateful to the man who's given you his name.

She discovered that holding a brush or a pencil in her fingers was the only way of keeping uncomfortable thoughts like that at bay. She sewed too, buying pretty remnants and stuffing them with rags and stockings that couldn't be darned any more to make cushions to brighten up their little home.

Worried by all this frantic activity, Robbie secretly consulted his mother. Agnes nodded wisely, told him about the nesting instinct and instructed him to let Kate get on with it, just not to let her overdo it or lift anything heavy. So he came home from work and helped his young wife with the stripping down of the sideboard, and made her put her feet up more often than she wanted to and brought her frequent cups of tea.

Then Grace put in her appearance, and Kate, blossoming into motherhood, achieved a calmness and serenity that made Robbie fall in love with her all over again. He didn't tell her, of course. He was learning how to hide his feelings, seeing how uncomfortable it made her when he expressed them. She was happy with him as a friend and companion. So that's what he tried to be. Most of the time. Sometimes those self-same feelings boiled over and he just couldn't help himself. He tried always, whatever it cost him, to be gentle – in word and deed.

For Kate, as time went on, it became easier to forget what might have been. There was a bit of a hiccup when the *Clydebank Press* reported, complete with picture, the wedding of Miss Marjorie Donaldson to Mr Jack Drummond. The couple, the paper informed its readers, were to enjoy an extended honeymoon in the United States, sailing to New York from Southampton before returning to set up home in a luxury flat in the West End of Glasgow.

A bit different from a few days in Millport and a single end in Kilbowie Road then. She wondered if Marjorie knew that it was Mr Donaldson's money which was paying for it all. Alone in her own house, Kate laid the paper out on the kitchen table and studied their faces in the wedding photograph. Marjorie looked deliriously happy, Jack his usual amused self.

Marjorie had tried several times to get in touch with Kate, had even invited her and Robbie to the wedding. She wasn't to know why that was completely out of the question. Kate had rejected each overture, had gone to elaborate lengths to make sure that Marjorie didn't know that she was pregnant. If she knew, then Jack would know, and that would be unbearable.

She had worried about Agnes Baxter telling Marjorie or her mother, but the wedding dress and trousseau had been made in London, where the Donaldsons had a flat. It was all far too grand to entrust to a local seamstress, no matter how gifted.

Bent over the table, Kate looked at his face again. Had he thought about her on his wedding night? She still believed that he cared for her, but he had chosen money over love. She straightened up and glanced across at the baby, sleeping snug as a bug in a well-lined drawer laid carefully on top of the box bed. Money over love. It was the work of a few seconds to move her hands to the diagonal corners of the paper and crumple it up between them. She had a fire to light.

Taking a defiant pleasure in setting a match to the paper and watching the flames lick up over the kindling and the coal, she forced herself to count her blessings.

She had Grace and her own home. It might be small, but she was mistress of all she surveyed. Now that she was out from under her mother's thumb, she had high hopes that she might be able to build a new and different relationship with Lily – as equals. There weren't many signs of that happening as yet, but Kate was eternally optimistic about it.

The rest of her family – and Robbie's – were frequent visitors to Kate's little domain. She had the knack of making everyone feel welcome. Her sister Jessie, in particular, flourished under Kate's encouragement. She was at teacher training college now, and enjoying it. Robbie, too, was solicitous with her. It was he who'd gently coaxed her into talking about Barbara again.

Pearl was a different kettle of fish entirely. There were too many pretty dresses which she claimed to have bought out of her own small pay packet, too many nights when, Jessie told her, Pearl came home late from work. Kate confronted her about it one day.

Exasperated by Pearl's bland refusal to tell her anything, Kate had finally yelled at her. 'For Pete's sake, Pearl! Do you not realise that you could get a reputation? Well, I just hope that if you can't be good, you'll at least be careful!'

Pearl put her cigarette to her lips and smiled sweetly at her sister. Robbie disapproved of women smoking. Kate was going to have to throw the window open wide before he got home from work.

'Careful?' asked Pearl. 'Like you were, you mean?' she said, nodding at Grace, who was sat at the table, happily drawing houses and suns and smiling mummies and daddies on rough sheets of paper with the crayons Kate always managed to find money for.

Kate drew her breath in sharply. Pearl wasn't clever like Jessie, but she was shrewd, and she had sharp eyes. Kate often wondered how much she knew and, being Kate, worried that she had set a bad example to her younger sister.

Her worries about Pearl apart, though, life was not bad. And if Robbie turned to her in bed more often than she wanted and much less often than he did, that was just something which had to be put up with. He was her husband, and he had the right to expect certain things.

It was harder, though, to put up with the hurt look in his grey eyes sometimes – the look he thought she didn't see. Robert Baxter was one of nature's gentlemen. He did his best to hide those feelings from his young wife, but in her more honest moments Kate knew that he was profoundly disappointed by the lack of passion in their marriage. She became very adept at shutting that thought away in the box in her head.

Fortunately, Robbie was in work, not at Donaldson's any more, but along the road at John Brown's, where the keel had been laid for a new Cunarder. Not just any old ship, but the biggest ever built – one thousand feet long, Robbie had told her proudly, a great liner for the Southampton-New York run. The keel had been laid just before Christmas 1930, the first rivet being driven home by the shipyard manager. All the men – including Neil Cameron, who had also taken his labour to Brown's – had cheered, because of the hope the new ship had brought them. Her job number was 534 and as the 534 she was to become famous.

In contrast to the happy hustle and bustle at Brown's, things were looking bad for Donaldson's. It seemed that the yard might well become one of the victims of the Depression. Kate sometimes wondered if Jack Drummond was disappointed with the bargain he'd made. She never saw Marjorie these days. Now and again she heard or read something about the pottery studio. Despite the problems facing other businesses, it seemed to be doing well, gaining orders and presumably managing to make a profit. That would suit Jack.

Kate hoped, quite genuinely, that the new Mrs Drummond was making a go of it. Sometimes she fell to wistfully remembering the conversations the two of them had enjoyed. She missed Marjorie. If things had been different, they could have been good friends.

Despite her plans to go back to classes, Kate got her

sketch book and paints out less and less often these days, pleading Grace as an excuse. Occasionally, his mouth set in a determined line, Robbie spread the table with newspapers, filled empty jam jars with water and put out his wife's water colours and paper, announcing firmly that he would look after Grace for a couple of hours.

Kate tried to respond, but her heart wasn't always in it. She thought, perhaps, that Grace had inherited some artistic talent. Maybe it would be better to encourage that and leave her own ambitions lying. She would get back to it one day. She was Robbie's wife and Grace's mother. That was going to have to be enough for her in the meantime.

Chapter 20

'Doesn't it look pretty, Auntie Jess?'

'It does that, Grace. Everything covered in snow. Even the 534 looks bonnie.'

Kate sent her sister a smile over Grace's head. '*Especially* the 534. Mind you don't slip now, Grace. You could go your length here.' She extended a hand to her daughter, who was happily skipping between the two young women. It was late on a winter's afternoon in early December and they were on the way home after a visit to Mary Deans, off work convalescing from having her tonsils out. Mary lived in Radnor Park up off Kilbowie Road. The area was nicknamed the Holy City because the flat roofs of the tenements there were said to resemble those of Jerusalem.

'Except that it's hot out there, is that no' right?' Mary's mother had asked wryly. 'I dinnae mind ever being taught at the Sunday School that the Good Lord had a problem wi' dampness in His hoose.'

She was right; the flat-roofed design was less than ideal for the damp climate of the west of Scotland, but the residents of the Holy City did have a great view. On a clear day you could see right across the Clyde Valley to the hills of Renfrewshire, or upriver to Glasgow, the spire of the university standing tall on Gilmorehill. Closer in, the view was dominated by Brown's, and the skeleton of the 534, which jutted up from the yard towards the sky like some great spire itself.

The street lamps had just been lit and the pavement in front of them as they walked down Kilbowie Road was already beginning to glisten with frost. The dips in the surface which had been puddles at midday were soon going to be lethal for anyone not watching their footing. Kate shivered in the cold and pulled the collar of her coat more tightly about her. Jessie smiled at her and then at Grace, so warmly wrapped up herself that she looked like a wee ball of wool on legs.

'Your Mammy would think the 534 looks bonnie,' Jessie told her niece, 'because your Daddy, who's helping to fit the ship out, has just given her the money to buy a nice new winter coat.'

Kate grinned. She was pleased with the coat, all the more so because she didn't often get new clothes. Robbie, however, had insisted that she buy it. He knew full well how much she'd come to hate the old herringbone tweed coat which she'd been wearing for years, and which had been second-hand when she got it. That would now be relegated to the foot of their bed, an extra bit of covering for the cold winter nights.

Jessie, on her Christmas holidays from college, had helped her choose the coat on a shopping trip that morning. It was dark green, with a big shawl collar in black velvet. The coat was well cut, hung beautifully and made her feel beautiful too. She couldn't wait to show it to Robbie.

Kate glanced up at the Singer's clock, rising above the huge complex of the sewing-machine factory. The imposing tower was a landmark for miles around, the clock face, so she'd been told, the second largest in the world. An hour till he was due home. Grace's feet slid on a patch of ice. Kate tightened her grip on her hand, smiling down reassuringly, and Jessie took the little girl's other hand.

'I wonder what they'll call her,' mused Kate, nodding towards the 534.

Jessie tossed her head. 'Andrew Baxter reckons that the

Queen Victoria is the best bet. Typical, he says, of this country's backward-looking stance to the glory days of Empire and its refusal to reach out and embrace the modern world.'

Kate bit her tongue. Jessie, however, said it for her, smiling ruefully.

'I know, I know, he does talk like a political manifesto sometimes, but I—'

She broke off, colour staining her pale cheeks. Kate changed the subject, asking her a question about her studies. That kept them going till they got down onto Dumbarton Road and she and Grace had waved Jessie off on the Yoker tram.

But I love him. Was that what Jessie had been about to say? Kate thought it over as she and Grace walked the short distance from the tram stop back to their little flat. Andrew Baxter might profess to love all of mankind, but Kate had a suspicion that he had a rather more personal interest in womankind. She had seen him several times with different girls – all flashy types like Pearl. Jessie didn't stand a chance against that sort of competition.

Quiet and studious, she just didn't make the most of herself. She was always clean and neat, but she took little interest in clothes and she wore her brown hair as she had done since she was a child, neatly combed back into a pony tail. For the umpteenth time, Kate wondered what would have happened if Barbara Baxter had lived. Would she have brought her friend out of her shell as the two of them approached womanhood, given her some of her own happy-go-lucky spirit? She sighed. No point in heading down the road of what might have been. She knew that better than anybody. She led Grace over the crossing at the bottom of Kilbowie Road.

She'd made one of Robbie's favourites for tonight's tea – mince and tatties. The mince, thick with gravy and rich with carrots and onion and turnip, had been cooked that morning before she went out, and the potatoes were peeled and steeped in water, just waiting to be boiled. She'd got some butter to cream them with. Normally she bought margarine to save money, but Robbie didn't like the taste of it. Since things did seem to be getting a bit easier, and the 534 looked set to guarantee work for the next couple of years, she'd lashed out on the butter.

Walking up the stone stairs to their flat on the second floor, Kate thought how funny it was that having just a wee bit of money could make all the difference between being miserable and being happy. Knowing that she could afford the supplies now as well as the modest fee, she had joined a local Saturday-afternoon art club in the spring. Getting back to some serious painting again had been great, and she quickly realised that she'd been fooling herself when she had thought she could put off her own ambitions indefinitely.

They'd done sketches of the river and street scenes of Clydebank, gone up to the Bluebell Woods above the town for a more rural subject. Now that they were back indoors for the winter, some of the students were working those up into paintings, while others were concentrating on portraits, using each other as models.

And a little extra money meant that she'd been able to buy Grace a doll for her Christmas. Granny Baxter, in on the big secret, had made two sets of clothes for it. Grace would be old enough to understand about hanging up her stocking this year and she'd waken up on Christmas morning to find it filled with an apple, an orange, a few sweets and a shiny new penny. Kate was looking forward to seeing her wee face – especially when she saw her dolly.

For most adults, who went to work on Christmas Day like any other, the big celebration was a week later at Hogmanay, but Kate liked the idea of celebrating them both. She'd bought Robbie a present, too – a fountain pen. He seemed to be doing a lot of writing these days. She wasn't quite sure what – he was being unusually secretive about it. Och well, no doubt he would tell her in his own good time.

She had just put her key in the lock when the heavy door swung open. Robbie stood there. Kate blinked. What on earth was he doing home so early? She looked closer. He was very pale. She reached out a hand to him and he grasped it between the two of his, pulling her and Grace into the flat.

'Are you ill?' she enquired anxiously.

Clutching her hand to his chest, he shook his head, started to speak, then had to swallow and gulp and take a second shot at it.

'We've all been laid off,' he told her. 'They've stopped work on the 534.'

Chapter 21

At the beginning of the second winter of unemployment, in November 1932, Kate sold the lovely green coat. She got half of what she had paid for it. She used the money to buy food, and a pair of shoes for Grace, second-hand but in reasonable condition. She hated not being able to buy them new, but she searched long and hard to find a pair that were as good a fit as possible. At least now Grace wasn't going around wearing shoes which were letting in water and really past repairing – like her own.

She took the old shabby herringbone tweed coat off the bottom of the bed and starting wearing it again. She hated doing that too, but there was nothing else for it. Oh, but Robbie was angry with her when he found out.

'What did you sell your coat for?' he asked, his mouth set in a tight line.

'Because Grace's shoes were falling off her feet! Because I wanted us all to have something nice to eat for a change!' Kate flung back at him. 'The dole money doesn't buy very much.'

'I'd have happily done without,' he replied, tossing his head. He looked so haughty, glaring at her, his eyes like grey steel. She had never thought she would ever be on the receiving end of a look like that. It made her want to shout at him, to point out how thin he was, how thin they both were. They were doing without as it was, not taking their own fair share so that Grace could have the nourishment a growing child needed.

Angry and tired of it all, she had squared up to him, hands on hips, ready to give it laldy. The ghost of a smile had touched his mouth as he looked down at her. Then, his eyes softening, he had uttered one simple sentence, his voice low and husky.

'I wanted you to have a bonnie coat – a new coat.'

She learned a little more about male pride that day. How a man felt when he couldn't provide properly for his wife and family. Especially when he had the strength and the skills and the willing hands – but the work just wasn't there. That didn't stop Robbie trying to find some. Every day he tramped around looking for 'homers' – carpentry jobs that he could do to earn a few extra shillings to supplement the dole money.

With hundreds of men doing exactly the same thing, finding the wee jobs that still needed doing wasn't easy. More often than not he came home footsore and weary, and with nothing to show for his efforts but another hole in the sole of his shoe.

Kate tried to make some money herself by selling her pictures, going up to Glasgow and doing the rounds of the private galleries. At the first two she tried she was looked up and down and shown the door. She was a young woman in a shabby coat trailing a child by the hand. What could she possibly have that would be of interest to them? At the third one she was more persistent, insisting on opening her small portfolio. The woman in charge pronounced the four water colours of the Bluebell Woods to be *quite pretty*. Kate's heart leapt until the woman went on to reject them. 'It's a bit of a hackneyed subject, isn't it, the bluebells of Scotland?'

Back out on the pavement, Kate pulled Grace into the doorway of an unoccupied shop. Tilting her head back against the heavy metal grille which guarded the door of the empty premises she closed her eyes briefly. This was awful. It was like trying to sell part of herself.

'Mammy?' Grace was tugging on her skirt, an anxious look on her little face. Kate smiled brightly down at her.

'A few more places to go, Grace, and then I'll buy you a bag of sweeties.' She could just about afford it. Gathering her courage, she took her daughter by the hand. Robbie was doing this all day, every day. The least she could do was to keep trying for a wee while longer.

At the fifth gallery there was no interest in her pictures of Clydebank or the river – *too realistic* – the man said, but she noticed that he too lingered over the Bluebell Woods paintings.

'Charming,' he said slowly. 'Not an uncommon subject, of course, but you've brought a certain freshness to it.' He hesitated. Then Kate's hopes were dashed once more.

'No,' he said decisively. 'No. They're not really what's selling at the moment.' He waved a hand at his walls. Grace was looking around her in fascination, entranced by all the pretty pictures. 'Sophisticated interiors, picturesque foreign landscapes – the Italian lakes, little villages in the Swiss Alps . . . that's the sort of thing I need at the moment. Have you got anything like that?' He glanced up, looking at her over pince-nez spectacles. Shades of Miss Nugent.

'No,' said Kate, tired and fed up and unable to keep the sarcasm out of her voice. 'I'm finding it a wee bit difficult scraping up the train fare to Italy at the moment.'

'Sorry,' he said. 'That's what people want. Something to help them shut out the gloom and doom of the Depression.'

'Some of us aren't able to do that,' said Kate sharply. 'Come on, Grace.' She began scooping her paintings back into the portfolio, but the man put a hand out to stop her.

'Not so fast, young lady.' He was studying the pictures

254

again. 'They've definitely got something . . . I'd need them framed, though.'

Kate swallowed. 'I can't afford to get them framed. My husband's out of work.'

The man hesitated. 'All right. I'll take them. Come back in a month and I'll let you know if I've sold any of them.'

Kate put her pride in her pocket. 'I need the money now.'

He quibbled about that. He didn't know if he would be able to sell them after all, and he was going to have the expense of framing them. With the persistence born of desperation, Kate pressed the point. Eventually he agreed to give her five pounds for the four of them. She'd been hoping for more, but it was a lot better than nothing, and she was well aware that she had very little bargaining power.

The five pounds didn't last very long, as they were in arrears with the rent. Back in her own less than sophisticated interior Kate took her frustrations out on keeping the tiny flat ferociously clean and on tramping around Clydebank with Grace in tow looking for bargains. She got to know the times when the butcher would have bones to sell off for a few pence, learned to buy the vegetables which were cheaper because they were bashed, compared notes with other women about which bakers were selling off yesterday's bread and rolls at half-price. They lived on soup and she wore out more and more shoe leather through scouring the town for the ingredients to make it.

It all seemed worse because of the 534, rusting there in Brown's yard. Birds had even started nesting in it. You couldn't escape it anywhere in Clydebank, towering over the town like a great white elephant. There had been such high hopes, the day the keel had been laid. Those hopes were dust and ashes now.

Cunard, in severe financial difficulties, had pleaded with

the government to advance it sufficient funds to allow construction to proceed. The government refused. Clydebank's MP, Davie Kirkwood, added his voice to those passionate pleas. A skilled orator, he was quick to see the symbolism. 'I believe,' he said, 'that as long as number 534 lies like a skeleton in my constituency, so long will the Depression last in this country.' The rusting hull of the 534, which was to have been the greatest passenger liner ever, did indeed become a symbol of the Depression, and of the despair which blighted so many lives in those years.

Kate felt that despair too. She fought against it, trying to stay cheerful and positive for Grace and Robbie's sakes, but it was hard. It was the hardest thing she'd ever done. Sometimes it overwhelmed her, especially when she thought of how very different her life might have been.

She gave herself a shake whenever she found her thoughts heading in that direction, refusing to allow herself to dwell on what might have been. That was all in the past, like everything else in that magical year when it had really seemed as though things might be going to turn out differently.

Whenever she started to feel miserable she reminded herself that she had Grace, who had brought so much joy into her life. The little girl could even make Robbie smile, no easy task these days.

Day after day he came home tired and dispirited from the search for work which just wasn't there, sitting silently for hours on end beside the range after they'd finished their frugal evening meal. Grace would study him gravely and then speak.

'Are you sad tonight, Daddy?'

'Not when I look at you, sweetheart,' he always replied, and she would climb up onto his knee and cuddle into him. Kate often wished that she could do the same, show him that physical affection which she knew he had once craved so much from her.

She was by no means sure that he still did. Their days devoted to the struggle to survive, they both tumbled exhausted into the box bed at night. He turned to her less often lately, but when he did his need was urgent and overwhelming. That scared her and, however much she tried to hide it, she knew that he felt her shrinking from his touch.

He was never rough with her — it was not in him to be that — but the tenderness had gone. She herself was partially responsible for that. Frightened by his passion, she had rebuffed his attempts to hold her afterwards once too often. The last time they had made love – a month ago now – he hadn't even kissed her or murmured the usual soft words of thanks before turning his back on her.

Choking back silent tears, Kate had stared at that rigid back for what seemed like hours, lifting her hand to touch it more than once – and dropping it again each time.

Their easy day-time companionship also became a thing of the past. Worn down by lack of money, worried for themselves and everybody else, two proud people who had hurt each other without meaning to were growing further and further apart. Kate had always shied away from physical contact. Now they had become emotionally tongue-tied with each other.

If it hadn't been for Grace, Kate sometimes thought the house would have been completely silent. She had tried, just a couple of weeks ago, not long after that dreadful night when he'd turned his back on her. Heart-sorry for her weary young husband, pale and tired and painfully easing his feet out of his boots after a day tramping around looking for work, she had asked him tentatively how he'd got on. He had bitten her head off. She hadn't asked again.

One Friday afternoon in December 1932, a year after the men had been laid off, Kate trudged home wearily from a prolonged shopping expedition, little to show in her message bag for the effort she'd put into it. She'd walked two miles to a baker's which had been recommended – to save the tram fare – only to find that everything was sold out. Deciding perversely to walk all the way home again to save a further few pennies, a passing delivery van had driven through an icy puddle and drenched her legs and feet.

The only blessing was that she hadn't had to drag Grace around with her today. She had gone to her Granny Baxter's till tomorrow. When Kate got in she peeled off the old herringbone tweed coat and spread it over the backs of two of the kitchen chairs to dry.

Yee-uch! The damp wool smelled like a wet collie dog. She hated that coat with a passion. Her shoes were sopping wet from the soaking she'd got, not surprising when one of them had a hole in the sole and the stitching of the other was beginning to come apart. Kate stuffed them with a couple of sheets of old newspaper which she kept for that purpose and set them down to dry at the side of the range. Then she started towelling her hair, looking at herself in the small mirror which hung to one side of the sink.

'You look like a drowned rat, Mrs Baxter,' she told her reflection.

There was a knock at the door. Who in the name of the wee man could that be? Padding over the hard floor on her damp stocking soles she opened the door.

'Kate?'

Dumbfounded, Kate stared at the two people who stood there: Marjorie Drummond – and behind her the tall elegant figure of her husband.

Chapter 22

Marjorie was beaming at her, the smile spreading all over her good-natured face.

'Aren't you going to ask us in, Kate? You look as if you've just seen a ghost!'

Bemused, Kate swung open the door and ushered them in. Seen a ghost? You bet she had. Except that ghosts were airy-fairy creatures, trailing white robes behind them. He was far more substantial than that, wearing a smart trenchcoat over a fashionable suit. He was as handsome as ever, and he was standing in her home, smiling politely at her.

'Welcome to my humble abode,' she said, letting the towel slide to her shoulders. She hoped she hadn't stuttered as she said it.

Humble was the word. How must her home look to the well-off young Mr and Mrs Drummond? Well, like her father before her, she would just have to rise to the occasion.

She whipped her old coat off the two chairs, crossing the room to hang it from one of the hooks on the back of the front door. His eyes were on her when she turned back. Was he remembering the times he had helped her on with it? The first time, perhaps – that day in the tearoom when he had slipped the box of chocolates into her bag? She should just have sent him a thank you letter, Kate thought wryly. It would have saved a lot of heartache.

'Won't you sit down? I'll put the kettle on.' It was funny

how you could come out with the polite phrases while your brain was thinking entirely different thoughts.

Marjorie hadn't stopped smiling. 'It's great to see you, Kate. It really is. How's life?'

'Och, fine.'

All too aware that her surroundings and clothes gave the lie to that particular polite phrase, she took her time about filling the kettle and setting it on the range. She wanted to allow them time to rearrange their faces, although it probably wasn't necessary. They were both adept at hiding their real opinions and feelings. People like them always were. Any minute now Marjorie would tell her how charming the flat was.

Her visitor was holding out a small package. Kate took it and opened it. It was a packet of chocolate biscuits, not too fancy, nothing to which her fierce pride could take exception – just a little gift between friends. She should have remembered how thoughtful Marjorie always was.

Suddenly Kate was ashamed of herself, remembering how the other girl had tried to keep in contact and how Kate had firmly rebuffed every approach. She wasn't to know why.

Kate knew. So did Jack Drummond – part of the reason, at least. Marjorie, however, knew nothing. She must have been hurt by the way Kate had so completely cut her off.

'It's good to see you too, Marjorie,' said Kate warmly. 'I've missed you.'

Marjorie's smile, which had grown tentative, came back in full force. 'We called at your parents' house – that's how we got your address. You have a little girl, I hear. Grace, is it? Where is she?' She looked eagerly around.

'She's at Yoker. You must have just missed her.' Yes, it was funny how you could come out with the polite phrases. Funny too, how your voice could sound perfectly calm when you said them.

Thank God you just missed her! Now that she saw him again,

Kate realised that an anxiety which had been building up in her for some time was well-founded. Not only did Grace have those same blue eyes, there was another resemblance. The little girl had a particular way of extending her hand to you. It was a very graceful gesture – and she had inherited it from Jack Drummond. Change the subject, thought Kate.

'Do you have children, Marjorie?'

'No . . . no, we don't.' The light died out of Marjorie's face and Kate cursed her tactlessness. It was obviously a delicate subject. Change it again, then.

'How are *you*, Jack?' There, she had said his name – and she was sure she hadn't stuttered this time. The gracious hostess – even though she was living in a shabby one-apartment house, and was dressed in washed-out clothes, with her chestnut locks hanging in rats' tails around her face. She couldn't have fixed a worse reunion with Jack Drummond if she'd tried.

Something of the grim amusement she felt at the thought must have shown in her face, for he was smiling at her. As handsome as ever, she thought again – and was surprised how unmoved she was by that fact.

He shrugged. 'Oh well, you know how it is, Kate. Times are hard. I'm afraid I lost my position when Donaldson's went quiet.'

Judging by his clothes, Jack Drummond's definition of hard times was a bit different from her own.

Jack turned to Marjorie, laying a proprietorial hand on her shoulder. 'By great good fortune, however, I married a clever wife.'

Marjorie dipped her head in pleased embarrassment. She still loves him then, thought Kate. Poor Marjorie.

'The pottery's doing well?'

Marjorie lifted her sleek head. Confident again now that she was on familiar territory, she answered Kate's question.

'Surprisingly enough, the answer's yes.'

She launched into a speech about how they were managing to weather the Depression. There were still people and organisations with money to spend. It was simply a case of researching the markets – there were always going to be discerning buyers for tableware and crockery of high quality and innovative design. You had, of course, to offer it at the right price to the right market.

'You see?' said Jack, when Marjorie paused for breath. 'Isn't she just the complete businesswoman?' Sitting at ease in one of Kate's rickety dining chairs, an arm slung casually over the back of it, he was ostensibly lost in admiration of his wife. Kate, however, was aware of an unpleasant undercurrent. She turned to him.

'Do you help Marjorie in the business, Jack?'

'Of course he does,' chipped in his wife before he could answer. 'He's particularly good at dealing with some of the male clients. They don't like to talk to a woman, you see. Jack takes them out for lunch or has a round of golf with them.'

'Darling!' said Jack, lifting Marjorie's hand to his mouth and kissing it. 'You're too kind. I do nothing compared with how hard you work. She's at that place from dawn till dusk, Kate, would you believe it? I hardly see her these days.' He dropped his wife's hand.

'Oh?' asked Kate politely. 'Don't you spend much time there then?'

He gave her a charming smile. 'I'd just be in the way, my dear. And you know me – I'm a stranger to hard work.'

He meant the comment to be amusing, Kate saw that. That was what had attracted her to him in the first place. He thought everything was amusing. Life was just one big joke. Only she knew now that it wasn't.

Studying him as he sat there in front of her, so relaxed, so elegant, so happy to let Marjorie do all the hard work, she saw something else too. Felt it, like a physical sensation, as though a steel buckle had snapped open inside her chest. It gave her a pang – bitter-sweet memories, a twinge of regret – but no pain. That lack of pain was a considerable revelation to her, so much so she barely realised that Marjorie had started to speak about the pottery again, giving her further details about the business.

'I'm glad to hear someone's doing well, Marjorie.' Kate meant every word of it, but try as she might she couldn't keep the wistful note out of her voice.

Marjorie took a deep breath.

'Kate, I'm telling you all this for a reason. I'm doing so well that I really need help – particularly new ideas. I'm getting stale, Kate. I need someone like you.'

'*Me?*'

Swiftly, Marjorie outlined her proposals. Kate would work for her two days a week, developing new designs.

Kate's heart was thumping with excitement, but she put up every argument against it that she could think of.

'I have a child, Marjorie. What would I do with her when I was working?'

'Leave her with your mother, or Mr Baxter's mother, of course. It's only two days a week. Or you could work at home if you prefer.'

No, that wasn't an option. Marjorie might see Grace one day. That had to be avoided at all costs. In any case, getting Grace looked after wasn't really a problem at all. She thought up another one.

'I'm out of practice.'

'But you're still painting,' Marjorie put in swiftly. 'One of my friends bought a picture of yours a few months ago – one of the Bluebell Woods. It was exquisite. I recognised where it was and then I looked at the signature, and I saw that you had painted it.' She beamed again at Kate. 'That's what made me think of coming to see you.'

'I don't have the practical knowledge,' Kate objected, secretly basking in the praise. 'I didn't do pottery for long enough at the Art School.'

'I want your design skills. You would get the practical experience quickly enough. I've got people working for me who could teach you. Learn while you earn.' Long and leggy, Marjorie clasped her hands around one silk-clad knee and leaned back in the chair, smiling at Kate.

'You would pay me?'

Marjorie laughed. 'Of course I would pay you, Kate. I'm offering you a job.' She mentioned a figure. It was a generous one. Kate took a deep breath, then let it out again. There *was* light at the end of the tunnel. A job, doing what she loved and paying good money. It was the answer to her prayers.

A sound broke into the silence which had fallen as Marjorie waited for Kate's answer. It was the scrape of a key in the lock.

Chapter 23

A dark, brooding raincloud came into the flat. Its name was Robert Baxter. Three heads swivelled round to look at him. Kate could see that he wasn't in the best of tempers. He'd been in Bearsden today, tramping around the big houses up there looking for homers. By the look on his face he hadn't had a successful day.

Finding Marjorie and Jack Drummond sitting in his kitchen clearly did not improve his mood. Marjorie, sensitive to the abrupt change in atmosphere, had a nervous smile on her face. Kate, knowing how close Robbie was to the end of his tether, felt a wave of anxiety sweep through her. Only Jack Drummond, looking cool, calm and collected, seemed to be choosing not to respond to the sudden lowering of the temperature.

Robert Baxter did, however, remember his manners. Just.

'Mrs Drummond,' he said. He unbent sufficiently to give her a tiny inclination of his dark head. Then he became ramrod stiff again. His cool grey eyes flickered over Jack. 'Drummond.'

'Good to see you, Robbie,' said Jack easily, relaxing back into his seat and stretching his long legs out in front of him. His ease in another man's house served only to pinpoint Robbie's lack of it.

Kate, who had temporarily lost her voice on her young husband's entrance, leapt to her feet. 'We're just having some tea. Marjorie brought us some lovely biscuits. I'll pour you a cup—'

'I'll get it myself.' He hadn't raised his voice. His tone was perfectly neutral. So why was Kate's hand shaking as she lifted her own cup to her lips?

Unable to stand the tension any longer, Marjorie rushed in where angels fear to tread.

'Are you having any luck in finding a position, Mr Baxter?'

Robbie got down a cup and saucer from the shelf, poured in milk and tea, carried it over and placed it on the high mantelpiece above the range before he answered.

'There's no work, Mrs Drummond. You of all people should know that.' Donaldson's had closed its gates for good some time before Brown's had suspended work on the 534.

Robbie took a sip of tea, replaced his cup carefully in the saucer and then stood there, looking down his nose at all three of them – like a prince of the blood royal reviewing his palace guard and finding it wanting. Robert Baxter, thought Kate grimly, you and I are going to have words later.

There was an uncomfortable silence. Robbie lifted his cup and took another mouthful of tea. Marjorie, frowning slightly, also drank some tea. Poor Marjorie, thought Kate, she's trying desperately to work out what to say to calm these troubled waters. Jack allowed a little smile to play about his handsome mouth. He was doing what he always had done, taking a malicious enjoyment in the scene unfolding before his eyes – making no effort to smooth things out.

Kate sneaked a look at Robbie, standing as still as a guardsman by the mantelpiece. He was thin and pale and his jacket was threadbare. It was still buttoned up, although he'd loosened the yellow muffler which he wore around his neck in the winter. He was badly in need of a haircut. He looked tired and restless and his mouth was tight and unsmiling. There were fine lines on his forehead which hadn't been there six months ago.

In contrast, Marjorie and Jack looked well-off, well-fed and well-dressed. Jack also looked completely relaxed, a man with no worries. Yet, when she compared the two men, Kate saw something else. For all his shabbiness and fatigue, there was strength in Robert Baxter – and courage, too. Life had flung everything it could at him, and he was still standing, facing up to it all with pride and dignity. If he was going down, he would do it fighting.

Struck by all this – and by another thought so unexpected it took her breath away – Kate was caught completely unawares when Marjorie, after a brief sideways glance at her, addressed herself to Robbie.

'Actually, Mr Baxter, I've just been putting a proposition to Kate which might help you out a bit.'

Kate groaned inwardly. Didn't Marjorie know *anything* about masculine pride, what a fragile flower it was? No, of course she didn't. She was married to a man who didn't have one iota of it. He never had done. Content to live off his mother's money, then his wife's, Jack was always ready to blame ill-fortune on anything but his own lack of effort and direction. Always ready to let someone else do the dirty work. Like Suzanne Douglas that night at the Art School. That had been no accident, as Jack had pretended. Funny how she had refused to admit that to herself until now . . .

Marjorie was in full flood. Kate picked out a few words.

'A wonderful opportunity for Kate . . . allow her to use her artistic skills . . . earn some money for the family . . .'

Once more, Kate groaned inwardly.

Robbie stood as still as a statue, apparently listening politely to Marjorie. Kate knew better. His tea, lying ignored on the mantelpiece, must be stone cold by now.

Kate could hear the subdued sound of Mr Asquith's purring

coming from the box bed. Jack Drummond looked up and caught her eye. She had a sudden memory, crystal clear in its intensity; Jack, sitting in the kitchen at Yoker, stroking Mr Asquith with those long, elegant fingers . . . She flushed and dropped her eyes. She never knew what gave her the courage to look up again. He had been smiling at her bowed head. She turned to gaze at Robbie.

I wish I could do portraits, she thought. I'd like to capture him like this. So handsome – so fierce. She loved him for it – loved his stubborn, infuriating pride. Aware, somehow, that Jack Drummond's eyes were still on her, she turned her head again. He wasn't smiling now.

Kate had always thought that Marjorie had a rather pleasant voice – deep for a woman and with the merest hint of a well-bred accent – but it was grating on her now. Shut up, Marjorie, she pleaded silently. Then a tiny thought, but intense. Oh God, please make Robbie agree to this. I want to do this so badly, and it would help so much. The money Marjorie was offering would make all the difference.

There was complete silence in the room when she finally stopped talking. It was Jack Drummond who broke the silence.

'Well, Robbie, what do you say? It would be a great opportunity for Kate. Give you some extra cash. Make things a trifle easier.'

Kate waited for Robbie to explode. He did it quietly, and without noticeable fuss, but he did it nevertheless. Politely to Marjorie and much less politely to Jack Drummond, he told them to go away, that the Baxter family was quite capable of looking after itself, thank you very much, that his wife wasn't going out to work. He didn't actually say, not while he had breath left in his body, but that was clearly what he meant.

'But Mr Baxter—' began Marjorie, dismayed.

Robbie's face darkened. 'I believe I've made the position clear, Mrs Drummond.'

'But Mr Baxter—' Marjorie began again.

Jack Drummond rose to his feet. 'Don't waste your breath, darling. I think we should probably leave now.' He raised those fair eyebrows, in the gesture Kate had once found so endearing.

Robbie looked steadily at them both. 'I think that would be best, yes.' Then he said, with magnificent condescension, 'My wife will see you out.' As though, thought Kate, I was showing them out of a palace instead of a single end at the bottom of Kilbowie Road.

Chapter 24

The big door swung heavily shut behind Marjorie and Jack Drummond. Coming back into the room, Kate saw that her husband was standing where he had remained throughout the visit, motionless by the range. He was staring into space, but he turned immediately at her step.

'Kate . . .'

She made a dismissive gesture with her hand, cutting him off. 'Don't speak to me! Just don't speak to me!'

He let out a long sigh. The stiffness went out of his body and he threw himself into the chair so recently vacated by Jack Drummond. Taking her at her word, he said nothing, adding fuel to Kate's smouldering anger.

'How could you?' she raged.

He smiled blandly up at her. 'How could I what? Tell that cocky bugger – excuse me – where to go?'

Infuriated by that smile, she yelled at him: 'You've just told some money where to go! Money that we could be doing with!'

The smile slid from his face as though someone had wiped it off with a cloth. 'You'd take money from *them*?'

'No! I'd earn money! Doing what I'm good at. Can't you understand that?'

'I can understand that you want to show me up in front of everybody. My wife going out to work while I can't get any?' He shook his dark head. 'I don't think so, Kathleen.'

For some unaccountable reason, his use of her full name riled Kate even further.

'So it's your pride that's hurt, Robert Baxter? You're not man enough to admit that I might be able to earn good money when you can't?'

She stomped across the room and stood over him, hands on hips. A strand of her shoulder-length hair strayed across her mouth. Angrily, she blew it away.

'Is that what this is about? Your pride?'

His head bowed, his voice was so quiet she had to strain to hear the words.

'Maybe my pride's all I've got left.'

She was too angry to hear the plea in his voice.

'Don't you speak to me about pride, Robert Baxter!' She was shouting at him now. 'Do you think I don't know anything about pride? What about having to tramp for miles to buy second day bread? What about having to ask for a bone for the dog, when the butcher knows damn' well that we don't have one – that I'm using it to make soup for ourselves? What about trying to sell my paintings and having people looking down their noses at them? What about having to sell my lovely coat and wear that horrible old thing?' She gestured wildly to the back of the door where the tweed coat hung. 'How many times do you think I've had to put *my* pride in my pocket? Answer me that, Robert Baxter!'

His shaggy head bent, Robbie was studying his hands, clasped loosely in his lap. Infuriated by his lack of response, she put her hands on his shoulders, and shook him hard. His head snapped up. Stormy grey eyes met furious green ones.

Then, shrugging off her hands, he stood up, suddenly not calm at all.

'I don't want you to work!' he yelled. 'It's the man's place to do that! Can you not understand that, woman?'

271

Kate was rendered momentarily speechless. She stared at him, not believing what he had just said.

'You don't want me to *work*?' Spluttering, she waved a hand to indicate the room in which they stood. 'What the hell do you think I do all day?'

Robbie winced. 'Don't swear,' he said.

Kate's chin went up. 'I'll swear worse than that before I've finished. So you don't want me to work. Do you have any idea what I do all day? I look after Grace, I keep this place clean, I dust, I polish, I scrub, I cook. I clean the fire, I set the fire, I put coal on it – and the coal dust gets everywhere. I go all over Clydebank trying to stretch what money we've got as far as it'll go. Then I come home and I start all over again. Washing clothes, scrubbing, cooking. Trying to put something tasty on the table every night with precious little money to do it with.'

Her voice wobbled, but she clamped her mouth tightly shut for a few seconds and began again.

'And you don't call that work? How dare you insult me like that, Robert Baxter!'

He had heard the tremble in her voice. He reached out a tentative hand towards her but she was too angry to allow him to speak.

'Have you seen the state of my hands?' She thrust them out to him and hastily withdrew them. Like her voice, they were trembling.

'They're red and dry and hard from scrubbing and cooking and everything else that I do. I keep this place like a wee palace. Have you any idea what it's like keeping a place clean and tidy and not even being able to afford a bunch of flowers to brighten it up? Have you? *Have you?*' Her voice rose with each question.

'Kate. I'm sorry . . .'

'I'm sorry too.' Abruptly, she walked away from him.

Brought up short by the jaw-box, she hugged herself and stood staring out. She took a big, shuddering deep breath. It lifted her shoulders and her breasts.

Behind her, Robbie was silent. Trying to work out how to deal with me, she thought, a part of her brain, as usual, taking a step back and observing what was going on, rather than being a part of it. They'd had disagreements before, but never anything as bitter as this. Well, thought Kate, lifting her chin and tossing her head, it's up to him to speak, up to him to offer me an apology.

When none was forthcoming, she swung around. He had obviously been staring intently at her back, but she couldn't read the expression on his face.

'I want to do this,' she said. 'I want to take the work Marjorie's offering me.'

Had his expression softened? If it had, it hardened again when she spoke.

'No. No wife of mine is going out to work. Particularly not while her husband's idle.' The grey eyes had grown steely.

Kate curled her lip. 'No wife of yours? How many have you got, Robbie? I want to do this.' She was too proud to plead with him, but she added one more sentence. 'It makes sense for me to do this.'

He gave her a stern look. 'No. And that's final.'

Provoked beyond all endurance, Kate bunched her fingers into fists.

'Oh, in the name of God! Marjorie's offering me a good job with good money, and you can't get a job at the moment. Don't be so bloody pig-headed!'

'That's right. Fling it at me that I'm out of work! That I can't support Grace and you properly! That I'm not a real man!'

Abruptly, with jerky movements, he strode over to the sideboard which Kate had repainted. Pulling open the middle drawer, he took out the contents of the emergency fund – paltry enough these days.

'And just where do you think you're going with that?' she demanded.

He gave her back stare for stare, flinging his next words at her. 'Maybe I'll just go and have a drink! It aye seems to work for your father!'

All the colour drained from Kate's face. She could feel it. She was pale to the lips.

'You do that, then!' she shouted.

'I will! Don't you worry about that!'

He pulled the front door behind him with a crash that echoed up and down the stairwell. Kate, drained and quite exhausted, slid into the armchair and buried her head in her hands.

By the time she heard the knock at the door two hours later, she had regained some measure of composure, fragile though it was. After she had finished crying she had splashed her burning face with cold water several times, and pressed a wet cloth against her puffy eyelids. Then she had washed her hair, made herself a cup of tea and got on with the chores. What else could she do?

She saw the bouquet of flowers before she saw Robbie. He was holding it in front of his face and it was a large one – properly wrapped up and tied with pink ribbon and a bow. He lowered it slowly and gave her a tentative smile.

'Haven't you got your key?' she demanded.

'Aye.' He tried another smile. 'But I thought maybe I should ask you whether or not I can come in.'

Kate shrugged. 'It's your house.' She turned on her heel, not looking to see if he was following her. Sitting down at the kitchen table she clasped her hands in front of her and stared down at her interlocked fingers. There were some children playing in the back court, their voices and laughter drifting up to them. Somewhere in the distance a dog barked. Robbie's voice was deep and measured.

'Would you look at me, Kathleen?'

The children were playing hide and seek. Kate recognised the voice of the little girl who was doing the counting. 'Ready or not, here I come!'

In the stillness of the flat, Robbie repeated his request.

'Would you look at me, Kathleen? Please?'

The calmness of his tone undid her as the previous yelling had not. Tears welled up like a fountain, sliding down her smooth cheeks and falling onto her hands. He was there in an instant. Down on one knee beside her, he laid the bouquet of flowers on the table, lifted her hands onto her lap and covered them with his own.

'I'm so sorry,' he whispered. 'Can you forgive me for shouting at you, Kate? And saying all those terrible things to you?'

She didn't answer him because she couldn't. There was a lump in her throat the size of a tennis ball. Taking her silence for refusal, Robbie squeezed her hands and redoubled his efforts.

'I shouldn't have shouted at you. It wasn't fair, I know that. I do know how hard you work, believe me, I do. And you've made this place real nice – doing up the sideboard and making wee cushions and things like that. I know that too – and I appreciate it. I really do.'

He squeezed her hands again. Kate gulped, swallowing the lump.

'Do you?' she managed.

'Aye,' he said simply. 'I do.' Stretching up from where he knelt on the floor he kissed her gently on the cheek. 'You've made a real home for us here.' He glanced around, his mouth curving in an affectionate smile. 'It may not be much, but it's ours. And I love it. Do you know why, Kate?'

She shook her head.

'Because you're in it,' he explained, his deep voice very soft, and his grey eyes fixed on her face. 'And Grace, too. If I can have the two of you – and our wee home – then I'll be a happy man. That's all I need.' His smile deepened. 'Mind you, I wouldn't say no to getting back to work again, either.'

Kate decided to let that one go. It was a long time since he'd been in a good enough mood to laugh at himself. It might be a fragile state. She looked doubtfully down at him, kneeling at her feet on the hard floor.

'Should you not maybe get up? You'll get a sore knee – or pins and needles, at least.'

He tossed his head, flicking back his hair. His voice was robust.

'Bugger my knee! Excuse my French,' he added. Then, his face clearing even further, 'What's so funny?'

For Kate had smiled at last. She was laughing down at him.

'We've just had the worst fight we've ever had and you're apologising for swearing. Always the gentleman.'

The momentary amusement which had brightened Robbie's face faded.

'I thought *he* was the gentleman. Jack Drummond. The man you might have married.'

Kate caught her breath. It had never been stated so baldly. Robbie gave her a quick, darting glance and went on speaking, his voice deliberately light.

'He's the gentleman and I'm the horny-handed son of toil, is that not right? Except that I'm not toiling at the moment. Makes a man feel a wee bit useless.'

'Does it?'

Very tentatively, she slid a hand out from under his and

276

raised it to his face, gently touching his mouth. He kissed her fingers. She let him do it, but then, suddenly shy, she tried to withdraw her hand. He wouldn't let her. Grasping her wrist he kept her hand where it was, lightly resting on his jawline. His next question made her heart race.

'Do you wish you *had* married him?'

'No.'

His fingers tightened their hold on her wrist. 'I want an honest answer. Not the one you think I want to hear.'

She studied his face. In some ways he hadn't changed much since they had played together as children. His dark hair was tousled, just as she always remembered it. He was frowning, his dark brows almost meeting over his long straight nose. It was how he always looked when he was trying to puzzle out the answer to some problem that was troubling him.

There was something different about his eyes, though. Where once there had been only youthful enthusiasm and zest for life, there was now caution. There was hurt too, in those deep grey pools – a man's hurt. Adversity had put it there – Barbara's death, unemployment, the struggle to survive . . . she herself?

Her gaze fell to his lips; her artist's eye saw their colour – a dark pink – and their beautiful shape. There was a tiny amount of extra fullness on the lower one and the lips were slightly parted. It was a man's mouth, not a boy's.

Kate Baxter realised something then, realised too that she had known it for some time. It had taken the catalyst of Marjorie and Jack Drummond's visit, and the tensions released by that visit, to make her see it. She looked up, and the green eyes met the grey ones once more.

'I married the right man.'

He grabbed her other hand, a spark of hope in his eyes.

'You're not crossing your fingers.'

'You know I do that?'

'I know you do that.' The gleam in his eyes was growing, but he was still cautious, scared to hope.

Kate leaned forward and kissed him, her own lips, like his, slightly open. 'I love you.'

'Oh, Kate,' he sighed against her mouth. She was startled when he gave a sudden yelp of pain.

'Robbie, what's the matter?'

Leaping to his feet, he yanked out one of the chairs from the table and sank down onto it.

'My knee's killing me, that's what's the matter. Oh, bloody hell – excuse me – oh, bugger – sorry – I have got the pins and needles!' He was rubbing furiously at his leg. Glancing up, he caught sight of Kate's face. 'Stop laughing! It isn't funny!'

But then he was laughing too and suddenly they were both standing up, having a fit of the giggles.

'I'd better put the flowers in water,' said Kate finally, wiping her eyes. 'Did you really walk through Clydebank carrying them?'

'I did,' he said, trying to look severe. 'The comments I had to put up with. Everyone's a comedian in this town, have you noticed?'

When she had arranged the flowers to her satisfaction – a task which they both knew had taken much longer than it merited – he produced a small package. Kate unwrapped it carefully. It contained a bottle of hand cream, perfumed with lily of the valley.

'Give me your poor wee rough hands and I'll rub it in for you,' said Robbie matter-of-factly. Before she could pro-test he took both her hands, laid them face down on the table and dropped a small bead of the lotion onto each one.

'Oh! That's cold.'

'Keep your hands still. It'll warm up soon.'

He was meticulous in his work, rubbing the cream carefully

into the backs of her hands and then instructing her to turn them over.

Kate allowed her head to fall back. Coldness again. Twice, as he dropped two spots of the scented cream onto her palms. He stroked it into her fingers, one by one, from base to tip, his work-roughened skin benefiting from the lotion as much as hers. Kate sighed contentedly.

'Nice?'

'More than nice,' she murmured. 'Oh!' Her eyes opened.

'What?' He was smiling. 'What are you feeling?'

She was breathless. 'Funny feelings . . . funny sensations in funny places . . .'

'Nice sensations?' His smile was slowly broadening and his eyes were beginning to sparkle. 'Fancy the same treatment somewhere else? Your back, for instance? Very relaxing, a back rub – so I'm told. Of course, you'd have to take some clothes off.' His eyes went to her breasts. 'Your blouse, for a start. And it might be more comfortable if you lay down.' His hands being fully occupied he made a gesture with his head. 'On the bed, that is.'

She went completely still, and he cursed himself for an idiot. He had rushed her. The sparkle died out of his eyes and he stopped massaging her fingers.

'You're still scared of it.'

'I've always been scared of it.'

He knew that was true, but he wasn't going to give up without a fight. Not this time. It was for her too, after all.

'I think, maybe,' he began, choosing his words, 'that if you let me try, I could make it nice for you. If we take it very, very slowly . . . if you allow me to woo you, to pay court to you.' His voice was a whisper. 'To make love to you.'

He was asking a lot. He knew that. If she turned him down,

he was just going to have to live with it. He loved her far too much to insist.

'Robbie, look at me . . .'

Her hand was at the collar of her blouse. She was beginning to undo the buttons.

'Slowly?' she asked, and he saw how scared she was. He hadn't thought that it was possible to love her any more than he did. He had been wrong.

'Slowly,' he promised. Her hand was trembling. He put his own over it to hold it steady. 'But would you consider letting me do this?'

'Be my guest,' she whispered.

Kate opened her eyes cautiously the next morning. He was awake, propped up on one elbow watching her.

'Good morning, Mrs Baxter.'

'Now I know why people make such a fuss about it.'

His smile, broad already, grew broader still.

'So I've done something right at last?' The guarded look had gone completely from his eyes. They were filled now with mischief. 'I kind of thought you were enjoying yourself – judging by the funny wee noises you were making.'

'I was *not* making funny wee noises,' said Kate indignantly, struggling up onto her elbows. Then she stopped. 'I was, wasn't I? I'm sorry,' she mumbled.

Robbie laughed and took her in his arms. 'I loved your funny wee noises, hen. In fact, I was hoping that I might hear them again sometime.' He raised his eyebrows in enquiry. 'How about tonight?' He kissed her. 'And maybe tomorrow night? And maybe the night after that, as well? Mmm?' He punctuated each question with a kiss.

Kate, safe and warm and loved in his arms, smiled.

'As often as you like.'

He smiled warmly back, turning with her in his arms so that

he lay on his back with her above him, her hand lying lightly on his chest. He played idly with a strand of her chestnut hair, tousled now as his so often was.

'Do you really mean that?'

'I do.' Then, seeing that he still needed reassurance, she bent and kissed him. 'You did good work last night, Robert Baxter. Maybe I'm going to become insatiable.'

His eyes lit up at her choice of word. 'Insatiable?'

'Aye. I'll be wanting you to m-make l-love to me all the time.' Kate stumbled over the phrase, shy still for all her bravado, but she went gamely on, poking him in the chest. 'You'll be worn out before I'm finished with you.'

His grin was a joy to behold. He kissed her again. Thoroughly.

'All the same, Kate,' he said when he had finally finished, 'much as I would like to, we can't just make love *all* the time.'

'No?' She lifted her head in mock-surprise, waiting for the joke.

'Not when you're at work, certainly.'

'What?' She jerked up, her heart beating too fast.

Robbie was trying for the pained look. 'Well, you don't think I'd have spent the emergency fund on frivolities like flowers and hand cream if I hadn't been planning to send you out to work, do you? You'd better go and see Marjorie first thing on Monday.'

Kate, her green eyes wide, came up on her knees onto the bed. 'You mean you don't mind? You'll agree to me going out to work?'

Robbie nodded smugly.

'You pig!' yelled Kate. 'You rotten pig!' Bending forward, she yanked the pillow out from under his head and began hitting him with it. Laughing, he fended her off.

'Help! Help! I'm being attacked by a wild woman. Ow! Stop

it, you wee bisom.' But he was laughing too much to stop her. When she paused for breath, he grabbed her by the waist and turned her neatly over so that she was lying beneath him, the pillow between their bodies.

'We'll just get rid of this.' He raised his body and pulled out the offending object.

'Ahhh . . .' breathed Kate a few seconds later.

'Going to stop hitting me now?'

Her eyes, which had closed, opened enough to show him a gleam of green. 'Not a chance, pal.'

'Wild woman, eh? I'll just have to use devious methods to pacify you, then.'

Which he did, to his and Kate's complete satisfaction, until it was time for them to go and fetch Grace.

Chapter 25

Robert Baxter was walking with a spring in his step these days. People who knew him saw that he smiled more readily and that the look of defeat had gone from his grey eyes. Those who met him for the first time saw a darkly handsome young man with a charming smile and an air of quiet self-assurance. It made him very attractive – to both sexes – and it got him more work. He had lost the air of desperation which had hung around him before.

When Kate started working in Marjorie's studio two days a week – Mondays and Wednesdays – Robbie matter-of-factly stated that he would confine his tramping around looking for homers to Tuesdays and Thursdays. On the other days he would look after Grace and do the housework and make the tea for Kate coming in. Kate had raised her eyebrows at that one, but wisely said nothing. The arrangement would give the three of them Fridays and all weekend to spend together. And if Grace's doting grandparents or equally besotted young aunts and uncles offered to take her for a few hours at the weekend to allow Kate and Robbie some time to themselves . . . well, so much the better.

What Marjorie paid Kate for the two days at the studio was a good wage, a lot more than the dole he'd been getting previously. If they were careful, it would allow them to live quite well. There was really no need for Robbie to wear out shoe leather and his own strength, searching for wee jobs. Except that there was every need for him to do it.

Kate said resignedly, 'I suppose you feel you have to?'

'Aye.' Grinning, he had dropped a kiss on the end of her nose. He wondered how he had never noticed before that it turned up very slightly at the end. He adored it, but then he adored everything about her, from her chestnut-brown hair, dancing very satisfactorily on her shoulders, through her trim but shapely figure to her neat, size five feet, now shod in smart little brown leather shoes with no leaks. On his insistence, that had been the first big purchase from her pay.

She came home after that first week working for Marjorie and handed over her pay packet to him. That made him laugh, but there was a rueful tinge to it, and he handed the small brown envelope straight back to her.

'No, hen, it's your money. You earned it fair and square.'

'It's *our* money,' Kate insisted. 'Just like the money *you* earn is our money.'

Robbie smiled at her logic, but shook his head. 'No, Kate. It's best if you deal with money matters.'

'But you'll take some money out of this.'

He didn't answer, and she saw that she was going to have a fight on her hands to get him to take any pocket money at all from her pay, but she was wise enough to bite her tongue for the moment.

'Aye, I need to go out and look for work. To prove my manhood, like.'

'I thought you had found other ways to do that,' murmured his wife. Smiling broadly, Robbie took her in his arms and kissed her. He couldn't believe how lucky he was. Sometimes he wanted to shout it out in the street.

'Kathleen Cameron loves me!'

He had found a poem in the course of his voracious reading which seemed to sum it up perfectly.

284

Jenny kissed me when we met,
Jumping from the chair she sat in;
Time, you thief, who love to get,
Sweets into your list, put that in:
Say I'm weary, say I'm sad,
Say that health and wealth have missed me,
Say I'm growing old, but add,
Jenny kissed me.

He didn't shout out his love to the heavens of course, but the knowledge gave him confidence, so that when he knocked on doors looking for any chairs that needed mending, or cupboards to be built, the householder felt confident too, and he got a lot more jobs than he had previously.

One morning about four months after Kate had started working for Marjorie, he knocked on the door of an elegant modern flat in the West End of Glasgow. A woman in her thirties answered. She was very attractive, with a mass of blonde hair loosely piled on top of her head. She initially opened the door just a crack, made as though to swing it wide, then seemed to hesitate when she saw him standing there in his working clothes. However, she listened attentively while he politely asked her if she had any carpentry jobs that needed doing, head cocked to one side, as though she were concentrating hard on what he was saying.

When she spoke, he understood why. She was foreign – French, he thought, her English heavily accented, but she nodded her head enthusiastically.

'Yes, yes, I do have some work for you. Come in.'

She led him to a bedroom where a wardrobe was half-built into an alcove. The original builders had gone bankrupt, she told him, and she had not been able to find anyone to finish the work. Could he do it, did he think? Gesturing vaguely at the pieces of wood stacked up neatly inside the structure, she said that she thought everything necessary was there.

He checked the wood lying around, evaluated the half-finished job with a practised eye and calculated that it would take him the better part of the day to complete. He quoted her a price and she accepted without demur.

'What is your name?' she asked.

'Baxter. Robbie Baxter.'

Busy unpacking his tool kit, his mind already on the job, he glanced up at the woman as she stood framed in the doorway. She wrinkled her nose.

'Robbie?'

'Robert,' he explained, smiling at her.

'Ah! Now I understand. *Robert*.' She said it in the French way, rolling the *r* softly on her lips and leaving the *t* unpronounced.

'Aye,' he grinned. *'Robert.'*

'I am *Jeanne*,' she told him. 'I shall fetch you to lunch at one o'clock.'

He had brought his own piece and a flask of tea with him, but if she wanted to feed him as well as pay him, he supposed that was all right.

Five minutes into lunch, he had worked out exactly what sort of a house he was in. If the rather racy paintings on the red-painted walls of the dining room hadn't given him enough of a clue, the fact that they were joined at the table by three young ladies wearing various forms of elegant sleeping attire left him in no doubt. How much sleep anyone got in this house was probably debatable, he thought, smiling as he applied himself to a bowl of the most delicious soup he had ever tasted.

He raised his eyes to find Jeanne surveying him with a smile.

'Are you shocked?'

Robbie shrugged his shoulders, filling out again now that he and Kate could afford to eat properly once more.

'Why should I be shocked?' The surroundings were pleasant, the girls were chatting happily to each other and to him. There didn't seem to be any compulsion. To be sure, it wasn't something he would have wanted for his own – or Kate's – sisters but nobody was in a position to judge anybody else, he reckoned. We all do what we have to in this world. He said as much to Jeanne. She smiled.

'I think you are a very nice man, *Robert*.'

Robbie asked what the soup was. When he learned that it was cream of mushroom he told her that he'd never tasted mushrooms before – in soup or in anything else. All four women around the table expressed surprise.

'Give him another plate, Jeanne,' said one of the girls, an attractive redhead. Her name was Marie-Louise, although she sounded as west of Scotland as himself. No doubt she put a French accent on for her clients. 'He could do with some fattening up.' She gave him a wink and cut him a second slice from the loaf which sat on a breadboard next to the white china tureen which held the soup.

Towards the end of his second helping of soup, he became aware that no one at the table was talking. Looking up, he saw that all four women were sizing him up with what looked like a professional eye. He had a horrible feeling that he knew what was coming next. He did.

Blushing a beautiful shade of dark red, he stammered an apologetic refusal of their offer to pay him for his day's work not in money, but in kind.

'One of my young ladies – or maybe all three?' enquired Jeanne, looking at him over the soup tureen. As though she was offering me three for the price of one at the greengrocer's, thought Robbie through a haze of embarrassment, shot through with an insane desire to burst into a hysterical fit of the giggles. That and the real terror that his anatomy was going to react to an all too vivid image of himself entwined on a bed with the three girls. What a story to tell Kate!

'It is not that we are short of money, you understand. We thought perhaps you might appreciate the offer.'

'Th-thank you. It's very kind of you. Th-thank you,' he stuttered again. *It's very kind of you?* What was he saying! 'But I'll have to say no.' Surely that was definite enough. They would take no for an answer – wouldn't they? He could feel the sweat breaking out on his forehead.

'*Quel dommage.* What a pity. My girls would have enjoyed a handsome young man for a change.' She swept him a glance which went from his head to his toes – and all points in between. 'And you would have enjoyed it too.'

'I-I'm s-sure . . . but I-I'm a married man, y-you k-know.'

One of the girls spoke. 'Darling, most of those we get in here are married men.'

The others laughed.

'Only not the sort who are madly in love with their wives,' said Marie-Louise, and just for a moment an expression of the most profound sadness passed over her face. It was gone so quickly that Robbie wondered if he had imagined it. He stood up.

'I-I'll be getting on then. Thank you for the meal. It was delicious.'

'Any time,' murmured the girl who had made the comment about married men. Somehow Robbie knew she wasn't talking about mushroom soup.

'Ow!' He had hit his thumb with the hammer. Swearing softly under his breath, he extracted a handkerchief from his pocket and bound it round the offending digit. Kate would have bawled him out if she'd seen it. It was none too clean. For a moment he toyed with the idea of asking one of the girls for a bandage. No, daft idea. Presenting himself as a wounded soldier might well lead to other things.

He swore again. He was as human as the next man and he was too honest to pretend that the image of himself entwined with the three girls hadn't flitted across the private picture screen in his brain several times that afternoon. Three of them together, just imagine it. He didn't doubt that they could teach him a thing or two . . . quite a few probably. But really tempted? Not in a million years.

Sitting on the floor by the almost finished wardrobe, he allowed his head to fall back against the wall and his mind to wander where his thoughts most often went these days – to Kate. Kate, her green eyes bright and expectant, turning at the sound of his key in the lock. Kate, standing at the range stirring something, sinking back against him as he slid his arms around her trim waist.

He heard the doorbell ring and then voices – one male, one female. He wondered idly if Jeanne rented out rooms by the hour. Then his mind went back to Kate.

She was turning in his embrace now, lifting her lovely face for his kiss. He could feel the soft warmth of her breasts against his chest. Now he could see them in his mind's eye, rising to the touch of his gently exploring fingers . . .

Something else was going to be rising soon if he didn't abandon this train of thought, he thought, his lips twisting in a wry smile. But not yet, not just yet. She was shy still – they both were – but she was beginning to offer him her own tentative caresses in return for his own. *Caress*. What a lovely word. He said it out loud, rolling it around his mouth.

'Caress.'

It was a rare word. Could he work it into a poem, somehow? He'd always liked reading poetry, now he was beginning to write it. He hadn't had the courage to show Kate any of his efforts yet, but he would soon. Most of them were about her. He didn't think she would laugh at him.

His mind drifted back to the mental image of her, beneath him in the gloom of the box bed, her hair shining against the dull gleam of a white pillow. She was so warm and willing, so loving . . . His eyes snapped open and he scrambled to his feet. He was the luckiest man alive, and he wanted to get home to her right now. It was early yet and the days were beginning to lengthen as spring approached. They could go for a walk by the river before tea.

It took him twenty more minutes to finish the job and pack away his tools. Jeanne pronounced herself delighted with his work and paid him what had been agreed, plus an extra half-crown.

'Call again in a month or two,' she told him, as they stood in the lobby of the flat. 'I might be able to find something else for you.'

'Aye, of course.' He wondered if he would. Maybe Kate would ban him from coming back once he'd told her the story. She'd be scared he wouldn't come home with his virtue intact the next time. Aye, this was going to make a rare story.

A door opened behind them. Swinging around in automatic reaction, Robert Baxter stared at the couple coming out. An untidy bed, testament to what they'd been doing for the last half hour, was visible behind them. The girl was still doing up her blouse. The man turned to kiss her, one hand resting, casually proprietorial, on her breast. He squeezed it, and she giggled.

Robbie looked at them with horrified eyes.

'Pearl Cameron!' he thundered. 'What the hell do you think you're doing here? You'd better have an explanation for this, young lady!' Which, as he reflected afterwards, was a bloody stupid thing to have said. The explanation for what she had been doing was only too obvious.

Pearl jumped as though she'd been stung by a wasp, and went as white as paper. Her companion, however, raised his head and looked Robbie in the eye.

'Well, if it isn't the puritanical Mr Baxter,' he drawled in his elegant, well-bred tones. 'How very nice to see you again, old chap.'

It was Jack Drummond.

Chapter 26

It had happened at last. Kate felt like dancing out of Dr MacMillan's surgery. Even when she had missed a period she hadn't dared to hope. She was beginning to think she and Robbie weren't meant to have any more children, but now the doctor had confirmed it.

She was walking on air as she went down Yoker Mill Road. It was March, but one of those days when you knew that spring was just around the corner. The sun was melting patches of snow on the top of walls, and crocuses were opening up in the gardens she passed.

Just like me, thought Kate happily. I've opened up to Robbie and now our child is opening up within me. He was going to be so happy. When they'd married he'd said that he wanted a house full of bairns.

She was going to miss the studio: the company, the sights and sounds, the smell of the clay, the satisfaction of seeing her designs transformed from paper into a three-dimensional object. Marjorie had given her a great deal of freedom to experiment and develop her ideas. Within a month of starting, Kate had developed a range of crockery which was to become known as *Rowan Tree Ware*. Marjorie was delighted with it and convinced it was going to become a huge success.

The two young women had developed an easy working relationship. Marjorie, Kate knew, would happily have taken it further. Kate had two objections to that. Politely but firmly she turned down every invitation to the Drummonds' flat in the West End of Glasgow. There was no way she could sit and drink tea or sip cocktails with Jack Drummond – and she knew damn' well that Robbie, normally the most amenable of husbands, would refuse point blank to do so. It was bad enough that she occasionally had to meet Jack at the studio, although he didn't call in often. His interest in the pottery was restricted to the profits it produced.

The greatest obstacle in the path of her friendship with Marjorie was Grace. Not only had she blithely knocked a year off her daughter's age when responding to Marjorie's friendly interest in the child – fingers firmly crossed behind her back of course – she had gone out of her way to avoid Marjorie ever catching a glimpse of the little girl. The resemblance was there. She just couldn't take the risk of Marjorie noticing it.

It took all the efforts of the madam and the three girls to stop Robbie punching Jack Drummond in the mouth there and then.

'You'll bring the police to the house and they'll close us down and my girls will be out on the streets,' said Jeanne urgently. 'You wouldn't do that to them, would you, *Robert*?' She was pleading with him, her lovely face troubled. She gestured towards Pearl. 'And she's willing, this girl—'

'My sister-in-law.' The words were innocuous, a mere explanation of the relationship between Robbie and Pearl. The look which accompanied them was anything but. Pearl flinched under the force of it. She hadn't known that Robert Baxter was capable of such anger. Neither had he.

'You won't tell Kate, will you, Robbie?'

He was breathing heavily. They had dragged him to a couch in the hall and sat him down on it – a girl at either side of him, hanging anxiously onto an arm each. He shook them off.

'It's all right. I'm not going to hit him. Not here, at any rate.'

The girls looked alarmed, but they released their hold on his arms, although they remained seated like sentinels beside him.

Jack Drummond, leaning nonchalantly against the door jamb of the bedroom which he and Pearl had been using, brought out his gold cigarette case. He took one out, lit up and blew several smoke rings before he spoke.

'Is that a threat, Baxter?'

'Take it any way you like, Drummond.'

The air crackled between them. There was something in it Robbie didn't quite understand, but one thing he knew. This man had hurt his Kate, and now he was hurting her sister – only the silly wee bisom couldn't see that. She was pleading with Robbie now, begging him again not to tell Kate. He lifted a hand to stem the flow of talk.

'He's a married man, Pearl. Doesn't that mean anything to you?' An image of Marjorie Drummond flashed across his mind's eye. This would crucify her, if she ever learned of it.

'I know what I'm doing.'

It was a front – he could see that. As much of a mask as her marcelled hair and the heavy make-up she wore. He looked sternly at his sister-in-law.

'You're only nineteen, for God's sake, Pearl. Nineteen!'

'Mmm. Old enough,' came the drawl he was learning to hate. 'And just *deliciously* young enough. You ought to try it sometime, Baxter. Variety is the spice of life, after all. But I hear from Jeanne that you're quite the old faithful married man. How touching.'

Robbie rose so quickly from his seat that he took his two guardians by complete surprise. As his fist made contact with Jack Drummond's face he felt nothing but satisfaction. The bastard was going to be nursing a beautiful black eye

294

tomorrow. Good. Let him explain *that* to his wife and their rich friends.

Jack Drummond, however, albeit pushed back against the wall by the force of Robbie's blow, was *smiling* at him. Then he began to speak. And as the words spilled from his mouth, Robert Baxter's world shattered into a thousand pieces.

As she came down onto Dumbarton Road an elderly man stopped at the sight of her.

'Have you come into money, hen? Naebody's got the right to look as happy as you do this afternoon.'

Kate beamed at him in passing. 'Much better than money,' she said. 'Much better.'

He smiled back. 'Well, God bless you, pet.'

Money, in fact, was going to be tight. However, she could go on working for the next three months – maybe four – and the emergency fund was healthy. A mile or so along the road, the hull of the 534 was still looming, rusting, over the town. Now and again the *Clydebank Press* reported plans to get work started on her again, but so far nothing had come of it.

Surely something would happen soon? Of course it would, Kate told herself firmly. On a day like today anything seemed possible. Work would restart, the men would be earning again. Once the baby was old enough, she could go back to working for Marjorie. Everything was going to be just fine. She walked across the road to the tram stop.

'Hello there, it's only me,' she called out as she pushed open the front door. The house seemed strangely quiet.

'Robbie, did you forget that you were to collect Grace today? Robbie?'

He was standing staring out of the window, his back to her, and he hadn't turned to greet her. Sharp as a shard of broken glass, a bolt of anxiety shot through Kate.

'Robbie, is something the matter?' She crossed the room and put a hand up to his shoulder, taking an involuntary step back when he whirled around and hissed at her through gritted teeth.

'Don't touch me!'

His face was pale, his eyes as cold and flat as the river in winter. She knew then. Knew even before he looked at her and asked the question which changed everything.

'Grace is Jack Drummond's daughter, isn't she?'

A terrible stillness descended on the kitchen.

He had worked it out on the way home. Done the sums. It was easy enough when he put his mind to it. The date of his sister's death was burned into his brain. He could pinpoint every event by relation to it. Funny how it had never occurred to him to do the calculations before.

A lot of things had never occurred to him. Like the fact that Grace had supposedly been born a good month early, yet she was a healthy bouncing baby. Like the real reason why Kate had been so terrified on their wedding night. Not the natural fear and embarrassment of a shy and innocent bride, as he had thought, but the fear of him finding out that her virginity, that most precious of gifts, had already been given to someone else. To Jack Drummond.

'You ought to listen to me, Baxter,' he had advised, ignoring the blood oozing from his nose. 'I'm by way of being a bit of an expert on the Cameron girls.' He had paused then, deliberately prolonging the agony, playing with Robbie as Mr Asquith might have played with a mouse, pushing Pearl's hand away as she dabbed with her handkerchief at his face.

'I've had this little trollop several times,' he said softly. Then, watching Robbie's stricken face grow paler and paler, 'And I've had your wife too.' Jack Drummond smiled, and his voice grew smooth as silk. 'Before you ever did, Baxter.'

Robbie wasn't entirely clear what had happened next, except that his brain and his tongue began frantically trying to deny what had just been said. Jack, still smiling, went on to supply him with the details: when and where and how, talking about Kate, his Kate, in a way that made Robbie's skin crawl. He had slumped back down onto the couch, and he had mumbled Kate's name. Then Grace's. Pearl, still kneeling beside Jack, had shot him a quick, sharp look.

He didn't remember leaving the flat. He found himself on the tram heading back to Clydebank, his brain doing somersaults and his heart growing heavier and heavier as each stop brought him closer to home. What had used to be home.

Kate's mouth had gone dry and she had to lick her lips before she could speak. The words came out as an agonised whisper.

'How did you find out?'

A grimace contorted Robbie's lips. 'Not going to deny it then?'

Kate shook her head, not trusting herself to speak. Robbie made a funny little noise in his throat and proceeded to tell her exactly how he had found out. He did it briefly and succinctly, relating it all in a flat, unemotional voice, but he left nothing out – including Pearl Cameron's involvement.

'Pearl – with Jack Drummond! Oh, no!' Kate shook her head. 'Tell me it's not true! Please, Robbie!'

Something flashed in the flat grey eyes.

'Don't use my name!' He put a hand up quickly to his face, bowing his head and pinching the bridge of his nose between his thumb and forefinger. Taking an instinctive step towards him, Kate was halted in her tracks when he raised his head again, looked her full in the face and spoke, his voice clear and unbroken.

'Why should it not be true? We all know that Pearl's a cheap wee tart, don't we?' He raised his dark eyebrows in interrogation. Then, his eyes locking with Kate's, he delivered the body blow. 'Following in her big sister's footsteps, you might say.'

It was as though he had struck her physically. She flinched, wrapped her arms about her body and clumsily found her way to a chair, her legs giving way just as she got there. She raised huge, hurt eyes to him.

'Robbie . . .'

'I asked you not to use my name.' He sounded perfectly calm.

'W-won't you let me try to explain? To apologise?' Her voice broke, and the shaking hand she was trying to extend towards him fell back uselessly into her lap.

'It's a bit late for that, do you not think?' He was looking impassively across the room at her. 'I'm going out,' he announced abruptly. 'You don't have to worry about Grace.' There had been a tiny pause just before he said his daughter's name. Jack Drummond's daughter's name. 'I'll ask my Ma to keep her for the night. I'll tell her you're not well.'

'You won't say anything to Grace, will you?'

His voice dripped contempt. 'What do you take me for? It's not the wee lassie's fault.'

The wee lassie. Could he not even bring himself to say her name a second time, then?

'When will you be back?' she asked miserably.

The expression in his grey eyes was unfathomable. 'When I see fit.'

An hour later there was a knock at the door. Kate flew to it. If he'd just give her a chance to explain, to apologise . . . She'd go down on her knees to him if she had to. She swung the door wide.

'Do you hate me, Kate?' asked Pearl. Her pretty face was streaked with tears.

'Och, Pearl,' said Kate wearily. 'You'd better come in.'

Turning, she led the way into the room. Then she sat down at the table and buried her head in her hands.

'Why should I hate you?' she asked.

'Because I've been . . . going with Jack.' Kate didn't lift her head. After a second or two Pearl spoke again. 'And because I've just been to see *her* – Marjorie Drummond.'

That brought Kate's gaze back to her sister's face.

'In the name of God, Pearl. What possessed you to do that?'

Pearl sniffed. 'It was the way he spoke to me – Jack Drummond, I mean. He called me a—. Well, what he said wasn't very nice. He might have given me lots of presents . . .'

Kate drew her breath in sharply. Pearl tossed her blonde head.

'It wasn't like that, Kate. Honest! He came into the shop about a year ago. Knew me straightaway, even remembered my name. Then we started seeing each other . . .' She caught sight of the expression on her sister's face. 'Och, I know, I know! But where's the harm in it really?'

'Pearl.' Kate shook her head.

'It wasn't nasty, Kate. It wasn't like being pressed up against the wall of a close with someone fumbling at your buttons and not knowing how to treat you right. I've had enough of that to last a lifetime. Jack took me to nice places, even bought me champagne sometimes.'

Champagne – of course. A tried and tested seduction technique.

'And he took you to that place where Robbie was today?' Kate asked, her voice a whisper. 'And you let him . . .' She didn't finish the question. The expression on Pearl's face was answer enough.

'There was no call to use that word about me. And he didn't need to tell Robbie about you and him. Robbie didn't need to know that.' Her voice trailed off. 'Och, Kate, if you had seen his face. He looked that shocked . . . white as a sheet. I think he just couldn't believe it at first.'

Well, he believed it now, didn't he?

'It was just so unfair! I thought she should know too – know exactly what sort of man her husband was.' Pearl's voice grew quieter. 'Once I'd told her I kind of wished I hadn't. She looked a bit like Robbie had . . .'

Kate squeezed her eyes tight shut for a moment. *Oh Marjorie, I'm sorry you had to find out like this!*

'I've just realised what a fool I've been,' said Pearl. With an abrupt, jerky movement, she pulled out a chair and sat down opposite Kate.

'Join the club,' said Kate softly.

Pearl gave her a wobbly smile. 'I thought you were in love with him.'

Kate shook her head. 'Once, maybe. Not any more. Not for a long time.'

'Robbie's been here?' Pearl asked after a pause.

Kate sniffed, and wiped her nose with the back of her hand like a child.

'Been and gone. Oh Pearl, I don't know if he's ever coming back!'

Pearl opened her bag and took out a handkerchief and a pack of cigarettes. She offered both of them to her sister, who took one and shook her head at the other.

'I don't smoke, Pearl.'

'Aye, well, maybe you should take it up.' She lit up herself, watching as Kate wiped her eyes with the scrap of lace-trimmed cloth. 'After you with the hanky, sister dear.'

Kate gave a half laugh. 'We're a right pair, aren't we?' She blew her nose heartily and then realised what she had done. 'Och, Pearl, I'm sorry. I can't give it back to you now, can I?'

'Keep it,' her sister said. 'I think I've stopped greeting now.'

Kate gave her a tremulous smile. 'What did Marjorie say?'

Pearl took several puffs on her cigarette before she answered. 'She asked me what age my niece was. Exactly.'

'Oh.'

So now Marjorie knew everything. Poor Marjorie. That was someone else Kate had betrayed, and she was sorry for it. She'd lost a husband and a friend today – and a job too, she supposed. She could hardly waltz into the studio tomorrow as though nothing had happened.

She bent forward so that her head was resting on the table, cushioned by her arms. Neither of them spoke for a long time, not until Pearl had smoked the first cigarette and lit a second one.

'What are you going to do, Kate?'

'I don't know.' It came out as a mumble, her voice muffled by her arms. 'I haven't a clue.'

'Well, I know what *I'm* going to do,' Pearl announced. She spoke so decisively that Kate lifted her head to look at her. Grinding out her cigarette, Pearl opened her handbag once more and brought out her powder compact, lipstick and mascara. She smiled grimly at the puzzled look on Kate's face.

'Jack Drummond's not the only fish in the sea – not by a long chalk. I've had other offers. There's a very nice fella – a bit old, forty if he's a day, but a real gent – who's been pestering me for months. Wants to set me up in a wee flat in Glasgow. He'd pay all the bills; I wouldn't even need to go out to work.' She spat on the brush, rubbed it on the block of mascara and applied it to her eyelashes. 'And if he's changed his mind there's a few others that might be interested. Jeanne

– the woman at the house – says that she could rent me out a room.'

Unable to believe what she was hearing, Kate struggled to find words. 'Pearl – you can't!'

Her sister stopped, lipstick in hand. 'How not?'

'It's not respectable, that's how not!'

Pearl laid the lipstick down on the table. She looked at Kate, then she glanced around the shabby flat, then she looked back at Kate.

'Respectable? You think respectable is the be-all and end-all? Well, I don't. I don't want to scrimp and save and never have anything nice to eat or to wear. I want the good things in life.' She waved her arm in the direction of the outside world. 'They're all out there, Kate. And I'm damn' sure I'm going to get my share.' Lifting the lipstick, she began to paint her mouth.

'Pearl – *think*! It'll break Mammy and Daddy's heart.'

Checking her mouth in the mirror of her compact, Pearl answered. 'Personally I don't think Mammy's got one. And Daddy doesn't have to know, does he?'

She snapped the powder compact shut and sent Kate a pleading look across the table. For all her air of insouciance, her voice had faltered when she had mentioned their father.

'What if I write a wee note, Kate? Tell them that I've gone down south with one of the girls at the shop to work in a hotel or something? Would you give it to them? Please?'

Kate looked at her for a long moment. 'Is there anything that I can do or say that would make you change your mind?'

Pearl shook her head. 'No, there's not.'

Kate's shoulders slumped. It was all her fault. She had set her sister a bad example. Robbie was quite right: Pearl *was* following in her footsteps. Only she was going a lot further down that road. Seeing Kate's complete dejection, Pearl stood up and came round the table, sliding an arm around her older sister's shoulders.

'I was always the wild one, Kate – you know that. It's not your fault that I've gone bad.'

'Oh, Pearl!' Turning, she threw her arms about her sister. Pearl patted her on the shoulder.

'We've had some good laughs together though, haven't we?' Kate nodded her head in agreement. 'And Robbie'll come back to you. I'm sure he will.'

He did come back – but not for long. It was seven o'clock that evening, on the day which was proving to be the longest of Kate's life. He dropped his bombshell as soon as he came into the house. He had been to the Pool – the Merchant Navy labour exchange up in Glasgow – had just made it before they closed for the day, and he had signed on for a trip aboard the *SS Border Reiver*, leaving the Clyde in two days' time for coastal trading on the other side of the Atlantic. Their carpenter had been taken off the ship with acute appendicitis, so Robbie's arrival couldn't have come at a better time. He wasn't sure how long he'd be away – maybe a year.

Open-mouthed, Kate stared at him. *A year!* He had brought a kitbag home with him and he began now to pack it with various bits and pieces: shirts, socks and underwear; his razor and shaving brush; two or three books. From a little cupboard above the box bed he took out a buff-coloured folder which seemed to contain several sheets of paper. Kate had never seen it before, but her attention left it when Robbie came over to where she sat and took an old envelope out of his inside pocket, setting it down on the table in front of her.

'I'm taking some of the emergency fund but I've made an arrangement for you to get money while I'm away.'

He was being very matter-of-fact, but the finger with which he pointed to the scrap of paper he had just laid on the table wasn't quite steady. 'If you go and see the company I've signed on with – that's the address – they'll tell you how it works.'

Kate swallowed. 'I don't want to take your money.'

He shrugged. 'Why not? You've taken much more from me.' He turned away from her, and she had to strain to make out the words. 'My pride for a start . . . and my manhood.'

Kate, her elbows on the table and her fingers interlaced with her hair, felt her heart turn over at those quietly uttered words. Was there no way she could get through to him? Tell him how much she loved him? Beg him to forgive her? His packing completed, he was standing staring out of the window again, his back to her. She stood up, her chair scraping on the floor. He turned at the noise, but the expression on his face was anything but welcoming. His features were set in forbidding lines. It was a mask, she knew – knew also how much pain it must be concealing.

Her throat ached. She yearned to open her arms to him, to draw his head down onto her breast. She knew she had forfeited the right to offer him any comfort by her betrayal of him. Yet she must try, all the same. She took a deep breath and looked him straight in the eye.

'I-I know you maybe won't believe this, but I really love you . . . and I'm so sorry.'

'Sorry that I found out?'

She was too honest to deny it. She dropped her eyes before the reproach she saw in his.

'You'll need money,' he said a few moments later. 'I doubt you'll be working for Marjorie any more. Especially not after I gave her husband a black eye.'

'You hit him?' Her voice rose in disbelief.

'Aye, I thumped him one.' A note of grim satisfaction crept into the carefully neutral voice.

She shook her head. She had thought him the most peaceable man in the world. In a society where male aggression

304

too frequently spilled over into violence, Robert Baxter had always seemed to Kate the last person to use his fists to resolve an argument.

'I'll be off, then,' he said at last.

They couldn't part like this. Casting around for something – anything – to delay him, she pointed at the folder lying on the table.

'You've forgotten that. Whatever it is.'

He went over to the table, flipped the folder open and took out the pages lying loose inside it. He held them in his hand for a moment. Then, with a quick movement, he screwed up the pages, twisted them and tossed them onto the range fire. The paper flared up brightly and he grabbed the long poker from its hook to hold them down and stop them falling onto the hearth rug. The paper twist uncurled as it burned. Standing beside the range, Kate could make out a few words on the top page. *To my emerald-eyed Kate.* She looked up at him.

'Poems,' he whispered. 'Mainly about you.'

Looking away from her, he stabbed viciously at the papers, holding them till they were burnt to blackened fragments. She hadn't thought it was possible for her heart to ache any more than it already did. She'd been wrong.

The destruction complete, he hung the poker back on its hook, and made once more as if to go.

'I thought your ship didn't sail for two days.'

'I can't stay here with you.' He drew his breath in. 'At this precise moment I don't know if I ever want to see you again.'

She flinched visibly, and thought she saw an answering reaction in his eyes. For his sake, for both their sakes, she had to stop him leaving, make him stay here and listen to her side of the story. Clutching at straws, she blurted out a protest he clearly thought unworthy of her, his grey eyes narrowing in disdain as she said the words.

'If you go to your Ma's she'll know that something's up.'

'I'm not going to my mother's.'

The mask, which had seemed to slip for a few seconds, was firmly back in place. Yet she couldn't give him up without a fight, she just couldn't! Then it came to her. The wonderful news Dr MacMillan had given her today. Why, she had almost forgotten it! She closed the distance between them, reaching out to grip his arm. She could feel the warmth of it through the rough cloth of his jacket.

'You can't go now. I went to see the doctor today.' She tried to smile. 'Robbie, we're going to have a baby.'

'Really? Do you tell me that, Kate?' It was the first time he had used her name during that whole terrible afternoon and evening. '*We're* going to have a baby? How nice. Are you sure it isn't another of Drummond's bastards you were planning to foist off on me?'

Kate Baxter lifted her hand from his sleeve, drew her arm back as far as it would go, and slapped her husband's face. The force of the blow sent him half a step backwards, but he kept his balance – and his equilibrium. Kate looked at the red mark she had raised on his cheek, horrified at what she had done.

He lifted the kitbag and slung it over his shoulder.

'I'll let you know where I am. Or maybe I'll not.'

Why had he said that to her? It was unforgivable, he knew that. He had absolutely no doubt that the child she was carrying was his. There had been so many joyful nights of love and passion. Or so he had thought. All a sham – all a bloody sham.

What she had done to him was unforgivable too. He'd never been in any doubt about Grace either. Until today. His mind was filled with images of his beautiful wee daughter – so bonnie, so clever, so loving. Her voice was ringing in his ears. *Daddy, Daddy! Lift me up, Daddy!* A single tear rolled down his cheek. He wasn't her Daddy at all. He gave an inarticulate sob and grasped the railing which separated the path from the river.

He sniffed, wiping his nose with the back of his hand. His little family had been the centre of his universe. More fool him. He had been an idiot – a blind, lovesick idiot. Now he saw his life for what it was – based on a lie.

He stood staring out at the Clyde, by the rowan tree where he had so often talked with her. He couldn't say her name. He couldn't even think it. Yet he knew very well why he had come to this place – to deliberately torture himself, to claw at the wound – to punish himself for living in a fool's paradise.

He had known, somewhere within himself, that she had married him on the rebound from Jack Drummond. But he had allowed himself to hope . . . and he had never dreamt that she would have let that bastard do what he had done to her.

He gripped the railing even more tightly. His all-too vivid imagination was torturing him with pictures of her with Drummond. He could see him kissing her, touching her, making love to her . . . He let out another sob and swayed wildly, anchored only by the vice-like grip he kept on the railing.

Maybe he should just slide into the river. Throw his arms above his head and let the water close over his face. Then she'd be sorry. Would she?

He shivered violently. It was raining heavily now and two droplets of water had just run down the back of his neck. He didn't bother turning the collar of his threadbare jacket up against it. Let it rain, let it fucking pour. He lifted his face to it, letting the water soak him, wondering if that's what it would feel like to give himself up to the Clyde. He never knew what stopped him doing it.

The Frenchwoman didn't look surprised to see him, or the

state he was in, but then he supposed in her business it didn't do to show surprise. She just opened the door and murmured his name in her soft accent.

'You have not come to cause more trouble?' she asked anxiously.

'No.' He shook his head, scattering water to both sides.

'Bah!' she said. 'You are like a dog which has been swimming. Come in, straight away. *Vite!*' She grabbed his arm, wrinkling her nose at the feel of the wet cloth, and pulled him into the flat.

'I've got money,' he said, leaning against the door, now closed behind him, his wet head tilted back against the smooth wood. 'I can pay.'

'You do not need money. Not tonight.' She clicked her fingers and Marie-Louise, the red-haired girl, came forward from a shadowy corner of the hall. Her face was full of sympathy and the accent she used to speak to him was their own.

'Ye cannae find it in your heart to forgive her?'

'I cannae find it in my heart to forgive her.' He got the words out, like a child repeating a lesson. Then he bit down furiously on his bottom lip. Marie-Louise made a tutting noise, lifted her hand to his face and traced the line of his lips.

'Don't do that. You've got a nice mouth.' She took a step back and held out her hand to him.

'Come wi' me,' she said. 'First we'll get you out of these wet clothes . . . and then I'll make you forget all your troubles. Come on, now.'

Robert Baxter looked down at her for a long moment. Then he let out a sigh, pushed himself off the door, and put his hand in hers. She led him to her bedroom as though he were a lost child.

Chapter 27

Without Grace, Kate knew she would have crawled into the box bed, drawn the curtains and cried for days. Only because she had to care for the little girl did she keep functioning: cooking, cleaning and washing as usual. As it was, she confined her weeping to the long and lonely nights, sobbing quietly so as not to disturb the child in her little hurly bed on the other side of the curtains.

She went to bed every night at the usual time, but she slept little. At first she just lay, curled up in pain, holding on to a pillow – his pillow. She put off washing the pillowcase for weeks because there clung to it, very faintly, the scent of his skin.

Then the thoughts began to torment her; guilt and remorse; an aching for Robbie and the hurt she had inflicted on him; and then finally a pain for herself. Would he ever come back? Or find it in his heart to forgive her? How could he? She had done the unforgivable.

It was hard too when she had to listen to everyone else expressing surprise at Robbie's sudden departure, even although, in the midst of his own hurt and anger, he had tried to put them off the scent.

'Robbie said the two of you had been planning this for a while, Kate,' said Agnes Baxter, looking anxiously at her daughter-in-law. She was worried about her. The lassie was looking pale and drawn.

'Aye, well, you know,' stumbled Kate, making it up as she went along. 'He hated being idle.'

'You'll miss him though.' There was the smallest of question marks at the end of the statement.

Miss him? Dear God!

Unable to speak, Kate nodded. Her mother-in-law put a comforting arm around her shoulders.

'That was a stupid question, eh? Well, never mind, the time'll go past quicker than you think. He'll be home soon. And you know you and Grace are always welcome here.'

And Kate, wracked with guilt, wondered how warm that welcome would have been if Agnes Baxter had known the truth.

One short week after Robbie's departure Kate knew that she was going to have to admit defeat, give up the tenancy of the flat and go back to live at her parents' house. It was the last thing in the world that she wanted, but she could see no alternative. There just wasn't enough money coming in. In fact, there was no money coming in.

She had received a formally polite letter from Marjorie, curtly terminating her employment with the studio and enclosing a week's pay in lieu of notice. She had wrestled with her stubborn pride for days over whether or not she should keep that money.

Pride, in the end, had to give way to practicality. If she and Grace were going to go back to Yoker she would have to pay for their upkeep. The longer she delayed, the more the emergency fund would be depleted. There was more space now that Granny was gone – she had died the previous summer – but with Pearl leaving, which had been another nine days' wonder, and her father on the dole, the Cameron family was in no position to feed another pair of mouths. Jessie, newly qualified as a teacher, was earning, but precious little.

There was Robbie's money, of course, but she was too proud to take it. No, that was the wrong word. She was too ashamed to take it – too ashamed to go up to the offices of the shipping company in the Broomielaw in Glasgow and ask for something from her husband's pay. She had no right. Yet, came a treacherous voice every so often, if she did that she could keep on the flat, maybe even have Jessie to live with her for company . . . not have to go back and live with her father's drinking and her mother's temper.

She might *have* to take some of Robbie's money for Grace's sake. He wouldn't mind that, would he? Often, during the hard times, she had sat and watched him put food from his own plate onto his daughter's. Then she would remember that Grace wasn't really his daughter, and the wound would open and bleed afresh.

It made her toss and turn at night, doing endless calculations in her head, as she'd done once before when she'd been planning how to get to the Art School. They had been happy sums, though. These ones just added to her misery.

Two weeks after the *SS Border Reiver* left the Clyde a listless Kate answered the door to a smart double knock. It was Jack Drummond. He didn't wait for an invitation, sweeping past her and into the flat.

'What are you doing here?'

Turning to face her as she followed him into the room, he raised his fair brows in a pained expression.

'Really, Kate, I might have expected a more friendly welcome than that. God,' he said, 'you look terrible. What happened?'

What happened?

She tucked a strand of hair behind her ear – she hadn't bothered combing it today – and wrapped her cardigan more tightly about herself.

'My cat died.' It wasn't a lie. The bairns who lived in the close had come clattering upstairs yesterday afternoon to tell her that 'the old cat' was lying out in the back court and, 'We think he's deid, Mrs Baxter.' He was, and Kate had lifted Mr Asquith's stiff little body onto her lap and, with Grace hanging around her neck, had cried inconsolable tears over it, alarming the children so much that they'd gone running for help. They'd cannoned into Peter Watt, coming through the close in search of her.

'Robbie came to see me before he left. Asked me to look in on you now and again,' he explained as Kate lifted her tear-stained face to him. That had set her off again and Peter had patted her shoulder, made her a cup of tea and then helped bury Mr Asquith under a lilac tree in a corner of the back court. The children had all been very solemn about it, conducting a brief but moving ceremony and putting a wee home-made cross on top of the freshly dug earth. Peter Watt had smiled at Kate over their heads and she had managed a shaky smile back.

'Was that the cat that sat on my lap? Oh, that's too bad,' said Jack Drummond. He looked around the room. 'Where's my daughter?'

Out playing with her friends, thank God, thought Kate, and only over my dead body are you going to see her. She folded her arms across her chest and gave him back look for look.

'She's not your daughter.'

'No? I understand from my aggrieved wife that she is.' Without waiting to be asked, he threw himself down into the armchair by the range. 'I also understand that's the reason why the gallant Robbie has taken himself off. Nursing his broken heart and his sense of betrayal on the high seas, so I hear. Sit down, Kate. We've got things to discuss.'

'You and I have nothing to discuss!'

'No?' He took out a cigarette and lit it, looking up at her

where she stood so stiff and unbending in the middle of the room. 'I have a proposition to put to you. It might be in your best interests to hear me out.'

Her heart began to thump. Was he going to offer her money to help pay for Grace's maintenance?

'My wife's left me, you see. Nursing *her* broken heart. Off to Southampton to take a boat to America. Oh, I've no doubt she'll come back eventually, but just temporarily it leaves me rather bereft. And I'm a normal man – with normal needs.'

Kate sucked her breath in sharply. 'I rather thought my sister had been meeting those.'

Jack Drummond shot her an odd look. He had misjudged her again – as he always had done. She could almost see the cogs turning as he re-evaluated, calculating what he could say to her to get what he wanted.

'Your charming sister and I have agreed to part.' His gaze swept once more round the flat. 'A woman like you shouldn't be living in a place like this, Kate.' It was shabbier than usual. She'd been going through the motions, doing the bare minimum of cleaning and tidying since Robbie had left.

'A woman like me? And just what sort of a woman is that?' Her voice was sharp.

He smiled up at her from the depths of the armchair, leaning forward, reaching out a hand to her.

'A woman nothing like her sister. A talented and very lovely woman. A woman I've missed very much.' His voice was very soft, his smile less confident – the little boy lost look. He was very good at it, she'd have to give him that. It was a pity she knew now that it was all an act.

Ignoring the outstretched hand, she looked him over. She wondered if she'd ever loved him, or if she'd simply been dazzled by what he had seemed to represent: elegance, ease, wealth – an escape route from the poverty of her childhood and towards her dream of artistic achievement.

313

'Come on, Kate.' His voice was a coaxing murmur. 'I can't believe you don't miss me, my darling. I've certainly missed you.'

That, thought Kate, was probably true. It changed nothing.

'I don't miss you.'

His eyebrows shot up in the amused gesture she remembered so well.

'Playing hard to get, Kate? I can see your sister must have shared a few tricks of the trade with you. Pity. You used to be such an innocent. No doubt experience has its compensations.' The blue eyes roamed from her face down over her body and back up again. The look sent shivers down her spine.

'Wouldn't you like to live somewhere a little more spacious? With a separate bedroom for the brat.' He paused and took a long pull on the cigarette. Then he looked her straight in the eye. 'And a bedroom for you – and perhaps, now and again, for me?'

The blood froze in her veins. There were so many things she wanted to scream at to him . . . She turned her back so that he couldn't see the expression on her face. Then: 'And what would happen when you got Marjorie back?'

'That would be up to you. I know how moral you are. Perhaps I would have to hope that Marjorie didn't come back to me *too* quickly. Just think about it though, Kate. A nice little flat in the West End – near the Botanic Gardens maybe, so that you could take the kid for walks in the fresh air. I daresay I could stretch to a nursemaid. You could go back to the Art School.'

Dear God, that was cruel. He knew exactly what to offer. Just for a few seconds Kate could see that spacious flat. There would be a wee room for Grace, space for herself to paint . . . It would be a short tram ride away from the Art School, maybe even walking distance.

She turned to face him, squaring her shoulders and drawing herself up to her full – if unimpressive – height.

'Get out of my house,' she said, her voice a splinter of ice. 'Don't ever come back.'

'I can't honestly believe you'd rather have him than me.'

That made her smile, as did the incredulous look on his handsome face.

'No, Jack, I don't suppose you can believe that, but it happens to be true.'

'You're turning me down and you don't even know if he'll ever come back to you?'

'I'm prepared to take that risk. I love him, you see. I think, probably, I always have done. It just took me a long time to realise it.'

Whatever Jack Drummond read in Kate's face and stance, it was enough to make him rise to his feet, pausing on his way to the door to stand in front of her.

'You know, Kate, I always thought you were like a lily on a dung heap. Now you're telling me you want to stay on the dung heap. Even if you do get him back – which I doubt – the two of you will never get out of this dump.'

He raised a hand to her face. She jerked back, but he was too quick for her. His free hand slid to the back of her neck, holding her rigid while his fingers traced the line of her lips. He spoke directly into her face, his voice a whisper.

'Such a pity – all that loveliness and talent going to waste.' His eyes dropped to her mouth. 'And me prepared to offer you a hand up.'

Her voice too was a whisper, but none the less definite for that. 'I don't care to pay your price.'

The blue eyes met hers. 'You're never going to do it on your own. You do know that, don't you?'

Straining against the hand imprisoning the back of her neck, she spat out the words. 'Just watch me.'

315

Jack Drummond laughed. 'So fierce, my little Clydebank girl.'

Bracing herself to resist the punishing kiss she felt sure was coming, Kate stared him out, daring him to do it. He laughed again, released his hold on her and kissed her so swiftly on the mouth she had no chance to pull back.

'Goodbye, Kate.' The eyebrows went up again. 'Or perhaps I should say *au revoir*. I'm going to enjoy it when you change your mind and come running to me for help.'

The door swung closed behind him. With a trembling hand, Kate wiped her mouth. She sank into a chair.

'Never,' she whispered, 'not in a million years. I'm going to make Robbie forgive me *and* I'll get back to the Art School. However long it takes. Even if I'm an old lady before I do it. And that's a promise, Jack Drummond.'

She tossed her head and ran her fingers through the dishevelled chestnut waves. Then, her head falling forward, she burst into tears.

Chapter 28

The brave words she had flung after Jack Drummond came to seem like a bad joke in the months that followed. If it hadn't been for Grace, Kate would have felt that her life had been a dream. Here she was back where she had started, living with her parents, putting up with her mother's temper, living a life of drudgery. Uncomfortably aware that she and Grace were an added burden on the household, she took the lion's share of the chores on her narrow shoulders, despite her increasing tiredness as her pregnancy advanced. Life was no longer a joy, it was something to be endured, every day an ordeal to be got through. Her father noticed.

'Is there aught amiss between you and Robbie, lass?' he asked one day, coming to stand behind her as she peeled potatoes at the jaw-box.

'No, of course not, Daddy. Why should you think that?' She stretched, arching her back. She was six months gone now, and beginning to show.

A hand came round in front of her. It held a brightly coloured postcard. 'Because your man writes to his daughter, but never to his wife.'

The next moment she was in her father's arms, sobbing on his shoulder as though her heart would break.

'There, there, my lass,' he soothed. 'There, there. I'm sure it's nothing that can't be sorted out.'

'Oh, Daddy! I did a terrible thing. I don't think Robbie will ever be able to forgive me for it.'

'Now, now.' His voice was deep and comforting, his big hand warm on her back. 'What could my girl have done that was so awful? I don't know what's gone wrong between you two, but I do know one thing. That lad loves you. He always has and he always will. You hold on to that and things'll come all right. You'll see. He's just gone off in the huff, that's all, but it'll come right, I know it will. Oh!'

He loosened his hold and Kate stepped out of his arms. Lily had come through from the front room and was tutting at their display of emotion.

'Are those tatties going to be ready for the tea?'

Kate, turning again to her task, bit her lip. She wasn't sure how much more she could stand of this. For the hundredth time she rehearsed the arguments about taking some of Robbie's pay and for the hundredth time rejected them.

'Don't you worry, Mammy,' she said, smoothing the hair back from her forehead with the back of her wrist, 'the tatties'll be ready on time.' She was no longer prepared to act the subservient child, but she wasn't going to snap back either. She had to stay calm – for the baby's sake.

Unobtrusively, out of sight of his wife, her father patted her arm. At least somebody appreciated her. She knew that Jessie did, too. The two sisters had initiated a ritual. Kate had a cup of tea waiting for her when she came in from school, but Jessie served it, making Kate put her feet up and take a rest while they chatted about their respective days. Kate's were getting less and less interesting, but she enjoyed hearing Jessie's chat about her colleagues and the children in her class.

Then, over-riding Kate's protests that Jessie had too much marking to do, her younger sister would help Lily get the evening meal, insisting that Kate stay where she was in front of the range, despite Lily's barbed comments about expectant mothers never being pampered like that in her day.

Kate went on with the peeling. Thank goodness they were onto the old tatties. She hated all the scraping that went with new ones. It was August now, and summer was slowly beginning to give way to autumn. *Oh God, please let him come home in time for the baby!*

She had written to him once, to let him know that they had moved back to Yoker. She had gone up to the shipping company in the Broomielaw after all, where a sharp-eyed clerkess in a frilly blouse and a well-lipsticked mouth had instructed her, as though she were a half-wit, to address any mail to Robbie care of the ship he was on.

'I think I could have worked that bit out,' murmured Kate, piqued by the way the girl was looking her up and down. She was, she had to admit, looking a bit shabby. She had bought two smart new outfits when she was working for Marjorie, but they were too tight now for her growing bulk. It was back to cast-offs, especially for maternity clothes. Grace, standing round-eyed and subdued by the unfamiliar surroundings at her side, wasn't much better. She seemed to be growing out of her clothes every second week.

The clerkess bristled. Kate didn't work too hard to hold back a smile.

'Then I hand the letter in to you, do I? Thanks for your help.'

She turned on her heel. She wasn't going to wait to be dismissed. Her feet, at least, were still well-shod – until her ankles began to swell, that was. Oh, the joys of pregnancy!

'Mrs Baxter, is it?' the girl called after her.

'Yes, that's right.' Kate went back to the counter which separated enquirers from the office staff.

The girl was consulting a file. She looked *very* important. She kept Kate waiting just a little too long as she scanned a

319

list of names. Two could play at that game. Kate tapped her fingers on the highly polished oak of the counter. Eventually Miss Frilly Blouse looked up.

'You don't seem to have made any claim on your husband's pay, heretofore.'

Heretofore? Oh dear, she did have a bad case of self-importance.

'No, I haven't. I fail to see that it's any of your business.'

The sharp eyes swept over her. 'All I'm saying is that most people do. You're quite unusual.'

'My dear young lady,' said Kate Baxter, with all the haughtiness of her twenty-four years, 'I'm so glad you're able to recognise that. Good afternoon.'

It took her several attempts to get the letter right. In the first one she poured everything out, begged his forgiveness for what she had done, told him how much she loved him and pleaded with him to come home. She didn't correct a thing. It was all from the heart. She was on the point of putting it in the envelope when it suddenly occurred to her that Robbie's might not be the first eyes to see her words. What if the letter followed him about from port to port or, horror of horrors, was returned to Glasgow, where Miss Frilly Blouse might open it?

She wrote a second one, more restrained this time. *Dear Robbie*, she started, and then remembered how he had asked her not to call him by his name that dreadful day. *Dear Robert*, then? She could hardly put *Dear Mr Baxter*. In the end she put nothing, just started the letter at the top of the page, below the Yoker address.

When she got to the end of the second page – the first letter had been four pages long – she encountered a similar problem to the one she'd had at the top. What should she put? She'd written *All my love, Kate* on the first one. She considered some others: *Your loving wife, Kate. Lots of love from Kate.* She had no reason to believe that he wanted to think of her in that way any more.

In the end, she wrote a brief one-page letter which told him very little.

> *This is to let you know that we have moved back to stay with my folks. I have given up the tenancy at Kilbowie Road. I have not drawn anything on your pay but may have to if we get really stuck. I hope you will not mind that too much.*
>
> *There is no word of work starting again on the 534 although everybody is hoping that it will not be long. I have seen Mary and Peter Watt a few times. It looks like being quite a hot summer this year.*
>
> *We are all well and hope that you are too.*
> *Kathleen Baxter.*

Kathleen Baxter. That was a daft way to sign herself. The whole letter was daft. She hadn't even told him that Mr Asquith had died, hadn't mentioned Grace by name, hadn't asked him when he was coming home . . .

She hadn't the heart to redo it, and he did need to know where they were. She supposed. She took the letter up to Miss Frilly Blouse, who accepted it as though it were something contagious and sniffily informed Kate that it could take a long time to reach the recipient.

It did not, however, take that long. Postcards began to arrive at the flat in Yoker, but always addressed only to Grace, never to her mother. She read them anyway, hungry to touch something which he had touched. His messages to Grace were brief but cheerful. *Hope you like the stamps on this card, sweetheart. I picked them especially.* He sent her pictures of towns and cities along the eastern seaboard of the United States: New York, Boston, Portland. He always signed himself *R. Baxter.* Kate agonised for hours over that and came to absolutely no conclusion at all.

'Hello there, lass. How were the bairns the day?'

Jessie took off her hat and hung up her coat, smiling at her father as she did so.

'Och, just the usual, Daddy – although Douglas MacPherson surpassed himself. First he dipped Lizzie Beaton's pigtails in the inkwell, then he put itching powder down the back of another wee boy's trousers while we were out in the playground having rounders.'

Neil Cameron threw his head back and laughed. 'Did you leather him, hen? Give him a touch o' the tawse?'

'Jessie doesn't believe in using the belt, Daddy,' put in Kate, throwing her sister a teasing smile. 'She's all for psychology. Isn't that right, Jess? Did you have a long serious talk with wee Douglas and make him see the error of his ways?'

'I did,' said Jessie, her mouth set in an expression of mock-severity. 'Sit down, Kate, and I'll bring you your tea. I got some nice tea-bread at the Co-op on my way home.'

'Shall I just put it out on the plates?' began Kate.

Jessie pointed sternly at the armchair. 'Sit, Kate Baxter. Dae as yer tellt.'

'Yes, miss,' said Kate, suiting the action to the words.

Neil Cameron's eyes were twinkling as he looked at his two daughters.

'Well, I don't know about the scholars,' he said in his soft Highland lilt, 'but the fearsome Miss Cameron certainly scares me half to death.' He patted his knee, and Grace clambered up on it. 'D'ye not think your Auntie's a terrifying woman, young Grace?' He rolled the double *r* in 'terrifying', bending forward and shaking his head from side to side as he said it.

'You're silly, Grandad,' chortled Grace, laughing up into his face.

'You see?' he said to Lily, who, engrossed in some mending, had taken no part in the conversation. 'All the women in my family think I'm daft.' He put his arm round Grace's waist and smiled broadly at her.

'Aye, well,' said Lily, not raising her head. 'Does that not tell you something?'

Neil's smile faded.

'So,' asked Kate, comfortably ensconced in the armchair with a stool at her feet. 'Did wee MacPherson see the error of his ways, Jessie?'

Jessie, distributing slices of fruit loaf, smiled grimly.

'Not exactly. Half an hour after I gave him the talking-to, I found him dipping another girl's pigtails in the inkwell. So *then* I leathered him – the wee toerag.'

Kate and Neil burst out laughing.

'So where's your psychology now, lassie?'

Jessie threw up her hands. 'I know, I know. That's only the second time since I started that I've used the belt. I hate doing it – but that child will be the death of me, he really will.'

While Neil was singing and talking nonsense to his grand-daughter, Kate tried to reassure her sister that she wasn't a monster because she'd delivered three of the best to wee MacPherson.

'There's no badness in him, Kate,' Jessie explained. 'It's just mischief – and he's a clever wee soul. He was funny after I'd belted him.'

'Did he cry?'

'Damn' the fear of it,' said Jessie. 'No, he went all pale and noble. Told me he understood why I'd felt the need to do it.'

Kate's green eyes opened wide in delight.

'So he made you feel guilty instead of him?' she suggested.

'Maybe it's wee MacPherson who's using the psychology, Jess.'

Jessie grinned. 'Aye, that child will go far, you mark my words. Right up on his high horse he was.'

'Well, we can all do that, I suppose,' said Kate, wetting her finger and picking up the last bits of fruit loaf from her plate. She sighed. She hadn't felt so relaxed in months. She'd needed a good laugh. She started telling Jessie about the girl in the shipping company office when she had gone to enquire about how to send a letter to Robbie. It had all been very raw at the time, but she was beginning to see the funny side of it.

She told the story exactly as she remembered it, putting on a silly pan-loaf voice for Miss Frilly Blouse.

'*"You don't seem to have made any claim on your husband's pay, heretofore."* Heretofore,' scoffed Kate. 'Can you believe it?'

'Do you mean to tell me,' came a voice from behind Jessie's chair, 'that there's money lying up in Glasgow that could have been coming into this house?'

Jessie jumped, and Kate looked up into her mother's face. She swallowed, coughing as a few of the cake crumbs went down the wrong way.

'It's Robbie's money,' she said quietly. 'I'm sure he's working hard for it. I'd like him to be able to collect it all when he pays off after his trip.'

'You're his wife,' said Lily. 'You're entitled to a share of it.'

'No, I'm not.'

Lily's blue eyes flickered. She half-turned, indicating Grace sitting on Neil's knee. 'Grace is entitled to it, then. She's his daughter.'

Kate opened her mouth and then, remembering that Jessie and Neil – and Grace herself – were listening in, shut it again without saying anything.

'I'll not make a claim on his pay,' she said finally, 'not unless I'm forced to. I'm sorry, Ma. I just won't.'

'Leave the lassie alone, Lily,' came a deep voice from behind them. 'She should not be badgered in her condition.'

Lily, her face contorted with anger, whirled round. 'You! You always take her part, Neil Cameron.'

She raised her arm as though to lunge forward and strike him. Neil hurriedly set Grace off his knee. Jessie darted up out of her chair and across the room, grabbing Grace and pulling her out of range. Kate raised herself up in the armchair.

'Ma! Don't! Please, Ma!' She pushed down on the arms of the chair, trying to get enough leverage to stand up. She'd done it awkwardly. She was all to one side like Gourock.

'Kate!' shouted Jessie. 'Don't! Just wait a wee minute and I'll help you.'

It was too late. Kate had made it to her feet. After a fashion. She was swaying. Then she fell, hard and heavy onto the cold oil-cloth. The last thing she heard was her sister screaming her name.

Chapter 29

Pain. Waves and waves of it. Like lying on a stony beach with the tide coming in and being unable to move – feeling it recede, taking a few quick deep breaths – but knowing that it would soon come sweeping back in again with renewed force.

She was in her parents' bed. It had been pulled out from the wall so that there was space on both sides of it. Jessie, holding her hand, was on her left, the midwife on the right. From somewhere in the room came the sound of someone crying.

Well, it wouldn't be the midwife. Kate turned her head – it seemed like an enormous effort to do it – and looked at Jessie.

'Are you remembering your breathing, Kate? Shallow when the pain's at its worst. That's what the midwife says.'

'I'll remember.' She got the words out with difficulty. Not Jessie, then. 'Grace?' She could only manage the name, but Jessie understood, giving her hand a reassuring squeeze.

'Downstairs with the Baxters. Flora and Alice said they would take her out to the park for the afternoon.'

Kate nodded, then wrinkled her brow in perplexity. 'Who's crying, Jessie?'

Then she heard her father's voice. It was very low-pitched, but Kate could just make out the coaxing, encouraging words.

'Come on, Lily, you're not helping the lassie by being here. Come on ben to the kitchen with me and we'll have ourselves a cup of tea.'

Kate, her head as heavy as a cannonball on the feather pillow, tilted her face so that she could look up. With her husband's arm about her shoulders, Lily was crossing slowly from the window. Her hair, escaping from its pins, was falling about her tear-stained face. Kate hadn't noticed before, but her mother had acquired quite a few white hairs. Funny how you sometimes knew people so well, and yet you never really looked at them properly, never noticed anything different about them. Lily paused on her way to the door.

'Kate . . .' She laid a hand on her daughter's bare forearm, Kate's hand still being entwined with Jessie's. It was the lightest of touches, Lily's fingers thin and cold. Then she was gone, ushered out of the room by her husband.

'Push, hen. Push now!'

'What do you think I am doing?' Kate grunted irritably.

'Save your breath, Kate!' Jessie was behind her, supporting her shoulders so that she could exert all her fading strength on pushing.

'One more big push,' the midwife commanded. 'Come on now, there's a good lassie!'

She gave one more big push and the baby was out. Then something else.

'Just the afterbirth, hen,' murmured the midwife. 'Now, I'll just get the cord tied and cut . . .' but the woman was talking to herself. With a cry of relief Kate fell back onto the pillow, Jessie's arms easing her down.

'Oh God, oh God, oh God,' she whispered, the words coming out on short, panting breaths. But it was over at last. The baby was born. She smiled up at Jessie. She'd stayed with her the whole time. Could any girl ever have had a better sister? If this baby was a girl, she definitely had to call her Jessie – or *Jessica* – aye, that would be nice. But maybe she'd had a wee boy. Jessie would soon tell her.

Why had her sister gone so pale? She had dropped Kate's hand and was staring at the little bundle the midwife was wrapping up in the cloth which had been warming on the clotheshorse in front of the fire in readiness.

The room had gone very quiet. Kate followed her sister's gaze. The midwife looked up. Her face told Kate everything she needed to know.

'Kate, lass, I'm sorry. I think he's just come too early, the wee soul. I'll send for Dr MacMillan, but I doubt he'll be able to do anything.'

Hustle and bustle then. Noise. Talk. The occupants of the room shifting and changing. The next thing Kate was aware of was a voice she couldn't quite make out. She had to strain to hear it. Something was wrong with the words. Then she realised it was her father, intoning something softly in Gaelic. The words flowed one into the other in a rhythmic chant.

Kate opened her eyes.

'Daddy?' she murmured through parched lips. He was beside her, holding something in his arms. No, not something – someone. Her baby – Robbie's baby. He was tiny, the merest scrap of humanity. Her father spoke again.

'I am saying a blessing over your son, Kathleen. I'm going to baptise him now.'

That could mean only one thing. She watched her father lean forward and make the sign of the cross over the cup of water by her bedside, remembering some long-ago Catholic past. He dipped his fingers in the cup and said the blessing now in English, stumbling over the translation of words which he'd only ever heard in the old language and half a lifetime away.

'*The little drop of the Father, on thy little forehead, beloved one. The little drop of the Son, on thy little forehead, beloved one. The little drop of the Spirit, on thy little forehead, beloved one . . .* In the name of the Father, the Son and the Holy Ghost,

I baptise thee—' He broke off suddenly and lifted his eyes to Kate.

'Neil James,' she whispered, 'after his two grandfathers.' Her voice tailed off. Just saying those few words had exhausted her. In a voice which shook, her father repeated the two names and made the sign of the cross once more, with his thumb, on the baby's forehead. Then he put the tiny bundle into Kate's arms.

I cannot weep. Not yet. I cannot weep because if I do I won't see you, won't be able to fix your face in my memory. We shall not have long together, my son. Shall I tell you about your father? But that was altogether too painful. She clutched the baby more tightly to her. He was very cold. So she had to tell him – before it was too late. *Your father is Robert – Robert Baxter – and he is a good man. I am your mother, Kate. You have a sister called Grace.*

She bent her head and pressed her lips to Neil James's forehead. It was smooth and cool, like an alabaster statue. She lifted her head and looked down into his face. Her son looked back at her.

Someone, somewhere in the room, was sobbing as though their heart was breaking. *I thought mine already had – till this moment.* The baby was looking up at her. He looked as though he was frowning, drawing his tiny eyebrows together in puzzlement. What did he see? Could he focus? See her face – her eyes, her mouth? Just in case, she smiled.

'I love you, Neil James Baxter,' she whispered.

Did she imagine the reaction in the tiny body she held, so light she was scarcely aware of any weight in her arms? Did a look of recognition pass over the perfect little face? She bent her head and kissed him again, breathing in the scent of him. *My son, my son. Our son.*

She listened to his breathing, soft and delicate, like the lightest of summer breezes moving among flowers. She heard it stop – quite suddenly, but quite peacefully. Still holding him close, she felt her father rise in his chair and stand over them. His hands gently separated mother and son, his fingers fluttering down to close the baby's eyes.

'Has he gone?' a voice whispered.

'Aye, he's gone.' Then, in the gentlest of voices, Neil spoke. 'Shall I take him from you, Kathleen lass?'

She could not tear her eyes away from her son.

'No, Daddy. Not yet. Let me hold him a bit longer.'

Her father's hand was warm on her shoulder.

'Aye, lass. Aye.'

Four days later she insisted on getting out of bed, much against her father's and Jessie's advice. They had absolutely refused to let her attend the baby's funeral the day before. The Baxter girls had sat with her while the other members of the two families had attended. Bitterly, knowing how weak she was, she had given in to that, but she wasn't prepared to have her wishes overridden a second time. Neil and Jessie, with Lily hovering in the background like a pale ghost, anxiously installed her in the armchair, with the foot-stool at her feet.

'I'm fine,' she kept saying. 'I'm fine.'

She was still telling everybody she felt fine at four o'clock that afternoon when she started to haemorrhage.

Her arms were empty. Not even Grace could fill them. She stood at the kitchen window watching her daughter playing with the other children down in the back court. She should have been standing here with a baby in her arms – tired and smelling of milk, but happy.

There were to be no more children. She had guessed as much when she had woken in the unfamiliar surroundings of the hospital and the doctor had pulled out a chair, sat beside her and reached for her hand. It was that gesture which had done it, and the way he had addressed her by her first name,

330

even although he didn't know her from Adam. She had known by those two things that he had bad news to deliver.

He had been very kind, had tried to break it to her gently, but there was no way of being gentle about the news he had to impart. She heard the words he spoke, understood what he meant about having to perform an emergency operation on her, knew what had been taken away from her. There was, he told her gravely, no reason why she shouldn't lead a normal married life in every other respect.

No reason except that her husband was on the other side of the world. No reason except that he no longer wanted her. What had he said that dreadful day? *At this precise moment I don't know whether I ever want to see you again.*

'You mark my words, lass,' said her father with cheerful bluster, 'your man'll be back just as soon as he can. Jessie's written to him to let him know what's happened. I'm sure he'll manage to find himself another ship to come home on as soon as he finds out.' Her father too had reached for her hand, lying listlessly on the spotless white hospital coverlet.

As the weeks rolled by, and her body began to recover from what she had been through, the fear that Robbie might never come back grew and grew. There had been no reply to Jessie's letter, although the cheerful postcards kept coming for Grace. That was hard to understand – real hard. Had he changed so much? Did he not care at all?

She wondered if she was being punished for what she had done to Robbie, wondered if God were really so vengeful. She didn't know. She only knew that He didn't listen. She heard Grace's prayers every night, but said none herself.

'Gentle Jesus, meek and mild, look upon a little child, pity my simplicity, suffer me to come to Thee.' Then Grace would go off into her own personal litany, asking: 'God bless Mammy and Daddy, Granny and Grandad Cameron, Granny and Grandad Baxter . . .' It went on, through her

331

young aunts and uncles, until she came to the end. 'And look after my wee brother, God. Amen.'

Neil James, Grace had declared firmly, reducing all the adults present to helpless tears, was in heaven now, playing with Mr Asquith.

Kate wished her own faith were still that simple. *Please God, bring Robbie home. Let him find it in his heart to forgive me so that we can start again.* It didn't work that way. She knew it didn't. She had tried.

Chapter 30

Kate felt manky. There was no other word to describe it. She was sweaty all over, and her hair, scraped back into a pony tail, was coming loose in wee wispy bits which were sticking themselves to the side of her head and neck. Well, there was nothing else for it. It was Hogmanay and the work had to be done. She had snapped Jessie's head off when her younger sister had anxiously asked if she really thought she was up to helping with the chores.

Of course she was. She'd been back to the hospital for a check-up at the end of November and everything was fine. Back to normal. Jessie, frowning, had finally agreed that Kate could help, but she wasn't to do anything heavy. When Kate had announced that she was going to wash the stairs, Jessie had briskly ordered wee Davie, now at secondary school and taller than both of his sisters, to fill the heavy galvanised steel bucket with soapy water and carry it out onto the landing for Kate.

'Och, Jessie,' he'd complained. 'That's women's work!'

She'd given him a swift clout on the back of the head and told him to get on with it.

'Psychology, eh?' Andrew Baxter had commented, grinning when Jessie had given him a rueful smile in return.

Kate, squeezing the mop out over the grille set into one half of the bucket, smiled at the memory. That pair needed a bomb underneath them – particularly Andrew. She was beginning to hope that, having sown his wild oats, he might eventually be coming to realise just what he had in Jessie, but he was taking his time. She'd encouraged Jessie to take more interest in her appearance, persuaded her to cut her hair and wear it in a more flattering style, not scraped back into that old pony tail. She was one to talk – considering the way she herself looked at this moment.

Well, she would sort that out once she had done the stairs; she would have a bath and wash her hair to get ready for the New Year. She had made some resolutions, too. Facts had to be faced. It made her feel sick to contemplate it, but Robbie might never be going to come back – and she and Grace couldn't stay with her parents for ever. If they were going to find a wee place of their own, Kate had to find a way of making a living. She had a talent. It was time she started using it. Life wasn't going to get any better unless she did.

Painting was a bit difficult in the confined quarters of the Cameron household, but she had started drawing again, using the illustrations of plants and flowers in Jessie's old Botany textbook for inspiration. Lifting the dirt from the floor with long regular strokes of the mop, Kate sighed. She could never stop herself working out how things would look, transferred to pottery. She had to get back to it somehow – but that might take a wee while. In the meantime, she needed to make some money. That meant she had to do some paintings – pictures that would sell.

She had an idea for a set of four paintings of different wild flowers – small enough for her to be able to do at the kitchen table but attractive grouped together on a wall for display. She would go up to Glasgow next week and ask the gallery owner who had bought her Bluebell Woods pictures what he thought of the idea – and if he didn't like it, she would think of something else. She would smarten herself up, do her hair nicely and borrow Jessie's new coat. There'd be no stopping her once she was suitably titivated.

Lifting the mop and swabbing it over the floor, a memory came back to her. Agnes Baxter had once encouraged her to do just that. *Laddies like to see a bit of sparkle. Especially a certain laddie we both know.* Kate stopped for a moment, leaning on the mop. She would write to him. Try one more time. However hard it was to compose the letter.

She heard footsteps coming into the close from the street two floors below, and dipped the mop once more in the soapy water. It was getting a bit grey now. She'd have to get Davie to change it for her. That would please him. Women's work, indeed!

The footsteps were getting closer. It couldn't be Pearl, could it, coming home to wish everybody a Happy New Year?

Gripping the dark wood of the banister, she leaned over to see. No, it was a man. 'Be careful if you're coming up,' she called. 'The floor's wet.'

The man ascended to the half-landing on the floor below and turned his face up to look at her.

'I'll be careful,' he said quietly.

Transfixed by that voice, Kate stared down at him.

'Hello,' said Robert Baxter, and started up the stairs towards her.

He was wearing an off-white sailor's polo-neck jersey with a navy jacket on top. His dark hair was unruly as usual, and a bit too long, but he looked fit and strong and tall, his pale skin tanned by months of exposure to the sun and the sea. He wasn't smiling. Somewhere nearby a door opened.

'Daddy!' There was a piercing shriek. Then all hell broke loose. In a flurry of curls and petticoats, Grace came hurtling out of the flat. She was hotly pursued by Towser, the Baxters' old dog, although you'd never have guessed his age from the

335

speed with which he was running after Grace. Woken from her trance, Kate yelled at her that the floor was slippy. Grace checked her speed not one jot. She did skid, in fact, but just before she reached Robbie. He laughed easily, caught her up and enfolded her in a great bear hug.

'Daddy, Daddy, Daddy!' Grace was delirious with joy. 'Oh Daddy, you're home!'

'Aye, sweetheart. I'm home.' He was hugging the little girl tightly, pulling her into his chest. He lifted his head and looked Kate in the eye. 'I'm home.'

What he might have meant by that, Kate had no chance of finding out. Grace's excited shouting had alerted everyone in the close. Doors were opened, faces broke into smiles, Towser tried to lick Robbie to death, and family and friends came out to shake him by the hand and clap him on the shoulders. He shot one final impenetrable look at Kate before they were both engulfed.

There were presents for everybody: ornaments for the parents; lengths of material for his sisters and Jessie; a simple camera each for Andrew and Davie; a Red Indian doll for Grace, complete with feathered head-dress.

'She's called Pocahontas,' he told the little girl, his arm loosely about her as she sat on his knee. 'Can you say that?'

Grace turned her face up towards him and repeated the difficult name.

He gave her a hug and dropped a kiss on her forehead. 'Well done, sweetheart.'

Kate had to look away. The little tableau of father and daughter was too much to bear. Up at the window Alice, Flora and Jessie were holding the lengths of fabric against each other, trying to decide who should have what. At the table Andrew and Davie were excitedly examining their cameras. Only one person had been left out. Kate wondered dully if anyone else had noticed. Neil Cameron had. His words fell heavily into the happy chatter in the room.

'Haven't you forgotten your wife, Robert?'

Robbie, who'd been watching Grace making friends with her new doll, looked up.

'No, I haven't forgotten my wife.'

He locked eyes with his father-in-law. It was a look which said as clearly as though the words had been spoken, 'And what business is it of yours anyway?' From the expression on Neil's face as the two men stared each other out, it was obvious that Kate's father thought otherwise. Agnes Baxter, with a lifetime's experience of defusing male aggression, rushed into the breach.

'Och, Kate, pet,' she said, 'I'm that pleased for you. To have Robbie back, I mean. After the baby and all that.'

Robbie's voice cut like a knife through all the other conversations going on in the room.

'And all that?' He was looking questioningly at Kate. 'Where *is* the baby, by the way? Through in the front room?'

She rose to her feet in one jerky movement. Jessie was beside her immediately.

'I'm going upstairs to have a bath and wash my hair, Jessie.' She smiled brightly at her younger sister. 'I can't go dirty into the New Year, now can I? Will you come up with me?'

'Aye, Kate. I will.' She slipped her arm through Kate's.

As the Cameron sisters left the room, Agnes Baxter began in a low voice to talk to her eldest son.

The two families were waiting together for the bells, as they had done so many times in the past. Money was tighter than ever but there was shortbread and black bun as usual and enough whisky for the men to toast the New Year, with lemonade for the women and children. The houses, stairs and close were as clean as many willing hands could make them. Every scrap of clothing had been washed. Everybody had washed themselves and their hair. The usual jokes were being told.

This Hogmanay, however, was like no other. Nothing had actually been said, although for a moment it had looked as though – astonishingly – Neil Cameron and Robert Baxter were about to exchange angry words. There were plenty of undercurrents, though: anxious looks and sudden silences.

Most members of the two families, especially the younger ones, felt the tension in the air without any idea of what was causing it. Agnes Baxter was unhappily aware that something had gone badly wrong between Kate and Robbie. She'd had her suspicions when he'd gone off like that, but the pair of them had managed to keep the full extent of the rift between them well hidden. Until now. Neil Cameron was on a knife-edge, she could see that. So could Lily. She kept clasping and unclasping her hands, darting anxious looks at her husband all the time.

Lily, Kate had to keep reminding herself, was the only person apart from herself and Robbie who knew what was really wrong. It had never been discussed – she didn't have those sort of conversations with her mother – but Lily was shrewd enough. She would have worked out why Robbie had gone off to sea.

Kate was certain, however, that her mother had never told her father the truth. His belligerent defence of his daughter against what he saw as Robbie's neglect of her tugged at Kate's heartstrings, but it was misguided. If he knew what she had done . . . but he did not, so she was not surprised when he could contain himself no longer.

It was well after eleven. Grace was sleeping soundly behind the curtains of the box bed. Davie was struggling to show how wide-awake he was, the last hour of the old year, as usual, dragging itself at a snail's pace towards oblivion.

'What are your intentions towards my daughter?' The words boomed out in the sleepy room.

Robbie stood up. Neil, too, rose from his chair. They were squaring up to each other, both almost exactly the same height, both as stubborn as mules – and neither prepared to give an inch. The atmosphere in the room was electric.

'My immediate intentions towards your daughter – who also happens to be my wife – are to take her out for a walk.' There was a very faint emphasis on that *my wife*. 'Do you have any objections to that, Neil? No? Good.' He wheeled round to Kate.

'Will you get your coat?' he asked quietly.

He hadn't given his father-in-law much time to answer. He'd never called him by his first name before, either. Kate fetched her coat. Her father spoke again.

'I'm not sure that Kathleen should be going out in the cold. She's been ill, you know. Or hadn't you heard?'

Robbie's voice was cool and unemotional. 'I'd heard. Although not until a few hours ago.' His grey eyes flickered over her as she stood doing up her coat and fastening a muffler about her neck. 'She's well wrapped up. A wee bit of fresh air will do her good.'

There was no need to discuss where they were heading. As they turned down Yoker Ferry Road Robbie spoke, his tone of voice calm and level.

'I think your father wants to rearrange my face.'

'He doesn't know,' Kate put in. They walked on in silence for a few paces. 'He doesn't know what I . . . what I did to you.'

She turned her face away, fixing her gaze on their surroundings, on the ferry and the river just coming into view, on anything but the face of the man walking beside her.

'But he knows what *I* did to you.'

She looked at him then, but his eyes were fixed on the lights of Renfrew on the other side of the river. The ferry was chugging its way across.

'You've no idea how much I've missed this river.' His voice was soft in the darkness.

And me, she wanted to ask, have you missed me?

They walked together without touching, in step but a foot or more apart. She had dreamed so often of having him home, had rehearsed what she would say, how she would explain it all to him. Now that he was here she couldn't seem to get a word out.

'We'll stop here.' They were at the rowan tree.

She halted immediately and saw, now that her eyes had grown used to the darkness, that there was a faint smile on his face.

'So obedient, aren't you? Come out when I ask you to, stop when I tell you to.'

She didn't know how to answer. He was so different from the Robert Baxter who had gone away nine months before. Oh, he looked more or less the same, but he had a different air to him somehow. He had acquired a polish, a sophistication. Was the real Robbie still there? Or was he buried so deep that she was never going to be able to find him again? She tucked a strand of hair behind her ear in the old, nervous gesture.

'Cat got your tongue?'

Her eyes filled with tears.

'You're crying.'

It was a statement of fact. Nothing more. No sympathy in his tone. No attempt to take her in his arms.

'I cried, you know.' There was still no expression in his voice. 'Down here. At this exact spot. The night we broke up.'

Kate found her voice at last. 'Broke up? Is that how you see it?'

He went on as though she hadn't spoken. 'It was pouring with rain that night, do you remember?'

Yes, she remembered. She had cried too, had thrown herself across the box bed and cried until she had made herself sick. She could remember the rain beating against the window panes . . .

'I stood here and cried and the rain ran down the back of my neck and I didn't give a damn. Nothing mattered.' He gave a short laugh. 'I got cold eventually – freezing cold. I started thinking of where I could go to be warm. Somewhere dark and secret. I suppose I was like an animal crawling away to lick its wounds.'

'Where did you go?' she whispered.

He turned then and looked at her. Was there still a faint smile on his mouth? 'I went back to where I had come from that day – where I had found out about you and Jack Drummond.'

Kate winced at that name – and at what came next.

'The woman there let me in – I must have looked like a drowned rat – and one of her girls took me to her room . . . and did what women in houses like that do best.' He *was* smiling. If you could call it that.

'I've learned to have great respect for women like her. I've done business with four or five of them since I've been away.'

'Four or five?' Kate's mouth went dry.

Robbie's smile broadened. 'Well, on one occasion I was too drunk to know whether I had been capable of anything the night before.'

'Drunk? You?'

'Och, I thought I would try it. See if it helped.' He paused, lifting his face to the night air. 'Take my word for it, it doesn't. Instead of just waking up miserable, you wake up miserable *and* with a thumping headache. I paid her though, it seemed the least I could do.' The cool, detached voice went on. Relentless. Ignoring Kate's growing distress. 'It's a business transaction, after all, and I had taken up space in her bed. She was entitled to her money. That's what I like about it. It's a straightforward deal – no emotions involved.'

Kate could take no more. She let out a cry of pain, like a small trapped animal in distress.

He lowered his head and looked directly at her. 'Hurts, does it?' he enquired pleasantly. 'Thinking of me with other women?'

Kate squeezed her eyes tight shut. Her voice was an agonised whisper. 'Yes, it hurts.'

'Good,' he said. 'Now you know how it feels.' He put a hand inside his jacket, took out a packet of cigarettes, extracted one and lit up.

She looked at him, so cool, so calm – so cruel. This was not the Robert Baxter she knew. This was a brittle elegant stranger. *Elegant?* It seemed a funny word to use about Robbie Baxter, but it was the one that fitted. He was studying her dispassionately, putting the cigarette to his lips, striking a match to light it.

'I didn't know you had taken up smoking.'

He shrugged. 'Maybe there's a lot you don't know about me. There was certainly a lot I didn't know about you. Wasn't there?'

Kate turned her head away and bit her lip, unable to meet that unforgiving gaze any longer.

Robbie swore. Coarsely and violently. Startled, Kate looked up. She had known he was capable of it. All the men in the yards did it, but few of them let a curse pass their lips when they were in female company. He gave another angry exclamation and tossed his cigarette into the river. She watched the glowing red tip as it fell in an arc towards the water. She even heard the tiny hiss as it was extinguished.

342

Then there was rapid breathing in her ear and Robbie was beside her, gripping her wrist, and looking down his long nose at her.

'Wasn't there?' he demanded. 'A lot of things I didn't know?'

'I'm sorry,' she said.

'Sorry?' he spat out. 'Sorry? For Christ's sake, Kathleen!'

Kate felt a sudden spark of anger. She tossed her head. 'Yes! I'm sorry! What else do you want me to say? I did a terrible thing to you, but by God I've been punished for it! And don't swear at me!'

He dropped her arm and took a step or two backwards. 'I'm sorry for swearing,' he said tersely. 'And for taking the Lord's name in vain.' He lit up again and then stood looking at her from under his dark brows. 'What was he like?' he asked abruptly. 'Our son?'

'Like you,' Kate said, caught off-balance by the suddenness of the question. 'He had this really curious look about him – inquisitive. You know?'

The man in front of her nodded, his lips pressed firmly together.

'I told him his name . . . and I told him about you . . . and Grace . . . and me . . . and he drew his wee eyebrows together, just like *you* do when you're trying to work something out.' She was silent, remembering those precious few moments with their son.

'What did you call him?'

'Neil James. After his two grandfathers. My father baptised him.'

Robbie nodded his head. 'You chose fine names.'

Somewhere deep inside Kate a tiny flame of hope flared into life. It was as small as the glowing end of Robbie's cigarette, and might be just as easily put out, but it was there.

'Why didn't someone write to me?' he demanded. 'Let me know what had happened?'

She stared at him. 'Jessie wrote to you. Did you not get the letter?'

'Jessie?' He shook his head from side to side. 'No, I got two letters from you.'

'No,' Kate insisted. 'The second one was from Jessie. I wasn't well enough to write. She wrote and told you what had happened.' Her voice broke. 'And you never replied. I waited and waited. I even thought you might come home as soon as you got the news. But you didn't.'

'I didn't know!' he burst out. 'I didn't open the second letter – I was so sure it was from you. The handwriting looked just the same.' He put the cigarette to his lips, then withdrew it, looking at it in disgust. 'God, I hate these bloody things.' It went the same way as the first one.

'You didn't open it?' Kate's voice rose on a note of mingled outrage and incredulity.

Robbie gave her a curious look. 'You're angry with me,' he observed.

'Yes,' she said slowly, realising it for the first time. 'Yes, I'm angry with you.'

He was watching her carefully. 'Because I wasn't there when you needed me?'

'That,' said Kate, thinking about it. 'And because you had me up on a pedestal. You thought I was perfect, that I couldn't make mistakes. Well, I can. And I did. Why did you not open the second letter?' she asked, her voice a little calmer.

'Because the first one was so . . .' He paused, searching for the right word. 'Cold. I just couldn't face another one like that.'

'Cold?'

'Well, what would you call it?' He quoted verbatim. ' "*It looks like being quite a hot summer this year. We are all well and*

344

hope that you are too." And the way you signed it! "*Kathleen Baxter.*" In the name of God, Kate! How do you think I felt when I read that?'

'I don't know. How did you feel?'

His answer came straight back at her. 'That you didn't love me any more. That you never really had loved me. That you still loved *him.*'

Kate was getting angry again. 'How could you think I didn't love you? How could you, after how it had been between us two? Are you stupid or something, Robert Baxter?'

He looked startled. Then his face relaxed.

'Yes,' he said softly. 'I'm stupid, a right eejit. I need things spelled out for me.'

She spelled them out for him. 'I love you. I always have done and I always will.'

'And Jack Drummond?' Robbie's voice was deceptively calm.

'I thought I loved him. I thought he loved me. That he wanted to marry me. I was wrong on all three counts.' She dropped her eyes, embarrassed at what she was going to say next, but knowing that it had to be said. 'But that's why I slept with him . . . and I did it once, Robbie. Just once.'

There was a long silence. Kate shivered as a little breeze off the water stung her cheek. She dared to look up. Robbie was slowly nodding his head.

'That's what I figured. When I had time to think about it. And he wouldn't marry you and your mother told you it was me or some old witch with a knitting needle.'

Kate flinched.

'I'm sorry,' he said. 'That was coarsely put. But that was what happened, wasn't it?'

She nodded, unable to speak.

'And you couldn't do it. You couldn't bear to end a life which had only just begun.' He paused. 'Grace's life.'

'No,' she whispered. 'No, I couldn't.' She coughed to clear her throat and went on, her voice stronger.

'I couldn't get rid of the baby, I just couldn't – and you were so upset about Barbara. I knew that you loved me, and I thought I could try to be a good wife to you, try to make you happy.'

She dared a look at him. Robbie was watching her intently.

'When Grace was born you loved her so much . . . just like she loves you so much. I knew that didn't make it right, but I thought – maybe – it made up a bit for what I had done to you.'

Robbie's grave expression hadn't altered. Kate forced herself to go on.

'Then I realised that I did love you, that it was you I had loved all along.' Her voice was a whisper. 'Maybe I've realised that too late.' She had tears in her eyes again. Turning her head away she looked out across the river to the lights of Renfrew. It must be nearly midnight. Almost the New Year.

His voice was gruff. 'You haven't realised it too late. Not as far as I'm concerned.' His next words were tentative and uncertain. 'Do you want to start again, Kate?'

Kate lifted her chin. It was courage that was needed here, not tears. Courage enough not to settle for second best. For both their sakes.

'Yes,' she said firmly. 'I do. But not if I have to go around apologising for the rest of my life. Not if it's always going to be cast up at me. Not if you don't allow me to make mistakes sometimes.'

There was a catch in his voice. 'Make as many as you like – just so long as you come back to me!'

'Oh, Robbie!' Was it her or him who closed the distance between them? No matter. They were in each other's arms.

'Hush, now. Hush. Don't fight me,' he added, for she was struggling a little in his embrace.

'Oh, Robbie!' She looked up at him, impatiently wiping away a tear. 'I was trying to be all grown-up and calm about it, and here I am crying on your shoulder. Just like I've always done.'

'That's what shoulders are for,' he said comfortably. 'And I've cried on yours too, haven't I?' He pulled her head down. 'Now cry. Cry for as long as you like.'

'But Robbie . . .'

His arms tightened around her. 'Dae as yer tellt, Kate Baxter.' He gave her back the words with which she had comforted him the night his beloved sister Barbara had died. 'It's all worth crying for, isn't it?'

There were to be many more tears in the days and weeks that followed – but no recriminations. That they had decided as they had stood by the Clyde at midnight, listening to the ships' foghorns heralding the arrival of 1934 in the time-honoured way. A new year, and a new start for them, Robbie had said.

It wasn't an easy time. Until they found a new place of their own, their only privacy was a nightly walk by the river. That was where they talked it all out. They were very frank with each other – and the tears were not all on Kate's side. Robbie got upset too, especially when he asked her to forgive him for breaking their wedding vows.

'I hated myself for doing it, Kate. Each time – afterwards, I mean – well, I felt disgusted with myself.' He paused, and reached for her hand as they walked. 'If it's any consolation, the last time was six months ago.' He swallowed, and she realised that he was forcing himself to tell her this. 'I did it all at the beginning. I think I went a wee bit mad after I left here . . .' His voice trailed off.

'I won't pretend that it doesn't hurt,' she said when she felt able to speak. 'It does. But I think – maybe – I can understand why you did it.'

He stopped and took her other hand in his. 'I don't deserve your forgiveness, Kate.'

'Yes you do,' she whispered, looking up into his troubled face.

'Och, Kate,' he said. 'Och, Kate.'

She took him to their baby's grave and he stood there for a long time with his head bowed. She gave him the time he needed, but when he raised his head at last she was beside him, wordlessly offering him the comfort of her arms. He arranged for the stone Kate hadn't been able to afford and when the spring came they went with Grace to lay daffodils in front of it in memory of Neil James Baxter.

'We'll plant some daffodil bulbs for your wee brother later on,' Robbie said, squeezing Kate's hand and smiling down at Grace. 'Flowers that'll go on living from year to year.'

In private, Kate had told him anxiously that there could be no more children.

'We've got Grace, haven't we?' He read the question in her eyes. 'Grace is my daughter,' he told her, '*our* daughter. In every way that matters.'

'Then why did you sign your postcards *R. Baxter*?'

He looked nonplussed. 'Because it didn't seem right to put *Daddy* on something that everyone was going to be reading.'

'That was all?'

'Did you worry about that? You're a daft bisom, Kate Baxter, d'you know that?' His smile slipped. 'Oh, but lassie, I'm sorry you had to go through so much on your own.'

He had listened gravely as she had recounted the story of her haemorrhage, and how she had woken up in hospital afterwards to be told of the operation. When she finished speaking, he pulled her soundlessly into his arms for a few moments, trying to imbue her with some of his own strength.

348

She was so thin . . . Maybe he would take her to Millport for a few days once the weather got a bit better. Shovel food and fresh air into her.

When he released her from his embrace his smile was wry. 'No wonder Neil wants to punch me in the mouth.'

Kate's father, in fact, had thawed a little. Watching like a hawk when they came back into the house on New Year's morning, he had relaxed visibly when he had seen that they were holding hands. He had unbent further the next day when Kate had shown the womenfolk of the two families the beautiful pearls Robbie had brought her back from America.

'I got them in Boston,' he told her when he gave them to her, 'and wondered if I would ever be able to give them to you. I felt so unworthy of you by then,' he went on, the grey eyes too bright. 'You made one mistake. I'd . . . Well, I'd deliberately gone and done what I did.'

'Don't torture yourself about it,' she said softly.

'If you promise me the same,' he said earnestly. 'Shall we agree to forgive each other, Kate?'

'Yes,' she said, 'we'll agree to forgive each other.'

Chapter 31

'Robert Baxter, why are you grinning like an eejit?'

He had just come through the door of their new flat in Dumbarton Road, not far from their first home at the foot of Kilbowie Road but with a bit more space this time. The two-apartment room and kitchen had been funded by Robbie's accumulated pay from his months on the *Border Reiver*.

His eyes were sparkling. He had swung the door shut and was leaning against it, his arms behind his back.

'Guess,' he told Kate who, a mixing bowl in the crook of her left arm, was creaming sugar and margarine together for the start of the sponge cake she was making.

'Och, I've no idea.' She glanced at the *Be-Ro* recipe book open on the table, propped the wooden spoon carefully against the side of the bowl and ran her index finger down the list of ingredients, more concerned with doing a mental check of her cupboards than in answering him.

'Shall I tell you then?'

'Aye, go on. Grace! A wee bit less raspberry, pet.' Grace was 'helping' her mother by finishing off the Eiffel Towers. Since this involved dipping the cooled baked cakes in a glaze made from raspberry jam and water and then rolling them in dessicated coconut, the potential for disaster was quite considerable. She should have known better. Kate set the mixing bowl down on the table and looked around for a damp cloth. There had been one here a minute ago.

'Kate, for Pete's sake. Pay attention!'

He was beside her, grabbing her by the waist and whirling her around the room. Grace clapped her sticky hands together in delight. Her father winked at her and kissed her mother soundly on the cheek. Grace chortled.

'Robbie! Put me down! I'm covered in flour!'

He laughed. 'Who cares? Now, are you going to ask me again why I'm grinning like an eejit?'

Kate raised her hands in surrender. His enthusiasm was infectious.

'All right! All right! Tell us what you've got to smile about.'

He released her and started ticking them off on his fingers.

'One. I'm married to the most beautiful girl in the world.' He kissed her again and then waltzed across the room to lift Grace into his arms. 'Two. I've got the bonniest wee daughter in the world.' He planted a kiss on her cheek too.

'You're daft, Daddy.' Grace laughed and took his chin between her small hands.

'As a brush,' he agreed. He paused for effect. Kate, also for effect, folded her arms over her flowery wrap-around pinny and tapped her foot. They grinned at each other.

'All right. I'll ask you. What's number three?'

'Number three, my dear girls,' he was going to burst if he didn't get it out soon, 'is that work is restarting on the 534! Next week! The day after Easter Monday!'

And then they were all three dancing round the room, and Robbie, tasting of raspberry jam, was kissing both of them and Kate was crying and laughing at the same time.

Clydebank was a town transformed. The Cunarder was to be launched that September and there was no time to be lost. Men streamed joyfully back to work. That first day back, at the beginning of April 1934, they were led through the gates

351

of Brown's by two kilted pipers, and the streets of the town were decorated with bunting.

Some were worried how they would cope with the hard work after so long being idle, but they set to work with a will. One man was told sternly by a foreman that his tools were a bit rusted.

'You should see my frying pan,' was the reply.

But the pots and pans were full again. The men were working and there was food on the table – and Clydebank was noisy once more. Living so close to the yard, Kate could hear it constantly: the clang of hammers and machinery and the constant hum of talk. It was more than that. In the yard and out in the town itself, people were light-hearted again, chatting and telling jokes. Men no longer stood aimlessly at street corners all day. The pall of despair had lifted. Maybe, folk said, work starting again on the 534 was the turning point for the whole country to get back on its feet. Maybe the great Depression itself would soon be over.

Kate Baxter was happy too. It wasn't just that she'd caught the general mood of optimism, powerful though that was. It was more that she started each day with a joyous thankfulness that she and Robbie had been given a second chance – that they had given each other that second chance.

They made good use of their fresh start. They took pleasure in each other's company by day and delighted in their nights together, private in the front room while Grace slept snugly in the box bed in the kitchen. They had bought a brass bedstead second-hand. They'd got it cheap – a real bargain. People were beginning to find them old-fashioned, but Kate had always wanted one of her own. She made the bedspread herself out of heavy white cotton which was on special offer at Clydebank Co-op, and used what was left to make pillowcases which she decorated with cutwork.

'Mmm,' murmured her young husband. 'What more does

a man need than you with your hair spread all over a white pillow, your arms flung up beside your head and your fingers tightening around the rails of the bedhead? Och, Kate, my bonnie lassie, my nut-brown maiden . . .'

They made time for their family and friends, seeing a lot of Mary and Peter Watt and their young son Adam, whom five-year-old Grace treated with great condescension. The two families went on trips together: up the West Highland line on the train on days out; 'doon the watter' on the pleasure steamers which plied the Firth of Clyde.

They worked hard and they played hard. Kate went back to the art club, experienced enough now that she could take on some tutoring of the newer members. Encouraged by Mary and Peter, she and Robbie got involved with a local drama group, Kate quickly becoming the set designer, painter and general stage manager. Robbie did the carpentry work for her and found time to write a play about the Cunarder which the group performed. It was sharp and witty and full of topical jokes and the plucky young lovers he put into it bore a remarkable resemblance to Kate and Robert Baxter.

He had re-written the poems he had burned, shyly offering them to her one Sunday evening and then having to leave the house while she read them because he was so embarrassed. He apologised profusely for them on his return, telling her how bad they were.

'They're very derivative,' he started. He'd been attending an evening class in English literature, and was beginning to acquire the vocabulary. 'There's a lot of the other Robbie in there – Burns, I mean.' He smiled sheepishly. She stopped him with a hand over his mouth.

'They're beautiful. They're from the heart. Your heart.'

They *were* derivative. She could see what he meant. But he had underrated himself. There was an originality in the poems and a way of using words that was all his own. She

353

told him so, and he blushed and kissed her and told her he'd write better ones for her one day.

'But not until after we put the *Queen* onto the river,' he added with a rueful grin.

She was launched less than six months after work had resumed. The whole town went Cunarder-daft for that, with special concerts and events of all sorts to celebrate the launch, including Robbie's play. The name had been a big secret up till the moment the Queen herself stepped forward on the platform. Forgetting that the ceremony was being broadcast to the nation on the wireless, she whispered anxiously to her husband the King, 'Which buttons do I press?'

Then she gave the 534 her own name. The Cunarder was to be called the *Queen Mary*.

Typically, it rained cats and dogs on the day of the launch. Everyone got soaked to the skin, but nobody minded. It was a great day all the same, even if Grace Baxter was disappointed.

'Why's the ship got no funnels?' she wailed. 'And why is she such a horrible colour?' The hull was painted a dull grey.

Her Uncle Davie, a Brown's apprentice now himself, crouched down to her and gave her the benefit of his knowledge.

'There's a lot of work to be done yet, wee yin. The engines and the boilers – aye, and the funnels, too – have all still to go in. Then they'll paint her in bonnie colours. And then there's all the fancy bits that the cabinet-makers like your Daddy do – the decks, and the bulkheads and the cabins and a' that.'

Robbie smiled at his brother-in-law.

'It's not the likes of me that does the really fancy bits. That's the interior designers and the artists and all those kind of folk.

Just wait till you see how fancy the *Mary*'s going to be. There's never been a ship like this one.'

After the launch the frantic activity resumed. They were all working towards the sailing date. She was the greatest liner ever seen, the world's largest. She was also to become the fastest, twice winning the coveted Blue Riband for the swiftest crossing of the Atlantic. Because of her great size she needed to leave the fitting-out basin on a high tide in order to get safely out – and safely down the river to the Tail of the Bank and the open sea. That high tide, occurring as it did only twice a year, made the date of completion of her interior of crucial importance.

Robbie often came home tired and worn out, but it was a happy tiredness. He was proud of what he was doing. All the men were. This ship was special.

He managed to get Kate on board for an organised tour of the ship shortly before she was due to sail. His wife was entranced. She'd been able to see for herself, from the outside, that the ship was huge. She hadn't realised that the vessel was like a floating town, supplied with everything the inhabitants of that town might need. Not only was the *Mary* fitted out with suites and cabins and restaurants and saloons – all as luxurious as you would expect – she also had a chapel, a hospital, a cinema and theatre, libraries, gymnasia and even tennis courts. There were playrooms for children, writing rooms for adults, a hairdresser's and a beauty parlour.

The *grand salon*, right in the centre of the vessel and going through three decks, was truly breathtaking. Like the other public rooms it was not only fitted out in the best of modern style – it was also decorated with paintings by some of the finest artists of the day.

There were maritime scenes, like the exquisite *Madonna of the Atlantic*, which showed Mary and Jesus in front of a group

355

of old high-masted sailing ships. Kate thought that was one of her favourites. There were bustling harbour scenes and pastoral views of the peaceful British countryside.

'Probably to help a' the rich folk forget where they are when they're feeling seasick,' one man said out of the corner of his mouth to Kate.

She flashed him an automatic smile, but barely heard him, stunned by the beauty and elegance of her surroundings. They were guided to one of the smaller lounges, where they were told of the attention paid to the details – down to the design of the ashtrays which also had to fit in with the overall theme: cutlery and crockery too, of course. Their guide opened a cupboard in illustration, showing them the cups and saucers from which the passengers in this particular lounge would be drinking their morning coffee.

Kate looked. Then she looked again. The crockery was her own *Rowan Tree Ware*.

She mentioned it that night, as the three of them sat at the table with their Friday treat: fish suppers bought from the chip shop along the road. Robbie was enthusiastic.

'Really? Och, that's great, Kate. I'll need to go and have a look. Which lounge did you say?'

She told him, and changed the subject.

Later, when he was helping her with the dishes, he brought it up again.

'With your pottery and my carpentry I reckon that makes the *Mary* a joint effort – a Baxter family production!'

'I suppose.' She laid another plate on the draining board.

He put down the plate he was drying and placed his hand on top of her wet and soapy one.

'What's the matter?'

Kate, one hand still in the sink, was staring out of the window at the back green. 'It's lovely to think that when she

356

sails away she'll have something of both of us on board,' she said softly.

'But?'

She took her hand back and washed the third plate, wiping her hands on her apron before she answered.

'I loved designing things and then seeing them become real. It's like a ship, I suppose. Only not on such a grand scale.'

He was drying the remaining plates, letting her talk, his eyes on her face as she struggled to put her thoughts into words.

'A ship starts as a drawing on a piece of paper, but if enough people work hard it becomes something real . . . and special. I worked hard at the designs for *Rowan Tree Ware* and I worked hard at learning the technical side. I used to dream of doing so much . . .' She gave him a sheepish smile. 'Even used to daydream about having my own pottery studio. And I love the art club, I really do, but I wanted to make a lot more pottery and maybe I never will.'

'Come here,' he said, putting the last plate down and tossing the damp cloth to one side. 'You,' he said, his hands on her waist, 'are most definitely going to do a lot more pottery. Would you not consider going back to the Art School extra-mural classes? I know they're expensive, but we could manage if we were careful. I'd look after Grace.'

Kate shook her head. 'No. We don't know if there's going to be any work once the *Mary* goes. And anyway, I'm a different person now – your wife and Grace's mother. The Kate who dreamed of being a great potter belongs in the past.'

Robbie made a rude noise. 'Just because you're a wife and mother doesn't mean you haven't still got your talent. You've proved that with becoming a tutor at the art club – and with your set designs for the drama club. Everyone's said how good they are.'

'Och, that,' said Kate dismissively. 'Well, it's fun, but it's

357

not exactly difficult. Not quite the same challenge as throwing a pot or making a lovely plate.'

He smiled and dropped a kiss on the end of her nose.

'Kate Baxter, you need some sorting out!'

What he meant by that she didn't find out till Sunday. He took Grace out for a walk in the morning and the little girl came back clutching a fistful of dandelions which she presented to her mother.

'Bonnie, aren't they?' asked Robbie, as Kate fetched an empty jam jar to put them in, the best green vase being far too big. 'Grace is like you. She finds beauty in the most unlikely things. I bet those dandelions would make a real nice picture. Unusual, like.' He walked over to the box bed in the kitchen where Grace slept and went down onto his knees.

'Robbie, what are you up to?'

He was pulling something out from the cupboard underneath the bed.

'It's taken me weeks to make this,' he grumbled. 'I could only work on it when I was sure you were going to be out for a couple of hours at the art club. I'll set it up through in the front room. You'll get more light there. Here Grace, take these bits.'

It was an easel. She could see that immediately. He went on talking as he pulled everything out.

'It'll sit on that table through there, and it's adjustable, so you'll be able to sit or stand, depending on what you're doing . . . and you can adjust the rake too, so that it can be completely perpendicular or like a sloping desk. You maybe wouldn't want it too sloped for water colours, would you? Although I was really thinking you might want to practise your oils if you had a bit more space to do it in, and not just once a week at the class.'

He stood up. There was a dirty mark on his cheek. She'd

have to remember to clean under the bed next time she was doing the floor. Grace marched off to her parents' bedroom carrying the parts of the easel which her father had given her.

'I've made the base a box where you can keep your paints. I didn't know what to do about canvases but we can maybe go up to Glasgow next weekend and get you some supplies?' He shot Kate a look of enquiry and then, in mock dismay, surveyed the base box and the other pieces of wood he held.

'With a bit of luck I'll manage to get everything put together in the right place. In about a fortnight.' He grinned at Kate. 'Are you coming ben the house to see how it works?'

'Robbie,' she whispered. 'You made this for me?'

'Well, I couldn't manage a potter's wheel or a kiln, but I thought maybe you could work on your painting until you can get back to that. It'll surely all help. Give you a proper studio, like.' He grinned again. 'Now that you're an art tutor and no' just a mere art student. Aye?'

'Oh, Robbie!'

'Hey, hey, hey!' He bent at the knees, laying the parts of the easel carefully down on the floor and then crossed the room to her, pulling her into his arms.

'You're a daft bisom, Kathleen Baxter. What are you greeting for?'

'Because I don't deserve you.'

'Well, that's true enough,' he said, and laughed softly when she punched him on the shoulder. He held her so that they could look at each other.

'It's a sin to waste talent, hen. Now, give me a kiss and let's get this thing assembled.'

A few weeks later, Robbie, just home from work, came into his house and looked around the kitchen in a way which made Kate, sitting at the range with Grace on her lap, laugh

359

out loud. A million miles away from being a domineering husband, he was nevertheless used to finding his meal ready for him to eat as soon as he came home. It was the way things were. Not tonight, though. The table was bare.

'We're having fish suppers tonight,' she announced gaily, lifting Grace off her knee and standing up to kiss his puzzled face.

'On a Tuesday?' he asked. 'Have you robbed a bank or something?'

'Better than that.' She crossed to the table, opened her handbag, took some notes out of her purse and counted them in front of his incredulous eyes. Forty pounds. Except when he'd paid off the *Border Reiver*, he'd never seen so much money all at once.

'Forty pounds?' Then realisation struck. 'You got forty pounds for your painting? The oil of the street scene? The one with the tram in it?'

Kate nodded, beaming all over her face. Inspired by his gift of the easel, she had not only immediately done a water colour of Grace's dandelions but also a large canvas of the view from their window on a wet summer's night: figures scuttling for shelter out of the rain; a brightly lit tram trundling through the twilight. She had revelled in using oil paints to capture the way the shiny puddles on the road reflected the warm yellow of the tram's interior lights. She had known it was good, had known the gallery would like it too.

'Not *too realistic*?' she had asked the man, her tongue firmly in her cheek.

The gallery owner had given her a look. 'Tastes change – as you know very well, Kate Baxter.' They were on good terms now. He had taken a few of her paintings over the past year, but he never paid her this much for them. The few pounds she had earned had gone into the housekeeping or the emergency fund, but there was enough to do something more this time.

Robbie, watching her, narrowed his eyes at the expression on her face. She was up to something. She made him wait, spinning it out, getting her revenge for all the times he had teased her and Grace by doing exactly the same.

'Right,' she began. 'Monday night,' she said, ticking it off on her fingers, 'you go to your literature class, and I stay at home with Grace. Yes?' He nodded. 'Thursday night Grace goes to Yoker and we both go to the drama group. Yes?' He nodded again, a cautious smile beginning to steal over his face. She was enjoying herself. Whatever was coming was going to be good. 'Saturday afternoon I go to the art club and Jessie usually takes Grace out somewhere.' Kate ticked off her fourth point. 'So can I take it you wouldn't mind looking after Grace on a *Wednesday* night? When I go to my pottery class at the Art School?' Like himself when he had told her about the resumption of work on the 534, she was bursting with the joy of it.

'You've enrolled? Och, Kate, that's great! That's just wonderful!' He threw his arms about her and kissed her soundly. 'I knew I was right to encourage you,' he said, laughing down at her. 'Paintings and pottery, eh? You'll be able to keep us all in the lap of luxury soon. We'll be that rich we won't know what to do with all the money. Right, Grace?' He extended a hand to their daughter, bringing her into the embrace.

Kate smiled down at Grace and then up at her husband.

'Huh! Maybe I'm hoping you'll become a famous writer first.'

His grey eyes grew soft, as soft as his deep and gentle voice. 'We've both got our dreams, lassie. Shall we dream them together?'

The following month they stood and watched another dream sail away from the Clyde: they and thousands of others. It was

March 1936 and the 534, the *Queen Mary* now, was leaving the river of her birth for ever.

Spectators filled every vantage point. They lined both banks of the river and watched from the high ground overlooking it. Peter Watt had organised a tour for a group of his workmates and their families. They crossed on the Yoker Ferry to Renfrew, where a specially hired bus took them down past Erskine to Bishopton.

The view they had from there was everything they could have wished for. Resplendent in the bonnie colours Grace Baxter had longed for, the *Queen Mary* glided past them, her hull black and red, her superstructure white, her three funnels red with black bands at the top. Mary Watt wasn't the only woman – nor man either – to have tears pouring down her face at the sight. The greatest liner ever built was steaming down the Clyde, taking a sure and steady course between the green hills, heading for the Firth and the open sea.

'Och, she's so lovely . . . but it's so sad to see her go!'

'It's what she was made for, Mary,' said Robbie, 'but you're right. It is sad.' His voice was husky. Kate, also unashamedly in tears, slipped her hand into his and gave his fingers a squeeze. He smiled at her and then raised his voice.

'Let's give her a proper send-off all the same. Three cheers for the *Queen Mary*, the pride of the Clyde!'

And the men who had helped build her opened their mouths and threw their bunnets in the air and did as he asked.

She had been part of their lives, in good times and bad, for almost six years. They had loved her and hated her, grown older in the building of her, put the skill of their hands and the strength of their backs into the work: aye, and their hearts and souls, too.

Two great *Queens* were to come after her. They would be proud of them too: proud to say that they were Clyde-built; that they had worked on them. There would be moist eyes and lumps in the throat when they left the river, but the *Mary* was special.

They had built her for this. Their eyes followed with pride her majestic progress towards the sea and her rendezvous with the ocean. That was her destiny. They had always known that.

Pride, then: overwhelming, intense and life-long. But sorrow too, the sweet sadness of farewell. One description of that day summed it up better than most. *She leaves a big gap in the landscape, and a hole in the hearts of thousands of Clydesiders.*

PART IV

1939

Chapter 32

A war was inevitable. Everybody knew that now. The policy of appeasement just hadn't worked. Robbie had never been in favour of it, declaring firmly that 'yon wee nyaff, Adolf Hitler' was a bully, and that bullies had to be dealt with. Never mind if the Prime Minister had come back from Munich waving a wee bit of paper and yattering on about peace in our time, sooner or later Great Britain was going to have to stand up to Herr Hitler and his Nazis.

Now, in the summer of 1939, frantic preparations were being made for war. Men were quietly being called up to the three services – the beginnings of the full-scale conscription which was to come in 1940 – and endless discussions were held about the advisability of evacuating women and children to the country. Places like Clydebank and Glasgow, filled with shipyards and other heavy industries crucial to the war effort, were bound to be targets. This war wasn't going to be like the last one, where the men marched off and the women and children stayed at home. This time home was going to be one of the main fronts.

Anxious to do his bit, Robbie had volunteered for the Navy several months before war was declared, asserting that it was only a matter of time before he would be called up anyway.

At thirty-two years old, he was in the prime of life, fit and healthy, and with valuable, if brief, experience in the Merchant Navy. He'd been whisked off at once for basic training.

Kate hadn't stood in his way, but she prayed every day that there wouldn't be a war, that the statesmen could still sit down together and work it all out. That was becoming an ever more forlorn hope, and Kate knew that as well as anybody.

As summer drew to an end, different emotions were evident among the younger members of the family. The Baxter girls were excited at the prospect of young single women being called up, seeing an escape from the future which had seemed to be mapped out for them. Wee Davie, at nineteen not quite so wee, was also unsuccessfully hiding wild enthusiasm at the thought of getting into uniform. Neil Cameron sat in his chair and shook his greying head as he listened to the news bulletins on the family's newly acquired wireless.

'I can remember the last time,' was all he said in his soft Highland accent, looking sadly up at the youngest member of his family, now as tall as himself. The nightmares had come back. It was Jessie now who had to help Lily calm him down.

Kate wasn't sure if her sister had finally given up on Andrew Baxter. He too was eager to join up. He'd taken himself off to Spain a year after the *Queen Mary* had sailed away, joining the International Brigade to defend the beleaguered Republican government there against the fascists. Jessie had gone completely white when she'd read the letter he'd left for her.

Pale to the lips, she had spoken in an agonised whisper to an anxiously hovering Kate.

'The silly bugger's going to get himself killed.'

It was the only time she ever heard Jessie swear. The silly bugger, however, had not got himself killed, but had come back from Spain with his enthusiasm for fighting fascism undimmed.

In August Robbie was allowed home on a forty-eight-hour

leave. They spent the second night of it alone, Grace safely dispatched to Yoker.

They ate, took a late evening walk by the river in the autumn twilight, and returned home to make love to each other in the big brass bed, falling asleep afterwards locked in each other's arms. Waking, cold and shivering, in the wee small hours, Kate pulled the blankets up over both of them. Then, sure that he was sound asleep, she turned on her side away from him and succumbed to silent sobs.

He felt them though, stirring awake a minute or two later. His arms, warm and heavy with sleep, came round her, pulling her towards him. She turned into his chest, her hand resting on the solid and reassuring thump of his heart. He kissed her hair and murmured little words of comfort and they fell asleep together once more.

He woke her early and made tender, fierce and silent love to her. Only when the sensations had faded and they lay facing each other did he speak.

'I don't want you to come to the station to see me off.'

She started to protest, but he kissed her to stop the words.

'Please, Kate. I want to remember you like this.' He kissed her again. 'Your lips soft and well-kissed.' Another kiss. 'Your body warm and well-loved.' And another, his hand stroking her arm from wrist to shoulder. 'Your hair needing combed.'

He smiled, trying to lighten the mood, but there was a plea in his grey eyes. She searched his face and answered it in mundane, ordinary words.

'All right, but I am getting up to make your breakfast.'

'What else do I keep you for, woman?'

Normally they sat opposite each other at the square table, with Grace between them. Today Kate, a pretty cotton dressing

369

gown over her nightdress, sat at Grace's place, although she couldn't bring herself to eat anything. She was finding it hard enough to swallow a few mouthfuls of tea. They were both very matter-of-fact. They discussed practicalities. How would they organise money while he was away? How would they keep in touch with each other? Should Kate allow Grace to be evacuated to the country?

'Maybe you should think of going too,' he suggested, spreading his second slice of toast with butter bought specially in honour of his brief homecoming. There were dire warnings going the rounds about rationing being introduced if the war did come, in which case, whether he liked it or not, Robbie was probably going to have to put up with margarine when he was on leave.

'I don't know,' she said. 'You're doing your bit and I think maybe that I want to do my bit too.'

'How, exactly?' He took a bite of toast.

Kate poured him another cup of tea. 'Mary Watt says Peter told her that Brown's are looking for more tracers – experienced ones. Apparently they think a lot of the young girls will join up if the war comes – they might even be called up like the men – so she says they're considering taking on married women. People like me, who were tracers before they got married.'

He nodded his head, thinking about it.

'Well, if they do, it would certainly keep you occupied. Stop you worrying so much about me.' He smiled and touched her hand, giving it a reassuring squeeze. 'And it's important work – you'd be doing your bit all right. If it does come to war, there's bound to be losses at sea. Oh!' Too late he realised what he had said. Kate bit her lip. He lifted her hand to his mouth and kissed her knuckles. 'I'll be as safe as houses. I'll lay you ten to one that I end up in Scapa Flow.'

'Scapa Flow?'

'Aye, it's way up north, in the Orkneys. A natural harbour formed by the islands. It's where the German fleet sank at the end of the Great War.'

'Thanks, Robbie, that's *very* reassuring.'

He grinned. 'They did it deliberately. Scuttled themselves because they were in enemy hands. The Flow's really safe – honestly, Kate. We've had lectures about it during training. Look, I'll show you.' He dropped her hand and starting rearranging the dishes which lay on the table.

'Right. Imagine that the teapot here is the main island. To the south-west of it there's a few small islands and a bigger one called Hoy. We'll use your saucer for that.' He positioned it. 'Then there's these three wee islands that form a sort of a chain round the eastern side, shielding it from anything coming from that direction – and that's where it would come from.'

His smile a little grim, he moved the milk jug, sugar bowl and butter dish into position.

'See? The wee islands form a natural defensive barrier.'

Kate lifted a teaspoon and drew it between the dishes. 'Why couldn't something come through here? Or here? They've got submarines, haven't they, the Germans?' She lifted her eyes from the tablecloth and looked anxiously at him.

'Because the channels are too narrow, and too shallow. They're also partially blocked with old wrecks. They did that the last time – to make a better barrier. Nothing's going to be able to get through. I'm telling you – it's as safe as houses up there.'

'But there's no guarantee you'll go to Scapa Flow.'

'No, but we'll hope for that, will we?' He changed the subject. 'Tell me what you and Grace are going to do today, so I can think about you both while I'm on the train.'

'Well, first I'll go and collect her from her Auntie Jessie. Then I'm taking her to the park. Jessie said she might come too, seeing as how it's Saturday. In the afternoon we're going

371

to the pictures, and Mary and Peter Watt have asked us to have tea with them tonight. Mary said Peter would see Grace and I home after.'

'They're good friends,' he said. His eyes strayed to the clock.

'What tram are you going for?' she asked.

'I think there's one about seven.'

'Ten minutes, then. Are you all ready?'

His eyes were soft. 'You're being gey brave, Kate Baxter.'

She sniffed, and raised the back of her hand to her mouth. 'I'm doing my best!'

'That's all any of us can do,' he said gravely, and rose from the table. 'Stand up and give me a hug.'

Only just before he left the house did her courage fail: when he kissed her and held her for the final embrace. She swayed against him, her body bending like a reed.

'Oh, Kate,' he breathed into her hair, 'my beautiful, lovely Kate. Be strong, lass. I need you to be strong . . .'

She took a great shuddering deep breath, forced the tears back and lifted her face to him. Her reward was to see that special slow smile which lit up his grey eyes, the smile that was reserved for her alone. He stroked the chestnut waves back from her forehead. 'My nut-brown maiden,' he murmured, and kissed her.

'I love you, Kate Baxter,' he said when he lifted his head.

'And I love you, Robert Baxter.'

Another kiss, deep and passionate.

'Will I not get dressed quickly and come down to the tram with you?' she whispered against his mouth.

'No. Don't wave to me either. Promise me you'll go back to bed for a wee while. It's early yet . . . and I want to think about you lying there, all warm and cosy.'

'Robbie—'

'Promise, Kate. Please?'

She could not refuse him.

One last longing look at each other, one last kiss, one last whispered *I love you*. Then he was gone. Kate put her back against the front door and listened to the sound of his footsteps going down the stairs and out of the close. *Oh Robbie, my love!*

She couldn't do it. She ran through to the front room. He was looking up at their window and she could see by the look on his face that he was glad she had broken her promise. He smiled and mouthed to her that the tram was coming. Kate smiled back and blew him a kiss. A grin lighting up his face, he returned the gesture. The tram trundled between them, blocking her view. It seemed to stop for no more than a few seconds before moving off again. Did she imagine a flash of white at one of the windows, a hand waving? She didn't know.

She watched it for as long as possible, her face pressed up against the glass. Then, with a groan at her own stupidity, she thrust up the sash window and stuck her head out, watching the progress of the tram along Dumbarton Road for another few precious yards until she could see it no more.

'Hello there, Kate,' called a familiar voice. 'Getting some fresh air?'

She turned her head. It was one of their neighbours, coming back from the shop with a newspaper and rolls for his family's breakfast.

'Robbie's just gone,' she called down. 'On the tram.'

The man looked along the road.

'Do you tell me that?' He looked up at Kate and smiled. 'Well, God bless him, eh? You'll mind and tell us if you need anything while he's away, hen?'

'I will,' she said, returned his wave and drew her head back through the window. She had promised Robbie that she would go back to bed, so she did. She managed ten minutes before she got up again. She got dressed and made the bed. Then she went through to the kitchen to tidy away the breakfast dishes.

'I just have to get on with it,' she told herself out loud, surveying the task without enthusiasm. Ah well, the sooner she was finished, the sooner she could go along to Yoker. What she needed today was company. Jessie wouldn't mind her turning up early. They would drink tea and then they would take Grace to the park. Being with her sister and her daughter would cheer her up.

She reached for the sugar bowl and the milk jug – removing Scapa Flow's defences, she thought with a wry smile. It's a good job the War Office doesn't know about me. Robbie seemed to think the real ones were pretty solid. Safe as houses, he'd said. Safe as houses.

'If that man Hitler thinks I'm leaving my house on his account, he's got another think coming.'

Kate laughed. 'What are you going to do, Agnes? Send him a strongly worded lawyer's letter?'

Thirty years old now, she was a mature woman, on an equal footing – and first-name terms – with her mother-in-law. War had finally been declared on 3 September and everyone was just waiting now for it all to start. Agnes Baxter, however, was not the only woman who had stoutly declared that if the yards were going to be working at full tilt for the war effort, she was going to do her bit too – at home in the Yoker. What would she do stuck out in the country? This Hitler was just a bloody nuisance. Like her two sons, she thought bullies had to be faced up to. Her granddaughter, however, was a different matter, and she was all in favour of the plans currently being laid for Grace to accompany her Aunt Jessie and her class to evacuation in Perthshire. She smiled at Kate.

'Speaking of letters, have you heard from that son o' mine since he went back after his leave?'

'I got a letter the other day.' A mature woman Kate Baxter might be, but she awaited her husband's letters like any lovesick schoolgirl, and she wrote lots to him.

Dear Robbie,

Well, I'm a working girl once more and guess what? The tracing apprenticeship has gone down to four years and they're going to give me credit for what I've already done, so I'll be time-served in six months – maybe by the next time you come home on leave! Isn't that great? The funny thing is that I'm one of the older ones, so the Chief Tracer relies on me to help keep what she calls 'the silly wee lassies' in order. She's nothing like Miss Nugent. (She, I hope and pray, was unique!) I'm enjoying it. There's a lot of work, but it's nice having company all day. We have some good laughs – even us 'oldies' who should know better!

She covered several pages, chatty and cheerful, giving him all the news of their families and their friends, keeping him up-to-date with the arrangements for Grace's evacuation to the country – probably somewhere in Perthshire, so they'd been told.

Everybody's asking for you, by the way. Grace gives you a special mention in her prayers every night. So does her mother. I've tried doing a picture of you, but I'm no good at portraits. Still, it keeps my beautiful easel in use. Have I ever told you about the really handsome man who made it for me?

I will close now so I can get this off first thing tomorrow. I love you always and I miss you more than words can say. Write soon.

All my love,
Kate.

She had no idea how long her letters took to reach him, no idea where he was. She'd got one letter from the training base at the end of August and then nothing for a while. She worried herself sick as news began to filter through of German U-boats attacking British ships, although she put a brave face on it for Grace's sake. She was going to miss her dreadfully when she went off with Jessie, but in some ways it was going to be a relief to be able to drop the air of cheerful unconcern once she was safely behind her own front door.

The broadcasters and commentators were calling this period the 'Phoney War'. Nothing much seemed to be happening on land or in the air, and it was to be several months before the two sides got to grips with each other in those areas. As far as the Navy was concerned, however, there was nothing phoney about it. The hostilities were becoming all too real.

When a second letter finally arrived from Robbie at the end of September, Kate pounced on it. She read it so often that it began to tear along the creases, waiting usually until Grace was safely tucked up in bed before she took it out of the envelope for the umpteenth time.

The hard-learned lesson that careless talk costs lives had not yet been fully understood. There were many, even in the forces themselves, who doubted that the war would last beyond Christmas, so the censorship was erratic, allowing Robbie to tell Kate which ship he was on – although not where he was. Well, not in so many words anyway.

Well, what did I tell you? I'm on a battleship called the Royal Oak *and I'm as safe as houses. Remember that? As safe as houses – so you can stop worrying about me.*

The sea is everywhere here, even when you're ashore you're never very far from it. It gives a particular quality to the light. I'm sure you'd love to paint here. There are lots of ancient monuments, all very mysterious and full of atmosphere. I went to this place called the Ring of Brodgar, a circle of standing stones, you would have loved it. Shall we come here after the war and you can paint them and I can write poetry about them?

I bet Grace will love the country, and it'll be good for her – all that fresh air and good food. I bet they never eat marge! Does the place in Perthshire know what's going to hit it? All those wee wildies from Yoker and Clydebank!

I try not to think about you all the time – after you gave me a row for not keeping my mind on the job! So instead I just think about you most of the time. Give Grace a big hug and a kiss from her Daddy before she goes off. We two will just have to wait for our hugs and kisses. How about staying in bed for about a month when I come home? (I can just see you blushing when you read that.)

All my love,
Your Robbie.
P.S. How's the job going? Hope you're keeping the silly wee lassies in order. If you see Peter Watt at work, tell him I was asking for him.

Carefully, with a smile, Kate folded the letter and slipped it back into the envelope. *So instead I just think about you most of the time.* Thank God. He was in Scapa Flow. As safe as houses.

Chapter 33

Everyone said that it couldn't be done. He was the kind of man for whom such a statement was a challenge. All the same, when the suggestion was put to him he asked for time to consider. He did, studying the charts and plans carefully before sleeping on it. The next day he told them that he would do it. They congratulated him on his bravery and daring. If he could pull this off it would strike a devastating blow right at the heart of the enemy.

They left their home port at the end of the first week in October. It took them five days to reach their destination. Just before midnight, carefully timed to avoid the strong currents of high and low tide, they squeezed their way between the two islands. It wasn't easy. They almost didn't make it. He had to risk coming to the surface to get past the obstacles deliberately placed in the narrow channel, but he did it, and remained undetected. Just after midnight on the morning of 14 October 1939, Lieutenant-Commander Günther Prien brought his U-boat into Scapa Flow. Then he went hunting for a target.

Robert Baxter was sound asleep when the first torpedo hit the hull of the *Royal Oak* about an hour later. So were most of the ship's company – well over a thousand men. After all, everyone knew that the Flow was impregnable – didn't they? There was no need to expect an attack in here, no need for nerves to be on edge. They were at night defence stations of course, the hatches battened down. That was to prove fatal.

Woken by the first explosion, Robbie was not at first too alarmed. It didn't sound like anything serious: a piece of machinery blowing somewhere on the ship. That would give the men on watch something to do, make the night pass quicker. He closed his eyes and settled himself more comfortably, trying to imagine himself back in bed with Kate.

Twenty minutes later the U-boat fired three torpedoes at the *Royal Oak*. They all hit home, tearing into the battleship. The lights went out and the ship quickly began to list to starboard. Everyone was awake then, all right, hastily pulling on clothes and making for the upper deck. With most of the hatches closed, there were only really two effective escape routes for those on the lower decks.

There was, however, little panic. Officers and men with torches stationed themselves at strategic points and urged their comrades to keep moving and keep calm.

Robbie, following others along an alleyway, groping his way towards the beam of a torch which seemed a long way off, heard a disturbance: raised and frantic young voices.

'What's going on here?' he asked, stopping at the door of a cabin and peering into the gloom. As long as nobody panicked and started a stampede, they might just all get out of here.

The voices stopped.

'We don't know how to get out, sir.'

He allowed himself a smile in the darkness. 'I'm not one o' the officers, son, but if you walk along this alleyway there's a man with a torch who's pointing the way up to an open hatch. Then I reckon we're all going for a nice swim.'

'It's Eric,' came another young voice. 'We can't leave Eric. Something's come loose and crushed his leg. It's bad.'

Robbie stepped over the high threshold. 'Can you lead me to him? Where are you?' He could distinguish their shapes in the darkness. He put out his hand and it was seized and guided to the shoulder of a man slumped against the bulkhead. Robbie's fingers passed over his face. It was smooth. Not a man, then, just a boy. Some mother's son. His hand travelled gently downwards. There was no response. The lad must be unconscious.

Robbie drew his breath in sharply at what he felt next. One knee was smashed, the leg beneath it almost severed, the other was trapped against the bulkhead by something that felt like a heavy piece of metal.

'We can't move it, sir. We've tried.' The speaker was close to tears.

'Let's all try.'

They were right. There was no budging the object. It seemed to have lodged itself in the bulkhead. The only way this boy was leaving the ship was without his legs. His friends, thought Robert Baxter, didn't need to know that. They were dangerously close to hysteria as it was; all credit to them for staying with their injured comrade.

He was moaning in pain now, having regained consciousness during their attempts to free him. Robbie rose to his feet and spoke calmly.

'You two go on,' he said 'and tell the first officer you come across that we need a medical team down here. All right? I'll stay with your mate till help comes.'

They argued, but he insisted, asking only that when he crouched down, they help guide the boy's head onto his lap, so that he could give him comfort. The ship gave another list to starboard. One of the boys whimpered.

'Go!' said Robbie. 'There's no time to lose!'

One of them gripped him soundlessly by the hand. Then he heard a 'God bless you, sir,' and they were gone. Hadn't he told them that he wasn't an officer? Ah well, maybe he deserved the promotion at that. He laid his hand on the boy's shoulder, a bit of human contact. The moans were growing quieter now.

He heard the water coming. It was whooshing along the alleyway, although it was some distance away yet. The great ship gave another lurch.

'Not long now.' He patted the boy's shoulder, but there was no answer. He must have slipped into unconsciousness. That was a mercy, at least.

The sound of the approaching water was growing louder. He knew that it was completely unstoppable. Funny, that. He had never felt so alive. Robert Baxter muttered a prayer and squeezed his eyes tight shut.

She was there, turning her head to smile at him, her green eyes bright and her bonnie hair being blown across her face by the wind off the river . . . His last conscious thought was of Kate, her name the last word on his lips. Then the sea took him.

Kate sat bolt upright, heart racing, blood pounding through her ears.

'Mammy?' Grace's voice was puzzled. Earlier that evening she had asked, in a very small voice, if she could sleep with her mother.

'It's all right, pet,' said Kate, patting her hand. 'Go back to sleep.'

Soon the quiet breathing told her that Grace was asleep again, but she herself slept only fitfully, rising early to open the blackout curtains on the misty October dawn. Icy fingers were clutching at her heart. Something had happened. She knew it had.

Chapter 34

Her grief was to be overwhelming – so total that Jessie Cameron began to secretly worry that her sister might never recover from the blow which fate had dealt her. Grief was not, however, the first emotion that Kate was to experience in those terrible days.

The first one was fear – a wave of cold terror which swept through her body when she heard the official announcement on the wireless, delivered in the measured tones of a BBC broadcaster.

'This is the BBC Home Service. Here is the news. The Secretary of the Admiralty regrets to announce that *HMS Royal Oak* has been sunk, it is believed by U-boat action.'

Kate's frozen brain heard one more word. *Survivors*. She heard it and she clung onto it, so there was hope – for a while. As the days wore on and lists of survivors' names were published, she searched in vain for his name. Even when the official letter finally came, she refused to give up.

'What if he managed to get ashore?' she speculated feverishly. 'Maybe he was hurt – or ill after being in the water. Maybe somebody up there's looking after him, in some wee isolated farmhouse on one of the islands. There's a lot of islands – Robbie told me there were. They can't have checked them all, can they?'

The people who loved her shook their heads, reluctant to take the lifeline away from her but not wanting to give her false hope either. Only Agnes Baxter, devastated by the loss of her eldest son, agreed with Kate. Something like that could easily have happened. In the weeks that followed the two women clung to each other in their shared grief.

Eventually, as winter drew on, Agnes began to shake her head too, frowning as she regarded her pale and thin daughter-in-law. The lassie was going to make herself seriously ill if she went on like this. She said as much to Jessie Cameron.

'Can you not do something, hen? She'll listen to you.'

Jessie didn't have Agnes's confidence, but she was desperately worried about Kate. She went ahead with the arrangements for the evacuation to Perthshire and then informed Kate that she was coming, too. Kate turned huge eyes on her.

'I can't, Jessie. What if he comes home and I'm not here? That would be terrible, don't you see?'

Jessie, crouching on the floor in front of Kate's chair, spoke gently.

'Aye, that would be terrible, but we'll tell all the neighbours where you're going. We'll leave the address of the house where we'll be. There's a telephone there, so he could go to a box and get in touch straight away.'

Jessie stopped short. Robbie was never going to get in touch, but Kate wasn't ready to admit that yet. She forced down the lump in her throat and reached for Kate's hand, lying lifelessly in her lap.

'Come on, Kate. Come with us. You know it would be good for Grace to be in the country, and she needs you with her, at least just now – for a few months.' As she had hoped, the mention of Grace's name had roused Kate. 'She misses her Daddy too, you know.' Jessie pressed her advantage. It's for her own good, she told herself firmly, although she wondered if she were a monster to push Kate like this.

Kate's eyes filled with tears. 'Oh, Jessie!'

'Wheesht now. Come on.' Rising swiftly to her feet, Jessie slid an arm around Kate's shoulders. 'We're going next Saturday. All right? You can help me control the wee horrors on the train. They'll be that excited, and all the posh folk on the train'll look down their noses at us.' She put on the pan loaf. '"*Oh dear, look at all these dreadful little lower-class children.*"' Jessie reverted to her own voice. 'I need your help, Kate. Honest. For the honour of Yoker. Now then, that's a bit better.'

For Kate had managed a watery smile.

So they went to Perthshire. Anniversaries came and went. Six months since the *Royal Oak* had sunk. A year. Kate found that you couldn't put a time limit on grief. One day she realised that she had just laughed at something Jessie had said. The next she was once more in the depths.

Being Kate, she kept most of it to herself. Jessie had been quite right. Grace did need her Mammy. *I need you to be strong.* That's what Robbie had said that last morning. For Grace and for him Kate did her level best.

With Jessie she began to build up a circle of acquaintances in their new home. They were billetted on a Mrs Robertson, a middle-aged widow who lived in a spacious Victorian villa in Pitlochry. Set on a road which climbed steeply up from the main street, it had a terraced garden at the front and a large green sward at the back surrounded by trees. Grace was entranced by it all. In the winter she and the three other children staying with them played endless games of hide and seek in the rambling old house. When the spring arrived she followed Mrs Robertson and her gardener about like a little dog, delighting their hostess by her eagerness to learn the names of all the flowers and by the charming little drawings she made of them.

Mrs Robertson, kind and inquisitive and sympathetic to the

young widow and her teacher sister, declared that it had given her a new lease of life having the young people in the house. She invited her friends to meet the Cameron girls and took them with her when she went visiting.

People wanted to be kind, but they didn't always know what to say to Kate, so she made it easy for them, forcing herself to make conversation about things which didn't seem to matter very much any more. Gradually that got easier.

Only with Jessie, once Grace and the other children were in bed and Mrs Robertson had retired for the night, did she really feel she could be herself.

'I torture myself,' she confessed one night, choking back the tears, 'wondering exactly how it happened. Did he know he wasn't going to get out? I wonder what he was doing, what he was thinking about.'

Jessie smiled. 'If I know Robert Baxter, he was probably trying to help someone else get out. That's the way Robbie was made. And as for what he was thinking about . . . He was thinking about you, Kate. I'm sure of that.'

Kate took her handkerchief out of her pocket and blew her nose, staring into the flames of the fire at which she and Jessie sat. It was autumn again and they were beginning to need the heat at night. She looked up, about to say something, but was stopped by the wistful look on Jessie's face.

'Have you ever thought, Kate, that . . . Well, I don't know if this is any consolation to you or not, but at least you've known what it is to be loved. Some people never do.'

Kate was instantly contrite. Jessie, she knew, had received three letters from Andrew Baxter during the past year. She knew because Jessie had let her read them all. There had been no reason not to. They were friendly and chatty – and contained not one single word of love. Kate leaned forward.

'Lots of people love you, Jessie. Me, for a start, and Grace – and the children you teach.'

Jessie smiled. 'That wasn't quite what I meant.'

'Oh, Jessie, I'm sorry. I really am.'

The girl leaned back in the chair and stretched her toes out to the fire. 'Och, I've got used to it, I suppose. Where there's life there's hope, eh?' She stopped, looking dismayed. 'Oh, Kate, I'm sorry. I shouldn't have said that.'

Kate Baxter was suddenly ashamed. For too long she had thought only of her loss whilst Jessie, with her own problems, had seemed to have a bottomless reservoir of support and comfort for Kate and Grace. Now here she was again – upset herself, but being so careful of Kate's feelings. *I need you to be strong*. Perhaps it was time to start fulfilling the promise she'd made to Robbie.

The next day she borrowed Grace's drawing block and some pencils and went off for the day, taking a flask and some sandwiches, heading for a spot down by the River Tummel which she and Jessie and Grace had discovered during the summer.

Although the previous night had been frosty the sun was beating down today – typical autumn weather in the Highlands, so Mrs Robertson had said. Kate spread her raincoat on the ground, sat down and put her back against an old oak overlooking the river and spent some time surveying what lay in front of her.

A light breeze caressed the surface of the river. The sun was catching the ripples. That would be hard to paint, but worth the challenge. In the distance were the mountains, dotted with patches of purple heather. Could that be fresh snow on their peaks?

Closer to her were green rolling hills and cultivated fields and all around her were wonderful old trees. Their leaves had turned to a glorious array of autumn colours – brown, yellow, red, purple and a hundred other shades besides.

'The world is beautiful,' she said out loud, and lifted the drawing pad.

By the end of the day, Kate had made several sketches and several decisions. Tomorrow she was going to buy a small set of water colours, a couple of brushes and some proper paper. She was quite pleased with her drawings, but she needed to capture the colours – and to feel a paintbrush in her fingers again.

She would give herself a month, till the weather got really cold. In that month she was going to walk and look and sketch and paint. She was going to eat properly too, build up her energy and strength. Then she was going back to Clydebank.

This war was going to go on for a while. She should be doing her bit. She would miss Grace dreadfully, but she would come back here as often as she could. It wasn't that far. She could probably manage it twice a month. And Grace was eleven now and would be able to understand, and she would have Jessie and Mrs Robertson to look after her.

Nothing could change what had happened. Nothing could bring Robbie back, but he had died because he had wanted to make his contribution. She owed it to his memory to make hers.

Chapter 35

Kate put in the last drawing pin and straightened up. Good. That was her all set up for tomorrow. Pinned out over the drawing, the tracing paper, which was actually very fine linen, would get the chance to stretch out properly overnight. As long as it doesn't get wet, she thought with a smile, saying good night and heading for the door. A month or so ago someone had tripped and spilled a glass of water over a batch of tracing paper. As soon as the water had hit it the paper turned back into cloth. It had been useless for tracing plans, but they'd saved it to be used for bandages. You didn't waste anything in wartime.

On the point of leaving the building, Kate jumped back as the door out to the yard swung open with some force.

'Where's the fire, Peter?'

Peter Watt came into the building and grinned at her.

'No fire, but they want us to work till midnight tonight. Another rush job. I just popped home for my tea, and to let Mary know.' The Watts lived close to Mary's mother in the Holy City, at the bottom of Kilbowie Hill. 'You know what she's like. Has me under the wheels o' a tram if I'm five minutes late home.'

Kate smiled. Mary was a worrier. She'd worried about young Adam staying in Clydebank, had agreed to him being evacuated and then, unable to bear the separation any longer, she'd gone and fetched him home again. Kate was beginning to wonder if she should do the same with Grace.

'I'll see you on Sunday then,' Kate said to Peter as he headed for the stairs to the drawing office. 'You're all coming to me for your dinner. Did Mary tell you?'

'She did,' he said. 'Are you off home now?'

'No, I'm going to Yoker for the evening.'

'Enjoy yourself then, Kate. See you on Sunday.' With a wave of his hand he was off, taking the stairs two at a time. The yards had never been so busy. They were turning out ship after ship. To his own disgust, and his parents' relief, Davie Cameron was one of the many young men who had been turned down for military service on the grounds that they were needed for the war effort at home – building new ships and replacing the ones which were being lost.

Kate left the yard, crossed Dumbarton Road and made her way to the tram stop. She glanced back at the window of her own flat, just along from the yard. She'd been lucky to get it back. Another couple had moved into it when she'd gone to Perthshire, but then the husband had been posted down south and the wife had gone, too. It had simply been a matter of collecting her own furniture and bits and pieces – dismantled and dispersed to the neighbours – and the flat was just as it had been before.

Well, not exactly. Kate's lips twisted in a wry smile. There was someone missing from it. There had been many nights when she had lain in a bed which was too big, longing for Robbie's kiss, aching for the touch of his hand . . .

She unbuttoned her coat. It was unseasonably warm for March – a bonus for the farmers throughout the country and for the many allotment owners in Clydebank. The clocks had just gone over to double summer time to allow those producing food as many daylight hours as possible to dig and grow for victory.

Kate took a deep breath. It was good to be out in the fresh air, instead of bent over a table tracing or lettering, although

389

she enjoyed her job. She'd been welcomed back with open arms. As expected, many of the young girls had gone off to join the services. An experienced tracer was worth her weight in gold and nobody cared whether you were married or had children. There was a war on. It was all hands to the pumps.

On balance, despite the lonely nights, she was glad she had re-established her home. It was good to have familiar things around her. There was the easel Robbie had made for her, and so many other things which reminded her of him, helped her feel his presence. Jessie had, however, insisted that some of Kate's paintings be taken to Pitlochry – for safekeeping, she said.

'So,' Kate had asked, arms folded and toe tapping, 'you want to make sure my paintings are safe from any air raids but I can take my chances?'

Jessie winked at Grace. 'Of course, sister dear. That way Grace and I will be set up for life. People will realise what a brilliant artist you were.' She struck a dramatic pose. 'What a loss to Scottish art! Then the two of us – as your heirs and successors – will be able to sell them for a fortune.' She grinned.

Kate turned to Grace and spread out her arms, palms uppermost, in a gesture of hopelessness.

'With friends like this, who needs enemies?'

Grace got the joke, but the smile she gave her mother was a little uncertain. Kate knew that she worried about her, especially after the raids which had taken place throughout the winter.

Clydebank and Glasgow had experienced some raids, but nothing like those London was suffering. Her heart went out to the folk down there. And last November Coventry had been almost obliterated. A new word had entered the language: the *blitz*. And a new expression: *a bomber's moon*. She glanced up just before she got onto the tram. There would be a bomber's moon tonight. The sky was clear, not a cloud to be seen.

Kate wondered how people could do it: drop death and destruction out of the night sky, killing and maiming men, women and children, mothers and fathers and wives not so very different from their own. She shivered.

The air-raid siren went off a little after nine o'clock, just as Kate was putting her coat on to go home.

'Here we go again,' muttered Davie Cameron. 'I bet it's another false alarm.' Twenty minutes later, when they heard the first explosion, they knew that it wasn't. Neil took command, insisting they all go down to the close to sit out the raid. Like many tenement dwellers in Clydebank, they had no Anderson shelter in the back court. Instead, their close had been 'strutted' – reinforced with steel bars along the roof. To counteract the effects of a nearby blast blowing debris in, protective screens known as baffle walls had also been built at front and back.

'Blankets,' Neil said to Lily. 'It'll be gey cold down there. Kathleen, will you make a big pot of tea? Davie, you can bring the milk and sugar. I'll take the cups and something to eat. This might be a long one. We'll need the hurricane lamp too, for afterwards. My God, would you listen to that?' Another one had fallen.

On the way downstairs, he persuaded the Baxters and the other residents of the close to join them.

'Aye, Neil,' said Jim Baxter, nodding and throwing a shout over his shoulder to Agnes. 'I think you're right.' He jumped as they heard the impact of another bomb. 'That one was bloody close. They'll be trying to get Rothesay Dock, eh?'

Agnes came out of the flat, dressed in what looked like her entire wardrobe, her coat buttons straining over the extra garments, and clutching her tins.

'Plenty in here for us all,' she said. 'I did a big baking yesterday.'

'You're a wee smasher, Agnes,' called Mrs MacLean. 'They'll not starve us out, anyway.'

Jim Baxter made as though to go back into his house.

'Where are you going, man?' asked Neil Cameron. 'Come on!' The bombardment was fast becoming intense.

'I'm just away to put my teeth in,' said Jim.

Davie Cameron leaned out from behind his father and grabbed Jim by the sleeve. 'Mr Baxter, you'll not need your teeth for your wife's cakes. They melt in the mouth. And that lot,' he gestured heavenwards, 'are no' dropping fish suppers. So come on!'

'Jesus Christ!'

'Buggeration!'

There was no need to apologise for the swearing. That one had definitely been too close for comfort. The building shook and they were showered in dust from the walls. Kate squeezed her eyes tight shut and tried not to think about the weight on top of them: the building itself, constructed out of heavy sandstone, the timbers of the floors, the lathe and plaster of the walls, the heavy cast-iron ranges, the furniture.

She shifted her weight. The floor was still hard and cold, even with layers of blankets down. She was sitting between her mother and Mrs MacLean. The comfortable bulk of the latter was absurdly reassuring. Not at the moment, though. At this precise moment all Kate was feeling was blind terror.

Funny that. When Robbie had died she had thought she wanted to go too. Now that somebody was trying to kill her, she rather thought she wanted to live. Life had suddenly become very precious. She was struck by the thought. Was this how *he* had felt in his last minutes?

'I'm scared, Kate.'

Startled by the quiet voice in her ear, she turned to her mother. She couldn't see her in the blackness, but she could feel her trembling. She fumbled for her hand. It felt old, thin and papery.

'I'm scared too, Mammy,' said Kate firmly. 'Shall we hold hands?'

'Something's on fire out there.'

'Well, of course something's on fire, you eejit. They're dropping incendiaries.'

Kate wasn't sure who the first speaker had been, but the second was her brother Davie. He went on, between blasts, to tell them what was happening. The first wave, he explained, were pathfinders, whose job it was to start fires to guide the next wave of aircraft to their targets.

'Oh, so that means that this end o' Yoker's really well lit up for them, then?'

Davie, full of his mission to explain, didn't catch the sarcasm.

'Aye, whatever that is burning out there, it's going to be a great marker for them.'

'Davie, lad,' came Neil's voice.

'Aye, Da?'

'Shut up, son, would you? Now, who knows some songs?'

They had survived. Kate thought that was all that mattered until, after the All Clear was sounded early the following morning, they staggered out of the close into the spring morning and saw the devastation the bombers had wrought. She and her father and Davie walked along Dumbarton Road – or what was left of it. A smoky haze hung in the air, and a very distinctive smell.

'My God!' said Neil. 'They hit Yoker distillery. A' that whisky gone up in smoke!'

The look of horror on his face was the only thing that made Kate laugh that morning. Nothing else did, especially not the knowledge that the bombers would be back tonight. Everybody knew that. It had been their pattern in raids on other cities. That's when the discussions started. Were they going or were they staying?

'I'm no' leaving my own house for that lot,' Agnes had said, folding her arms across her chest and gesturing towards the sky. 'I wouldn't give them the satisfaction!'

They'd got word that buses were to be laid on for those wanting to leave Clydebank but, despite the devastation, some folk still felt safer staying in their own homes. Lily, Kate could see, was terrified of going and terrified of staying. Neil Cameron slipped an arm about his wife's trembling shoulders.

'We'll stay too, lass. Take our chances together, eh?'

Lily, her eyes brimming with tears, had looked up at him and nodded. That's when Davie had said, 'Oh, Da . . .' and the argument had started up again.

Kate slipped out. She was undecided herself as to what to do, but she did know that she had to get in touch with Jessie and Grace. Raids weren't always reported straight away – news like this was bad for morale – but she couldn't take the risk. They'd both be worried sick if they'd heard anything about it on the wireless.

From the looks of it there weren't going to be any phone boxes working in Clydebank so she walked back along to Scotstoun. Her luck was in: the damage wasn't nearly so bad in that direction and Miss Noble and Esmé MacGregor, hugely relieved to see Kate safe and sound, were still at home, with a working telephone, although like everyone else they were considering whether or not to move out.

'Come to Pitlochry,' Jessie urged Kate, her voice crackling over the phone line. 'Mrs Robertson says she can squeeze everybody in. Grace is up to high doh about you – and everyone else.'

Which might, thought Kate as she walked back to Yoker, be the only thing that would influence Grace's grandparents to make a move. She walked up the stairs and pushed open the door. It was on the latch.

'Daddy . . .' she began, walking into the kitchen. Then she stopped dead. Peter Watt was sitting in her father's chair staring into space. He was filthy, his face covered in dirt and smears of blood. Neil took her to one side.

'The Holy City's flattened, lass. Nothing but a pile of rubble.'

Kate searched her father's face. 'Mary and Adam?'

His face etched with lines of sadness, Neil nodded and put a hand on her shoulder. 'I'm sorry, Kathleen. Seemingly they brought their bodies out about an hour ago.' He gestured towards the man sitting so silently in his own chair. 'They asked him if there was anyone he could go to and all he could say was "Kate Baxter at Yoker". So they brought him here.'

Kate went to stand by him. 'Peter,' she said softly.

His eyes filled with tears when he saw her. 'Kate,' he said, through cracked lips. 'Oh, Kate . . .'

'Hush, now,' she said, putting her arms around him.

He looked up at her, his dirty face streaked with tears. 'I wasn't with them, Kate. That's what I can't bear. They must have been so scared.'

She lifted one of his hands. It was bleeding, his skin shredded and his fingernails jagged. Oh God, he must have tried to dig them out with his bare hands . . .

'What am I going to do, Kate?'

Her arms tightening around him, she pulled him into the warmth of her body. 'What we're all going to do, Peter. Keep going. That's all. Just keep going. That's all any of us can do.'

Chapter 36

Two years after the war ended Kate visited the islands. The Orcadians welcomed her with open hearts and quiet sympathy. She saw the sights Robbie must have seen: the burial chamber of Maes Howe with its runic inscriptions; the Stone Age village of Skara Brae; St Magnus's Cathedral. She saw Scapa Flow, still full of British warships but with a hole at its heart, a marker buoy indicating where the *Royal Oak* lay under the water.

She took a bus down over the Churchill barriers, the defences built in response to that tragedy by Italian prisoners of war. She visited the Italian chapel, made by those prisoners out of a Nissen hut. With only scrap materials to work with, they had created an exquisite little place of worship in the style of the churches of their homeland. Kate found it in her heart to admire the men who had conquered their homesickness by making something beautiful out of nothing.

'I'm glad you're going,' Peter had said when he'd seen her off. 'You see, I know that Mary and Adam are dead, because I saw them. But I don't think you know that Robbie is. Not really. In here, maybe.' He tapped her forehead. 'But not in your heart. You're still hoping he'll walk through the door one day.'

'Och, Peter,' said Kate, her green eyes soft. 'You're not going to ask me again, are you?'

She had hoped at first that their increasing closeness over the war years had been because of their tragic bond, strengthening their friendship because they had both known the pain of losing partners. On VE Day, however, as the whole country had celebrated, Peter had turned to Kate and asked her to marry him. They were not old, and he was sure that neither Mary nor Robbie would have begrudged them some happiness. Kate thought that was true. It made no difference.

She valued Peter as a friend, and she told him so. Robbie had been her husband – her soulmate, her lover, her best friend. There couldn't be another relationship like that. Not for her.

Peter, however, hadn't been prepared to take no for an answer and brought the subject up at frequent intervals. Not, apparently, on this occasion.

'Credit me with some sensitivity, Kate. I'd hardly ask you when you were about to go off to the Orkneys, would I now? Now, mind and take travel sickness pills wi' you. I hear that the Pentland Firth's gey rough.'

She left the Ring of Brodgar till the day before she quitted the islands, going there in the early morning, a lift having been arranged for her with one of the local posties in his van. It was a remarkable place. She counted the stones – thirty-six of them – all much, much taller than herself and arranged in a huge circle – more than 300 hundred feet in diameter, the postman had told her. She walked round it, on the inside of the stones, and then obeyed a childish impulse to do it twice more. Three times for luck.

She stood then with her back against one of the stones and looked about her: heather-clad hills in the distance, two sparkling blue lochans in the hollow between the stones and the hills. The countryside was quite different, but it reminded her of how she had felt the day she had looked out over the Tummel at Pitlochry. It had been a turning point, the day she had decided to start living again. After a fashion. But she was tired now. It had been a long war.

Abruptly, she slid down the stone to sit on the grass, closing her eyes and letting the wind caress her face.

Her mind was full of images of him: helping her save Mr Asquith from a watery grave; offering her first bite of a shiny red apple; his eyes softening as he leaned forward to kiss her; his face alight with love and wonder when he had seen Grace for the first time . . .

With a sob, she drew her knees up and let her head fall forward. *I need you to be strong.* She had been strong. For Robbie, for Grace, for herself, for Peter, for everybody. She was tired of being strong. It had been easier while the war was on. Then there had seemed to be some purpose to her life. Now there didn't. Was there any point in living on without him? Grace was almost a woman now, about to start at the Art School. Soon she wouldn't need her mother.

The breeze danced on the nape of her neck. It was the lightest of touches, like a couple of fingertips delicately brushing her hair to one side. It happened again. Slowly Kate raised her tear-stained face and looked into the middle of the great circle of stones. With an exclamation, she dashed away the moisture from her eyes. It was making her see things.

Two figures stood there, some distance away from her. Then, without any apparent movement, they were right in front of her. She was dreaming. She must be. His smile, however, was just as she remembered it – wide and slow, lighting up his grey eyes as he looked at her.

You daft bisom, you've still got work to do, but I'll be waiting for you once you're done.

She heard the words in her head. Her eyes went to the other figure. A handsome young man, tall and straight, with a smile just like his father's.

The voice in her head came once more. *Neil James, of course.*

Who else did you think it would be? She could hear the rumble of amusement. *He's a fine lad, this son of ours.*

Her heart full, she stretched out a hand. Could this really be happening? She had felt that featherlight touch – she knew she had. The figures were fading.

We'll be waiting for you . . .

She was alone again. The stone circle was empty. There was only the wind and the sun on her face and the plaintive cry of a bird, hidden somewhere in the heather.

'Thank you,' said Kate softly, the words directed to whoever was listening. 'Thank you.'

Kate took a step back and looked critically at the arrangement of her plates and bowls on the felt-covered table. She'd sold quite a lot today, and got an order for wall plaques from a city-centre shop – but it meant there were a few gaps now in her display. Never mind. Jessie, off school for the Christmas holidays, was going to help her bring some more stuff in tomorrow.

Thinking of her sister, Kate sighed. Some things just didn't work out. Andrew Baxter hadn't got himself killed in his second war against fascism either, but he'd come home from it with a wife – a cheerful girl from York called Gwen. Like generations of her family before and since, Jessie Cameron had risen to the occasion, congratulating the newly-weds and shaking them both warmly by the hand.

'It would be easier,' she had confessed to Kate afterwards, 'if I could hate her, but she's a really nice girl.' Only then, in privacy, had she burst into tears and cried it all out on Kate's shoulder.

That's what shoulders are for. Kate moved a small bowl from the side of the table to the middle and smiled. He was never very far from her thoughts. *You've got work to do.* Well, she was doing it now. She hoped he would be proud of her if he could see her. She smiled again. Maybe he could.

Even with her paintings beginning to fetch good prices, it had been a financial struggle to set herself up in business: buying the kiln and the other equipment, renting a small workshop, paying out for the clay. She was getting there though, pleased as punch to have been invited to exhibit her pottery at this pre-Christmas arts and crafts fair in Glasgow. Still working part-time at Brown's – she couldn't afford to give her notice in just yet – life was hard going but satisfying. And she had good friends.

'Friends,' Peter had said in a flat voice, when she had come back from the Orkneys and told him that no meant no. 'You want us to stay friends.' Then he had relented and kissed her on the forehead. 'I suppose so. If I'm allowed to do that occasionally, and to walk arm in arm with you now and again.'

Kate had wanted to cry.

'You're a good man, Peter Watt.'

'Oh, aye,' he had said in a resigned tone. 'It's a pity I'm no' a Catholic. Otherwise you could have put me forward to the Pope for canonisation.'

He did deliveries for her at the weekends and Grace helped out when she could, although her own art studies kept her busy. Kate had no complaints about that. From the looks of it, her daughter was developing into a fine portrait painter.

She moved the bowl back to its original position. Esmé MacGregor had bought a larger version of the same design that morning and then had tried to make Kate take the money for it. Frances Noble, looking on with a smile, had advised her friend to give up the fight.

'Don't you remember my telling you about a very stubborn pupil of mine? The girl who never gave up?'

Kate had won, of course, insisting that the bowl had to be

a gift – a thanks for everything the two women had done for her. She was glad she had vindicated their faith in her, even if it had taken her a long time to do so.

Making a final adjustment to her display, Kate turned – and found herself face to face with Marjorie Drummond.

'Oh, Kate!' she said, her thin face lighting up with pleasure. 'It is you! I saw the poster about the craft fair outside the hall and I just wondered if you might be here. Come and have tea with me.'

Dumbfounded, Kate could only stare at her. Marjorie actually sounded pleased to see her.

'What about Jack?' she got out at last, peering cautiously over Marjorie's shoulder. 'Is he with you?'

'Nope,' said Marjorie cheerfully. 'I left him in South Africa. We sat the war out down there.' She lifted her shoulders in a self-deprecating gesture. 'At this moment I should imagine he's with his new wife in Cape Town – another rich man's daughter. Now, isn't that a surprise?' She smiled wryly. 'That seems to be Jack's type. Only she's not as gullible as I was. I give them five years – maybe not even that long.'

Kate was still having difficulty in speaking.

'Close your mouth, Kate, you'll catch flies,' said Marjorie, an impish grin spreading over her face. 'I divorced him,' she added calmly. 'He was a rat.'

Kate stared at her. Then she began to chuckle.

'Y-yes, he was, wasn't he?' Her laughter stopped as abruptly as it had started, and her voice grew wistful. 'But don't you hate me, Marjorie? For what I did to you?'

'Oh, Kate,' Marjorie said. 'You didn't do anything to me – *he* did. With a little help from Suzanne Douglas. She's out there too. I don't think Jack's new wife cares very much for the way she hangs around – especially when she's supposed to be married to someone else.' Marjorie's smile was once more rueful. 'I can't say I blame the new Mrs Drummond. I didn't care for that very much either.'

'Oh, Marjorie,' said Kate, her face full of sympathy for her old friend.

'You didn't do anything to me, Kate,' Marjorie repeated softly. 'He did it to both of us.' She stepped forward, flung her arms around Kate's neck and gave her a hug.

'You're not crying, Kate, are you? Oh, drat, so am I!' She fished a handkerchief out of her neat little bag. 'Here, you'd better use it first. Now come on, Mrs Baxter. Get someone else to look after your stand for an hour. You and I have matters to discuss.'

'We do?'

Marjorie's smile grew a little tentative. 'How do you fancy taking me on as a partner, Kate? I've a good business head. I used to run a pottery studio, you know,' she said wryly. 'And I've still got a little capital. I've even thought up a name for us – the Phoenix Pottery. To symbolise a new start after the war, and a new start for the two of us.'

A slow smile spread across Kate's face. 'I had forgotten just how persuasive you can be.'

Marjorie grinned and stuck out her hand. Kate took it – and the Phoenix Pottery was born.

Epilogue 1997

Kate was drifting in and out of consciousness. She had always heard that hearing was the last of the five senses to go. That seemed to be true. Her vision was certainly fading, although she could make out a square of light which must be a window. When they'd brought her in here last week she had asked the nurse if you could see the river through it, the hospital being a tall, modern building and the floor she was on so high up.

'The whole of the Clyde Valley,' the girl had confirmed. 'New York on a clear day. Depending on what you've been drinking the night before, of course!'

This town is full of comedians. That was right enough.

She was still aware of touch, had known it when the doctor had sat on her bed, held her hand and called her by her first name. Always a bad sign, that.

'Can you hear me, Kathleen?' the young woman had said.

'Kate,' Grace had corrected. 'She's never been called Kathleen.' But Grace was wrong. There had been two people who had called her Kathleen . . .

She thought she knew who was in the room with her – Jessie, of course. Davie and his family had visited last week, while she had still been able to talk to them. That had been good. Her Baxter nieces and nephews had been in too. They were a lively bunch.

Pearl had sent a card and a huge bouquet of flowers. She

403

lived in Birmingham now – a respectable widow as far as her neighbours were concerned. That's all they knew.

Grace was here, with her children and two grown-up granddaughters. Not young Michael, of course. His mother had brought him in last week, but he would be with her and his baby sister today. Better, by far, that he remember his Grandma Kate from that trip they'd had down the coast last summer. That had been a lovely day . . .

Michael's father was sitting by the bed, now and again lifting his hand to gently stroke his grandmother's forehead and smooth her hair back from her brow. That felt nice.

Kate's eyes were closed, but she was still aware through her closed lids of the light from the window. They were talking about her, going over her life. Another bad sign.

'So why did Grandma Kate and Uncle Peter never get married?'

'I think,' said Grace slowly, 'because she wouldn't. She was devoted to your great-grandfather, you know. That was a real love match. You've seen that painting I did of him, haven't you?'

Ah yes, the portrait of Robbie. Grace had caught him exactly – casual in unbuttoned waistcoat, collarless shirt and rolled-up sleeves, his hair tousled. He was in the act of turning, and he was smiling, a twinkle in his grey eyes.

'Mmm,' came the appreciative answer. That was young Barbara, who'd taken over from Kate at the Phoenix Pottery, running it along with one of her Baxter cousins. 'I've always thought Grandad Robert looks *dead* sexy in that picture!'

They all laughed. Well, Robbie would have laughed at that too.

He was a real person to them all because of that portrait, hung in pride of place in their Grandma Kate's home. They often talked of him – asked about his writing, asked about his life. They spoke of how half the family had taken after Kate

404

by going in for art or pottery, while the other half had become journalists – taking after Grandad Robert. Kate always smiled when she heard them say that.

'I was only ten when he died.' Grace's voice was very soft.

'So how did you manage the portrait, then?'

'Well, I had the old photos . . . but it was how I remembered him too. Life was hard back then, but he always had time for me. He used to take me out for walks, pointed things out, told me stories . . .' Grace's voice had grown softer still, '. . . and whenever he saw your Grandma Kate, his whole face just lit up.'

'So you don't think she and Uncle Peter ever . . . you know . . .'

That was Barbara again. Cheeky wee bisom. No, there had never been anything like that between her and Peter, but he'd been a faithful companion to her over the years, and she had missed him after he'd gone.

'So exactly when did Grandma and Aunt Marjorie start the Phoenix Pottery?' That was Barbara's sister. Asking a journalist's question.

'A couple of years after the war,' said Grace.

'But I thought they had worked together before that. In the 1930s.' The reporter in action. Always trying to get at the truth. Just like Robbie.

'Yes,' said Grace vaguely. 'Do you remember anything about that, Aunt Jess? I think there was some sort of a falling-out.'

Well, that was one way of putting it. They didn't know the half of it.

'Look,' said Michael's father. 'She's smiling.'

'Maybe we'd better watch what we say then!'

The voices faded. How strange, that her family should have come to call Marjorie 'Aunt'! She had missed her too these past few years. Even after Marjorie had got married again –

405

to a straightforward and uncomplicated man who worshipped the ground she walked on – the friendship between her and Kate had strengthened and deepened.

They had made a go of the Phoenix Pottery too, pulling off the difficult trick of being commercially successful and critically acclaimed. It was a good feeling to think that you were leaving something beautiful behind you, that you had done your work well.

The voices came back again, like someone turning the sound up on a radio. They were laughing softly. She had missed the joke. Damn.

She was walking by the river, coming up to the rowan tree. She took a deep breath. That felt good. The air was clean and clear. The river was clean too, much more now than it had ever been, flowing to the sea, flowing as her life had done, always coming back to the same place.

'Kathleen,' he said.

He was standing under the rowan tree.

'It's time, is it?'

'Aye, it's time, hen. And I think I've waited long enough. Don't you?'

'Who else is there with you?' There was a bright light behind his head. It was dazzling her, but she could make out some faces – her father, her mother, her face younger and softer, a child in either hand – the twins, of course – Eliza and Ewen. Was that Neil James she saw beside them?

'Have you said all your goodbyes?'

Kathleen Cameron Baxter smiled. 'Just one last one.' She turned for a final look at the Clyde, flowing on as it always had done. As it always would.

'Come on then, lass. Time to go.'

Kate turned to Robbie, her face filled with joy. Then she put her hand in his, and together they walked towards the light.